PRAISE FOR

Lost and Found in Prague

"Many layered, intelligent and atmospheric, with an unusual cast of characters, this is addictive stuff from Kelly Jones."—Elizabeth Cook, author of *Rutherford Park*

". . . intriguing thriller . . . Jones has a real gift for creating well-limned characters and describing the streets and buildings of Prague."—*Publishers Weekly*, January 2015

Evel Knievel Jumps the Snake River Canyon . . .
and Other Stories Close to Home

"These stories are deftly told character-driven tales set in quiet towns, with sensitivity and affection for the characters."—*Publishers Weekly, Booklife*, February 2015

". . . Jones tells an endearing story . . . a fast and pleasantly bumpy ride through the lives of idiosyncratic characters trying to find their way across one kind of chasm or another,"—Bill Wolfe, *Read her Like an Open Book*, April 2015

The Woman Who Heard Color

". . . intense and richly detailed . . . puts a wonderfully imaginative spin on art and history."—*Publishers Weekly*, October 2011

"You will not be able to put down this extraordinary story of condemned art, unshakable family loyalty, and secret passion in a time gone mad."—Stephanie Cowell, author of *Claude & Camille*

continued . . .

The Lost Madonna

". . . truly a hidden treasure, written with dedication and intricacy that readers will surely appreciate."—Tracy Zappala, *Contemporary Romance Writers*, April 2007

"Jones' vivid descriptions of Florence, and the involving story, will captivate art and fiction lovers."—Kristine Huntley, *Booklist*, 2007

The Seventh Unicorn

"The Seventh Unicorn is one of those rare reading experiences; page-turning and insightful, it explores the human condition in a way that few novels do. Kelly Jones is a wonderful writer, and definitely one to watch."—Nicholas Sparks, author of *The Notebook, A Walk to Remember, The Longest Ride*

"Intriguing debut full of interesting details and history . . . a haunting and breathtaking story."—Jory Reedy. *Fresh FICTION*, 2005

Also by Kelly Jones

Lost and Found in Prague
(a Dana Pierson novel)
Evel Knievel Jumps the Snake River Canyon
The Woman Who Heard Color
The Lost Madonna
The Seventh Unicorn

Bloodline and Wine

Kelly Jones

Ninth Avenue Press

This is a work of fiction. Characters, places, and events are products of the author's imagination and any real names or locales are used fictitiously.

Bloodline and Wine

For more information, contact kelly@kellyjonesbooks.com

ISBN 978-0-9914468-2-7
Cover Design by Brian Florence, Steamroller Studios
Author Photo by Jim Jones

ACKNOWLEDGMENTS

I have many to thank for making this story into a book. I am especially grateful for the Aero writers who have contributed in many ways, guiding me through versions and revisions. Thank you to Erin Anchustegui, Glida Bothwell, Judy Frederick, Maureen Harty, and Laura Kelly Robb, not only for the writing stuff, but for sharing our life events, our ups and downs, as we connect through our stories. To Weldon Stutzman and the crew at AeroCaffé in Boise, I'm grateful for the cozy room to create, the coffee, and the quiche. A big thank you also to Renie Hays who has helped me through many of my books with her thoughtful readings.

To my husband, Jim, for the trips to Italy, the gifts of wine, for reading all the drafts, and for always being there to lift me up, thank you!

PROLOGUE

Wine, the color of blood. Not crimson fresh pouring from an open wound, but *Bruno.* The color of dried blood.

Yet, it gushes with life as a gloved hand opens the spigot of the first oak barrel, then the next, moving quickly. A dozen now. Barrels as tall as one man stacked upon the shoulders of another.

Wine slaps the tile floor. It swirls toward the drain. Then the shriek of ripping plastic, knife splitting wide the cover encasing rows of bottled wine. Hands grabbing one, then another, by the neck, smashing them violently against the metal rack.

The early morning silence of the cellar has been interrupted, though it disturbs no one. The cry of destruction will not permeate the thick stone walls of the cellar, even as glass shards fly and rain down upon the Tuscan tile, and the open taps of the wooden barrels continue to pour forth precious liquid. *Borelli Brunello.*

CHAPTER ONE

For over sixty years, Paolo Paluzzi has worked at the Borelli estate in the municipality of Montalcino, in the province of Siena, just south of the Renaissance City of Florence. Originally hired by Vittorio Borelli, Paolo has served loyally as the business passed to Vittorio's children, Giovanni Borelli and Estella Borelli Antonelli.

In the early days, the estate was small but has grown to over 1,000 hectares, less than a third planted with vines. The villa, home now to three generations of Borellis, sits on more than a hectare, and within resides much history. Yet, the Borelli name itself will live on only through the legacy of the label. A son who has become a priest, and a daughter who has become an Antonelli, will produce no heirs to carry on the family name.

Paolo labors not in the vineyards, but in the intimate gardens of the estate, tending the rows of tomatoes, squash, and fresh herbs, trimming the hedges in the labyrinth of the garden open to the public, pruning the flowering bougainvillea and wisteria vines that climb along the villa walls, the arbors and entry to the visitors' center.

Each morning Paolo sits in the garden on one of the elaborately carved benches, perched next to a putto or figure of a Roman woman draped in stone, the fountain's open-mouthed fish gently spewing water, creating a soothing rhythm for Paolo to begin his day. Sitting for a smoke before tending to his gardens, he watches the rising sun, streaking the sky with rays of Tuscan gold and pink, glazing the hills with a patina of extraordinary light. Gazing out toward the vineyards and orchards, the dips in the land where natural forests of pine and oak spring forth, he never wonders what lies beyond, content with his life just as it is.

It is generally a peaceful, quiet time, but this morning he notices the gathering clouds, an unfamiliar movement in the air, and he senses something amiss. He rises and slowly makes his way along the garden path, passing through the perfect arch of the trimmed greenery separating the villa grounds from the cellar. He casts his gaze about, though he sees nothing out of place.

Arriving at the cellar, he immediately notices that the lock has been broken. Cautiously, he pushes the heavy wooden door open and steps over the threshold, pausing, listening a moment before entering. He hears not human voices, but a sound that sends a shock of fear through him, as does the smell. Not the familiar aroma of wine contained in oak, but wine let loose. Taking a deep breath, he snaps on the lights and sees the spigots on the large oak barrels have been opened, wine rushing forth. Quickly, intent on stopping the flow, he steps toward the first barrel, losing his balance, foot slipping along the tile floor, made slick by the flow of wine. Steadying himself, he takes another step, slipping again, hitting his head on the metal edge of the large wooden barrel. Staggering, he attempts to right himself, hand reaching out to grab something that isn't there. Dizzy, he groans, feeling the damp warm blood oozing from his head. As he reaches up, the weight of his body, the fogginess of his mind, pulls him down. He is on the floor, trying desperately to hold on, but he is slipping, fading, vanishing.

BLOODLINE AND WINE

Blood, mingling now, red with red, the fermented Sangiovese grapes mixing with true blood.

Paolo's body, face down, gurgling, attempting to draw breath, breathing in the wine.

Broken glass, broken dreams. Clogging the drain, as the wine, the lifeblood of the Borelli family, rises higher and higher.

CHAPTER TWO

Dana Pierson stopped on the footpath where she and Father Giovanni Borelli walked between the vines.

"It's beautiful," she said, gazing down toward neighboring vineyards winding rhythmically along the hillside, rising above pockets of olive groves and forested land. It was October, just after the harvest and the autumn colors had yet to alter the lush green landscape. Clouds that had earlier threatened their morning excursion had parted, revealing cypress trees casting thin shadows across narrow roads below. Stone farmhouses and red-tiled villas dotted the landscape. Borelli had also slowed his pace to take in the vista, though it was one he knew well.

"I am still amazed," he replied as they continued their stroll, "by the beauty of the land. I find myself at peace when I am here." He'd grown up on the estate, had studied and lived in Rome for many years, but was now retired and living in the family villa with his sister, Estella, her son, Leonardo Antonelli, and Leo's daughter, Mia.

After many invitations to visit the Borelli Vineyards, Dana had accepted. She would spend a week, then planned on meeting two old college girlfriends in Rome.

"Would you like to visit one of the cellars?" Borelli asked, but before Dana could answer he exclaimed, "No, no, we must take advantage of the day!" He gazed upward. "Let's drive into Montalcino."

They had arrived at the base of the hill where they'd parked Borelli's truck. He reached into his pocket, pulled out his keys and presented them to Dana. Reluctantly, she took them, realizing they would have to return to the villa for a driver unless she was willing to take the wheel. Borelli no longer possessed a valid driver's license, though he had explained it was perfectly legal for him to drive on the family's private land, the vastness of which Dana had experienced that morning as she began her official Borelli Vineyards tour.

"We could visit the *fortezza,*" he suggested, "the church, do some shopping if you wish. We will visit the cellars later this afternoon."

"Sounds like a good plan." Dana slid into the driver's seat and started the motor of the truck which she might have described as either vintage or old beat-up clunker. "Do you think Mia would like to go with us?"

"She has always enjoyed these excursions, but lately . . . I imagine she has something planned with her friends for the weekend."

"She no longer enjoys the company of adults?" Dana smiled, remembering a time long ago when she'd rather hang out with friends, certainly not parents or grandparents. She would do anything now to spend time with her father. Dana thought of Mia's father, Leo, and the obvious rift between them. Dana had overheard a conversation—in Italian, which she didn't understand—though it was obvious the two were arguing. Then, the lack of warmth between them at dinner was palpable. Yet, Dana sensed a special bond between Mia and her great uncle as they'd exchanged glances, a whisper, a quick grin, over the course of the evening.

Dana and Father Borelli had a bond, too, one that might be

difficult to define or explain. She certainly couldn't claim he reminded her of her father, though he was close to the age her dad would have been. Her father was a quiet, thoughtful man, a professional athlete at one time, a baseball player. He'd had a second career as a sports writer and had been instrumental in getting Dana into the profession of journalism.

Borelli, on the other hand, was loquacious, unafraid to express his opinions, and if he had not told Dana he'd been a skillful soccer player in his youth, she would not have thought of him as an athlete.

Years ago, Borelli had been sent to Boston as a representative of the Vatican. Their paths had intersected, but he and Dana had not met until she visited her cousin, a nun with the community of the Discalced Carmelites in Prague. Father Borelli was visiting his childhood friend, Father Giuseppe Ruffino. Dana and Borelli had been forced to work together when an ancient fifteenth-century icon, an image of the Christ Child, had disappeared from a small church in the Mala Strana. With her background in investigative journalism and Borelli's not-completely-explained past role as a canon lawyer and researcher for the Vatican, their joining forces was inevitable.

They had not seen each other for over four years, but they had written during this time. Old-fashioned letters, delivered through the U.S. and not-always-reliable Italian postal systems, had been their sole means of communication.

While the tenor of the letters could in no way be described as intimate—they wrote of current events, history, and occasionally of family—their friendship had continued to grow. Dana wasn't even sure why, though he was one of the few she had spoken with openly about her greatest loss. One might expect to lose a parent, but never a child. And this was the loss that continued to define Dana's life—the disappearance of her son, Joel. At times, she perceived a deep loss within Giovanni Borelli, too. Though it remained unspoken, she sensed a sadness, a searching for something missing. And maybe this was the very aspect of their lives that had drawn them together.

Mia Antonelli sat in the kitchen, perched on a wooden stool at the long marble counter, stomach rumbling with hunger. On awakening, she'd slipped on her flip-flops, not bothering to change from the flannel shorts and T-shirt in which she'd slept, and made her way down to the kitchen where she found the estate cook, Renata Paluzzi, going about her mid-morning routine.

Mia had slept late, something her father generally would not have approved of, even on a weekend, as it was now, when early rising was not necessary. Mia guessed that after their blowup—they had a stupid argument about her wearing too much make-up—he would not want to spend time with her anyway. She knew he sat in his office now, just off the reception lobby for the tourists. Later in the day, visitors would be spilling out of the vans, eager for a tour of the Borelli Vineyards and a taste of the world-renowned wines.

Mia thought of the young man, recently hired, an apprentice learning the trade, and wondered if she would see him that morning. Often, he worked in the office, but generally, he could be found out in the vineyards. Fabrizio Rossi was handsome, well spoken, and Mia's father Leo had taken a special interest in him. So had Mia, and the thought made her smile. She would never tell her father of these strange new feelings, or her grandmother, or her great uncle, Zio Giovanni. Not even Renata. Though her father called this new employee a boy, he was eighteen, truly a man. Mia was thirteen.

"Zio Giovanni left very early this morning," Mia told Renata. She'd heard the old truck revving and had pulled her pillow up over her head to muffle the sound. "With our guest," she added, catching Renata's eye.

The cook stood on the opposite side of the island, easing a fresh loaf of bread out of the pan. "Yes, I suppose he'd like to show her around. Your grandmother and father will be busy today with the buyers coming."

There would be much activity this evening, but it was quiet now.

Mia tucked a strand of long, dark hair behind her ear, tore a chunk of bread from the warm loaf and took a bite. Renata rolled her eyes, but she did not protest as she sliced through a lush, ripe tomato, then licked the juices from her plump fingers.

"What do you think of the American woman?" Mia asked. She reached over, picked up a sprig of basil, tore off a leaf, held it to her nose, then stuck it in her mouth and sucked.

The visitor was model thin, not beautiful, but pretty in an American way. There was something about the manner in which she moved, carrying herself with a hint of superiority. Because her luggage had been delayed at the airport, she'd come to dinner wearing jeans and a T-shirt. Yet, even in this casual attire, she radiated a confidence that Mia admired.

Guests at the Borelli estate were generally exporters, buyers or distributors, on occasion an ancient cousin, whose family relationship was never fully clear to Mia. But Dana Pierson was different. A single woman, a writer from America, about her father's age, arriving as a guest of her great uncle, Father Giovanni Borelli. She knew her grandmother, Estella Antonelli, had concerns about her brother, a priest, inviting a single American woman as a week-long guest. Mia had overheard a conversation between her grandmother and Zio Giovanni in which Estella had questioned the wisdom of entertaining this woman. "What will the neighbors think?" she'd asked, and Zio had come back roughly, "What? You do not believe a celibate man should be allowed a friend? If anyone asks, which I dare say they will not, the *family* is entertaining an *Americana.* We've done this often enough, invited female guests," he'd added dryly. Mia found it rather exciting.

"What do I think?" Renata repeated the question as she plucked the remaining basil leaves off the stem. "She seems nice. I believe they are friends. Do you think otherwise?" She pursed her lips as she glanced up at Mia.

The American was much younger than Zio Giovanni. Surely, they were not lovers. Mia could not imagine such a thing. "Yes, they are just friends." But, now, she was intrigued. "Do you think my uncle, *the priest*, has ever been in love?" she asked.

Renata did not look up from the plate on which she artfully arranged layers of sliced tomatoes, mozzarella, and basil. "Years ago," she said, sliding the plate across the counter to Mia. With an unhurried gait, Renata sauntered to the sink, her plastic clogs slapping along the stone floor. She turned on the faucet and rinsed off a knife, her back to Mia as she gazed out the window toward the herb and vegetable garden, then the distant hills. "It might be a nice day after all," she said.

"Really?" Mia asked, feeling a curious grin curve her lips, though she had no interest in the weather, but in this new revelation. "Zio Giovanni was in love?"

Renata turned, her expression giving away nothing. Neither judgment, nor excitement revealed along the fixed line of her mouth, or within her deep, dark eyes, set like tiny seeds into her fleshy round face. She wiped her thick hands on her apron as she made her way back to the counter.

Mia had always been able to sit comfortably with Renata, sometimes speaking of little or nothing as the woman offered a taste from her kitchen. At times, they would speak of events in Mia's life—her desire to get a new kitten, an unfair chore requested by her father. Renata listened well. The kitchen had become a safe place for Mia to share her thoughts, which had become more and more complicated each day.

Speaking to her grandmother was difficult. Estella had an old-fashioned attitude about how a woman should behave, continually attempting to groom Mia, to make her behave like a fine young lady. Her grandmother had always played the role of the dutiful wife, the dutiful mother, allowing the men in her life to make the major decisions. Mia's own mother had been different. When she was well, she would rise early, go out into the vineyards, taste the grapes, touch the soil. Her mother had played an important role in managing and running the business. She had been gone for over two years. Mia missed her terribly, yet sometimes she couldn't remember the details of her face, her touch, her smell, no matter how hard she tried.

"Was he very young, Zio Giovanni?" Mia wasn't yet ready to let go of this conversation. "When he fell in love? It was before he became a priest?" she asked, attempting to hide her desire for scandal.

"Yes, they were young. Engaged to be married. And, *yes*," Renata emphasized, "this was *before* he became a priest."

"Engaged?" Mia's voice rose with this revelation. Why had she never heard of this? "Did he break her heart?"

"I'm not sure . . . it is not always the man who breaks the woman's heart. It might happen either way. I've seldom heard of a mutual parting." Renata lifted her eyes from the wooden board on which she was slicing the bread and looked at Mia somberly as if this bit of information and insight was important.

"How very sad," Mia said after a moment. "He became a priest because of a broken heart?"

Renata continued her work with an even, unhurried rhythm, layering tomatoes and cheese on a piece of bread. "She was a beauty. Gia Veronesi."

"From the Veronesi family on the hill?" Mia's shoulders straightened in alertness at this. "Gia Veronesi?"

"Yes," Renata said. "The family on the hill."

Mia wondered why they had always referred to the Veronesi estate as *on the hill*. It wasn't even the highest hill in the region—that was the city of Montalcino itself. She knew at one time the Veronesis were the largest producers in the area, though this was no longer true. Yet, there was a certain self-imposed superiority understood with the mention of the name. Mia knew enough to know the Borellis did not get along with the Veronesis. There was something strange about the family, stories about mental derangement. Possibly even prisoners held in the attic and cellars of the home. Mia guessed these were merely myths and stories exaggerated over the years.

"Zio Giovanni and Gia Veronesi?" she asked, delighted with this odd discovery. "A Romeo and Juliet story," she added, feeling a tug at her heart at the thought of a perfect, surely forbidden love. Yet, at the same time, she realized if Zio Giovanni was young, as Renata told her, it would have been many years ago. They had recently celebrated his seventy-fourth birthday. It was difficult to imagine Zio Giovanni had once been young, let alone in love.

Mia slid a slice of tomato topped with fresh mozzarella and basil into her mouth and chewed thoughtfully. Renata finished wrapping a sandwich for her father-in-law, Paolo. It was too early for lunch, but he generally came in for a snack to break the labor of the morning. He was still a robust man, nearing eighty now, but at times his memory faltered. Often, he forgot to eat, and his daughter-in-law made sure something was sent out to him on the estate. "You're off now," she told Mia. "Go find Signor Paolo and take him a bite to eat."

CHAPTER THREE

"Didn't you see that bump?" Borelli's voice rose as they traveled toward the main highway. The lack of a valid driver's license, as well as the lack of a back seat, did not preclude him from backseat driving. "You are able to see without your glasses?" he added.

"Laser surgery," Dana explained. For years she'd worn glasses, and she recalled how she and Borelli had spent a day in Prague searching for an optometrist's shop when she'd broken her glasses. Maybe cause for him to be concerned now, though she felt she was doing just fine with her driving. "The eyes are great. No glasses needed. Don't worry about your ol' truck," she teased. "Eyes are fine."

She'd never felt particularly self-conscious wearing glasses. They seemed a natural part of her self-proclaimed nerdiness. A badge of her nerdiness, in fact. But, as she aged, she'd had a desire to make some changes, slow things down. She'd recently changed her hairstyle, too—given up on attempts to straighten her waves. She'd begun using a non-permanent tint when she'd first noticed a hint of gray in her brown hair—she was just mid-forties, much too young for gray. Later, her hairdresser had suggested some golden highlights and so, here she was . . . almost blonde.

Borelli, too, had changed over the past four years. He had lost at least fifty pounds since she'd last seen him, though she thought he was still too heavy for his health. His decision to limit his consumption of alcohol to one glass of wine with dinner—at least that was what he'd told her—likely contributed to his weight loss. Dana had observed in Prague that he could devour a bottle of wine during a slow-paced meal with little help, and a good spot of whiskey seemed essential when sitting down for a serious talk. He also appreciated a good meal, something she'd witnessed a time or two, though he'd told her during their early morning walk that his doctor had put him on a healthy diet. Yet, Dana had noticed at dinner the previous evening, as well as at breakfast that morning, he had indulged and quite enjoyed it.

His hairline had neither receded farther nor had the sparse remaining dark hair grayed any more in the past four years.

The narrow road wound along the hills, offering a breathtaking view at every turn, vineyards, villas, and finger-like trees, brushstrokes of green, umber, and cerulean blue that could have been plucked from a Renaissance landscape. They were soon twisting up to the hilltop city.

After finding parking, they continued on foot toward the city center, taking the designated path and stairs. Dana noted the ascent was made without Borelli's familiar wheezing. Another change he'd made on doctor's orders—no smoking. Even without the laborious breathing, it was a slow journey up to the old city center.

They wandered the narrow streets, most allowing foot traffic only, past one shop, then another, each displaying wines from the many vineyards in the area. Signs in each shop declared *We ship anywhere in the world.* Bottles of the famous Brunello—all in high-shouldered green Bordeaux bottles, a requirement, according to Borelli—along with Rosso di Montalcino and Moscadello di

Montalcino, were artfully arranged atop wooden crates, some horizontally in custom made wine racks. She noticed the Borelli wines featured in many shops, easily identified by the drawing of the family villa on the label.

Borelli pointed out the colorful banners displayed on each street. "Part of the fun during the upcoming festivities of the *Sagra del Tordo*. There are four sections of the village, each represented by their colors, which, as you can see, are displayed on the standards. An old-fashioned medieval archery competition will take place this coming weekend. Red and white for *Quartiere* Borgetto," Borelli explained. "Red and yellow for the Travaglio Quarter, blue and white for the Pianello, and blue and yellow for *Quartiere* Ruga. The competition can become quite fierce, though all in good fun."

"Which are you?" Dana asked. "How do the Borellis fit into all of this?"

"It's mostly made up of the townspeople, tradesmen, those who live inside the village, though a good number of them work in the vineyards. More than half of the residents are employed in the wineries. The bulk of the others in the tourist trades, the shops, restaurants, hotels, which, of course, are dependent on the wine industry. The tourists come for the wine and inevitably support the economy of the entire region. We landowners," he said in a playfully mocking voice, which Dana noted verged on a real sense of superiority, "can pick a team. It's a friendly though competitive rivalry, team members eating, drinking, celebrating with those from competing quarters, until the main event."

"Sounds like fun," Dana said.

"Yes, we'll definitely put the competition on our schedule."

Dana suggested they find a shop to get a postcard to send her mom. She'd promised her brothers and sister-in-law she'd keep in touch through email. She hadn't bothered to bring her cellphone, though she'd packed her iPad for connecting with family. But, for her mom, a postcard. Her mother hadn't been particularly happy about Dana's plans to visit Father Borelli. She had nothing against

Borelli, though she often mentioned Dana's propensity for choosing male friends who were ineligible. Which, in a way, was true. The team she worked with in Boston was made up of two married men and a single man who was one of Dana's best friends though definitely not relationship material. He was fond of voluptuous blondes, a category in which Dana definitely did not fit, despite her recent transformation into *blondishness.*

Dana knew her mother wished her to find a nice, young man, but at this point in her life, a middle-aged man would be more appropriate, though Dana certainly wasn't looking. She'd dated off and on since her divorce, had brief affairs with men she could now admit she hadn't even cared for. She wasn't good at relationships. Or maybe she was merely content with being single. And maybe this was another aspect of her life that had drawn her to Borelli and to this odd friendship. Borelli's *singleness* by virtue of his chosen vocation, Dana's by virtue of what her mother called Dana's reluctance to "put herself out there."

After finding a postcard, they sat for coffee, choosing an outdoor table where they could watch the growing crowds as Dana jotted a note to her mom. Tourists, with their sturdy walking shoes, guidebooks, and backpacks were easily identified. Locals could be picked out by their quick steps as they rushed by window displays. A group of teens, both boys and girls in tight jeans, laughed and puffed innocently on cigarettes on the opposite side of the street. A girl with long dark hair, streaked with an unnatural shade of red, nuzzled up against one of the boys, the tallest one. Playfully, she snatched the cigarette from his mouth and took a slow, sensual drag, then placed it back in his mouth.

Borelli waved to the young man, who waved back. He said something to the girl, handed her the cigarette, then started toward them, hands in the pockets of his leather jacket, broad shoulders swaying, exuding a youthful confidence in his swagger.

He approached the table and greeted Father Borelli, then smiled at Dana. She guessed he was about eighteen or nineteen, a handsome young man with wavy black hair and dark eyes hooded under thick brows.

"Ms. Dana Pierson," Borelli said. "Our guest at the estate this week," he explained, and then introduced the young man as Fabrizio Rossi, an apprentice at the Borelli Vineyards.

"Very pleased to meet you," the boy said as Dana extended her hand. He smelled of leather, tobacco, and spicy cologne. "Welcome to Montalcino. A lovely time to visit the region." His English was accented, but his words came out with self-assurance and he looked directly in her eyes as he spoke. An almost-adult who was in no way intimidated by older adults, even a Borelli, part-owner of the estate on which he was employed. Dana had never seen herself as threatening, which had certainly proved to be an asset in her work. But Borelli, with his deep, gravelly voice, overflowing with self-importance, as well as his size, might come across as a bit overwhelming.

"You are enjoying your stay?" the young man asked.

"I arrived just yesterday," Dana answered, "but, yes, I am enjoying my stay."

"You have an excellent tour guide in Father Borelli."

"Yes, it doesn't get any better," Dana replied.

"The weather, very agreeable." Fabrizio glanced toward the sky.

"Ordered just for our guest," Borelli said.

"Very nice seeing you, Father Borelli, and meeting you, Ms. Pierson." He smiled at each as he pronounced their names, then glanced back toward his friends. The girl with the dark hair streaked with red waved toward the trio, cigarette clasped between her fingers. "Perhaps we will see you at the estate." Fabrizio offered another warm smile before joining his friends.

"It appears Leo has given him the day off." Borelli's eyes narrowed, and Dana couldn't tell if he was adjusting for the sun, which was working its way across the sky, or if there was more to it than that. A puzzled look stretched across the priest's face, but he added nothing more.

Dana tucked her postcard in her bag and, after finishing their coffee, they found a place to mail the card. Borelli suggested they visit the *fortezza* and then drive into Siena for lunch.

As they walked up toward the fortress, they came upon a large metal plaque, the upper right embossed with a colorful logo for the *Consorzio del Vino Brunello Di Montalcino,* a stylized green vine sitting proudly atop a mound of golden Tuscan earth. An expansive map, red dots marking locations and gold print designating names of the wine producers, stretched across the face of the plaque.

"Consorzio del Vino Brunello Di Montalcino," Borelli pronounced the words dramatically with a wave of his arm, "an organization formed in the late nineteen-sixties to protect the integrity of the Brunello wines, to ensure that prescribed standards of production are met, that only Sangiovese from within the Montalcino growing zone are used."

"The first Brunellos," Dana added, "were produced by the Santi family in the mid-eighteen hundreds." She was letting Borelli know she had done her pre-trip reading. "Yet, there was no guidance, no overseeing until the mid-nineteen hundreds?"

"Yes, but the first Brunellos were not commonly available," Borelli explained. "Reserved for a few wealthy connoisseurs."

Dana wondered if it was possible for Borelli to pronounce the word *connoisseurs* without giving the impression that he was one of them.

"The Brunello wine," he went on, "was not made available to the general public until the mid-nineteen hundreds, and only a select group was producing the wine at that time. Now, over two hundred fifty growers are producing Brunello Di Montalcino." He pointed out the location of the Borelli Vineyards on the map.

Additional words on the sign—*Zona di produzione con ubicazione delle aziende imbottigliatrici*—were translated from Italian into English. *Production area and site of bottling estates.*

"It's amazing the region is able to support this many," Dana said.

"Most are small. Some, such as the Borellis', over a thousand hectares, the equivalent of just under two and a half thousand acres," he explained. "Not all planted vineyards. Many, for environmental concerns, lay fallow."

"Two hundred fifty producers?" she asked. "Are their roots as deeply planted in the land as the Borellis'?"

"A few. But many have sold out," he said, hesitating a moment, and Dana was sure she detected something in the words—*sold out*—as if he saw this as a betrayal. "It seems to be trendy these days," Borelli snorted, "to own a vineyard. Many of the families have sold their best wine-producing land to celebrities, rock, film and TV stars, artists, American corporate executives, who seem to enjoy escorting their friends through their Tuscan vineyards." He shook his head. "It seems anyone with money to spare wants to get into the winemaking business these days. Perhaps nothing more than a status symbol. *I own a small vineyard in Tuscany,*" he said in a mocking voice. "Quite trendy. Like a celebrity carrying a miniature dog around in a purse. Now, the trend is a mini vineyard in Tuscany."

Dana couldn't help but smile. "It's the smaller vineyards that are being sold?"

"Generally." He sighed. "Some of the smaller vineyards feel they have been rescued. With the price of producing wine, old equipment giving out, expensive oak barrels that have to be replaced more often than one would imagine, and yes, everything—if one hopes to keep up with the industry—is computerized now. Very expensive to keep up. These celebrity owners generally keep the producers intact, those who know the art of winemaking. Fortunately, some of the new owners realize that simply because one has the money to buy something, one does not have the knowledge or necessary passion to run the business. Many—the Italian families—are doing better in letting the ownership go. The infusion of money, it's been good for some. They are able to stay with the land, continue to produce without the constant worry of how they will finance from year to year."

Borelli motioned toward the fortress and they continued up

toward the massive stone building. Entering through the open gate, they crossed through the courtyard, past a small group of tourists, then through the *enoteca*, the wine bar and shop on the lower level. After climbing to the top of the ancient building, they strolled leisurely along the rampart, taking in the view of miles and miles of rolling green hills, vineyards, olive groves, mini forests of evergreens as well as patches of deciduous trees. Borelli spouted the expected history, explaining the origin of the fortress in the mid-fourteenth century, designed by the Sienese architects Mino Foresi and Domenico di Feo. Just as they were about to continue on to the city side of the upper level, they were startled by what sounded to Dana like a digitalized Gregorian chant.

Borelli reached into his pocket and pulled out a tiny cellphone, surprising Dana because she was aware that, though he was not averse to modern technology, he was not ready to fully embrace it.

"Oh, Mia, *buon giorno,*" he said in a friendly tone. "Siena, *si, si.*" He nodded, grinning, then said to Dana, "The poor girl is bored. If we are going to Siena for lunch, Mia would like us to come fetch her."

Dana smiled at the thought, and then she heard a high-pitched scream coming from the phone, so loud and shrill it caused Borelli's hand to quiver, even as he reached for his chest, all color draining from his face.

CHAPTER FOUR

"Mia, Mia," the priest shouted into the phone, but Dana could tell from Borelli's frightened tone that he received no reply. "Get the truck," he commanded, pointing to the main street below. "Meet me there."

Sensing the urgency, Dana turned and sprinted down the stairs of the *fortezza*, nearly knocking over a couple as she passed. She rushed through the enoteca, startling the small group of tourists leisurely perusing the wines displayed along the wall, darted into the street, dodging vehicles as she made her way to the other side. She ran down the steep, grass-covered hill, not bothering to take the designated path, choosing the shortest route, slipping once as she made her way to the parking area. Finding Borelli's truck, she unlocked the door, jumped in, revved the motor, zoomed out into the street, climbed up the hill, and found the spot on the main road where Borelli had pointed. She could see him, making his way toward her with great effort, winded, cellphone to his ear.

Slipping the phone in his pocket, he motioned her to move over, which she did without hesitation, lifting her legs over the gear shift, snapping on her seatbelt. License or not, Borelli intended to drive.

"I called Leo," he said, gasping for air between each word. He paused for a quick moment, glancing one direction, then the other, and pulled out into traffic. "He hasn't seen Mia this morning. I called Renata, our cook. This is the first place Mia heads each morning, Renata's kitchen. She told me she sent Mia out to take something to Paolo, Renata's father-in-law."

"Mia called you from the estate?"

Borelli nodded.

Dana knew what they heard over the phone was a young girl's scream. "No one heard her scream?"

Borelli shook his head, leaning forward as if this would increase their speed, though Dana was sure his foot could press with no greater force on the gas pedal as they veered onto the narrow, two-lane highway leading out of the village. They passed one car then another, one of the drivers offering Borelli a hand sign that did not appear to be one of approval. Dana grasped the door handle as they began their steep descent.

"The phone went dead?" she asked.

"Not dead," Borelli replied. "It sounded . . ." He hesitated, searching for the words. "At first a crackling sound. Then, yes, nothing."

When they arrived at the estate, after a tense, but speedy drive, Borelli pulled into the parking area in front of the villa, gravel spraying, brakes screeching.

Mia sat on an outdoor bench, her father at her side, his arm wrapped protectively around her shoulder.

Borelli and Dana jumped out and rushed toward them. Mia wore a T-shirt and shorts, a jacket that appeared to be too large—possibly her father's—draped over her shoulders. The girl was rubbing her eyes, pushing her hair away from her damp face, her eyes swollen with tears. Her legs and bare feet were oddly stained and spotted with cuts. Bright red blood oozed from several wounds. Then Dana noticed that Leo's shoes and the bottoms of his jeans were damp.

Leo's hands bore cuts similar to those on Mia's legs. His pressed white shirt was spotted with blood. Or wine? Dana smelled both, but it was the fruity, fermented scent that overpowered.

"Paolo," Leo said, motioning across the driveway. He spoke rapidly to Borelli in Italian, then switched to a few English words, allowing Dana into the conversation. "I called the police. Renata is outside the cellar with . . . We tried . . ." Leo took a deep breath. His lower lip trembled. He reached up and ran his fingers quickly over his mouth, leaving a trace of blood. "We tried to revive him. I wanted Renata to come to the house."

Dana could see both father and daughter were in shock. Mia had not uttered a word, and the look on her face was hollow and blank. Her tiny body rocked back and forth as her hands moved nervously along her upper legs.

Mia's grandmother, Estella, appeared with a bowl of water, the liquid sloshing, her entire body shaking. A towel draped over one arm. A box of bandages and a bottle of disinfectant were tucked awkwardly under the other. The old woman's face was as pale as her white hair pulled back in an old-fashioned bun. The natural, outdoor light deepened every line in her face, her creased brow, and her tightly pinched lips. Such a stark contrast to the dignified, composed woman Dana had met the previous evening.

Dana reached over to help with the items Estella struggled to hold and motioned for her to sit. Dana knelt in front of Mia, dampening the hand towel, rinsing the girl's legs and cuts as gently as possible. Mia, still wordless, flinched and buried her face into her father's shoulder. In one of the deepest cuts, Dana saw something sharp and ragged. Slowly and carefully, she removed it. Mia stiffened, emitting the soft sounds of a wounded animal.

Placing the object in the palm of her hand, Dana saw it was a small shard of translucent green glass, the color of the bottles of Brunello wine she had seen in the shops of Montalcino. She glanced back at Borelli, who had taken a protective stance in front of the bench, even as his eyes darted about. Estella sat rigidly, one hand grasping Mia's, the other quivering on her lap, legs shaking.

A dark vehicle with tinted windows pulled up. Leo motioned for Borelli to sit, as he jumped up and hurried toward the car. Borelli lowered himself to the bench, enclosing the girl protectively between himself and Estella.

A large man emerged from the passenger side of the car. A wrinkled suit jacket that appeared too large, as if he'd recently lost weight, hung from his thick shoulders. His pants draped over his shoes. His dark brown hair was threaded with gray, but his mustache was pure white and as thick as a janitor's broom. A second man, the driver, much younger and thinner, stepped out, moving with an uneven gait as if one leg was shorter than the other. He followed the first man in a stoop-shouldered manner that left no doubt which was the chief. They spoke to Leo, voices rising and falling, Leo gesturing toward the bench, then out toward the cellar.

A second vehicle arrived. Several men jumped out. One of the men sprinted toward them, medical bag in hand. He knelt down in front of Mia, next to Dana, and took over tending the girl.

As Leo and the two men headed toward the cellar, Dana asked, "Would she be more comfortable in the house?"

"I want to go to Renata," Mia cried. "To Signor Paolo." An uneven sob came from somewhere deep within, her chest heaving uncontrollably. Estella tightened her arm around the girl, wiping a tear rolling down her granddaughter's cheek, as the medic patched Mia's wounds.

Borelli spoke in a soft voice, in Italian, to Mia and she replied with the same even tone, stopping now and then, gazing toward the path her father and the two men had followed.

Shortly, Leo returned, along with the younger man, a plain-clothes detective Dana guessed, as he did not wear a police uniform. Leo spoke to Mia, then to the young medic who had carefully and silently tended her. Mia nodded and her father swept her up and started toward the house. Glancing back, he said, "Detective Perotti would like to speak to each of us inside." Mia had melted into his arms and said nothing. "Inspector DeLuca asks that we stay away from the cellar. I'm taking Mia up to her room. If they want to talk to her it can be done later," he added with a sharp edge. Dana looked over at Borelli, back at the detective. No one spoke.

Estella followed Mia and her father up to the second floor of the villa while Borelli, the younger detective, and Dana waited downstairs in the living room.

Borelli paced anxiously in front of the unlit fireplace, beneath a painting of a long-necked woman in a modern, semi-abstract style. A number of tapestry pillows nestled along the backs of two identical sofas perpendicular to the fireplace. Dana sat on the edge of one, after checking the back of her jeans to make sure they were not stained with blood or wine. Aware that her knees were damp, she made every effort to sit carefully. As the priest and detective spoke, Dana knew, from the sharp tone of their words, that they were arguing. Borelli turned to her and said, "He'd like you to wait in the library, which is ridiculous since I informed him you do not speak nor understand Italian. Detective Perotti wants to remove any possibility that we are collaborating our stories." Borelli rolled his eyes. "Then I am to act as translator for your interview, which adds to the absurdity of his request."

"I'll do whatever I can to help," Dana said, though she doubted she had anything to offer. She rose and made her way down the hall to the library, where she examined books on the shelves—a mixture of Italian and English—and then gazed out the window, where she could see no human activity, parked vehicles only. She thought of poor Mia, her screams coming from Borelli's phone, the girl sitting on the bench, legs bloody and cut.

About twenty minutes later, Borelli appeared, inviting Dana back for her interview.

"He wishes to ask you a few questions," Borelli said, motioning for Dana to sit. The officer stood as Borelli settled into the sofa, across the coffee table from Dana. The detective cleared his throat.

A short interview was conducted, Borelli acting as interpreter.

The questions were simple, though it seemed Borelli was adding to her answers as he translated her brief replies into Italian for the detective. "I arrived just last evening . . . I work as a journalist in Boston, Massachusetts . . . the reason for my trip is pleasure . . . this morning, I awoke, had breakfast, went for a walk with my host, Father Borelli, then we drove into Montalcino."

If it hadn't been for the seriousness of the situation it might have been great comedy fodder. Dana's short concise answers seemed to turn into elaborate, wordy interpretations when Borelli spoke. She wondered if the detective realized this. He held a pad and a pen that he twirled in his fingers, only occasionally taking down notes. She guessed that he was hearing exactly what Borelli had shared with him in his interview.

After the detective thanked Dana and shook her hand with a *"Grazie, Signora,"* he left the room.

"What happened in the cellar?" Dana asked.

"Paolo," Borelli replied. "He's dead."

"Dead?" From what Leo had said, from Mia's obvious distress, and the seriousness of the police officers, this did not completely surprise Dana.

"When Mia went looking for Paolo this morning," Borelli explained, "she noticed the lock on the cellar had been broken. She entered and found Paolo lying in front of the first barrel. Someone had opened all the spigots on over a dozen large barrels." He closed his eyes, rubbed his head before he could continue. "The produce from one entire year destroyed. Most of it would have been bottled early next year as Brunello. A small percentage would have been left in barrel for an additional year to be labeled Riserva." Again, Borelli paused. His eyes tightened. "Mia found him face down in—"

"The wine?" Dana took in a deep breath as this image formed in her mind.

"They also destroyed a number of bottles of Rosso di Montalcino stored on racks in the cellar. Millions of dollars of destruction. Such viciousness."

"Paolo was murdered?" she asked.

"I believe that is what the police are attempting to determine. Leo said he had a gash on his head."

"How awful. I'm so sorry." She was grateful for this explanation. Much of the conversation among Leo, Borelli, Estella, and Mia had been lost in the Italian. She'd understood nothing of the conversation between Leo and the detectives. "Poor Mia," Dana said.

"Yes, poor girl. As you can see, she is—oh, Lord—" Borelli placed an open hand against his head then clenched his fist, pressing into his temple. "She saw no one . . . but, of course, Paolo—"

"Uncle Giovanni." Leo stood in the doorway of the living room. "Mia is asking for you," he said, and then he motioned for Dana to follow him.

CHAPTER FIVE

"Please," Leo said to Dana as they entered the kitchen. "Please, if you will." He pulled out a stool at the long marble counter in the middle of the room and directed her to sit, and then he said, "*Momento*," and left her alone.

He did not explain where he was going, but the kitchen was not an unpleasant place to wait with its warm, dark wooden cupboards, pots and pans hanging from a rack above the island, the aroma of fresh bread. The three stools along the marble island faced toward another counter with a deep-set country sink and three nice-sized windows looking out into the garden. Ceramic containers lined the counter on either side of the sink and bunches of drying herbs and garlic hung in front of the windows. A large six-burner range stood against a backsplash of yellow and blue tile and took up a good part of the counter to her left. An unattended pot, red sauce dripping from the side, complete with spoon as if it had been left in mid-stir, sat on one of the back burners.

Leo returned carrying a bottle of wine and, after wiping off a thin layer of dust, he reached into a drawer and drew out a corkscrew embellished with the family logo, a drawing of the Borelli villa.

He uncorked the bottle with a practiced gesture and set it on the counter. Without words, he opened a cupboard, selected two matching wineglasses. He poured wine into each, pulled out a stool, and sat beside Dana as an uncomfortable silence surrounded the two.

After several moments, Leo said, "This is how the Borellis face a crisis. With a glass of wine." There was something in the tone of his voice she could not interpret. Surely not sarcasm. Perhaps anger? Mixed with frustration and sadness?

Dana wondered if they were waiting for the wine to breathe. It seemed Leo himself had ceased to breathe as he sat without motion, without words, staring out toward the garden.

Finally, he said, "The police have requested I wait in the house." He rose. His posture was erect, though his finely pressed, white, long-sleeve shirt as well as his jeans were stained with blood and wine. Yet, even in his obviously troubled state of mind, there was a dignity about the man, definitely a Borelli trait.

Leo pulled his cellphone from his pocket, punched the screen, and spoke rapidly. The cadence of his Italian words carried a hollow, lifeless tone that gave Dana the impression he was speaking to no one, merely leaving a message. She picked up a few words—*Roma, aeropòrto, Americani.* Leo paced the room. Setting the phone on the counter, he glanced over at her. "We have potential buyers coming this afternoon." His eyes were very dark brown, so deep in color she saw little distinction between his pupils and irises, which made it difficult to read his eyes. "Americans," he explained, his gaze wandering about the room. "And tourists. This is a busy time of year with the upcoming *festa.* the *Sagra del Tordo.* Many visitors in the area." He rubbed his head, pushed back his hair, which she'd noticed was just beginning to thin, though he had much more hair than his uncle Giovanni. "Perhaps we must cancel."

Dana wasn't sure if he was speaking of the tourists or buyers, or both. She wanted to do something to help. She knew Estella and Borelli were with Mia and questioned why her father had not gone back up, though he obviously had business to attend to.

Leo grabbed the phone, pressed a key with his thumb. Again, his tone indicated he was leaving a message. He placed the phone back in his pocket.

"I have no means of contacting them until they arrive. Important buyers from the United States. My intention—to pick them up myself at the airport in Rome. With a driver. Our driver, he speaks little English. Our enologist, Marco Dardi, is away on a family matter and will not return until later this evening." Leo spoke English, not Italian, so Dana knew his words were for her, yet it seemed as if he were speaking to himself. "Uncle Giovanni could go, but better that he remains here with Mia. I must answer questions for the police. They are Americans, these buyers. None speak Italian."

Dana guessed Leo's calls were an effort—unsuccessful—to find an English speaker to go with the driver.

"I could go," she offered.

Leo turned, looking at her with an expression of surprise as if he hadn't even known she was there. Then the corners of his mouth lifted. Not quite a smile but certainly a look of amusement. His eyebrows, thick and perfectly symmetrical, shot up for a second. He said nothing, yet his expression might have said, *Yes, but you know nothing about wine. About Tuscany. About the history of the Borelli Vineyards.*

"That is very kind of you." He rubbed his head as if thinking this through, perhaps mentally putting together the words to gracefully tell her this was not a good idea.

He walked toward the window. Unlike the front of the villa that looked out toward the rolling fields and vineyards, the kitchen opened out into a small area, the family herb and vegetable garden, a much more intimate setting. He turned back to her and said, "Your bag arrived. Perhaps you have something . . . I do not wish to offend you, Ms. Pierson, but perhaps you have something more suitable to wear to meet our guests?"

Surprisingly, he was accepting her offer. Dana looked down at her jeans, which she'd been wearing for three days now—on her flight from Boston, her flight from Rome to the Peretola Airport near Florence, then all day yesterday and for her morning walk with Borelli and their trip into Montalcino. A grass stain, unnoticed until now, discolored her jeans. The knees were stained with blood and wine. If she was going to the airport as a representative of the Borelli Vineyards, she could understand Leo's concern. He wouldn't want his important guests to think that Leonardo Antonelli had sent one of his laborers, fresh from the vineyard or grape stomping vat to pick them up.

"Yes," she said. "If my bag has arrived, I could find something more appropriate to wear."

"That would be very kind of you." She might be his last resort, but she sensed Leo was grateful for her offer. She wondered if the police investigator would allow her to leave.

"I will call the driver to pick you up in front of the house," Leo said, and then, "I will inform Alberto, Inspector DeLuca. He should be informed that you are leaving the estate. I do not see that this will create a problem." Leo reached for his phone, glanced at the digital time on the screen. "Half an hour. Would this be possible?"

Dana nodded as she started to rise from the stool. He reached over, placed a hand on her arm.

"Please," he said. "Join me for a glass of wine." As he handed her a glass, then picked up the other for himself, she half expected him to perform some involuntary, unconscious ritual, a sniffing, a swirling, a slow thoughtful drink, but he didn't. He took a substantial swallow, then another, like a frat boy chugging beer. Under ordinary circumstances, this would have startled Dana, but the events of the morning had been anything but ordinary.

She sat and sipped her wine, Leo waiting, staring out the window.

After her glass was empty, a process both too slow and too quick for Dana that involved little further conversation, she wondered if she'd used up a good portion of the time she would be allowed to change.

"Perhaps a little extra time," Leo said, offering a gracious smile. "Half an hour from now?" His perfect brows rose.

Dana returned a smile, nodded and went up to her room and found her bag. Quickly, she unpacked the contents, attempting to shake out the wrinkles. After a very quick shower and hastily towel drying her hair, she put on a clean blouse and her black slacks. She always traveled light—a couple pair of jeans, T-shirts, two blouses, a black pants suit, which she could wear when something more formal than jeans was expected. She dabbed on gloss and blush. As she slipped on the matching black jacket and arranged one of the two scarves she'd packed, she heard a knock on the door as a familiar voice called out, "I have brought you something to eat. I apologize that we were unable to have a proper meal in Siena."

Dana opened the door to find Borelli, standing with a tray filled with a bowl of olives, some cheese, salami, bread, a wineglass, and a decanter of wine.

"Thank you," she said, motioning him in. He placed the tray on the small table near the window and poured a glass of wine.

"I'll pass on the wine," she said. The glass she'd had with Leo on a near empty stomach was more than enough.

He took no offense at her refusal of wine, but sat down in one of the chairs flanking the table and placed a folder, which she hadn't noticed until then, on the table. He fingered the base of the wine glass tentatively, as if thinking—*since I poured it, someone will have to drink it.*

"Mia?" Dana asked. She sat in the chair opposite Borelli.

"Estella called the family doctor," Borelli told her. "He arrived a short time ago. Mia has been sedated. Estella, too."

"What a terrible experience for both," Dana said.

"If only," Borelli said after several moments, "if I had followed my original plan—if only we'd gone directly from vineyard to cellar, we might have come upon Paulo. We might have saved him." He picked up the glass of wine. "May I?" he asked.

Dana nodded.

He took a sip. "If only we, instead of Mia, had entered the cellar first, at least we might have saved her the pain . . ."

The past cannot be altered, one cannot save another from pain, Dana thought, but in her mind she was echoing Borelli's words, and then, *If only we had not stayed at my mother's that night . . . if only I had heard a sound in the night . . .*

"How is Renata?" she asked.

"She wanted to accompany Paolo. She has not returned yet."

"Does Paolo have a wife?"

"She passed some time ago."

"Renata is married to Paolo's son?"

"He is no longer with us either. Gone for several years now." Borelli shook his head, rubbed his bald spot. He lifted a piece of cheese off the tray. "Leo said you offered to go with the driver to pick up the Americans." He handed her the folder. She opened it and found several papers inside the pockets. Literature on the Borelli Vineyards, reprints of articles from American wine magazines, a list of prestigious sounding awards, as well as an itinerary of events for the guests over the next few days.

Dana wondered if they would be able to follow this schedule, if the American visitors would be allowed on the estate. She also realized Borelli had presented her with this information to study if the Americans had questions on the drive from Rome.

"I know I can rely on you, Ms. Pierson," Borelli said as he rose. Then, as if an afterthought, "Perhaps you should not mention what happened in the cellar this morning."

CHAPTER SIX

The driver, a stiff, formal man in uniform and cap, and apparently a religious man—a rosary hung from the rearview mirror—spoke little English. Just as Leo had explained. He introduced himself as Claudio, and then, after a brief conversation with few words, Dana opened the folder Borelli had given her, intent on learning as much as she could before their arrival in Rome, hoping this might provide a diversion, something to keep her mind busy.

Several sheets in the folder presented details about local wine production that Borelli had shared with Dana earlier, and general information she'd learned from her pre-trip reading. She reviewed the schedule set out for the guests. Dinner that evening at the villa at eight o'clock. The menu was printed in an italic-like script. Borelli wines were paired with each course. The following day would be dedicated to a vineyard tour, both barrel and bottle tasting, followed by dinner at one of the local restaurants in the city of Montalcino.

She wondered how the Borellis would handle the arrival of the guests. Surely someone would explain what had happened that morning. She was grateful it wouldn't be up to her to share this information. The police might even insist the dinner scheduled that evening be canceled.

Attempting to concentrate on the information in the folder, she questioned if her offer to pick up the guests had come too quickly. At the time it seemed like the best way to help. She scanned a list of wines currently available: Several vintages of Brunello with and without the Riserva label, a selection of Rosso di Montalcino, a wine also produced from Sangiovese, but with a much shorter aging period than the five years required for the Brunello. This allowed producers to release a wine sooner to generate cash flow. The list also included a white wine, the Borelli Moscadello di Montalcino.

When she came across the description of the Borelli Brunello to be sampled in barrel the following day, she took in a deep breath, exhaling slowly, realizing it was the wine that had been destroyed. The wine in which Mia had found Paolo.

A number of articles from American wine magazines that featured the Borelli Vineyards were included in the file, one from almost thirty years ago with a black and white photo of Leonardo Antonelli, his father Angelo Antonelli, and the enologist, Marco Dardi. Leo looked very young, ready to take on the world. There was something intriguing, appealing, in the tilt of his head, his subtle but open smile.

She nibbled on bread and cheese she'd lifted from the tray Borelli had brought up to her room, though she wouldn't have needed to bring it along. The van was equipped with a basket of snacks and wine, a cooler of water, juice and soda.

About halfway to Rome, Dana checked the cellphone Borelli had handed her before she left and found that the flight was a few minutes late. When Borelli gave her the phone, he'd told Dana that Mia had suggested it, had set it up for her several days before her arrival. Borelli had not thought to give it to her earlier. "I didn't believe you'd need it," he'd said. "But now . . ."

All information and apps in English. Curious, Dana clicked on *contacts*. Mia had listed Father Borelli, Leo, and Mia. Dana was touched that the young girl had listed herself as a contact for Dana.

When they arrived at the airport, the driver let her out and told her where to meet him after she greeted their guests. She had been informed that there would be three representatives from Simonelli Distributors, none of them a Simonelli. A Mr. Richard Jones, a Mr. David Ryder, and a Ms. Octavia Fleenor.

Dana tucked the cardboard sign identifying her as a representative of the winery under her arm and proceeded to the passenger pickup area. BORELLI VINEYARDS was written across the top, the company logo in the middle, WELCOME, SIMONELLI DISTRIBUTORS, in broad caps across the bottom. A nice little free airport advertisement.

She'd been given no physical descriptions of the representatives and would have to rely on them identifying her. Standing among hoteliers and tourist company reps, Dana held up her sign, grinning stupidly as passengers flocked in, nodding at those who smiled back, waiting for the Americans. She wondered if they would be surprised, possibly disappointed after traveling all the way from New York. They would likely expect more authenticity than this. She might be able to fake her knowledge of wine, but surely not the fact that she was an American.

Then she saw them, a trio she was sure was hers—two obviously American men, one tall and thin with dark, plastic-framed glasses, the other stout and bald, looking about expectantly, appearing oddly both cheerful and weary. He smiled broadly as he spotted Dana. The third was a tall blonde wearing tight slacks, a silky blouse, and high heeled shoes, looking like a starlet fresh from makeup and wardrobe. Dana wondered how she'd managed that on an eight-hour flight.

The stout, bald man wore a maroon pullover sweater over a white, collared shirt that had come loose and hung untidily below his round belly. The other man wore khakis, looking youthful and preppy in a navy polo shirt. She guessed he was the youngest of the trio, maybe in his mid-thirties.

"*Buon giorno,* Borelli Vineyards," the man in the maroon sweater called out, confirming Dana had guessed correctly.

As they approached, Dana said, "I'm Dana Pierson. Welcome to Italy."

The weary, but jovial, plump traveler introduced himself as David Ryder, his companions as Rich Jones, and Octavia Fleenor. "Seems we've picked up a hitchhiker on our way over," he added. "You don't mind if Winkie comes along to Montalcino?"

A short man with a mass of curly hair that looked like it had just gone through a wind tunnel stood beside David Ryder, staring down at his cellphone, fingers flying. He glanced up and nodded, then back to his phone. Now, *he* definitely looked like he'd made that transatlantic flight and hadn't bothered to comb his hair before deplaning. With his head bent toward the phone, a circle of scalp was clearly visible in the middle of the messy swirl of salt-and-pepper hair, a bald spot probably unnoticeable if it weren't for this peculiar angle, and the fact that Dana was several inches taller than the man.

"I'm sure that won't be a problem," Dana replied as she moved closer to offer her guests a hand with their bags. The van was a seven-passenger with plenty of room, and she knew her assigned task was being a gracious host. "We have a room for each of you in Montalcino. Should we call ahead for an additional room?" She glanced at Winkie.

"No need," Winkie said, finally looking up at Dana. Oddly, he looked very much like Winkie Dalton, the famous comedian, movie star, and producer. As she studied his face, Dana could see—that was exactly who he was. Winkie Dalton. He was heavier than she would have thought, definitely carrying some extra weight, a middle-aged paunch. But then, she realized he hadn't appeared in a movie recently, being mostly behind the camera in various roles. Writer. Producer. Director. She wondered why he didn't have his own transportation, maybe an entourage.

"We've got everything?" she asked taking a quick inventory of luggage. A small carry-on for each of the men, a couple of briefcases. A good-sized, wheeled piece for Octavia, plus a matching carry-on and an enormous bag hung over her shoulder. Dana reached out to take the carry-on, and Octavia offered a thank-you smile.

"We have a driver waiting." Dana motioned, then called Claudio, who showed up within minutes of their arrival at the passenger pickup area.

The two fellow wine buyers climbed in the back of the van, and Octavia settled in the middle two-passenger seat, as Claudio lifted the bags into the storage compartment in the back. Dana asked Winkie if he'd like to sit up front, but he shook his head and slid in next to Octavia. Dana sat in front with the driver.

As they exited the terminal area, Dana looked back and asked, "You had a pleasant flight?"

"You're American?" Mr. Ryder asked. She detected no disappointment in his voice.

"Yes," she answered, then, as a means of distraction, she offered a glass of wine, water, something to eat. Dana poured drinks for each passenger at their request, placed several snacks on a tray, feeling very much like a flight attendant. Conversation was sparse as they made their way out of the maze of airport traffic.

"Beautiful country," Mr. Jones said gazing out the window as they sped along on the Autostrada. "The weather's been nice?"

"A little cloudy early this morning, but it looks like it will be nice for the next couple of days." The weather app she'd checked predicted warm weather for their stay in Montalcino—three days according to the itinerary in the folder.

"Wonderful, wonderful," Mr. Ryder said. "I've always loved Italy. We're certainly looking forward to visiting the Borelli Vineyards."

"I've thought about buying a home here," Octavia joined in, then added with a laugh, "Or perhaps a villa or vineyard."

The men chatted back and forth. No one asked why Leo had not come to pick them up or inquired why she had been sent.

Within minutes, Mr. Ryder was snoring heavily from the back seat, and the others seemed content with a silent drive. Winkie Dalton continued to work away on his cellphone. From the quick movement of his fingers, Dana guessed he was texting, or maybe playing a game. Shortly, his head was pressed to the window and she wondered if Winkie too was catching a wink.

Piece of cake getting this little group to Montalcino, Dana thought. She wouldn't have needed Borelli's crib sheets. She could have winged it.

As they picked up speed on the Autostrada, passing farmland, orchards, and a number of old boarded-up, deserted villas, they continued on in relative silence, snoring down to a faint buzz, the hum of the motor adding an even, soothing rhythm.

About half an hour into the drive, the quiet was interrupted. "How is it that you've come to be employed by this Italian, family-owned business?" Dana turned to see Winkie had awakened . . . if he'd even been asleep. The others had all nodded off. "Being an American?" he added.

"A family friendship," she replied. She could probably tell him she was visiting and had been asked to accompany the driver who spoke little English, but then she might have to explain why Leo couldn't come. She knew eventually the news would get out. A death, the wine destruction, could hardly be kept a secret. She wondered why Winkie was here, why he knew that the Borelli estate was family owned if he was just a "hitchhiker" the distributors had picked up on the way over.

"First time visiting Montalcino?" she asked.

He nodded vaguely.

"You traveled from New York with the Simonelli group?" Dana was curious to know how he ended up here with this trio.

"Just a coincidence," Winkie offered. "Octavia and I go back . . . oh, some time. Her brother and I were at Yale together. I used to spend weekends at their place in the Hamptons. Octavia was such a cute little girl. At first, I didn't recognize her. Seems we were all headed to the same place. She told me they had a driver coming and offered a ride. So here I am."

"You're on holiday?" Dana asked.

"Well, uh," he replied, hesitating. "Working, more or less."

"You're working on a new project?" He'd piqued her interest. She'd always liked his movies, his characters. He often played the role of a nerdy, well-educated, intellectual. A sensitive man.

"I need a quiet place to work," he replied. "To write."

"I've always enjoyed your films," she said. "I'm a fan of your work." She thought that might keep the conversation going, but when Winkie said, "Thank you," it was with a touch of aloofness that told her he was finished with the conversation. He stared out the window. As a journalist, she had a sense of when to end an interview and she sensed it now. She knew he didn't intend to share anything more.

As they got closer to Montalcino, a group of about a dozen men and women, most young and unkempt, marched along the side of the road, carrying signs. Italian words in red slashed circles. One of the signs contained a heart symbol, like that made famous during the *I Heart New York* craze. The symbol was followed by a sphere with swirls of blues and greens. I *heart* the earth? Dana wondered. An environmental protest?

"Has that created a problem for the vineyards?" Winkie asked.

The graphics, including the universal skull-and-crossbones, looked like they might represent chemicals or poisons. Signs with the symbolic red slashed circles might be indicating fertilizers or pesticides.

Dana wasn't sure if he was asking if the protesters or the environmental concerns were a problem. After a moment, she said, "Many of the wineries, such as the Borelli's, have been handed down from generation to generation, and there is pride and a sense of stewardship in caring for the land."

Winkie nodded, but he said nothing more, and Dana wondered again why he had asked.

When they arrived in Montalcino, the driver went directly to the hotel where arrangements had been made for the guests.

"Dinner at eight?" Dana said, glancing from Richard, to David, to Octavia, who were all awake now, in various stages of shaking off the weariness from their long journey. Claudio jumped out and hustled back to get the luggage. "We'll drop by about seven-forty-five?" Dana wasn't sure why she was saying *we*. Surely Leo would have something worked out by then.

"Sounds perfect," David Ryder answered in a groggy voice, a not-quite-here-yet expression, eyelids drooping. He looked like he could use a shave. He smiled. "Thank you for the ride. We'll see you about a quarter to eight then."

"Can we drop you off somewhere?" Dana asked Winkie as the driver helped Octavia with her bags, taking them up to the hotel and turning them over to the young man who had come out to greet them.

Winkie was digging around in his carry-on, still sitting in the middle seat as if expecting he would be delivered to his hotel. He pulled out a folded paper and opened it. "Veronesi Vineyards," he said, handing Dana what appeared to be a map. She studied it for a moment, aware it was similar to the map she'd seen earlier that day in Montalcino on the large metal plaque near the *fortezza*, each red dot marking one of the 250 Brunello wineries in the area. The Veronesi Vineyards appeared to be just a short distance from the Borelli estate.

"Shouldn't be a problem," she said.

She handed the map to Claudio, who had returned to his driver's seat. His eyes widened. He stared at Dana, eyes narrowing and said, "No." The defiance in his voice startled her.

Winkie had settled back into the van, legs stretched out, arms draped over the back of the seat, staring out the window. She sensed he was aware of Claudio's negative response to her request, though she didn't think it was that far out of their way. She wondered if the driver was concerned about deviating from the prescribed plan—pick up guests at airport, deliver to hotel in Montalcino, return to Borelli estate.

She grabbed her cellphone, hit *contacts*, and called Borelli. He answered right away.

"Mission accomplished," she said. "We've dropped our guests off in Montalcino. It seems we picked up an additional passenger." She explained who he was, but Dana wasn't sure Borelli understood that he was an American celebrity. "He's staying at a neighboring vineyard. Veronesi. From the map, it appears to be close to the Borelli villa. I'd like to drop him off, but Claudio seems hesitant. I don't want to upset him. I'd like to have your permission to take him."

Borelli was quiet for so long that Dana thought he'd turned off his phone or was somewhere with sketchy reception.

Then, finally, Borelli said, "Return to the villa, then we can take this American fellow. Winkie, you said?"

"Winkie Dalton."

"We will deliver him ourselves. You are correct, the Veronesi Vineyards appear very close to the Borelli estate on the map, and yes, it is as the crow flies—as you Americans say—but it is a greater distance on the road, which truthfully is not kept up as well as those here on our property."

Dana clearly detected some hesitance in Borelli's voice, and then that familiar tone of superiority, and she wondered if she'd overstepped. Surely, Winkie could get his own ride.

"Mia?" Dana asked. "Is she doing okay?"

"She's sleeping. Estella, too. We can talk later." Dana sensed Borelli didn't want to share anything more over the phone. "Let me speak with Claudio."

Dana handed her phone to Claudio who listened, saying little. A slight nod as he handed the phone back to Dana. She turned to Winkie. "Your destination is very close to ours and we will continue from there to the Veronesi Vineyards."

Winkie was back on his phone. He glanced up, blinking nervously. He nodded.

CHAPTER SEVEN

Back on the highway, Dana noticed the protesters had inched closer to the sign announcing the Borelli Vineyards. As several in the group sprinted toward them, waving their signs in the air, she was well aware that the logo and name on the outside of the van identified it as belonging to the Borelli Vineyards.

Claudio slowed as they approached the turnoff to the villa, allowing oncoming traffic—a small truck and another vehicle—to pass. Suddenly, one of the protesters, a young man with a scruffy beard and French-like tam perched on his head, was so close to Dana's window she could see the anger in his eyes. Claudio accelerated quickly to turn, just as the man slapped the side of the van. Dana's heart took a leap.

"What the—?" Winkie looked up from his phone as Dana glanced back to catch his surprise as well as the protester raising one fist in the air, his other hand placed in the crook of his raised arm. She didn't need an interpreter to understand the gesture. Although safe within the vehicle, she felt a tightening in her gut. Catching Winkie's eye, she detected a quick, nervous blink, a moment of distress from him, too, though he didn't say anything. They continued on in silence.

As they neared the estate, Winkie asked, "Will we be detained here?"

"We'll have you at your destination soon," Dana replied as Claudio took an abrupt turn onto a side road, causing Dana to brace with her leg and grab onto the arm rest. When they approached the garage from the back, and Dana saw Borelli making his way toward them, she realized he wanted them to avoid driving to the villa or near the cellar, where the police were likely still conducting their investigation. She wondered if the media had arrived, though there were no obvious signs of TV or press as they'd driven up the road.

"Grazie," she thanked Claudio as he got out, leaving the keys in the ignition. He straightened his tie as if it had become twisted on the long drive, nodded, and, nostrils flaring, turned and walked away. Borelli approached, breathing heavily. He motioned Dana to switch over to the driver's side, and she got out and hurried around as he slid into the front passenger seat. She glanced at him, seeing the worry and fatigue in the lines radiating from his eyes and etched around his mouth. She wanted desperately to ask if the police had made any progress, how Mia and Estella were doing, but she knew this must wait until after they delivered Winkie.

"Mr. Dalton, this is Father Giovanni Borelli," Dana said.

"Pleased to meet you, Father Borelli," Winkie replied, and then, oddly, he started speaking Italian. Soon he and Borelli were engaged in a lively conversation, though Dana understood not a word. Now and then, Borelli would point or gesture, directing Dana along the highway, shimmering with groves of olive trees, a patch of shrubs or trees here and there, more vineyards. The sun was slipping. The protesters lacing the highway just a short time ago had disappeared.

They veered off onto a narrow road, then began climbing a hill, passing several small areas of well-pruned vines, an ancient looking tractor parked on a steep incline, tilting as if it might tumble down. Soon they approached a sign, slightly worn, but still proudly presenting a family crest—a crown intertwined with grapevines—the words *Veronesi Vineyards.* As they rose, they passed more vineyards, though these appeared to have had limited recent care. She turned at the next marker that displayed a small arrow with Veronesi Vineyards printed in block letters. Bumping along, they hit one pothole, then a rut and a rocky patch, the priest and actor chatting away. Borelli gave no further instructions, so Dana guessed she was on the right track. They passed patches of what appeared to be abandoned vineyards, an untended grove of olive trees.

After a short while, they crested the hill and a large, imposing, three-story stone structure came into sight. As they got closer, Dana saw the exterior cream-colored stucco was stained and flaking. Paint curled off the green shutters. An older model Mercedes, with a ROMA license plate, sat out front in a wide circular driveway. A stone path, flanked with large urns containing mere skeletons of plants and miniatures, led up to enormous double wooden doors. Dana thought about Winkie telling her he'd come to Tuscany for a quiet place to work. This certainly might fit the bill, though she wondered why a wealthy movie producer would pick such an obviously deteriorating site. She glanced back at him to gauge his reaction, but as Winkie studied the surroundings, she saw no visible signs of disappointment.

Winkie gathered his bag and carry-on as Dana cast her gaze toward the upper floors of the building. Most of the windows on the third floor were boarded up, as were several on the second level. Then she noticed a quick movement behind a slim gap in an interior shutter. She attempted to catch Borelli's eye as he exited the van and reached out to shake Winkie's hand. When her eyes rose again, she saw nothing and the window had been shuttered from inside.

The two men exchanged a few words, and then Borelli was back in the van as Winkie walked up and rapped on the door. It opened and he stepped inside.

"Are the police coming up with anything?" Dana asked as she pulled around the Mercedes in the driveway. She was curious about what was going on with Winkie Dalton, why he was staying at this rundown estate, but first she wanted to know if Borelli had learned anything more while she was away.

"The police, no. Nothing they are sharing." He glanced quickly back at the house, then at Dana, eyes narrowed.

"Will the events of this morning . . ." She hated to call what had happened in the wine cellar an event, but she wondered how they were to continue the entertainment as planned. "Will what happened change the schedule? Will dinner be canceled?" She was also thinking, *Will the guests be informed?*

"Yes, we will continue with our plans, with business, as much as possible."

As they started back down the hill, Dana said, "I found that interesting, that Winkie was speaking to you in Italian, that a wealthy movie star would stay at—"

"A place in such obviously poor condition?"

"Well, yes."

"It was not always so," Borelli replied thoughtfully, and then, "Yes, interesting."

"I thought it was rude."

Borelli shot her a puzzled look.

"His speaking Italian," she said.

"Perhaps Winkie thought you speak Italian," Borelli said.

"The few words he said to me on the way from Rome were in English. Everyone in the van knew I was American. I made no attempt to convince them otherwise. Don't you think when I didn't join in your conversation, he—Winkie—would have realized I didn't understand?"

"Chauffeurs are generally instructed not to speak unless they are answering questions or providing pertinent information." Borelli chuckled, and then so did Dana.

"Did Winkie explain why he was here?" Dana asked.

"Writing," Borelli said.

"Working on a new movie script?"

"I assume. That's what he does. Isn't it?"

"Yes." Dana guessed there was more to Winkie and Borelli's lengthy conversation than that. "What else were you talking about? You were chatting right along as if thoroughly engaged, quite enjoying your conversation."

"The area. The wine industry."

"You think he's doing a movie about a vineyard, the story set in this area? He said he was here to find a quiet place to work, and, truthfully, it doesn't look like much is going on at the Veronesi estate."

"Currently, they are producing little wine, but years ago they were one of the largest, one of the best. The house on the hill was the liveliest place in the entire Siena Province. Events, parties, harvest celebrations." He shut his eyes for a moment as if imagining one of these parties. *That* Dana could picture. She sensed that Borelli might have enjoyed a good party in his youth.

"The Veronesi family," Borelli went on, "claims a royal bloodline. But, of course, hundreds of years ago, titles were awarded for favors. Nothing to do with bloodlines. Large parcels of land given to favored families. Such titles go back to the kingdom of Sardinia, the two kingdoms of Sicilies, the Papal State, the grand duchies of Tuscany, Parma, and Modena. But, these mean nothing now. The last Italian monarch was deposed in 1946. Land owned by some of these *noble families*"—Borelli exaggerated the words—"lost or sold off over the years. To lowlifes like the Borellis. Titles do not necessarily imply honor or intelligence." His chin rose.

"The Veronesis have fallen on hard times?" Dana asked, though this was obvious.

Borelli gazed pensively back up the hill, but the villa was no longer visible. "The Veronesi have often fallen on hard times." There was an edge to his words that Dana might have described as *hard* in itself.

"Oh?" she asked, but when she glanced at Borelli, his expression was flat and he didn't respond.

As they turned on to the main highway, reflected light from the retreating sun created a lush softness in the hills. The cypress trees pressed long dark shadows along the highway.

"I imagine it will be reported this evening in the news," Borelli said, "probably already on the internet."

Dana knew the conversation had shifted again, that he was speaking of what had taken place on the Borelli estate. She would check online news sources when she got back to her room. Surely the police would have issued a report. She assumed if they were to continue with the dinner, they had the police inspector's okay. "How well does Leo know the police inspector?" she asked. "He called him by his first name—Alberto."

"Alberto DeLuca? They were school friends. He's from the area. He and his officers spent the better part of the afternoon in the cellar. Neither Leo nor I were permitted to enter. I have no idea how long they will insist on keeping it closed off. Though, of course, the four-year-old wine in those barrels cannot be replaced. It's not as if we can go in and fill them up again tomorrow." She could hear the frustration in his voice, the helplessness he surely felt. "Produced from the perfect vines, one-hundred percent Sangiovese." He sighed, then repeated, "Sangiovese. From the Latin *sanguis Jovis*, the blood of Jove. Roman king of the gods, the mythical Jupiter. Even with proper insurance, there is no way of replacing the wine."

"Alberto grew up in Montalcino?" she asked.

"Yes, so naturally he knows how devastating this is to the entire area. Our economy is based on wine."

Dana wondered if DeLuca might be sympathetic and allow business to continue with as few interruptions as possible, but before she could ask, Borelli said, "Though I am still a primary owner of the vineyards and estate, I haven't been involved in the day-to-day activities for years. I left to study in Rome, first secular law, eventually canon law. Each quarter a nice little deposit is made to my account, but I have no part in running the business. Some years are good, others not so good. I know how business is going based on the size of the deposits. But I leave it up to Leo. The poor boy hardly needs the interference of an old uncle who has contributed little over the years, who voluntarily left the family business for other pursuits." He threw her a cautious glance. "The last deposit, smaller than usual."

Dana wondered why he was sharing this with her. Was he telling her that, like the Veronesis, they were suffering? She'd seen no evidence of this.

"As far as I know, we are doing fine," he said, answering the question she had not asked. "But the business has had substantial capital investments over these past two years. Keeping up with technology, modern production, a new cellar . . . a behemoth corrugated warehouse." He snorted with disapproval, shaking his head. Dana gathered from his tenor that Borelli had ill feelings about storing the Borelli wines in a corrugated warehouse.

"This is where the destruction took place?"

"Oh, no, no. We've kept the ancient stone cellar. Partially for show, for the tourists, but still completely functional." He gazed out the window as they passed one of the numerous areas planted with vines. "This is all very expensive. This loss will certainly set us back." He paused for a moment and added, "The loss of a human life can never be evaluated in financial terms."

Human life cannot be measured, Dana thought, but she also thought for one not involved in running the business he seemed to know a great deal about it.

"I do not rely solely on my income from the vineyards. My life as a priest requires little in a material sense, though I've made wise investments over the years." She remembered a conversation they had once when he'd told her that he did not belong to an order that required a vow of poverty. He'd implied that he had invested well and had significant financial resources.

There was little traffic and they were soon behind a slow-moving tractor. The numerous curves prevented Dana from passing.

"How is Leo doing?" she asked.

Borelli paused as if searching for the proper reply. "Leo has become adept at masking his feelings. He's been through so much." Again, he hesitated, and Dana sensed he was speaking of more than this recent loss. She knew he had lost his wife, Teresa, just over two years ago, and she knew personally that losing a loved one was not something a person could get over easily. Time was not a cure for loss. One changed, perhaps adjusted, but each individual must do it in his or her own way.

"Sometimes I feel as if Leo is hiding something," Borelli said.

"Hiding something?" she asked, definitely interested.

"There is a young man," Borelli said. "Well, you met him in Montalcino. Recently hired by Leo."

"The handsome young Fabrizio."

"Yes, the handsome young Fabrizio Rossi." Borelli's eyebrows rose as he tipped his head, acknowledging that a woman would certainly take note of a handsome young man. "As I said, I have no part in running the business, no decisions in hiring. But this young man who has recently joined the employment of the Borelli Vineyards, Leo has taken him in almost as if he were a member of the family." Borelli was quiet as if considering how much to share with Dana. "When he first arrived, Leo invited him to stay in the villa. Just took him in." The pitch of his voice rose. "Living with the family as if he were one of us."

Dana saw an opportunity and pulled around the tractor. The driver and Borelli exchanged waves.

"He's not staying in the house now?" she asked, back in the proper lane. Surely, she would have seen him—last night at dinner, this morning at breakfast.

"Oh, no, no, no," Borelli replied. "As soon as an estate cottage became available, he moved out. As I understand, it caused quite a stir. Leo got into it with a long-time employee who felt entitled to the cottage. Ended up firing him."

"Leo fired him over the boy?"

"I'm not sure," Borelli answered thoughtfully. "There might have been more to it than that."

Dana wondered if Borelli thought this man being fired had something to do with what had happened in the cellar. "Was this information shared with the police detectives?"

"I'm sure Leo mentioned it. He turned over records with all recent employees' names, including Carlo Porcini, whom he had just fired."

"Would this be enough to motivate the vicious destruction of the wine?" Dana asked.

"I can't imagine it would," Borelli replied, "but there's something else I find rather disturbing. Leo attempted to contact Fabrizio this morning. To accompany Claudio to pick up the guests."

Dana thought of the calls Leo had made as they sat in the kitchen, then of meeting Fabrizio that morning in Montalcino. His English was good, he seemed personable, a good choice to meet Leo's guests in Rome.

"But the boy failed to answer his phone. Since we saw him this morning, I find that odd. He was friendly enough, coming over to our table to say hello."

"You think he might—"

"Have had something to do with what happened this morning?" Borelli raised his hands in a dramatic gesture. "I don't know what to think." He stroked his head, running his fingers over his sparse hair. "Leo told me he had given him the weekend off."

"He was with his friends, having fun. Maybe he didn't feel obliged to return a call from his boss since he had given him the weekend off."

"You are probably correct," Borelli conceded. "This most likely has nothing to do with what happened this morning, but I've had some concerns since Fabrizio arrived. There's something strange about the situation. The boy shows up one day. Becomes an apprentice. Extremely smart with definite leadership skills. He's taking some classes at the University in Siena at Leo's urging. And he seems to have a sense for the wine. This is the only way I can explain it. A natural talent, according to Estella. But where did he come from? It is almost as if . . ." Borelli stared out the window, taking his time. "Leo loved his wife dearly, but the early years of their marriage were fraught with difficulties. They did not conceive for many years. It's just that, well, truthfully Leo treats the boy as if he is grooming him to take over the business, as if he is one of us." Borelli paused. "As if he is family."

"Family?" Dana asked, and Borelli tilted his head, raised his shoulders and shot her a questioning look. Was Borelli implying that his apprehension had nothing to do with the destruction in the cellar? "You think he's Leo's son?" she asked.

"For many years I served in various positions within the Vatican. One thing I know, it is unwise to make a decision or pronouncement, particularly one with lasting effects, one that can profoundly shape the future, affect real people's lives, based on . . . well on a hunch, on mere suspicion." He cast her an apprehensive look. "You, too, as a journalist, as one who endeavors to find and share the truth, well, we do not base our work on mere hunches."

"No, we don't," she agreed, "but, isn't this often the starting point?"

They had reached the sign announcing the Borelli Vineyards. Dana turned off the highway.

"Leo should open his eyes," Borelli said. "Mia has become quite taken by the young man."

Is this why Leo had moved Fabrizio into the cottage? He did not wish this handsome young man living that close to his beautiful, impressionable, thirteen-year-old daughter. But then Dana realized Borelli's true fear and perhaps Leo's too. Borelli was concerned that Mia might be developing a crush on her own brother.

As they approached the villa, Dana could see that only two of the vehicles parked near the villa earlier in the day remained.

To lighten the mood, she asked, "So, how was Winkie's Italian?"

"Rather good, though definitely a northern dialect. His family has roots in Italy, his mother's family from a small village just outside of Milan. They were farmers. He said he learned Italian as a child."

"So, he's returned to his Italian roots," Dana said just as they pulled up to the garage behind the villa. "Should I plan on picking up the guests in Montalcino for dinner this evening?"

"We'll arrange for someone else to go along with Claudio. Our guests will be apprised of the situation." Dana took this to mean they would be given the option of canceling their visit. "But, please," Borelli added, "you are to join us."

"You'll hardly need me there this evening for what is strictly a business dinner. Don't you think your wine buyers might think it strange that the hired help has been invited to dine? I could scrounge something up in the kitchen on my own."

"Oh, Renata is not fond of scroungers in her kitchen," he said and then stopped abruptly. "I don't imagine she will be preparing our meal tonight. Her assistant, Lala, came in earlier this afternoon, so I assume she will be cooking this evening. You are aware that in Italy dinner is never strictly business. You are our guest, and you are to be included." He smiled as if to say, you can make no excuses. "Dinner at eight. You might want to get some rest," he advised her. "A proper Italian dinner can go on for hours."

CHAPTER EIGHT

Winkie Dalton sat alone in the living room of the Veronesi villa, slowly sipping a glass of water. He gazed up at the frescoed ceiling, faded but still beautiful. Plump little putti cavorted in a sea of clouds against a cerulean sky. Even with minimal care, a fifteenth-century fresco could survive if the atmospheric surroundings were suitable. The room was fairly cool, and any dampness that might have seeped in was kept out by the stone walls as thick as those in a medieval prison.

The rest of the room had not fared as well. The wallpaper was peeling, the furniture was worn, as were the rugs arranged about the dark tile floors. Several tapestries hung on the walls, threadbare patches confirming their authenticity.

Winkie wondered if it was pride that kept the Veronesis from selling these valuable pieces. He was well aware they were experiencing financial difficulties.

He also knew the history of the family, once the wealthiest in the region in both land and other holdings.

Two sons. One daughter. Then, no further generations of

Veronesis.

Vincenzo Veronesi, deceased.

Lorenzo Veronesi, in ill health. Or possibly dead. Winkie wouldn't be surprised if the announcement of Lorenzo's demise had been delayed to avoid estate taxes. The family was land rich and dirt poor.

Winkie was aware that Giovanna Veronesi claimed her primary residence in Rome, and that she was recently widowed upon the death of her third husband, a deposed Romanian prince who had nothing remaining from his prior life other than a worthless title. Giovanna had the misfortune of finding husbands whose assets were in old names, empty titles, and nothing more.

"Signore, you wish to go to your room?" The man who had greeted him at the door when he arrived addressed him. He wore a dark, well-tailored suit, a red and blue striped silk tie, and displayed a stiff, dignified posture. Though he appeared to be in his mid-seventies and had likely been with the family for years, he had the robust, commanding voice of a much younger man.

On arrival, the man had offered Winkie something to drink and then abandoned him to take his bags up to the second floor. The man spoke a few words of English and, as Winkie often found when traveling abroad, the locals often wished to impress their American visitors by speaking English. They had stumbled along during their initial conversation in a mixture of simple words, both English and Italian.

A woman in a dark uniform and white apron had brought him a glass of water and then left without speaking.

"Yes," Winkie said, "if Signora Veronesi is not available, I believe I would like to go to my room." He had expected to be greeted by Giovanna Veronesi with whom he had corresponded through her attorney in Rome.

"This evening," the man said as Winkie rose, "at dinner. Signora Veronesi with you at eight." He motioned, indicating that the dining room was at the other end of the villa.

The man led Winkie back to the main hall. An intricate iron staircase led up from the front entrance to the upper floors. Together they climbed the winding staircase, stepped into the hall on the second level, and Winkie was shown to his room, which smelled of lemon polish. Fresh flowers sat on the small table next to the bed. The room was sparsely, though nicely, furnished. A tall, narrow, shuttered window looked out toward what Winkie guessed, if he had his bearings correct, was the front of the villa. It was a corner room and the other window should offer a view toward the west. He stepped over and opened the front shutter. Fading light made its way into the room. Gazing out, Winkie took in a perfect view of the evening shadows on the Tuscan landscape below. "Very nice," he said aloud.

"Your bath," the man announced, motioning toward the hallway. He walked back to the door and gestured directly across the hall. "No others. Only you. Visitors not often here. You wish to see?" the man asked. *"Il bagno?"*

"No," Winkie replied. "I'm sure I can find it."

After the man left the room, his footsteps echoing down the hallway, Winkie opened his bag and settled his underwear and socks into the small dresser. As he hung his slacks, jacket, and shirts, shaking out the wrinkles, he heard a creak above him. It dawned on him now that the staircase had not continued on to an additional floor. There must be a back staircase to the top floor, used for the servants' quarters. He assumed Signora Giovanna Veronesi had a bedroom on the first level, that she wouldn't be climbing stairs to her room. He knew she was seventy, though he had no idea of her present health.

Settled in, he pulled out his phone to give Audra and Sam each a call. Damn if it didn't need to be recharged. The battery was dead. He found an outlet but realized he forgot to pack his adaptor, so the plugs were all wrong. He was used to staying in hotels that would provide them for forgetful travelers. He didn't imagine such amenities were supplied here.

"Damn," he said out loud. But Sam and Audra knew he'd arrived as he'd texted them both, and he was exhausted from his travels, so calls could wait. Glancing at his watch, he was grateful he had time for a nap before dinner.

Just as he was about to doze off, he heard a rumble in the driveway, a spray of gravel. He shook the drowsiness from his head, rose slowly and stepped to the window. Opening the shutters, he gazed out. In the dim light he saw a large, late model vehicle, some off-European brand, had stopped in the driveway behind the Mercedes.

A thin man with a limp got out of the passenger side, then a larger man swung one leg, then another, out of the driver's side. Both wore overcoats and sunglasses, the latter surely unnecessary at this time of day. The larger man's slacks pooled around his shoes and Winkie thought he could use a good tailor. His head swiveled from side to side and the other man too seemed to be looking for something as they lumbered up to the front door. He heard a rap, then the butler's muffled voice, then the slow creak of the closing door.

Winkie returned to the bed and lay down, his jet lag pulling him into a restless slumber. When he woke, the room was dark, no light filtering through the slats in the shutters. He heard a vehicle outside and wondered if the two visitors were leaving, but when he rose, went to the window, and opened the shutters he could see in the dim glow from a light on the post near the driveway that it was a completely different car—an older Volvo. A man at the wheel, possibly a passenger, but Winkie couldn't tell for sure or make out any details. The car pulled out and started down the hill.

Shortly after this vehicle left, another arrived, a sporty two-door—possibly an Alfa Romeo. A man carrying a briefcase emerged. The lawyer from Rome? Winkie got no more than a quick glance at the figure in silhouette as he approached the front door and entered.

Well, Winkie mused, *the Veronesi villa is a rather busy place on this particular October evening, though, according to the butler, they seldom had guests.*

CHAPTER NINE

Back in her room at the Borelli villa, Dana pulled her iPad out of her carry-on, settled down on the bed, and entered the Wi-Fi password she'd received shortly after her arrival. Using a search engine, she typed in *Borelli Vineyards destruction*. Scrolling down, she saw nothing in English, but an article in Italian, dated that day, popped out at her from the second page. Quickly she clicked on a translating program. The article reported what had happened that morning and seemed to be a reliable news source, a print paper that would likely run a version of the article the following day.

The story stated that someone had broken into the Borelli cellars the previous night and opened a dozen of the large barrels containing Brunello valued at over eight million euros.

Dana stopped reading, struck by the amount. Borelli had mentioned millions, but *eight* million?

She continued to read. An employee of the estate, Paolo Paluzzi, had died, though there were no details on how he had passed. An autopsy would be performed because of the circumstances of his death. Inspector Alberto DeLuca was quoted as saying that employees, as well as recent visitors, were being interviewed. The officer said they had not yet established a motive, but he did not believe others were in imminent danger.

According to the owner, Leo Antonelli, the lost wine was a Brunello that had been aging for the required four years for the DOCG designation. A portion would have been bottled in January as prescribed by the Consortium, some aged another year for the Riserva label. The lost wine would have produced up to 100,000 bottles. Dana wondered if the eight-million-dollar figure had come from Leo. That would average out to $80 per bottle.

As she continued to pick through the article's translation, she noticed the word *murder* was not used. Dana wished she could read the original Italian. As a writer, she understood the nuance of language. She wondered if the information coming from both Leo and Alberto DeLuca was slanted to make it appear there was little danger to anyone else. The wine industry, the thousands of tourists who visited each year, *was* the area's economy. According to Borelli, all local hotels, restaurants, and shops depended on the visitors who came for the wine.

After going through the article a second time, Dana checked her personal emails, found nothing important, and then decided to send a quick email to her brothers and sister-in-law. She didn't mention what had happened—it didn't appear to be coming up on any English-language news sources, so she'd hold off until she knew more. And she surely didn't want them to say anything to her mother, who always had concerns when Dana traveled, particularly on this first European venture since Prague.

Visited Montalcino with Father Borelli, she wrote. *Looking forward to Siena and Florence. Beautiful scenery, great food and wine. I'm dining with the wine connoisseurs tonight, so I'll raise a glass in your honor!*

Her brother Ben would appreciate this. He'd enjoy a fine Brunello. Jeff would consider it a waste of money. He was a beer and pretzels guy. Dana thought of herself as the most flexible of the trio of siblings. She wasn't much of a drinker, and certainly no expert at choosing a wine, though she enjoyed a glass with a fine meal. For casual dining, pizza or burgers, a beer would do just fine.

Sitting on the edge of the bed, she considered slipping under the covers for some rest as Borelli had advised. With dinner at eight, it could be a late evening. She fell back on the bed and closed her eyes, trying to clear her mind, to vanquish visions of wine flowing from barrels, an old man face down in the dark red liquid. Borelli's recent revelation, his concerns about Fabrizio Rossi, an image of the young man she'd been introduced to that morning in Montalcino, buzzed in her mind. She was curious about the boy, especially after what Borelli had told her.

She sat up and reached for her iPad again, typed in the name *Fabrizio Rossi*, the word *Italy*. It appeared that Rossi was a common family name. There were thousands of Rossis. She looked at several images, finding nothing, no photos of Fabrizio Rossi. Then she typed in *Winkie Dalton* to see if there was anything about his trip to Italy, but of course there was not. A bio confirmed what he'd told Borelli—his maternal grandparents were Italian. Winkie, Winston Antonio Dalton, had been born in New York. He was five years older than Dana.

Shortly before eight, she reapplied her makeup, slipped on a fresh blouse, her suit jacket, a different scarf, and went down for dinner. Though the guests had not yet arrived, Leo greeted her in the formal room where she had been questioned by the police officer earlier. He offered her a drink, a sparkling wine which he said was not available to the public, something they served only to special guests. She sipped slowly, imagining there would be plenty of wine offered throughout the evening. Leo told her his uncle had gone to pick up the guests.

"How's Mia doing?" Dana asked.

"Still resting. I had hoped to have her join us for dinner tonight. Well, before this morning . . . but after . . . I think it best we wait. My mother, too, she enjoys having visitors, but she is in no condition to entertain guests."

"Are the police coming up with anything?"

"They have spent the day collecting any possible evidence from the cellar, interviewing those who have been working on the estate, those visiting—I do apologize that you have become involved. Also, I wish to thank you for going to the airport this afternoon and escorting our guests to their hotel in Montalcino." His voice was sincere, if a little shaky, and the stress was evident in the tightness around his eyes and mouth. Dana thought of the photo of the young Leonardo Antonelli in the folder Borelli had given her.

"You were able to enjoy the scenery on the drive?" Leo asked. "Possibly Uncle Giovanni will take you to Siena tomorrow."

"A beautiful drive." Dana wanted to ask him about what she'd read on the internet, but she could see he was attempting to veer the conversation away from what had happened that morning.

"I am pleased the weather is cooperating," Leo continued. "Fall is a pleasant time here in Tuscany. Perhaps you can enjoy the festivities of the *Sagra del Tordo* this weekend."

"I understand there's an archery competition scheduled for Sunday," Dana said, yielding to Leo's obvious desire to limit the conversation to light chatter, though she cared little about an archery competition when a man had just died, when the livelihood of a family was being threatened. As an investigative reporter, she'd spent much of her career interviewing victims. In her early days, she'd often talked too much, asked too many questions, but she soon learned that a victim might feel victimized once more by an intrusive or overly eager reporter. Leo, too, was a victim, and she would let him lead the conversation.

Father Borelli's deep, gravelly voice resonated from the entry hall, and Dana was grateful that the discomfort of speaking of weather and upcoming festivities would be cut short by the guests' arrival. Borelli was explaining how the villa had been in the family for centuries, how he grew up in this very house as had his father and grandfather.

"There is little left of the original home," Leo said to Dana in a low voice with a conspiratorial half smile, as if he knew that she too was aware of his uncle's tendency to exaggerate. "Many renovations and additions."

Leo started out toward the foyer to welcome his guests. Dana could hear the introductions, and then the trio of wine buyers, along with Leo and Borelli, entered the room.

Octavia Fleenor wore a pencil-thin, black skirt with a slit up one side, very high-heeled, open-toed shoes, a light-colored silk blouse and a structured wine-colored jacket with an Asian-style collar. The blouse was cut low, and a nice-sized diamond hung on a chain from her slender neck. The men wore dark suits, business-like ties. Borelli wore his clerical collar, and Dana imagined this was the way he dressed for a semi-formal occasion, such as it was this evening. She was definitely underdressed. She adjusted her scarf, hoping the label wasn't showing.

"Buona sera," Octavia exclaimed, kissing Dana on one cheek and then the other, as if they were best friends, as if they were both European and bound by this two-cheek kissing ritual.

"You've found your hotel satisfactory?" Dana asked, feeling stupidly formal and subservient as soon as the words came out of her mouth.

"Yes, very nice," Octavia replied kindly. "Thank you for coming to the airport to pick us up. Father Borelli explained the situation, that you are a guest here, too. I'm afraid we were all exhausted when we arrived."

"The flight tends to wear you out," Dana agreed.

"How long have you been here?" Octavia asked.

Dana had to think for a moment. She'd only been in Italy since the previous day, but so much had happened in such a short time. "I arrived yesterday."

"I'm afraid Ms. Pierson," Leo joined the conversation, "hasn't arrived at the best time for a holiday. With the destruction in the cellar . . ." He glanced at Dana and it seemed he was telling her that Borelli had informed the guests. Probably a good idea as the news had already hit an online news source. It seemed none of them had decided to opt out of the dinner invitation.

"I assume there's insurance," Octavia said.

"Yes, yes, of course," Leo replied, "but that will not replace the wine." There was such sadness in his words Dana could feel the ache of this loss. What would it be like to lose something that had come from the land, aged for years to produce the perfect wine? Money would surely not replace this loss.

"Yes, of course," Octavia said, the regret of her question evident in her tone. "We are so sorry for your loss. A man died in the cellar?"

"A trusted employee." Leo paused, and Dana was fully aware, as she had been earlier, that he wished to discuss this no further. "Tomorrow, we will go out into the vineyards, and then visit one of the cellars. Our enologist, Marco Dardi, is unable to join us this evening, but will be available tomorrow."

After drinks and antipasti, olives, salami, and crostini, and no further talk of the destruction that day, Leo ushered everyone into the dining room.

Guests were seated. Leo at the head of the table, Borelli at the other end. Dana beside Richard Jones. Octavia on the other side with David Ryder.

Dana was impressed by Leo's breadth of knowledge and his sudden ease of conversation as they spoke of Italian history, film, art, cities of Italy, particularly Florence, which Octavia especially loved, having spent a year there studying Renaissance art. Uncharacteristically, Borelli yielded to his nephew in allowing the younger man to lead the conversation. Leo made a point of mentioning that Dana was a well-respected journalist for a prestigious newspaper in Boston.

Salad greens with vinegar and oil arrived as a first course to accommodate the Americans, followed by gnocchi with pesto, a main course of fresh sautéed vegetables and a delicious roasted veal with mushrooms, *Vitello Arrosta con Funghi*. By the time dessert, *torta di cioccolato*, arrived, they had gone through several bottles of wine, with sniffing and swirling, and words that were beginning to blur. Talk soon turned to business, though much was indecipherable to Dana, the only one who didn't have a wine-based pedigree. Talk of vintage, acidity, aroma, tannins, was slipping right through her brain as were Italian words such as *biologico, affinamento, argilla*. She glanced over at Leo who nodded and offered her a quiet smile, as if to say, I hope you do not find this talk too boring. She returned his smile, thinking what a gracious host he was, realizing how much effort this required, particularly after what had happened that morning.

And then she thought of what Borelli had spoken of earlier that day. Was Leo a master at deception? What had Borelli said? That at times he felt Leo was hiding something?

CHAPTER TEN

Though dinner was scheduled for eight, Winkie Dalton sat alone *again* in the living room until almost nine, his impatience growing, as he fought the fatigue that threatened to send him back to his room. But he was starving and certainly entitled to eat. It had been hours since his meal on the plane, then his light snack in the Borelli van.

Yet, an even greater sense of determination kept him anchored to his elegant yet well-worn chair. He had waited, not just hours, but years to meet this woman, and he would not give up now.

Then, suddenly, she stepped into the room, appearing exactly as he had envisioned her. Petite, stylishly dressed in a teal blue pantsuit with wide, flared legs and a fitted jacket that showed off her still attractive figure. Perfectly coiffed, smelling of expensive perfume, she reached for his hand with a nod of apology, then kissed him on each cheek as he stood.

"Please, forgive me for I am late, Mr. Dalton," she said in stilted English. She looked at him deeply, her expression verging on affection, studying his face for a moment, and then she took his arm and guided him into the dining room. A large table with a suite of chairs took up a good share of the space. Above a matching buffet hung a large painting of the Virgin and Child. Classic, authentic Renaissance, Winkie determined with a quick glance.

The gentleman who had assisted Winkie earlier appeared, pulled out a chair for Giovanna, then for Winkie.

"*Grazie,* Andrea," she told the man, then turned to Winkie. "My English, not good."

Winkie considered for a moment before admitting, *"Parlo Italiano."* He realized if he were to accomplish anything during this visit, he would have to converse in Italian.

Giovanna smiled, relieved. *"Bene. Parliamo Italiano."*

Winkie returned her smile and they continued in Italian.

"I'm afraid we have had a number of visitors today," Giovanna said, "which is most unusual. I do apologize for keeping you waiting so long."

Winkie knew three vehicles, at least four men, had arrived over the course of the evening. He had no idea how long any of them had stayed, or if the visits had overlapped, because he had napped off and on.

"We seldom have guests," Giovanna said.

But today, Winkie thought, the visitors had poured in and out of the villa flowing as freely as wine on a Tuscan estate. It appeared he was the only one invited for dinner and offered accommodations at the villa, though it was he who had requested the opportunity to stay at the estate for a few days as he considered his offer. He was somewhat surprised that he had been extended the invitation.

Winkie wondered how many others were interested in the Veronesi Vineyards. The first two men hardly looked like investors. Cops, he thought now. Yes, plainclothes police officers. That's exactly what they looked like. It was dark by the time the others arrived, but he guessed one of them might have been the attorney from Rome.

The table was set with fine china, crystal, and silver for two, though it was large enough to seat a dozen people. Winkie and Giovanna sat facing one another for ease of conversation at the end of the table closest to the door that opened to what he assumed was the kitchen. A woman stepped out with a large plate filled with salami, olives, and marinated vegetables. Wine was poured.

The conversation came easily, that of two people just getting to know one another as Giovanna led, asking about his flight, his latest project, his work in the entertainment industry.

At seventy she was still a beautiful, engaging woman. Her olive skin barely showed a wrinkle, and her hair had been softened from the original dark raven color to a deep, caramel brown with golden highlights. Winkie thought of the much-admired actress, Elizabeth Taylor. As she aged, she had gone from her signature dark hair to blonde. Winkie had met her once. He could only describe himself as star-struck.

The feeling now was something quite similar, yet completely different. He had seen photos of Giovanna Veronesi from her younger days, then during her marriage to the Romanian prince. Even a photograph with the pope. Though he had seen nothing from recent years, he believed that he would have recognized her. She had aged extremely well.

Dinner was served by the young woman who, other than the dignified butler Andrea, appeared to be the only other employee in the house. Pasta, then a steak perfectly pink in the middle, with potatoes nicely broiled, and a green salad, arrived at precise intervals as Giovanna led the discussion with the grace of a practiced hostess. She asked about his family. He was single now after the demise of a second marriage, though he quickly skimmed over that. His children, Audra and Sam, were the lights of his life, and he had no difficulty speaking of them. Sam was at NYU. He wished to study film, but his father had encouraged him to take as many business courses as possible. Audra was still in high school and was the most perfect girl ever to walk this earth. As he spoke of his children, he felt overwhelmed with great satisfaction and knew this was why he was here. It was for his children that he had come to Giovanna. It was for his children's legacy.

They spoke of film, his and others. Of travel, lightly touching on politics. He sensed she was testing him, and Winkie felt he was passing with honors.

It was not until they had finished dessert, and were sipping coffee, that Giovanna spoke of the present condition of the winery.

"As you know, through correspondence with our lawyer in Rome, my brother Lorenzo has been very ill. Though he has attempted to run the estate, the vineyards, the winery, on his own since our brother, Vincenzo, passed, it has become impossible." Giovanna shook her head slowly, then took a small sip of coffee. "For years," she added without further explanation.

Winkie had done extensive research on the two brothers and had found a nice article from years ago in a prestigious wine magazine, along with a photo of a proud, but obviously aging Vincenzo Veronesi, who was the true force behind the success of the business. He was as rough and rugged looking as Giovanna was delicate and refined.

Putting together a history of the Veronesi Vineyards, Winkie learned it was one of the first to produce the famous Brunello wine for public consumption. Vincenzo had died over twenty years ago and, from what Winkie had seen and read, the estate had begun, and then continued, its decline from there. The second brother, Lorenzo, seemed to have disappeared. Giovanna indicated that until recently he was running the winery, but Winkie didn't know if that was true. The family attorney in Rome, Raffaelo Sabatini, wrote that Lorenzo was ill, but offered no details on the nature of the illness. Winkie had not been able to find anything, other than the mention of Lorenzo's name, in any of the materials he'd found in his research.

"Much of the land lies fallow now, while other producers are vigorously planting new vineyards." Giovanna laughed sadly. "At least that has kept us in a favorable position with the environmentalists and their concerns of soil erosion and landslides." She sighed. "There have been recent accusations that the land here in Montalcino, into Montepulciano, has been overproducing, overused. A dangerous *monoculture*, it's been called." She straightened the jeweled cross hanging from her neck. "But much of the land, if properly cared for, could be put to use." She was still for a moment. "As you surely noticed, the land in the region also supports olive production, and we used to grow sunflowers." Her face lit up, her eyes sparkled. They were a deep brown.

"Oh, the sunflowers are so beautiful earlier in the summer," she went on. "In the fall, they begin to fade. But so beautiful." She looked along the table at the fine silk cloth, candles flickering in silver holders. A bouquet of rosebuds graced the center of the table, a substantial distance from where the two sat. "All beauty does not fade, but it must be cared for. The silver polished." She picked up a fork and examined the intricate pattern. Winkie could tell it had recently been polished and imagined old Andrea shining away, meticulously preparing for guests who seldom came.

"The gardens must be tended," Giovanna said. Winkie had noticed no gardens as they drove up, though the pathway up to the front door was lined with large terracotta pots filled with soil and spent plants and miniature trees.

"With the proper placing of various crops," Giovanna went on, "careful management of the land, the Veronesi estate could be revived, brought back to its prior glory and its rightful place in the world of fine wine production."

Winkie sat listening, nodding his head.

"Do you know that a vine can produce for over one hundred years? It might reach a peak. Thirty years perhaps." She laughed lightly. "As a child, the concept of thirty years seemed almost impossible. But, do you know, the past thirty years . . . slipped by as if in a blink." She looked at him again the way she had when she first entered the room. "One must cherish time." Her voice had softened, then it rose again. "A new planting will take four years to produce grapes for wine. Great patience is required to produce a fine wine. Great patience, yes. Do you possess great patience, Mr. Dalton?"

Winkie smiled and offered Giovanna a slight nod. *If only you knew*, he was tempted to say. *If only you knew.*

They were both silent and then Giovanna offered, "One of my visitors this afternoon." She stared directly at Winkie, perhaps aware that he had peered from his window and watched as the visitors came in and out. "Represented a group of environmentalists. They wish to make an offer. It is their intention to devote a portion of the land to organic vineyards." She shook her head. "Whatever that means. We've never used chemicals, though I understand some of the progressive vineyards are doing just that. They—these environmentalists—wish to return a good portion to its natural state."

"You're considering the offer?"

Her lips lifted into a tentative smile, but she did not reply. Winkie wondered if she was merely letting him know that she had other offers. He considered the possibility that she might have put him in the room on the second level where he could easily see and hear the comings and goings, where he would be aware that others were visiting. Did she think he would see them all as potential buyers?

"I grew up here," Giovanna said. "I have wonderful memories. My brothers and I running along the hillsides, going out into the vineyards with the crews, participating in the harvest celebrations, greeting guests. Tasting the grapes. Do you know, Mr. Dalton, if one has the gift, it is possible to tell from tasting a single grape if the wine will be worthy." She sounded very serious, but then her voice shifted again, taking on a less somber tone. "Oh, once this was a lively place, full of parties and fun!" She smiled as her eyes moved about the room. On either side of the painting of the Virgin and Child, above the buffet, hung a gold wall sconce. Light shimmered against the wall.

"It is with sadness that we consider letting it go. There are no heirs." Her eyes glistened. "No one to continue the family business. I'm too old to come back home. Rome is now my home. We must let it go."

Her continued reference to *we* made Winkie wonder if she was referring to the brother or the attorney in Rome.

"If you will excuse me now, Mr. Dalton," she said. "It is late. We can talk more tomorrow. I will attend Mass in Montalcino at ten a.m. Perhaps we could have brunch at eleven-thirty when I return. Then I will escort you around the estate."

"Yes, that would be very nice." He'd planned on asking her if she had an adaptor he could use to charge his phone, but somehow he couldn't because the latter part of the conversation—in which Winkie had said very little—seemed much too grave, too emotional, to bring up something so trivial. He'd ask Andrea. If there was an adaptor in the house, he was the one who would know.

Giovanna rose and started out of the room. She turned abruptly. "I noticed you were delivered in the Borelli Vineyard's van." There was a noticeable quiver in her voice. "Is there something I should know before we proceed?"

CHAPTER ELEVEN

Coffee had been served in the Borelli villa living room, comfortable and warm with a snapping fire. Again, talk had brushed lightly on business, the arrangements for the following day, a tour through the vineyards and cellar. It was near midnight when Leo offered to accompany the dinner guests back to their hotel in Montalcino. He called Claudio to come around to pick them up.

Embers in the fire fading, Borelli and Dana sat alone. She was about to describe what she'd read in the internet news article when he asked if she'd like another dessert or more coffee. Without waiting for an answer, he rose and motioned for her to follow.

The kitchen was quiet and cleaned, no abandoned pots on the stove as Dana had seen earlier in the day.

"I used to enjoy a midnight raid of the kitchen with my brothers," she said, "but honestly I can't eat another bite."

"Then sit and talk to me while I have a piece of cake. Coffee?"

"I'm good." Dana pulled out a stool at the long marble counter and sat as Borelli opened the cupboard, took out a plate, then slid out a drawer, grabbed a fork and a knife, and carefully lifted the glass dome from the half-eaten cake on the counter and cut himself a slice.

He sat. "Thank you for your help today," he told her, taking an enormous bite. He'd evidently decided against brewing more coffee. She didn't understand how he could still be hungry.

"I found an online article," Dana said, "about the destruction in the cellar. In Italian."

Borelli looked up from his cake, swallowed. "Yes?" he asked with interest. "You want me to translate?"

"I used an online translator," Dana explained, "so I understand the general content of the article."

Borelli's brow wrinkled as if she'd just told him a little Italian translator, an actual person, had jumped out of her iPad.

"It's a program to translate the original text into, well in this case English. Sometimes too literal, but—"

"It was a reliable source?"

"I believe so. It's an online site for a local daily newspaper." She told him the name of the newspaper and the reporter, and he nodded as if he wished her to continue. "Some of it was merely reporting what we already know. The inspector seemed to be downplaying Paolo's death—reassuring those concerned that there was no threat to others."

Borelli nodded again—in agreement, or as encouragement for her to go on, she wasn't sure.

"The article quoted Inspector DeLuca as saying they were interviewing those on the estate, employees, and visitors over the past several days, to determine if anyone saw anything. There was a quote from Leo about the number of bottles lost."

When Dana told him the quoted value, Borelli shook his head in disbelief. "That's a conservative estimate. It was an outstanding vintage, a perfect ripening season that year, and one bottle of the Brunello might be priced at one hundred fifty dollars. The lost wine included a good portion that would have been aged another year and labeled Brunello Riserva. It would not be unusual for a bottle to sell for over three hundred American dollars in a nice restaurant." He took another large bite of cake. "The Brunello *Normale* would have been bottled early next year, the fifth year after harvest, then released to market after the required four months in bottle. The portion designated as Brunello Riserva, another year aging, then six months in bottle."

Dana was attempting to calculate in her head. If 100,000 bottles were lost, as the article stated, at $150 per bottle that would be 15 million. She had no idea how much of the wine was Riserva, but, according to Borelli, it was worth $300 a bottle. She guessed that the figure given in the article, 8 million euros, was for wholesale, not retail . . . her mind was overloading, so she didn't even attempt to convert to American dollars.

"The article mentioned the DOCG designation," she told Borelli.

"Denominazione di Origine Controllata e Garantita," he said, "Denomination of Controlled and Guaranteed Origin."

"The designation guarantees certain standards are met?" Dana guessed the designation would contribute to the astonishing price of the wine. She remembered the official-looking seal on the neck of the bottle Leo had opened as they sat in the kitchen earlier. He'd drained his glass in a few large gulps as if they were drinking cheap beer.

"Very strict standards," Borelli said. "The origin of the Sangiovese grapes must be within the communal territory of Montalcino. To earn the DOCG designation, the producer must adhere to strict rules of not only origin, production, and aging, but even bottling, which must be done within the production area." Borelli wiped his mouth with the back of his hand. At times the man could conduct himself with dignity and refinement, yet at times he seemed to have the manners of a five-year-old. Dana reached for a napkin in a ceramic holder on the counter and handed it to him.

He nodded a thank you and continued to clean the crumbs along the corners of his mouth.

"The emphasis of the article was certainly on the loss of wine," Dana said. "You believe Paolo just happened to be in the wrong place at the wrong time?"

"I see no reason someone would want to hurt him. He was a harmless old man. The viciousness of the destruction certainly implies it was someone with a personal vendetta." Borelli's jaw tightened. He pushed his plate aside. "I don't believe it was against Paolo."

"A vendetta against the Borellis?"

Borelli seemed ready to offer more in the way of explanation, but then he said, "Well, I suppose we should get some rest." He picked up his plate and plodded over to the sink.

As Dana stood, the door leading from the kitchen to the garden opened quietly, and a draft of cool autumn air slid into the room.

As Borelli turned, both he and Dana gasped at what they saw.

CHAPTER TWELVE

Mia appeared in the kitchen doorway, impossibly small but surprisingly sturdy as she supported Fabrizio, his arm draped over her tiny shoulder, blood oozing from his stomach, spilling onto the tile floor, the boy groaning, still conscious but slipping quickly. Mia, too, was covered with blood, though it was impossible to tell if it was hers or Fabrizio's.

Borelli rushed over with more speed and agility than Dana realized the man possessed. Relieving Mia of the weight, with Dana's help he lowered the young man to the floor, Borelli keeping his head elevated in the crook of his arm. What appeared to be a broken arrow shaft protruded from his abdomen. He wore his leather jacket, but it was unzipped, and the fabric of his shirt was ripped at the point of impact, the blood spilling out, turning the pale blue of his shirt a bright red. Dana grabbed several kitchen towels from a bar on the stove and applied pressure around the wound.

Fabrizio's body twisted in pain. The metallic smell of blood lay heavy in the air, even as it puddled on the floor. The boy groaned.

After a frantic exchange of words with Borelli, Mia jumped up and hurried over to a small built-in desk, picked up the phone and punched in a number. She spoke rapidly, urgently into the receiver. It didn't appear the girl was injured; Dana could see that now. The blood was all Fabrizio's.

"They are coming," Mia said as she returned and knelt at Fabrizio's side. Borelli spoke to her in Italian, in a voice more frightened than harsh, yet Dana sensed he was asking, *what the hell were you doing outside?* She could not decipher Mia's reply. Dana wanted to know, too, but as Fabrizio faded in and out of consciousness, she knew they must concentrate on keeping him alive until help arrived. When blood slid down the side of his mouth, Dana shivered, realizing if they didn't get help soon, the boy would die.

Mia gathered more towels and arranged them under Fabrizio's head, relieving Borelli of the weight. "Should we remove the arrow?" she asked, voice quivering.

"No," Dana replied, and Borelli agreed with a shake of his head. Removing the broken arrow would likely make it worse. Borelli closed his eyes as if praying. Maybe he was. Mia held a damp towel to Fabrizio's head, her cheeks moist with tears, his thick, dark hair curling from the damp of his sweat.

The minutes dragged on. Mia spoke softly to Fabrizio as she ran her hand gently over his damp forehead. Dana could tell from the tone of her voice that she was telling him everything would be okay, that help was on the way.

Dana wondered if the two had become friends, or if Mia had a romantic thirteen-year-old's crush on this almost-man as Borelli feared. A young man who was possibly her half-brother.

The hum of a motor came from outside. "They have arrived." Borelli stood with some difficulty, rubbing his leg, then stomping his foot as if attempting to dismiss a cramp. He lumbered across the kitchen toward the hallway to the front of the house, as Dana and Mia stayed with the boy.

Hurried footsteps echoed in the hall, into the kitchen. The medics worked quickly, efficiently, one on his cellphone, assisting the other, inserting an IV, hooking Fabrizio up to oxygen. As they carefully secured him on a gurney, Borelli told Dana he would accompany Fabrizio to the hospital. She wondered if he wished to administer last rites, something he might have done earlier if they hadn't been so concerned with merely keeping the boy alive.

After what sounded like an argument with Mia, Borelli asked Dana if she would stay with his niece and assured her the police were on their way.

"I'll call Leo," he said just as he left.

As soon as the motor started back up, Mia rummaged through a drawer, pulled out a flashlight, and before Dana could say a word, she'd crossed the room, opened the door and stepped outside.

Dana followed, calling out, "Mia, please, let's stay inside. The police will be here soon." Dana picked up her step. "Your father, too," she added, but Mia apparently saw this as no threat. She moved even faster.

"Do you have your phone?" the girl asked, glancing back. "Mine was . . ." Mia stopped, swallowed deeply. "Lost in the cellar."

"Yes," Dana said, fingering the phone in her jacket pocket, remembering it was Mia who'd set it up for her. "Where are you going?"

"I'll show you," Mia replied, moving quickly, not slowing until she stopped abruptly and shined the flashlight beam on a small stone structure. "This is Fabrizio's cottage." She circled light over the front of the building. "And this is where I found him." The beam moved along the ground several feet in front of the door, a swing of light encompassing a small area. Then it ceased to move, steady now, shining on what appeared to be blood. Dana wondered what the girl had been doing out here so late at night.

As if reading her thoughts Mia glanced back and said, "I couldn't sleep, but I did not want to take the pills the doctor gave me. They confuse my thinking. I needed to breathe fresh air. I heard a sound, an animal whimpering. It came from near the cottages, so I started over."

Dana thought the girl was either very brave or stupid. After what had happened in the wine cellar, she shouldn't have gone out in the first place, and then she should have come back to the house for help, not attempted to support the boy who must have been almost double the girl's weight. Dana glanced around, wondering if whoever had shot Fabrizio was still out there.

"We should go back to the house," she said. But she knew, as Mia took several steps away from the building, studying the ground with the beam, the traces of blood, that the girl had other plans.

"The arrow broke off before I found him," Mia said.

"You're looking for the rest of the shaft?" Dana asked as Mia followed the path of blood.

About twenty yards from the cottage, she exclaimed, "Here it is!"

"Don't touch it," Dana warned. *Where were the police?* "We don't want to tamper with evidence," Dana cautioned as she approached.

Mia stooped, examining the broken arrow in a stream of light. "We could take a picture."

Dana hesitated for a moment and then pulled the phone from her pocket and knelt down. She took several quick shots from various angles without touching or moving the broken shaft. It was partially covered with dirt, but she could make out blue and white fletchings and stripes around the circumference in the same colors.

"Yes," Mia whispered, and Dana could hear a conspiratorial grin in her voice. "We should leave the arrow for the police to find." Dana felt a surge of adrenaline.

"Let's return to the house," she said, but Mia was already sprinting back toward Fabrizio's cottage. Before Dana knew it, the girl was at the front door, Dana moving quickly to keep up.

Mia twisted the doorknob, and then jerked it up and down in a practiced way. "Ancient doors," she said, "and the lock, not that great."

"This isn't a good idea, Mia," Dana said, but even as she spoke, she considered the possibility that Mia had been here before, that she hadn't merely come out for fresh air.

Mia had worked the door open. Dana knew she should get her back to the house, but she'd already stepped inside, and Dana's own curiosity was pushing her sense of good judgment aside as she too entered.

Immediately, a strong, unpleasant odor hit them.

"There's something dead in here," Mia gasped, putting her hand to her nose. She scanned the room with the flashlight beam, keeping the shaft low.

"Oh, shit," Dana replied under her breath. Quickly, she took in the room as Mia swung the light beam. Dana's heart skipped a beat. What if whoever had shot Fabrizio was inside the cottage? Damn, she should have picked that girl up and hauled her back to the house. But, now that they were inside . . . there was no sound, no movement, only the smell.

The interior appeared to be nothing more than a small square consisting of a single room with a bed and a tiny kitchen with a two-burner stove, a microwave that seemed at odds with the obvious age of the building, and a miniature refrigerator that appeared as if it had been designed for a college dorm room. A table with two chairs butted up against the window on the kitchen side of the room. Dana stepped over and, as Mia swung the beam, they both knew where the smell was coming from. An overflowing trashcan reeked of rotting food, and the sink, filled with dirty dishes, bits of leftovers, and stagnant water, gave off a ghastly smell.

"That explains the stink," Mia said, turning.

Jeans, underwear, a shirt were strewn about on the floor. The boy was not particularly tidy. The place was a mess, though it didn't look like someone had rummaged through it. No open drawers or cupboards or papers thrown about. Just typical kid, tossing clothes on the floor. But no dead bodies.

No trace of blood, either. The boy had not been shot inside the cottage.

Mia, along with Dana, moved over to the bed covered with rumpled blankets. Carefully, Dana drew the blankets aside. Just checking. The girl pulled out the single drawer on the nightstand, flashed the light inside. A couple of packages of mints and a stack of condoms were the only things in the nightstand. Dana felt herself blush and wondered if Mia was doing the same. At least the boy practiced safe sex. She envisioned Fabrizio as she had seen him that afternoon in Montalcino with his group of beautiful young friends. His charm was obvious, though she certainly hoped he'd tidy up if he brought his conquests here to his cottage. She prayed Mia wasn't one of them. Then she pictured Mia, arm around the boy, holding him up, bringing him to the house, blood dripping from his wound, broken arrow shaft protruding.

Dana's imagination spiraled, spinning out images. The police arriving at the villa, Mia's father, searching the house—panicking because they found it empty. Leo, stricken with fear that something had happened to his daughter.

Without a word or any visible reaction to the content of the drawer, Mia slid it shut and crossed the room to the table where they could see, with the help of the flashlight, a stack of papers and what appeared to be textbooks. Dana opened one. In Italian, but from the illustrations and diagrams, she thought it might be a college-level botany book. Computer printout sheets were tucked into the other book, possibly a chemistry book. Dana glanced around, but she didn't see a computer or electronic tablet.

Mia picked up an envelope underneath several papers, shining the light beam for Dana to see. The postmark was blurred. No name or return address printed on the envelope. Carefully Mia slid the letter out. In a whisper, she translated:

"My dearest Fabrizio, we are happy that you have settled in and received such a warm welcome and that you feel you are among family. I do know you have always wanted to have a little brother or sister, and you barely remember your father. I am happy that you are content with the Borelli family and that you are finding satisfaction in your work."

Dana guessed it was a letter from an older family member; she didn't think kids wrote letters anymore. She wondered what Mia was thinking as she translated the words in a whisper. The girl stopped for a second as if listening for outside sounds, but hearing nothing she continued. "It goes on . . . something about a desire for Fabrizio to continue his university education, but that there is value in learning from the land, too. Then something about keeping his Locri family in his heart even when he is far away, and then it is signed, Nonna."

"Grandmother?" Dana asked and Mia nodded. The encouraging, thoughtful words in the letter certainly sounded like a grandmother.

"Locri?" Dana asked unsure if the girl was unable to translate this word from Italian to English. "A family name?"

As Mia turned back to her, they heard a rustle, the crack of a twig, footsteps as if someone was approaching the cottage. Then voices. Men's voices. Within seconds they sounded as if they were just outside the cottage.

"Is there a back door?" Dana asked in a low voice, glancing to a door that she thought might lead into the bathroom, not outside.

Mia shook her head, and then she bent over and scooped up a pile of clothing from the floor. The front door opened. The light flicked on.

Dana blinked, adjusting to the brightness. She was only slightly relieved that it was Leo and two other men, one she recognized as Alberto DeLuca, who stood just inside the doorway. Leo rushed to his daughter, threw his arms around her and said something in Italian that Dana was sure was *What are you doing here? You scared me to death when we couldn't find you.*

The police officers seemed to be reacting to the awful smell and left the questioning of his daughter to Leo. A conversation went back and forth between Mia and Leo, voices rising, Mia holding up the bundle of Fabrizio's clothes she'd picked up off the floor.

The younger officer said something in Italian that Dana interpreted as, *What's that awful smell?* DeLuca coughed, but stepped deeper into the room, glancing about at the mess.

Leo's voice grew harsh and Mia started to cry.

The two police officers moved cautiously about the room.

Mia held tight to the bundle of clothes as her father stepped toward the bed. Dana wanted to put her arm around the girl, but she feared Leo was already furious with them both, and she didn't want it to appear that she and Mia had planned this together. Mia leaned into Dana and whispered through her tears, "I told father I came for clothes to take to Fabrizio." Dana realized the boy's clothing was covered with blood, also that Mia was a quick thinker.

Dana grabbed the pillow on the bed, pulled off the pillowcase and, taking the clothing from Mia, began folding the items into the makeshift bag. Leo glared at Dana, even as she attempted to gather words of apology, but Mia jumped in before she could speak. "She tried to stop me."

The younger officer had found the source of the smell. He held his nose as he examined the trashcan and sink.

"You could have waited until morning," Leo said to Mia, shooting another quick, disapproving glance at Dana. "You could have asked for my permission." His words were heavy with fatigue, but edged with anger.

"I knew I wouldn't be able to sleep," Mia explained. "I wanted to do something. I wanted to go to the hospital, but Zio Giovanni wouldn't—"

Leo held up a hand as if to tell her that was enough, and then he turned to DeLuca and said something in Italian, motioning to his daughter, then Dana, then back toward the villa.

"I want to get his toothbrush," Mia replied defiantly. "Some things from the bathroom."

Leo said a few words to DeLuca. The detective nodded and then motioned with a quick jerk toward the bathroom.

"I'll help," Dana said. The younger officer followed them, standing near the bathroom doorway, arms folded over his chest as if he wished to impress or intimidate them with his sense of authority.

It was a small room with toilet, sink, and a shower that was little more than a drain in the corner with a rod and shower curtain. Mia opened the cabinet above the sink, took a toothbrush and toothpaste out of a glass cup. Dana grabbed a razor, comb, and stick deodorant. There was little else in the cabinet. A small plastic bottle of eye drops, a glass bottle of red cough syrup, some aftershave.

"Not so sure those clothes on the floor are clean," Dana whispered, and then, "We should tell the police where we found the arrow shaft."

"They'll find it. If they don't, they are idiots. Who couldn't follow a blood trail?"

The girl was right. She and Mia had found it without difficulty, and Leo would be even more upset if he knew they had been snooping around in the dark.

They stepped back into the room and placed the items in the pillowcase. The younger officer stood in the open doorway, looking outside where DeLuca and Leo crouched down several yards from the front door of the cottage. Quickly, Dana stepped over to the dresser, grabbed a couple pair of clean undershorts and stuffed them in the pillowcase.

Leo returned to the cottage and after another tense conversation with his daughter, none of which Dana understood, he handed the full pillowcase to DeLuca.

The younger detective escorted Mia and Dana back to the villa, while Leo and DeLuca stayed at the cottage. There were three vehicles parked near the house.

No one spoke. Dana was grateful they hadn't touched the arrow shaft, and Mia was right—the police would find it.

When they stepped inside, they could hear activity in the kitchen, footsteps above. As they approached the staircase, a uniformed officer hurried down and spoke rapidly to the young detective, who then spoke to Mia in Italian.

"I've been instructed to return to my room," Mia told Dana without emotion. Dana gave her a quick hug, the girl small and fragile in her embrace. Mia kissed Dana on each cheek and started up the stairs. She glanced back once, her expression vague, then a quick smile, definitely a thank you, flickered across her face.

The detective motioned for Dana to wait in the living room, which she did. She was exhausted and felt that she might fall asleep in the chair where she sat, though one of the officers checked on her every five or ten minutes. Eventually, a thin, somber-faced woman entered, told Dana she spoke English, and then sat silently.

A weary-looking DeLuca walked in.

Through the interpreter, he asked Dana what she had seen that evening. She told them about Mia coming into the kitchen with Fabrizio, Borelli going to the hospital with the young man, Dana following Mia, unable to convince her to come back to the house.

"Did you see anyone outside?" the woman asked.

"No."

"Hear anything unusual?"

"No."

"Did you remove anything from the cottage?"

"Only the items that the investigator okayed." Dana eyed DeLuca, who listened calmly, stroking his thick mustache as the woman spoke to him in Italian.

After several more questions, Dana answering the best she could, she was asked again how long she planned to stay. When she told the interpreter she was scheduled to stay a week, leaving next Sunday, DeLuca stood and left the room. The interpreter told Dana she could go upstairs and thanked her for her cooperation.

Dana started out of the room. DeLuca stood in the hallway.

"Fabrizio?" Dana asked.

DeLuca shook his head, then stared down at the floor. Dana had no idea if this meant he was dead or barely hanging on, but she knew it wasn't good.

The officer she'd seen coming down the stairs earlier was pacing the hall upstairs. He let her go to her room, where she sat alone, turning the events of the past few days over and over in her head, praying Fabrizio was still alive, feeling such heartache for the Borelli family, and especially for Mia. And then, a guilty twinge of excitement.

CHAPTER THIRTEEN

A sound awakened him from his fitful, sporadic sleep and from a dream in which he fell from a steep cliff into something vague and undefined. At first, Winkie thought the noise was part of the dream, but soon realized it came from outside. He rose, feet to the cold floor, and made his way to the window, peering through the slats of the shutter. The Mercedes was pulling out, Giovanna at the wheel.

Last night when she'd asked about his arriving in a Borelli van, he'd explained that he'd met a friend on the flight from New York who was visiting the Borelli Vineyards and had been offered a ride. She seemed to accept this explanation for why he had arrived in a rival winemaker's vehicle—possibly because it was true?

He watched Giovanna's Mercedes disappear down the road, then he returned to the nightstand and glanced at the time on his watch. It was too early for her to be taking off for ten o'clock Mass but perhaps she had other errands to run. Maybe she was going for coffee. Headed out to Starbucks, he thought with a laugh.

Coffee. He could certainly use a cup. He felt a headache coming. He dressed, crossed the hall to the bathroom, then descended to the first floor.

The woman who had served dinner last night was puttering around in the kitchen, placing the silver flatware into a large wooden box. She looked up, surprised to see him.

"Cappuccino?" she offered. "Coffee?"

"*Sì, grazie,* coffee." He might enjoy a cup of cappuccino later, but now he wanted coffee without the fluff. Straight black coffee. She motioned him into the dining room, indicating she would serve him there. *"Non c'é pane,"* she said, her face blushing lightly with embarrassment. *"La Signora va . . ."* She pointed toward the direction of town.

"Grazie," he said and headed toward the dining room. Giovanna had gone to the bakery to get some bread, maybe some pastries, a typical Italian breakfast, which Winkie had always enjoyed, though it felt like mere hours ago that he had finished eating dinner and he wasn't hungry.

The dining room had lost the glow and ambiance of the previous night when soft light flickered against the walls. In daylight, which was creeping in through the gap in the heavy, tattered drapes, he could see how worn the room was. The tablecloth remained, as well as the flowers in the center of the table, but everything else, remnants of the elegant dinner—wineglasses, silver, china—had been cleared away. As he sat and waited, he wondered if the room's ambiance had diminished partially because of Giovanna's absence. The woman had a radiance, a glow about her. He liked her, and he smiled at the thought.

A mug of coffee arrived, with more apologies from the Signorina. Winkie assured her this was fine. The coffee was served in a sturdy mug, for which he was grateful as he was not in the mood for delicacy. She sat a small pitcher of milk and a bowl of sugar next to him on the table, along with a single spoon and napkin. The bowl, a muted green, was chipped along one side of the rim, which gave him an odd satisfaction he couldn't explain.

He drank the coffee straight without sugar or milk. It was strong and dark and richly fragrant. Shortly, the woman returned to offer a refill. After she'd gone back to the kitchen, Winkie rose, coffee in hand, and stepped out into the hall, then through the main entryway, down the corridor off to the opposite side of the kitchen and dining wing. First, he passed by a room with the door ajar. He did not enter but gazed in. Bookshelves lined three walls. The other opened up to the courtyard which could be seen through the glass doors. He continued down the hall, passing a closed door that he guessed led to Giovanna's suite.

He returned to the kitchen, finding no sign of the kitchen helper. He refilled his coffee, stepped back into the entry foyer, then out the front door. The driveway was empty. Ruts in the gravel revealed several sets of tire tracks, maybe from the Borelli van or from the trio of vehicles, the mysterious guests.

Sipping his coffee, Winkie walked along the side of the house and out into the closest vineyard, gazing down over the landscape. The grapes had all been harvested. A good freeze and the hillside would be covered with the gold of autumn. In the distance, he could see a grove of sturdy, thick oak trees. It was a beautiful morning. Sunday morning, a time to spend outdoors, not inside a dank, medieval church, a priest chanting ancient prayers.

He crested a hill and stared down as the soft morning light spread a glow over the vineyards below. He could see the Borelli villa in the distance. He strolled leisurely along the side of the hill, then down into a dip, following a path lined with olive trees. It felt good to get out, take in the scent of the autumn day, the earth. He could get used to this.

He started up another hill, realizing he was some distance from the villa. He felt slightly disoriented though he guessed he could retrace his steps when he was ready to return. As he reached the top of the hill, he saw several outbuildings below him. He started down and, as he approached, he saw the buildings were dilapidated and appeared to be abandoned. He wasn't sure if he was still on Veronesi land or if he had crossed over a property line.

A car was parked along a gravel road leading up to the buildings, but no one was in sight. It was an older model vehicle, dusty, with a dirty windshield. It looked familiar and then Winkie realized he had seen it before. The Volvo, the second car that had come up to the house last night. Curious, he stepped closer and stood hidden behind the nearest building. He heard voices, though he could see no one. They spoke Italian, but he couldn't make out what they were saying. From the tone of the voices, he gathered it was two men. Arguing.

A man stepped out from the adjacent building, his back to Winkie. The man wore a cap. He took it off and scratched his head. "She won't implicate anyone. She's too deep into this herself."

The other man, the younger of the two, looked toward where Winkie stood. For a moment he thought the man had seen him, but then he turned back to the other man whose features were obscured in the shadow of the building.

"We did not know about the old man," the younger man said. "He wasn't in the cellar when we got there." His voice quivered. "This wasn't the way we planned it. We didn't know until . . ." He kicked the dirt with his boot. "We will still get the second payment?"

"Stupido cretino," the older man growled. "You should have left the bottled wine alone. If you'd just followed the original plan." He let out a string of angry words, some Winkie didn't understand, but from the gruff, angry tone he knew they were swear words.

It appeared the younger man was about to speak, but then thought better of offering a defense. Something about this fellow seemed familiar to Winkie, and then he realized the person who'd come to visit last night, who'd come in the same vehicle parked in front of the building now, was the angry protester they had seen along the roadside, the man who had rushed up to the Borelli van.

He wasn't wearing the tam he'd worn then, but his jeans were tattered, his beard scruffy, and he wore the same hooded coat. The other man wore jeans, a windbreaker-type jacket, but appeared much better dressed, tidier.

The older man stood silently for several moments, adjusted his cap, looked down, then gazed out toward a far hillside. He shook his head, said something in a low voice, and started down the hill. The other man lingered for several moments, and when the older man was no longer in sight, he got in his car.

Winkie waited until the vehicle had disappeared, wondering about the strange conversation he'd heard, remembering Giovanna had told him a group of environmentalists was interested in buying the vineyard. He stood several minutes making sure no one else was in sight, casting his glance slowly along the hillsides around him. A flutter, a movement, a twitter startled him, but when half a dozen birds shot up nearby, he realized it was just sparrows. Noting the location and angle of the sun to get his bearings, Winkie started back to the house.

When he arrived, Giovanna's car was parked out front. He went to the kitchen, realizing after his walk he was hungry. A box of pastries sat on the counter. A fresh pot of coffee had been brewed. Winkie poured himself another cup and ate a pastry with a lemon crème filling, not bothering to return to the dining room, but eating over the sink without using a plate or napkin.

Just as he finished, licked his fingers, and turned to leave, Giovanna walked into the room.

"You're up," she said. She smiled and it grew into a small laugh. She picked up a pastry and took a bite. "After your flight, the time change, as well as a very late dinner, I hoped you might be able to catch up on your sleep."

"I'm afraid I'm not much of a sleeper," he said.

"Yes," she replied, "I know the frustration." She paused for a moment and gazed at him as if there was something more to say. "I'm headed into town."

"I'd like to go with you," he said, not really thinking it through.

"To Mass? To church?"

He had no desire to go to church, but he might look around the town. He hoped to find someplace to get an adaptor. "I'm afraid I left my adaptor at home. Maybe I can find one in town. My phone is dead."

"Oh, dear," she said, glancing about the room. "I'm sure we don't have one here. I apologize. We seldom have guests, particularly from America. I didn't think about the converters, the adaptors. Yes, surely you are welcome to ride along into town." She finished off the pastry with a large, unladylike bite, which made Winkie like her all the more. "I don't know if there is anywhere in Montalcino on a Sunday." She waved a hand in the air. "So much has changed over the years. But, with all the tourists, perhaps there are places to shop. I'd enjoy your company. Yes, please come along."

CHAPTER FOURTEEN

Blood. Then wine. Flowing. She and Mia stood above the body of a man, face down in the deep red liquid. It wasn't Paolo, but a younger man. And then, a boy. Dana smelled both blood and wine, as the boy turned and rose. Effortlessly, as if he were a ghost. He was faceless. Dana awoke. She was sweating. Was the faceless boy Fabrizio? Or was it her son? Was it Joel? She lay still, silent.

The dreams came unexpectedly. Often nightmares. And yet Joel would come sometimes to comfort her, to let her know he was okay. Not now. She felt no comfort. Was Fabrizio a lost boy too? Someone's son.

Her cellphone rang.

"Yes," she said, pushing her damp hair out of her eyes, rubbing her head.

"Are you awake?" Borelli asked.

"Yes." Both her body and mind needed more sleep, yet she feared her sleep when the nightmares came. At times she longed for them, for any possibility her son would appear.

"You did not sleep well." It wasn't a question and she guessed Borelli hadn't slept well either.

Sitting up, she attempted to shake herself more fully awake. So many questions shot through her head. Was Fabrizio still alive? Had Borelli spoken to Leo? Did he know what she and Mia did last night?

"Are you at the hospital?" she asked. "Is he going to be okay?"

"He made it through the night. Through surgery." Borelli's tone told her the boy's condition was still tenuous. "I'm here, downstairs," he said. "Come down. Bring a jacket, whatever you need for the day."

"What time is it?"

"Almost nine."

"Give me half an hour," she said. She needed to shower. She remembered, she'd showered before falling into bed, but she was damp with sweat. "It's almost nine?" She couldn't believe she'd slept this late. Yet, she realized it must have been past three a.m. when she returned to her room.

She showered quickly, towel dried her hair, dressed, didn't bother to put on any makeup, grabbed her bag, and hurried down. Borelli met her at the bottom of the stairs.

"We're going to Siena," he said.

"Is Leo okay with this?" she asked. "Where's Mia?" They stepped outside. Two of the vehicles she had seen last night were still parked in the driveway. "Are the police okay if we leave?"

"Have you been arrested?" Borelli asked.

Only slightly stunned by his question, she shook her head.

"Well, neither have I. We are free to come and go as we please. So, I'm taking you to Siena. You are on holiday, and I am your host."

"You don't have to do this for me," she said. "There is so much happening, with your family, the business—"

"We are going to Siena," he said firmly, cutting her off.

They walked out to the garage to get Borelli's truck. The van was gone, no sign of Claudio or anyone else. Dana glanced around the interior where tools were arranged on hooks above a tidy workbench. No mechanic's type pin-up calendars, but oddly, a small religious picture of Christ with a glowing heart hung on the wall.

"Leo came to the hospital late last night—no, it was morning by then," Borelli said. "The boy made it through surgery, but no one has been allowed to visit yet. Leo returned home for a short while. Claudio will take Leo and Mia into Montalcino for Mass. I'm sure she will attempt to convince her father to take her to visit Fabrizio, but I know Leo will not take her until—"

"Until Fabrizio is better?"

"Yes, better. We will attempt to keep doing things the way we always do. Mass on Sunday—the boy can certainly use the prayers. Brunch when they return." He opened the driver's side of the truck, handed Dana the keys, and motioned her to get in.

"You're not going to Mass?"

"I said Mass in the estate chapel when I returned from the hospital. Too early for others, particularly on Sunday. Estella often attends a chapel Mass, though never on Sunday as she enjoys going into town."

"Was your sister able to accompany them?" Dana asked as she slid in behind the wheel.

"Estella is not doing well."

Borelli settled into the passenger seat, yanked the seatbelt out, and then with some effort arranged it around his girth.

"Does she know?" Dana asked. "About Fabrizio?"

"Yes," Borelli replied with a catch in his voice. "Estella was told this morning." Dana realized that Estella had most likely slept through all the commotion last night if, unlike Mia, she'd taken the medication the doctor had prescribed.

"Do you believe there is a connection between what happened in the cellar and what happened to Fabrizio?" she asked.

"It's generally rather quiet around here," Borelli said, and Dana took it that was his answer.

They were nearing the exit from the Borelli property. A vehicle was parked just this side of the main highway, a Subaru marked Carabinieri, another unmarked within a short distance. Two men stood conversing. One of them caught Borelli's eye, tilted his head and waved them on.

"Police?" Dana asked.

"Yes, and possibly a reporter," Borelli speculated, then said, "Tell me about last night."

They pulled out onto the main highway as Dana explained about Mia. The arrow shaft. Inside the cottage.

"Then Leo and Alberto DeLuca arrived?" Borelli asked. "Talk about incompetence. Mia's call alerted the medical responders, but since there was an officer here already—probably snoozing in the wine cellar—there was some confusion and DeLuca was not notified right away."

Dana had wondered why it took the police so long to arrive.

She told Borelli how Mia had scooped up the clothes, explaining to her father and DeLuca that they had come to the cottage to get some personal items for Fabrizio.

"I'm sure that's the last thing the boy needs now—clothes and his toothbrush." Borelli snorted, but then he smiled. "She's a clever girl. Isn't she?" There was a layer of pride in his voice. "Now tell me more about the arrow shaft."

"We didn't touch it. I knew better than to move or contaminate it. Did the police find it?" she asked hopefully.

"It has been taken to the evidence lab in Siena." He glanced over at her expectantly as if he knew she'd examined it, even without picking it up. "Any markings on the arrow?"

"Blue and white fletchings."

"The shaft itself, any markings?"

"Blue and white stripes."

Borelli thought for a moment. "Any symbols or other marks?"

"Possibly. I took several photos," she said, knowing this would meet his approval.

"Very good." He grinned. "May I?"

"Phone's in the pocket of my bag," she said, pointing.

He attempted to reach down to where she'd placed her bag near his feet, finally undoing the seatbelt, then lifting the bag, rebuckling the seatbelt. He pulled out the phone, struggled with it for a few moments, touching the screen, then tapping. His nose twitched with irritation and impatience. She reached over and, one eye on the road, one on the phone, she found the first picture and handed it back to Borelli.

He studied it carefully. "Can you expand the photo."

She motioned with her fingers indicating how he could enlarge the image, and he was able to do this without more help. "The blue and white fletchings and stripes," he said thoughtfully, "the colors of the Pianello quarter."

Pianello? Then Dana realized that Pianello was the name of one of the four groups competing in the archery event at the *Sagra del Tordo.*

"Something perhaps rubbed off here?" Borelli asked. "Is it possible to send this photo to my phone?"

"Yes, but please may we wait until we park?" She grimaced.

"Yes, yes, of course," he agreed. "Now, tell me more about the cottage."

She described how easily they had entered, how the place was a mess, though no sign that anyone had rummaged through drawers or cabinets. She told him about finding the letter from the grandmother, how Leo and the detectives had arrived just after that.

Borelli said, "Leo told me Fabrizio's grandmother is on her way, but he didn't tell me any more than that, as if oddly he didn't know much about her. He said she—Fabrizio's grandmother—is a friend of his mother's."

"Estella's friend? You didn't know this?"

"I did not," he replied indignantly.

"Can you ask your sister?" Dana said. "You could clear this up." She caught Borelli's eye, and wondered . . . if Fabrizio was Leo's son, had Estella been keeping this secret, too? Estella would be his grandmother. If true, this might be devastating to Mia.

"There is obviously a reason Estella has not shared this information about Fabrizio with me, that is, if she knows," Borelli said with little emotion. "I certainly haven't been informed, and I would prefer to have some facts before I approach her. Particularly in her fragile emotional, as well as physical, state. If she'd intended to share this with me—"

"You think she's hiding something? Covering something?"

"I just want to have facts in hand when I—was there anything in the letter you and Mia found? A postmark?"

"Unreadable, though Italian I'm sure," Dana said. "Mia translated the letter for me."

Dana told Borelli, as close as she could remember, what the grandmother had written. She told him about the references to family, Fabrizio's desire to have a sibling. Were these merely musings from a grandmother wishing a favorite grandson well in a new adventure away from home, hoping that he would be taken in as family. Or *was* Fabrizio family?

"There was a reference to his Locri family," Dana said. "Could that be a family name? I was about to ask Mia when Leo and the police arrived. Does that mean anything to you? Locri?"

Borelli thought for a moment, repeating the word, *Locri*, once, then twice.

"It does mean something to you, then?" Dana asked.

"In Calabria. A region in the southern part of Italy."

"This being where Fabrizio and his grandmother come from?"

"Perhaps," he replied. "Calabria, on the very tip of the boot. The toe. Kicking Sicily."

"Some distance, then."

"Driving would take a good . . ." He paused, calculating. "Nine hours. Flying to Rome or to Florence, a much shorter journey."

Dana wondered if he was attempting to determine how long it would take the grandmother to arrive, but knowing Borelli as she did, it was more likely he was planning a trip down to Calabria himself.

CHAPTER FIFTEEN

When they arrived in Siena, they walked around the city, Borelli playing the role of guide, Dana the tourist. She could tell he was distracted, as was she, even as he explained the history of the Piazza del Campo where they stopped for a mid-morning coffee and pastry.

"The site of the Palio," he said, arm sweeping in a wide gesture, taking in the fan-shaped, concave space where tourists gathered, many sitting on the red-brick piazza as if it were a grassy picnic area. "Twice a year, during the warmer weather, a horse race is held in which the seventeen neighborhoods of the city compete."

Dana couldn't help but think of a similar competition which was scheduled for the coming weekend in Montalcino. The archery competition of the *Sagra del Tordo*, in which the four quarters of the city would compete. She envisioned the broken arrow shaft protruding from Fabrizio's bloody body, then the fletched end, which she and Mia discovered, displaying blue and white feathers, colors of the Pianello quarter. She caught Borelli's eye and wondered if he was thinking the same.

After finishing their coffee, a slow leisurely stroll around the exterior of the piazza, Borelli announced they would have lunch with friends. Dana wasn't completely surprised; she had wondered if he had something planned other than a touristy little jaunt to Siena.

Taking one of the numerous streets radiating out from the square, Borelli veered through pedestrian traffic, led Dana down a narrow street and, after numerous turns, he stepped up to a door, announcing their arrival with a vigorous knock. Soon, footsteps sounded from inside, someone coming down the stairs, and a man about Borelli's age swung the door open and greeted them. A child, about four years old, wrapped his arms around the man's legs, looking up at the guests with large, dark brown eyes. After quick kisses and smiles were exchanged, Borelli introduced his friend as Francesco Treponti, the boy as his grandson, Peppe. They were led up a narrow staircase into an apartment and greeted by a younger man, and an older woman, Francesco's wife. Plump with graying hair wrapped around the back of her head, she could have been an actress for a commercial advertising authentic Italian spaghetti sauce. Red stains on her apron gave the impression she'd been in the kitchen all morning, preparing marinara from scratch, and the aroma wafting through the room seemed to confirm this.

They stepped into the living room. Two children, maybe about seven and nine, eyes glued to the TV, reminded Dana of her youngest nephew and niece. After quick introductions, the older man invited them to sit. He called out to the children who obediently turned the sound down on the TV.

Dana could understand little of the conversation between the priest and his friend, but picked up a few words like *Americana, Boston, Prague,* and realized Borelli must be explaining to Francesco how they had met.

A decanter of wine, along with a plate of salami and cheese, was brought into the living room by a younger woman, introduced as Regina. Dana rose and followed her back to the kitchen to see if she could help. Francesco's wife put Dana to work cutting bread and arranging it in a basket. The younger woman, a daughter or perhaps daughter-in-law, spoke English, asking Dana if she was staying with the Borellis, how long she'd be in Italy. Signora Treponti dipped a spoon into the luscious, spicy smelling sauce simmering on the stove, and offered Dana a bite. *"Delizioso,"* Dana said with a smile.

As they worked side by side in the kitchen, Dana heard a lively conversation, ever increasing in volume, coming from the living room and guessed that others had arrived. Soon another young woman joined them in the kitchen, bringing in a dish that she slid into the refrigerator. Introductions were made by the woman who spoke English.

When all was ready, those in the living room were invited into the dining room, a small space filled wall to wall with a large table and mismatched chairs to accommodate the numerous family members. Photos of children and grandchildren, as well as couples, including the elder two, in wedding pictures, lined the walls. One of the photos showed a much younger Francesco Treponti, standing proud and erect, dressed in a police uniform. Dana threw a side glance to Borelli, who dipped his head, aware that she knew their visit was more than a social call.

After several courses, including pasta, bread, chicken and green beans, the two older men, Borelli and their host, rose and stepped out on the small balcony looking out to the street. Though he'd told Dana he'd quit smoking, she could see Borelli lighting up, pinching a cigarette between two fingers, the other gesturing in animated conversation. Their host had also lit one up.

The women, Dana included, cleared off the table and cleaned up the kitchen. Though Dana had no sisters, she had a sister-in-law, aunts and girl cousins, and when gathering for similar family dinners, they would gravitate toward the kitchen. She enjoyed the company of these friendly Italian women, particularly Regina, who took an interest in Dana and asked about her writing for an

American newspaper. Even as they conversed, Dana was curious about what Borelli and Signor Treponti were discussing out on the balcony. When the women returned to the dining room, the two men had come back in and were enjoying another glass of wine.

Borelli said they should be going and rose to thank their host and hostess, who walked them back down to the street level. Dana expressed her gratitude while attempting to suppress her curiosity.

They had barely stepped out onto the street when she said, "You and Francesco were talking about what happened in the cellar?"

"Everyone is talking about it. Yes, Francesco had heard."

"He's a police officer?"

"Retired, but he still has connections within the *Questura*, the provincial branch of the police force."

"Which is headquartered here in Siena."

A nod from Borelli.

"What did he tell you?"

"He said there was no sign of a struggle in the cellar, though Paolo did, as Leo told me, have a deep cut on his head." Borelli picked up his pace as if this conversation required an urgency to move forward. "It appears that he hit his head on the metal edge of one of the barrels. The cellar floors are all equipped with drains. Because of the broken glass from the destroyed bottles, the drains were partially clogged."

"Paolo fell and hit his head?"

"Yes," Borelli said. "It appears that he drowned in the wine."

"They've already completed the autopsy?" Dana asked.

"Conjecture now. But yes, they are conducting an autopsy," Borelli said, motioning to take a turn on the next narrow street.

"Do the police believe he came across whoever released the–"

"Likely he entered the cellar after."

"If the motive was purely the destruction of the wine, the vandals,"—Dana didn't know what else to call them— "had no intention of killing a man."

"Vandals," Borelli said, shaking his head, "probably not an accurate word. This was no childish prank. Whoever opened the spigots and smashed the bottles had the intention of destroying the wine. The viciousness of the act . . ."

"Was there any talk of who might have done it?" Dana asked.

"Francesco said the police are questioning other producers, other members of the Consortium."

"Another wine producer might be responsible?"

"It's a viable theory." He stopped for a moment, glanced up at the street sign, then continued walking.

Dana thought of the 250 names on the plaque in Montalcino, those vineyards in the area that produced the Brunello wine. Though Borelli had explained the Consortium was a group of producers working together, she imagined there was competition among those 250, particularly the larger producers. "Have there been problems within the Consortium?"

"Hints of conflict are not unusual, jealousies over one producer being rated higher than another. When working with a variety of producers, an assortment of personalities and with so many of the vineyards now under new management, problems arise."

"What kinds of problems?"

"Over the past years, subgroups have popped up, factions including those made up of several board members, who were intent on changing the production codes, allowing a small percentage of grapes other than Sangiovese in the Brunello. Discussions have become heated. As I understand," he added as if he had no direct knowledge of this.

"Where do the Borellis fit into these discussions?" Dana asked.

"Leo is a purist. A traditionalist when it comes to Brunello."

"Could someone taste the difference?" she asked. "I mean if the wine contained grapes other than the Sangiovese?" She was quite sure she wouldn't be able to tell, but she wished as soon as she asked the question that she hadn't because Borelli glanced over, giving her a look—his head tilted at an angle. He was definitely looking down his nose at her.

"Might one distinguish between a diamond and zirconia?" He waved an arm dramatically, then stopped as if he needed a moment to rest. "A collar trimmed with mink, one made from the fur of an otter?"

She knew he didn't expect an answer, so she said nothing.

"Probably not," he said, surprising her. He reached into his pocket as if searching for something. Dana wondered if he felt the need for another cigarette. When he produced nothing, he continued, "If the amount was small. Only detected by the most discerning palate. But one willing to pay three to four hundred dollars for a bottle of wine might expect to receive what he has paid for."

Dana noted that the price was inching up. Last night he'd claimed a bottle of the Brunello Riserva would be priced at $300 in a nice restaurant.

Again, they walked, shouldering through the crowded area of the Piazza del Campo. Eventually, they emerged on a street that Dana recognized as the one on which they had parked the truck.

"Francesco said the state financial police are involved, too," Borelli told her, "as well as the *carabinieri*. I pray they can all work together. At times there is so much division, squabbling over whose jurisdiction, whose authority."

"Joining forces, surely they can resolve this?" Dana said, her inflection clearly indicating the desired response from Borelli. *Maybe we should just butt out, let the authorities handle this?*

Borelli emitted a sound, equal parts snort and laugh, but he didn't answer her question. "Regarding Fabrizio," he finally said, "that may be a matter that requires a more personal investigation."

"Francesco said nothing about what happened to Fabrizio?" Dana sensed that Borelli was still concerned about the boy in a way that went beyond the fact that someone had tried to kill him.

"With Fabrizio being shot late last night, the news evidently hasn't traveled, and Francesco was not aware. I didn't bring it up. I was waiting to see if he knew anything about it. So, no, he knew nothing about Fabrizio."

They continued down the street headed in the direction of their parked vehicle.

"I'm concerned about Estella," Borelli said. "She's been hit especially hard by all this. Paolo. Now, Fabrizio."

"They were good friends? Paolo and Estella?"

"I don't know that one could say 'good friends,' but Paolo has worked for the family for many years, and my sister was fond of him. Her interaction is more with his daughter-in-law, Renata, because she works in the home directly with Estella who supervises the household help. Renata has looked after her father-in-law, particularly since her husband's passing."

"Paolo's son?"

"Yes, also named Paolo."

"Did the younger Paolo work for the Borellis?"

"As the viticulturist. A fancy word for the grape farmer. He oversaw the planting, pruning, harvesting. A position of great responsibility."

"This is the position that Marco Dardi now holds?" Though she had yet to meet Marco, both Leo and Borelli had spoken of him. And she knew he'd been with the Borelli Vineyards for many years. His photo, taken some time ago, had been in one of the magazine articles Borelli had placed in the folder he'd given her.

"No, no, Dardi oversees the making of the wine. He is the estate's enologist. On the small vineyards both positions might be held by the same person, often the owner. Many of those now producing in Montalcino have just a few hectares, not a great number of employees."

"But the Borellis—"

"Larger than most. A business this size takes many working together." The sadness in Borelli's voice was evident. The family had just lost a trusted long-time employee. They might also be on the verge of losing a more recent employee. A young man whose employment was a mystery in itself.

CHAPTER SIXTEEN

Borelli was on his phone for the better part of the drive back to the estate, at first examining the photo of the arrow shaft that Dana had forwarded to his phone, then making calls. Speaking rapidly in Italian, Dana could pick up only a few words, but she knew he was speaking to someone called Luigi, then a Marco, who she assumed was the enologist Marco Dardi.

When they pulled onto the road leading up to the villa and winery, the police officer they'd seen earlier conversing with the man Borelli thought was a reporter, stepped out of his vehicle and waved them through. Borelli motioned for Dana to take a left turn into the vineyards. The Borelli van soon came into view, parked on a dirt path next to a row of vines.

Claudio sat stiffly at the wheel, another man sat on the passenger side, turned away, gesturing toward the hillside. Octavia smiled and waved from the middle seat. Richard sat in the back, along with David, who appeared to be reading something.

Borelli directed Dana to pull alongside the van. He rolled down the window and called out, "Claudio, *come stai? Buon giorno*, Marco."

Claudio tipped his hat. The passenger in the front seat turned and smiled. "*Buon giorno,* Giovanni," he said.

"Dana, this is our enologist, Marco Dardi. Marco, our American guest, Dana Pierson."

"Buon giorno," Dana replied, but the words going through her head were, *Well, Marco Dardi, you were certainly worth the wait!* There was something instantly pleasing about him. Strong jaw, softened by something around the eyes, his mouth, a welcoming approachability. He was in his mid-to-late forties with the type of looks that often become more attractive for a man as he reaches middle age. His thick dark hair was touched with a hint of silver. He was much better looking than the younger man in the magazine photo.

A brief conversation followed between the men that Dana could not understand. From the somber tone, she guessed they were speaking of the recent events.

"Why don't you go along with them, Dana." Borelli's voice had shifted, ready to move on to more pleasant conversation.

"Yes, please, join us," Marco said in English. His voice, too, had relaxed. He shot Dana a warm smile.

Borelli said, "Going with Marco and the others would be a perfect opportunity for you to learn more about the vineyards from an expert."

"Sure, I'd like to go along," Dana said.

"They've sampled barrel wine in the new cellar," Borelli explained, "certainly not the experience we wish for our guests." Dana recalled Borelli's description of what he'd called a behemoth corrugated warehouse. "They are now going out to examine the vines. A rather backward way to do a tour, but . . ." He waved a dismissive hand. "Perhaps we should feel fortunate to be allowed guests at all."

Dardi got out of the van and stepped over to the truck and around to open the door for Dana. He reached for her hand to help her out. He had a nice touch—not too forceful, yet firm. He released her hand. The others were getting out of the van.

"Father Borelli," Marco asked, "will you join us?"

Borelli had already eased himself out and around the vehicle to the driver's side. "I have business to attend to. Enjoy the afternoon."

"I'll catch up with you later," Dana said, and Borelli nodded. She had no doubt that his business had something to do with the information he had acquired from retired police officer Francesco Treponti that afternoon, or maybe from one of his recent calls.

As Borelli pulled out, the others started up the hillside on foot, Marco leading the way, Dana noticing that his jeans fit him nicely. He wore a polo shirt and dark green windbreaker. He had an appealing way of looking rugged and refined at the same time.

Dana walked alongside Octavia, who wore slim jeans, heavy boots and a vest that made her appear as if she was set for a serious safari. She still managed to look like a fashion model. A camera hung around her neck adding to the safari illusion.

Dana asked, "You are enjoying your stay?"

"I took a stroll through Montalcino this morning, up to the *fortezza*. Beautiful view of the area. I got some great shots." She patted her camera. "I ran into Winkie in town, which reminds me." She dug around in her bag. "Oh darn, I forgot it."

"Forgot what?"

"I have something I want you to give to Winkie."

"I'm not sure I'll see him again."

"He said he needed to talk to you."

"About what?"

"I'm not sure." Octavia stopped, focused her camera on a distant hillside. "He'd forgotten his adaptor for his phone and the battery was dead."

Dana wondered where this conversation was going. It wasn't hard to believe the phone was dead. He'd been fiddling with it all the way from Rome.

"He was trying to find one," Octavia explained, "an adaptor, to charge his phone. I told him I had one in my room and we were leaving tomorrow and if I charged my phone, then he could take it with him, and he said he was catching a ride back to the villa where he was staying, so he couldn't wait. But he came up to use my phone to have some privacy to call his kids." She slowed, focused, and took several more shots. "Anyway, I charged my phone and I'm fine 'til I get home."

"But he didn't say why he wanted to talk to me?"

"He didn't, but he said you knew where he was staying, so maybe you could drop it off."

"What?" Dana asked, voice rising. The men looked back. She smiled and waved, letting them know everything was fine. "Winkie wants me to be his delivery girl?" she asked Octavia, calming her voice. "He wants to talk to me, but he didn't tell you why?"

"I think it has something to do with some environmental protesters. He was telling me about a group we'd seen on the way into Montalcino, and I said, 'I have no idea what you are talking about,' and he said, 'Oh, you were asleep.' But then, he said you saw them."

This conversation seemed to be circling round and round. Of course, Dana saw the protesters, particularly the one who nearly pushed his face through the window, then slapped the side of the van.

"He said, well he said he needed to talk to you," Octavia went on. "He asked that I not mention this to anyone except you. I'll bring the adaptor this evening at dinner, and then maybe you could get it to him?"

Dana was too curious to refuse, though she didn't know if she was invited to dinner.

Octavia said, "Do they know who did it—released the wine? Killed the old man?"

"I haven't heard anything more," Dana said.

"It's so awful. I hope they find out soon. Is there danger of more destruction?"

"I don't know," Dana answered, realizing that Octavia and the others didn't know about Fabrizio.

The men, now just steps ahead of the women, had stopped and were conversing. Marco motioned for Dana and Octavia to join them. When they had gathered in a tight little group, he explained that the vines they were now looking at were some of the older plantings, that they had produced some of the estate's highest ranked wines.

"After the harvest, the grapes go through a destemming and crushing process, then a 10- to 12-day alcoholic fermentation, followed by malolactic fermentation, and several months of racking. In March or April, the wine is ready for aging in oak barrels. With a wine such as the Brunello, it is all about the wait. As you know, Brunello Riserva is aged for over five years before it is released, and often reaches its peak years after this." He paused and a quick smile flicked across his face. "Brunello is designed for aging."

Worth the wait, Dana thought, aware that Marco was smiling at her, even as he spoke of weather patterns, of how the soil from one vineyard to another might have a different makeup, how this could affect the taste of the grapes, the wine, how even a subtle variance could make all the difference. He described the Sangiovese grapes, with an apology that they were unable to see grapes on the vines this late in the year. "The defining grape of Italy," he said affectionately. "Thickly skinned on the outside, but ah so delicate, the fruit."

Richard and David walked ahead again, stopping now and then to chat, examine the vines, pick up a sample of soil and run it through their fingers or lift it to their noses. Another man, shorter, and substantially stouter than Marco, but dressed in a similar fashion—windbreaker and jeans—was making his way toward them. He stopped to converse with the two men.

As the trio—Marco, Dana, and Octavia—approached, the man said something to Richard, they laughed, and then he started down the row of vines.

"Our viticulturist," Marco said, waving at the man, who looked back briefly. "If the quality of the grapes is not to our standards, the wine will not be to our standards. This is the most important person on the Borelli estate," he said fondly. The man, at some distance now, smiled, his face shadowed beneath the rim of his cap which he tapped in a half salute, then continued down the row.

Marco described the cycles of the grapes, the tending and pruning through the seasons, the harvest, all done by hand. He explained that the number of vines per hectare was limited in order to produce the finest grapes, and then spoke of production limits per vine, how each was pruned to very specific standards in order not to overproduce and affect the quality of the grapes.

"We like to think of winemaking as art, but truthfully, it is the math and science that will take a vineyard down. The number of vines per hectare, the exact number of bottles produced from each vine, a specified time in barrel. And the science. Biology and chemistry. Weather patterns. Soil makeup. Sun and wind exposure. These all contribute to making the perfect wine. In Montalcino we produce a Sangiovese grape like nowhere else in the entire world."

They continued along the vines, with more questions and technical discussion, Dana's mind drifting . . . why did Winkie want to talk to her? Did it have something to do with the protesters?

"Research has been done to determine the exact origin of the Sangiovese grapes," Marco said. "Many respected viticultural academics agree that the roots are Tuscan."

Richard asked about the clonal research done back in the mid-sixties, and Marco continued with a detailed explanation of the research involved.

After several more questions from the group, Marco motioned them back down the hill toward where they'd parked. When they arrived at the van, he told Dana, "We will return you to the villa, then take the guests back to their hotel in Montalcino."

"I'll walk to the house," Dana offered. "No need to circle back to the villa just for me."

Richard and David slid into the far seat, as Marco held the door for Octavia and spoke to Claudio who had remained with the van.

"I'll see you later this evening," Octavia whispered to Dana.

"You are sure you do not want a ride?" Marco asked approaching Dana, guests all settled back in the van. He gazed off to the west, the sun slowly dipping. "It will be dark soon. Would you like company? Claudio can successfully return our guests to their hotel."

"Company would be nice," Dana replied.

The two of them started back to the villa. It had been a fairly warm day, but was starting to cool. They picked up their pace as Marco waved toward a path winding through a grove of olive trees. A light breeze rustled the leaves, showing a lovely underside of silver.

"This is such a beautiful place," Dana said. "How lucky you are to call this home."

"I grew up here on the Borelli estate," Marco replied. "My father worked for the Borelli's when I was a child. This is all I've ever known."

"You still live here on the Borelli estate?"

"You are filled with questions," he replied with a laugh.

"I guess it is my nature," she returned with a smile.

"Yes, I hear you write for a newspaper. An investigative reporter?"

"Oh, there's always a bit of investigation involved," she said.

"You enjoy your work?"

"I do."

They were moving up a steep incline and he reached for her hand to help her up. Dropping her hand as they crested the top, they stopped to take in the view, the cottages, the Borelli villa. Especially beautiful in the late afternoon light. The angle of the sun brought out the contrast of colors, softening the various shades of gold and green. The shadowing clouds added another dimension to the landscape. A row of cypress trees cast long thin fingers over a distant path.

"To answer your question," he said, "I no longer live here on the estate. I have a small piece of property. A very small farm."

"What do you raise on your farm?" she asked with interest.

"A cow. A pig. Some chickens," he answered with a laugh. "So many questions. A very small farm with an insignificant number of vines."

"Sangiovese of Montalcino?"

"No. No." He laughed again, but this laughter carried a hint of his awareness of her ignorance. "There are a limited number of hectares registered to the Brunello grapes. Though the Sangiovese required for Brunello di Montalcino can only be grown within a prescribed area, the soil varies greatly, as does the altitude, and not every property will successfully produce the grapes of the quality required for the Brunello for which we are known."

They headed back down the hill. Stopping, Marco pointed out where the Borelli land ended, the neighboring landowner's began.

"No fences?" Dana asked.

"The landowners know the property lines well. It may be a dip in the land, a tree, even a rock. The land has become part of who they are after generations of ownership." He gestured again. "It happens infrequently, but a good-sized estate that has been owned by one family for centuries is presently up for sale. Smaller than the original piece of land, but still many hectares." His eyes moved slowly over the adjacent hillsides. Dana wondered if someone who had worked for one family for his entire life, rising to an important position, might one day want to own his own vineyard.

"The Veronesi family at one time owned just about everything you can see from here." His eyes moved slowly across the landscape, the sun settling now on the horizon.

"This is the family that is selling?"

"Yes," he said.

Dana thought about what Borelli had said about the Veronesis. She'd sensed some friction between the families. Suddenly, it hit her that this was the reason Winkie was here. She remembered what Borelli had told her about wealthy Americans and particularly celebrities buying up "hobby" vineyards in the area. Yes, this was why Winkie was here. Somehow his explanation about a quiet place to write didn't ring true. Again, Dana thought of his strange request sent to her through Octavia.

They dipped, then crested a hill and several vehicles came into view, still parked about the estate. It was almost dark now, but Dana could make out a man sitting on a bench and two others standing in front of him. The bench where Leo had taken Mia the morning of the destruction in the cellar. The flicker of a cigarette flashed in his hand. As they got closer, the men standing departed, and she saw the man with the cigarette was Leo. He stubbed his cigarette in a potted plant as if embarrassed to be caught. He stood and walked over to meet them.

"There is a problem with transportation?" he asked, concerned.

"No problem. I wanted to walk," Dana said. "Marco was gracious enough to accompany me. Claudio is returning the others to their hotel."

"We will see you this evening at dinner," Marco said, and Dana thought he was talking to Leo, but when she caught his eye, she realized Marco was talking to her. "Thank you for joining us on our tour," he said.

"My pleasure," Dana replied, offering him a smile.

"This evening, then," Marco said. He spoke briefly in Italian to Leo before he nodded at Dana and headed toward the direction of the garage.

When he was out of sight, Leo said, "You enjoyed the vineyard tour?"

She nodded a yes. "Marco is a gracious representative of the vineyards, so knowledgeable."

"We have come to rely on him. Particularly over the past few years." He rubbed his hands together nervously, then reached into his pocket and withdrew two cigarettes. Dana guessed anyone who carried single cigarettes was not a regular smoker. He offered her one. When she declined, he slipped them both back in his pocket.

"Giovanni took me to Siena this morning," Dana said. "I wish he didn't feel the need to entertain me after what has happened."

"But, it is your holiday," Leo said with a sad smile. "I feel I should offer an apology," he added sincerely.

"Any word on Fabrizio?" she asked.

"The doctors are amazed that he made it to the hospital alive."

Dana watched his facial expression to see if she could read anything more than an employer's concern.

"His grandmother is here?"

"Yes."

"His parents?"

"Both deceased."

"Is she taking him back home?" Dana asked.

"He is too weak for that. As I understand, he has not been able to provide any information to the police." Then with a shift in tone, he said, "I hope he will be able to continue here at the vineyards. My mother has grown very fond of him, as have I. He is a likable boy."

And your daughter has grown fond of him, too, Dana thought, again attempting to read beneath his words as he spoke of the boy.

"For one so young," Leo said, "he seems to have a natural instinct for the wine."

Because he is your son? Dana wondered.

Leo motioned toward the house. "What happened in the cellar has become big news," he told her. "The incident with Fabrizio, Inspector DeLuca wishes to keep this . . ." He paused as if searching for a word. "He wishes that we do not let this information get out yet. If anyone asks about Fabrizio . . . perhaps he has returned home."

It sounded like a warning that she was to keep quiet. Since Fabrizio had not grown up here and had no family nearby, this news might not get out as quickly as the news of the cellar vandalism.

Was it Leo or Inspector DeLuca who wished to keep this quiet? Dana knew the police often refused to release particulars about an investigation. Sometimes they would go to the public for help, but generally, during the initial stages of an investigation, they would attempt to release as little as possible. The most successful investigations were often the ones where the police were able to keep certain aspects of the crime out of the press. Though it was always the reporter's job to uncover as much as she could, Dana would have to agree that this wasn't always in the best interest of the police or in solving the crime.

"Thank you for going out with Mia last night," Leo said as they drew near the front door of the villa.

Dana had thought he was angry with her for going, but from the tone of his voice she didn't think that anymore. "I could see she had every intention of going, and I didn't want her to go alone."

"She is stubborn," Leo said. "I do not think children were so . . . defiant—is that the correct word? —so lacking in respect for their elders when I was growing up. It seems since her mother's passing she is more and more difficult. I sometimes do not know the best way to . . . Raising a child on my own, one of the most difficult tasks I—" He glanced at Dana as if she might add to this conversation, and then she could see on his face—in the light that had flicked on as they approached the front door of the villa—instant regret. *How cruel,* she could see he was thinking, *to speak of the difficulties of raising a child to a woman who has lost her only child.*

"I apologize," Leo said. "It is an honor to raise a daughter such as Mia. She is bright, ambitious."

"She is," Dana agreed. They lingered for just a moment, and then Leo opened the door and they stepped inside.

"We leave for Montalcino at half past seven," he said. "We will dine at our favorite restaurant with our Simonelli guests at eight. It is our custom to complete our business dealings with a special dinner. I would like you to attend." He offered her a warm smile, and Dana returned the same.

Well, she thought, *looks like I'm going to dinner this evening.* She was definitely curious why Winkie wanted to speak with her, and this would give her an opportunity to talk to Octavia.

And then she realized, Marco Dardi would be there too.

CHAPTER SEVENTEEN

When Dana arrived at her room, she realized that in her exhaustion last night after what had happened to Fabrizio, going to the cottage with Mia, being questioned by the police, then her rush to meet Borelli that morning, she hadn't bothered to hang up her pants or jacket. She'd thrown them on the bathroom floor, then fallen into bed. As she picked up the slacks, she could feel the stiffness and smell a rusty metallic scent. After examining them, she realized they were spotted with dried blood. Fabrizio's blood. The jacket was also stained. Too late to send them out to be cleaned, and the stains had most likely set by now.

In light of what had happened over the past few days, she should hardly be stressed over a ruined suit, but she had nothing to wear to dinner that evening. Jeans were definitely not suitable. She flung herself on the bed, rubbing her head, staring up at the ceiling.

Maybe she should pack up and leave. She thought of poor Father Borelli. This was hardly the holiday either of them had envisioned. Borelli's sister, Estella, was so distraught she hadn't made it out of her bedroom since the destruction in the cellar, let alone join her brother and their guest for some sightseeing. Dana couldn't imagine what Leo was going through, attempting to operate the business, hosting American buyers, dealing with the police, all while trying to father a rebellious daughter. The family didn't need the added worry of entertaining Dana. Maybe it would be best to cut her visit short. She could head down to Rome, do some exploring on her own until her friends arrived.

But, then she thought of her strange conversation with Octavia, Winkie's need to speak with her.

She sat up, thinking . . . *I must go to dinner this evening.* And then another thought—*I have nothing to wear.*

She glanced over toward the chair where she'd dropped her purse. She stood, slung the bag over her shoulder, and left the room, intent on finding Borelli and asking to borrow his truck. As she hurried down the stairs, she wondered if it was too late to find an open shop. She checked for Borelli in the kitchen, then the living room, the library. The entire house felt empty, deserted. She knew a meal would not be prepared that evening, and the help had obviously been dismissed.

She made her way out to the garage, keeping on the path, led by the light from the villa, then a light on the outside of the garage. She found Claudio, wearing a pair of coveralls, changing the oil in one of the numerous estate vehicles.

"Father Borelli?" she asked.

"No," Claudio said, wiping his hands with a rag. He motioned toward the area of the garage where Borelli usually parked the truck. The space was empty.

"Grazie," Dana said as she started back to the house. It was probably too late to do any shopping. This was a stupid idea. She'd stay at the villa with the excuse that she was not feeling well. Yet, she wanted to talk to Octavia. Maybe it would make more sense to call her at her hotel.

As she approached the front door of the house and stepped inside, Mia was coming down the stairs.

"Ciao," Mia said. "You are going to dinner tonight?"

"I've been invited," Dana said.

A quick smile flickered across the girl's face. "I'm going, too." Mia glanced back up the staircase. "I wish Grandmother would go, but she's not well." She turned to Dana, hesitating for a long moment before continuing in a low voice, "That was . . . fun last night." Her eyebrows rose and she looked a little like her father as she tilted her head. "With these terrible things happening—Paolo, Fabrizio—I shouldn't be having fun."

Dana was about to say she understood because she did, but before she could reply, Mia said, "I want to visit Fabrizio. But Father will not allow it."

"You and Fabrizio are *very* good friends?" she asked. The word *very* came out with an emphasis that Dana had not fully intended. But then, maybe she did. If the girl, who seemed to trust her, would confide in her, maybe she could offer some motherly advice.

"Yes, like you and Zio Giovanni are very good friends," Mia came back.

It took Dana a moment to gather her thoughts. "Yes, we do enjoy each other's company." How clever this little girl was, Dana thought.

"He's much too old for me," Mia said.

"Yes, and your uncle is too old for me." They exchanged glances, and then simultaneously, they both laughed.

"And, also a priest," Mia added.

"He's a good friend," Dana said, hoping Mia understood that's what it was, nothing more. While Dana and Borelli's friendship might seem odd to some, the notion of a romance? Mia and Fabrizio, on the other hand . . . someday he would not be too old for her.

"You saved him," Dana said, touching Mia's hand. "If you hadn't found him, he would have died."

"He'll be okay," Mia said, but both the conviction and levity had slipped from her voice.

"Yes, he will."

"I didn't tell the truth," Mia said quietly, gazing down, then back upstairs as if checking to make sure they were alone, "about going out for fresh air." Her eyes met Dana's. "I did go out to talk to Fabrizio. I trust him. I like him. But there is nothing going on between us that my father would not approve of. Fabrizio would never do anything—"

"It is nice to have a friend." Dana believed the girl was telling the truth.

"Yes." Mia smiled and bit her lip. "Zio Giovanni took you to Siena today?"

"Yes, then a tour of the vineyards with Marco Dardi. I was looking for your uncle to ask if I could borrow his truck, but it seems he has taken off."

"He's driving?" Mia threw her head back, hand on her forehead as if to say, oh dear, that's not good. "Where do you want to go?" she asked with a touch of excitement.

"I want to find something to wear this evening. But, I wonder if it is too late to shop. Your father said the van leaves at seven-thirty."

"Yes, and father is always punctual," she replied. "You spoke to him? My father?"

"I was walking back from the vineyards and saw him."

"He said he wanted you to come to dinner this evening?" Mia seemed pleased. "We have many cars. We will borrow one."

After a brief conversation in the garage between Mia and Claudio, who didn't even acknowledge Dana, he handed a set of keys to the girl. Dana got the impression that Mia generally got what she wanted. She could be quite charming, and this was evident as she spoke to Claudio, thanking him profusely as he handed her the keys. For a moment Dana thought Mia was going to drive, but then she passed the keys to Dana along with a big grin.

They pulled out of the garage and started down the road, Mia gazing out the window into the darkness, the headlights catching a vineyard, then another as they maneuvered the turns down toward the highway.

"I hope Fabrizio will return to work soon," Mia said, turning to Dana. "Both Father and Grandmother say he is reliable, very smart, and a fast learner. I think he could one day run the business."

Dana wasn't sure how to respond to this. "I've heard good things about him. How well he is doing, learning about the wine industry." Dana wondered if Mia had any interest in running the vineyards. Maybe she was too young to give this much thought. "What about you?" Dana said. "Would you eventually be interested in running the family business?"

"I wish to pursue other interests, as Zio Giovanni has."

"You wish to pursue a religious vocation?"

"No, no." Mia laughed. "But, I do not wish to spend my entire life here. I want to be like you and see the world."

Dana could hear the admiration in the girl's voice. It probably appeared that Dana led an exciting life—writing for a well-respected newspaper, traveling the world. Mia didn't see that Dana was a middle-aged, single woman, longing for her lost child.

"Do you think it could have been an accident?" Mia asked. "Fabrizio being shot? Hunters often come onto the land, and the owners are not unhappy because the deer destroy the vines and come into the family gardens. Poor Renata chased two away with her broom just days ago."

"Would they be hunting at night? With a bow?"

"It's possible. A bow is silent. The hunters would be protected by the darkness of night."

Dana could understand why Mia didn't want to believe someone had hurt Fabrizio on purpose. But, the vandalism in the cellar was certainly not an accident.

Dana considered asking Mia about Carlo Porcini, the man forced to give up the cottage for Fabrizio, but they had arrived in the village, and Mia was directing her down a street where she said they could park. Because it was late in the day, a Sunday at that, Dana thought they might have difficulty finding a place to shop, but Mia knew exactly where to go. They found a small shop on a side street just off the main town square. Mia pressed the button next to the door and a thin woman greeted them warmly and invited them inside.

Racks of colorful clothes, displays of shoes, shelves of accessories, jewelry and perfumes, filled the small space. Mia immediately went to work, pulling one item, then another from the rack, holding them up for Dana to express her approval or disapproval. The woman, about fiftyish with short, salt-and-pepper pixie hair and red-framed glasses, joined in, speaking rapidly to Mia in Italian as they selected several outfits for Dana to try.

Dana laughed and shook her head as Mia held up a low-cut, gold, sparkly, sequined blouse, a skirt with a slit up one side. Dana had always preferred pants to skirts, black and white, or khaki and tan. As a reporter, she dressed to disappear, not to stand out.

After trying on several outfits, they settled on a lovely violet colored blouse and a patterned skirt with splashes of a similar color, some gold and teal, along with a textured, form-fitting jacket in a color somewhere between golden and taupe, a color that Dana would never think to wear. She liked the way it set off the highlights in her hair. But, purple? She had never worn this color before, but she was pleased when she looked at herself in the mirror. Since she had brought only her walking shoes and a pair of black flats, Mia decided she also needed shoes in a neutral color. Mia tried to talk her into some very high heels, but Dana said she was more the slip-on-a-flat-and-run-with-it type, which made Mia laugh. They picked out a pair of flats and a necklace that set everything off. The girl had some sense of style. Then, before Dana could object, Mia grabbed a bottle of perfume and gave her a good spray.

"Oh, no," Dana protested, "I'm not a perfume kind of girl either."

"Oh, dear," Mia gasped. "You are allergic?"

"No, it's not that—"

"Today you wear perfume." Mia laughed and handed the bottle to the woman attendant who put it in a bag.

By the time they left the shop, Dana having loaded her credit card with what she generally spent in a year on her wardrobe, they were both laughing and checking the time. Mia had insisted on buying her the bottle of perfume, and it appeared the woman had charged it to an account, no card or money exchanged. Just as Dana thought, Mia could get just about anything she wanted around here.

Heading back to the car, which they'd parked in a secret place that Mia knew about behind a wine shop, Dana spotted a couple, intertwined, lips locked, leaning up against the side of a building, barely visible in the dim light of the single bulb near the back door.

The girl glanced over, not even embarrassed. She looked familiar to Dana. The girl nodded toward Mia.

"Do you know that couple?" Dana asked in a low voice.

"Of course," Mia replied. "Silvio Gallo and his girlfriend Elena Moretti. Everyone knows everyone in Montalcino. One of the reasons I'd like to leave." As they approached the car, Mia glanced back. "Silvio is . . . how to put this into American terms? Silvio is full of himself."

"How's that?" Dana asked, smiling at Mia's use of the American idiom.

"He is one of the archers who hopes to win the competition for the *Quartiere* Pianello during the *festa*."

"Is he good?"

Mia laughed. "He certainly thinks he is."

As they hopped in the car, Dana remembered why the girl looked familiar. It was the girl with the streaks of fake red in her hair whom she'd seen wrapped around Fabrizio Rossi the day before.

CHAPTER EIGHTEEN

Giovanni woke, confused and groggy, sitting in his truck on a hillside overlooking his favorite vineyard. The sun had slipped down over the horizon, and the sky was streaked with ribbons of gold. There was something peaceful and soothing about the scene, though he felt little inner peace.

After dropping Dana off at the vineyards, he'd driven around, thinking, stopping now and then to make a phone call, setting up his plan for the following day. He realized now, as he adjusted himself, ran his hand over his stiff neck, that he had fallen asleep. Concerned that he had slept through dinner, he glanced at his watch. Still plenty of time. He started the motor and returned to the villa.

When he stepped into the upstairs hall, he heard voices coming from Estella's room, though he could not make out the words. At first, he thought it was Leo but then realized the voices were both women's. He stopped outside her room, trying to determine to whom she was speaking. He knew it was not Renata. She had not been back to the estate since Paolo's death. The woman who came twice each week to clean was not scheduled for today. The voice sounded too stilted to be Lala's, Renata's sometimes-helper, who was filling in for her now, and too mature to be Mia's.

Giovanni knocked on the door.

"Sì?" Estella called out in a frail voice.

"It's Giovanni. May I come in?"

"Sì," Estella answered. "Please come in."

An older woman with meticulously styled short, wavy white hair sat in a chair next to Estella's bed. She wore a well-tailored grey suit. A black leather bag sat on the floor next to her chair. Estella introduced her as Fabrizio's grandmother, Flavia.

"Your grandson?" Giovanni asked with concern.

"Better," the woman answered. "The doctors still have some serious . . ." She rubbed a finger nervously over her lower lip. "Concerns about his recovery." The words caught in her throat. She reached down and took a tissue from her bag, wiping her mouth, then held it tightly in one hand.

"If there is anything we might do to help," Giovanni said.

"Estella has generously offered me a room here at the villa," Flavia replied, "but I have found accommodations at a hotel much closer to the hospital."

Giovanni wished they could offer her a meal, but they had scheduled dinner in town with the American buyers. How terrible this woman might feel if she knew they were entertaining in grand style as her grandson lay in the hospital nearby struggling for his life. Giovanni didn't even know what to say now.

"You remember Flavia?" Estella asked Giovanni. "We were in school together many years ago."

Giovanni studied the woman, but he had no recollection of her. Their father had sent Estella to a convent school when she was in her teens. On occasion she would bring a friend home or visit a classmate. So many years ago, and Flavia would look very different now. For a moment Giovanni wondered if his sister was lying to him. Yet, the two women were about the same age.

"That was some time ago," Flavia said with a gentle smile.

"Yes, many years ago," Giovanni agreed, still trying to determine, with a glance at Estella, if this was a fabricated story. If so, for what reason?

"I was about to leave." The woman reached for her purse, stood, tugged on her suit jacket, adjusting it. She was shorter than Giovanni would have imagined, but her posture was erect and dignified. She leaned over and kissed Estella on the cheek.

"We will pray for his continuing recovery," Estella said, her voice little more than a whisper. "Please call me if there is anything we can do." Giovanni wondered if Flavia was blaming the Borelli's for what had happened to her grandson. If he was indeed her grandson.

He offered to walk her downstairs. When they arrived in the foyer, she glanced outside. "My ride is here."

Giovanni opened the door for her and they stepped out. A late model Mercedes with driver had pulled into the driveway.

"I understand you are a priest," Flavia said as the driver got out and came around to open the door.

"Yes," Giovanni answered, "though I'm now retired."

"Will you say a Mass for my grandson?" She unlatched her purse as if to make an offering. Giovanni reached out and placed his hand over hers to stop her. The gesture seemed to startle the woman.

"He's a very good boy," Flavia said with an ache in her voice. There was something in her eyes, a sincerity and at the same time a pleading, as if she wished Giovanni to confirm this. As if he might have reason to believe this wasn't true.

"Yes," Giovanni said, "he is a very good boy."

Dana rushed into the shower, hopped out quickly, catching a glimpse of herself in the full-length mirror. She had little time to get ready for dinner after her shopping spree in town with Mia, but something made her stop and examine herself. She was still thin, had not put on the after-forty weight like many of her friends. Yet, there was clear evidence of the life she had lived. Stretch marks from giving birth to a child she had lost. This was especially painful. And then . . . the scar from Prague.

She turned away, pushing these thoughts from her mind, wrapping herself in a towel.

Quickly, she dried and fluffed her hair, reapplied her makeup before dressing in her new outfit. Again, she stood before the full-length mirror, assessing herself, pleased now with what she saw. Though she seldom wore skirts, she had nice legs. Before she left the room, she spritzed a dab of perfume on her wrists and behind her ears. How thoughtful of Mia to buy her the perfume. She liked the scent. She liked Mia. They had had fun shopping that afternoon.

When she went down, she found Borelli and Leo waiting in the entryway. Borelli looked very much the priest in his clerical collar and pressed suit. Leo wore a well-tailored dark suit with a silk tie and perfectly polished dress shoes.

"You look very nice this evening," Leo said with a nod of approval. Dana was glad she had gone shopping.

Borelli studied her with a quizzical look. *Oh, dear,* Dana thought, *is he thinking I don't look much like myself this evening?*

"Yes, you look lovely," he agreed with an awkward twitch of his nose as he stepped closer to kiss her quickly on each cheek. She got the impression he did not approve of Mia's selection of perfume.

Leo glanced at his watch, then at Borelli. "Did you speak with Mia? She is coming this evening?" His troubled tone broke the mood—if this strained sense of festivity could be described as a mood. The frightening events over the past few days provided more than sufficient reason to stir up concern over a Borelli or Antonelli being late. "Did you see her this afternoon?" Leo asked, biting down on his lip, glancing from his uncle to Dana.

But before anyone could answer, Mia glided down the stairs, her normally straight hair in a more formal style, curls falling to her shoulders. She wore a short dress, with a fitted bodice and full skirt, with sparkly flats. The cuts on her legs were barely noticeable. She had on just a hint of makeup, some mascara, a touch of blush, appropriate for a modern thirteen-year-old girl, if not perhaps for her father. Dana thought she looked darling.

"Bella. Bellisima," Leo said. *"Andiamo."*

When they arrived at the restaurant, they were shown into a private room, tables set with crisp white linens. Richard, David, and Octavia stood conversing, drinks in hand. A waiter glided by with a tray of antipasti.

Leo and Borelli greeted their guests, and Leo introduced them to Mia. Dana said hello. Octavia, as always, looked beautiful in a peach colored dress with a royal blue jacket, an odd duo of colors that Dana would never have thought of combining. Dana wondered if she'd brought the adaptor for Winkie, but just as she was about to ask, Marco Dardi arrived.

Like Leo, he wore a nicely tailored dark suit with a silk tie, and if Dana had not met him earlier during the vineyard tour, she would have thought this was his everyday attire. The man had a natural ease and confidence about him, no matter how he was dressed. Marco greeted the men, then the women, quickly kissing each with the expected Italian graciousness and attentiveness. He smelled musky and warm, his cheeks smooth and freshly shaved. Was it just Dana's imagination that he took a little sniff of her, too? Stepping back, he shot her a puzzled look that she couldn't read at all, and then he smiled. Was he, too, comparing her more formal look this evening with her casual attire that afternoon? His smile indicated he was pleased with what he saw.

Marco offered Dana a glass of sparkling wine, then picked up one for himself.

"Lovely," he told her, "You look lovely this evening."

"Thank you." She took a drink, swallowed, feeling a flutter in her stomach that she knew she couldn't attribute to hunger or even the bubbly quality of the pre-dinner wine. *"Grazie."*

Leo was soon directing guests to their seats, Marco between Dana and Octavia, Mia between Richard and David, perhaps the place that might have been reserved for Estella had she been up to attending. Leo, as host, took the head of the table, and Borelli sat at the other end.

As Mia conversed with the two American men, she seemed completely comfortable. She smiled across the table at Dana, who wondered if the girl had often been placed in situations where she was in the company of grownups. This might have been one of the reasons she liked to go out to the cottage to talk to Fabrizio—to get away from the old people. Dana was sure that Mia had friends her own age, but this evening she seemed more mature and aware than most thirteen-year-olds. After what the girl had gone through, Dana was amazed that she was doing so well. She thought of what Marco had said earlier in the vineyards about the Sangiovese grapes being thick-skinned, and she wondered, as she gazed around the table, if this might be an accurate description of the Borelli-Antonelli family, too.

Wine flowed freely, Mia slowly sipping a single glass. A Rosso del Montalcino was served with the pasta in a rich, spicy tomato sauce, a Brunello Riserva with the main course, each accompanied by sniffing, twirling, sipping, and much discussion. Borelli, whose position at the end opposite Leo, placed him next to Dana at the oval-shaped table, explained that the Riserva had come from the Borellis' private cellar, implying that this particular vintage was no longer available.

As the conversation flowed, Dana sensed that Leo was pleased with what they had accomplished during the visit, though no one spoke of the specifics of a business deal. Or the prized Brunello that had literally gone down the drain.

Marco skillfully included both Dana and Octavia in conversation with a mixture of flirtatiousness and business-like courtesy.

"You must return next year," he told Octavia, "during the late summer or early fall before the harvest. You will find it much different than coming this time of year when the grapes have been harvested. Tasting grapes on the vine . . ." His raised his fingertips to his lips, kissed them, then released them like a flower. "It is a wonderful experience to taste the grapes and anticipate the wine itself."

Octavia smiled. "Yes, I'd love to visit again."

"Yes," Leo, said. "You must all come again. Richard and David are invited, too." He grinned and David, then Richard, lifted a glass in a toast.

The small group, the intimacy of the setting encouraged all to join in the conversation.

"It will take little to convince me to visit again, Leo," Octavia said with a laugh that verged on a giggle.

"I enjoyed our walk this afternoon," Marco said turning to Dana, Octavia now engaged in conversation with their host.

"So did I," Dana replied.

"How long are you staying here in Montalcino?"

"The original plan was until Sunday, a week from today, but with all that has happened, I feel as if I'm more in the way than anything. Father Borelli is making every attempt to entertain me. We spent this morning in Siena."

"It is a shame that your holiday has been ruined. Perhaps if you have some free time," he said, touching her hand. "I know many interesting places to visit that the Borellis might not be aware of."

Before Dana could reply—and she wasn't sure how to reply because she would like to spend more time with Marco, but did not wish to offend Borelli—Leo called out to Marco in Italian, and then again shifted back to English and the group was talking about an award-winning vintage and the rating it had been given, and the opportunity to continue her conversation with Marco had been interrupted.

The guests marveled over the delicious *Brasato di Cinghiale,* braised wild boar, and Leo called the restaurant owner to come out to meet his guests and accept their praise. The grand finale was a *Limoncello Tiramisu,* and after several hours of enjoying one course, then another, each paired with a Borelli wine, finishing with a

Moscadello di Montalcino, plates were being carried away. Octavia looked directly at Dana. "Need to use the girls' room?"

After the copious amounts of wine that had been poured throughout the evening, Dana didn't need an invitation to visit the restroom. She glanced over at Mia, attempting to catch her eye, but unable to do so, Dana rose, realizing it would probably be best to talk to Octavia alone. Feeling a tiny bit tipsy even in her flats, Dana noticed that Octavia didn't seem to teeter at all on her four-inch heels.

After they had used the facilities, washed their hands, and Octavia had freshened her lipstick, she reached into her mini bag and pulled out an adaptor. She handed it to Dana. "We are leaving early in the morning, so please if you could take it to Winkie? You know where he's staying?"

"Yes." Dana stuck it in her purse, curious. "Tell me again why Winkie wants to speak with me."

Octavia repeated her story about running into Winkie in town, how he'd left his adaptor at home. "So then, I guess I was telling him about what had happened in the cellar, with the wine being released, the old man being killed, and I was surprised that he didn't know, but he said with his phone dead, no TV, or internet access, and we were talking about how we've all come to rely on our electronic devices, and—"

"Then he asked about the protesters we'd seen along the highway?" Dana asked.

"I told him I hadn't seen them, and he realized everyone, other than you and Winkie, was asleep."

"But, he didn't say exactly why he wants to speak with me?"

"No, but he did ask that I tell no one about this request."

"What do you make of that?"

Octavia shrugged, rolled her eyes. "Celebrities, always concerned about their privacy. Well, guess we'd better get back or they will wonder what happened to us." She took one last look in the mirror, rubbing a lipstick mark off her teeth.

Coffee was being served when they returned to the dining room. Marco Dardi had already left, and Dana's earlier expectations drifted toward disappointment with an equal portion of embarrassment. Was it merely light dinner chatter, his talking about showing her around? Was he simply being polite? Marco would have stayed to talk with her if he'd really meant it.

Plans were being made for the guests to be picked up the following morning. It would require an early pickup, about 5:00 a.m. and since it was now nearing midnight, the Simonelli guests were ready to return to their hotel. It was a short distance and they could walk.

On the ride back to the villa, Leo seemed surprisingly at ease as he sat next to Dana. Mia had crawled into the back seat, insisting her dad and Dana take the middle two passenger seats. Borelli sat in the front seat next to Claudio.

"You enjoyed the evening?" Leo asked Dana, touching her on the arm.

"Yes, very much," she said. "Thank you for including me."

"Our pleasure," he replied with a smile, slowly drawing his hand away.

Dana had had more to drink than usual. She sensed Leo had too. He seemed relaxed, and the mood of the evening had verged on celebratory, perhaps an attempt to forget for a short time the terrible events of the past days.

There was little chatter as they turned off the main highway to the Borelli estate. As they passed the cluster of vehicles that had been swelling near the property over the past twenty-four hours, then the sign announcing the vineyards, Leo's phone rang. He pulled it out of his pocket. *"Pronto."* He listened, speaking but a few words.

Slipping it back into his pocket, he said, "That was Alberto, Inspector DeLuca. They have made an arrest in the attempted murder of Fabrizio Rossi. Silvio Gallo was taken into custody this evening."

"Silvio Gallo?" Mia shrieked, grabbing the back of Dana's seat, pulling herself forward. "We saw him today."

"Gallo?" Borelli asked, his voice troubled, but much calmer than Mia's.

"The archer for the Pianello Quarter," Mia offered, her voice pitched with excitement and disbelief.

Dana pictured the couple she and Mia had seen as they left the dress shop, the archer who hoped to win the *Sagra del Tordo* competition and claim the trophy for the Pianello quarter, and the same young women she and Borelli had seen with Fabrizio.

CHAPTER NINETEEN

After the initial excitement of learning about Silvio Gallo's arrest, they had continued on to the Borelli villa in a subdued state of shock. One of their own, a young man from the village, had shot Fabrizio. Attempting to carry on as usual was a true farce at this point.

Leo accompanied Mia upstairs, his arm wrapped around her protectively. Borelli shot Dana a look as he lingered at the base of the stairs. She sensed he had something he wanted to tell her in private. She wondered if he was about to suggest a midnight raid on the kitchen. Over the past few days his intentions of a healthy diet had vanished, though she wondered if he could possibly be hungry after their large meal.

"Meet me at the garage tomorrow morning at five-thirty," he whispered to her when Mia and Leo had reached the top of the staircase and were out of sight.

The following morning, Dana rose early, dressed, grabbed her handbag, and tiptoed down the stairs, and out toward the garage, making her way easily in the dark on the now familiar path. Two of the unmarked police vehicles that had been parked around the estate for the past few days remained outside the villa. No drivers in sight.

As she approached the garage, Dana realized that Claudio would have left by now to pick up the Simonelli buyers and drive them to the airport. The garage door was locked and there was no sign of anyone nearby. Within minutes, Borelli arrived, wearing a dark suit and his clerical collar. He was going on this mission in the role of a priest. A bag and a thermos were tucked under his arm. He unlocked the garage, asked her to pull the truck out, and told her he'd lock the garage behind her.

Tasks completed, he lumbered over to the truck, opened the passenger side and placed the bag and thermos on the floor. Curious, Dana leaned over and glanced in the bag. It contained several small bread rolls and a couple of pears. "Is this breakfast or lunch?" she asked.

"Breakfast," he said, pocketing the garage keys, and then settling in with a grunt as he yanked out the worn seatbelt. "This is breakfast." He snapped the belt. "We should be in Locri in plenty of time for lunch." He unscrewed the top from the thermos. "Coffee?" Then, like a magician creating something from nothing, he extracted a small bundle from his pocket, an item wrapped in a cloth napkin. A careful unwrapping revealed a delicate espresso cup.

"Not sure I can drink and drive at the same time." She shifted the gears. "Ah, we're going to Locri?"

"Something to eat," he said reaching in the bag.

"A pear would be nice."

He handed her one, which she set on the seat beside her. Borelli pulled out one for himself along with a roll. In a gesture worthy of his dramatic showmanship, he spread the cloth napkin out on his wide lap.

"Locri," she said again. "Home of Fabrizio Rossi and his

grandmother."

Borelli nodded, poured steaming coffee for himself and took a cautious sip. He bit into the hard roll with a crunch, sending crumbs cascading down onto the napkin.

"I met Fabrizio's grandmother last evening," he said. "Estella told me they were in school together."

"I didn't think the family was from this area," Dana said.

"No, no, they are not. Father sent Estella away to a convent school. It was a normal way of educating a girl back then. Estella asked if I remembered Flavia, as if we had met before. My sister brought friends to visit at times. I tried desperately to bring up a memory of the woman."

"And did you?" Dana asked.

"No," he said. "But that was many years ago."

"You're still intent on learning more about Fabrizio?" she asked. "Even though a man has been arrested?" She guessed that the news of the attempt on Fabrizio's life would hit the local media, if not the national, and international too. "Even though his grandmother is here?"

"I still believe there is something strange about the situation. With this latest development, Silvio being arrested, I believe Fabrizio's identity has become even more relevant." He motioned for Dana to turn onto the road that wound down toward the highway. Still dark, she didn't see the police vehicle parked along the road until they were passing. An officer waved from inside. They continued on toward the highway.

"I'm not convinced that it was Silvio who shot Fabrizio," Borelli said. "Do you think the boy would use an arrow that might easily be traced back to him, then pick up where he left off with the girl after he shot Fabrizio? Right there for anyone to see."

It wasn't exactly right there for anyone to see. There hadn't been anyone else on that particular street by the dress shop when Mia and Dana stepped out and saw the young couple.

"Easily traced?" she asked.

"The blue and white fletchings and stripes, the colors of the Pianello quarter," Borelli explained.

"It doesn't seem that the blue and white would necessarily point to Silvio," Dana said skeptically.

"When I reexamined the photo, I believe I detected what appeared to be a portion of a Pianello marking—a horizontal bar, with two blue bars above, and two below—mostly scratched off to make it appear he was attempting to hide the identity. Ridiculous," he snorted. "A custom-made arrow, most likely with Silvio's fingerprints all over it."

"Maybe in the heat of passion," she suggested. "Something not planned. Catching his lover in the arms of the handsome young Fabrizio."

"A viable theory, perhaps," Borelli replied thoughtfully. "One often does irrevocable deeds in the heat of passion." He took a large bite of the pear, then wiped the juice from his chin with the back of his hand. "But, who would be walking around in the dark, bow slung over his shoulder?"

Dana visualized what she had seen when Fabrizio and Mia stumbled into the kitchen. So much blood. The sharp rip through his clothing, the broken arrow still protruding from his abdomen. Then she thought of the conversation she'd had with Mia who wondered if Fabrizio had been shot accidentally by an archery hunter out in the night. Then a thought came to her—something she should have been aware of much earlier.

When she was in her teens, she used to go to an indoor archery range with her dad and brothers. She was a good shot, better than her brothers. The guys went deer hunting in the fall and never invited her to go along. She hadn't objected as she often did when the "men" excluded her. Because she knew she couldn't kill a helpless animal. The thought of one of the hunting arrows with its razor-like blade made her shiver, even now.

"Silvio is a target shooter?" she asked Borelli.

"Yes. A skilled shooter."

"From what we observed, this might invalidate the heat of passion theory."

"Continue." Borelli blinked, and a twitch of his mouth indicated he was aware she was about to offer a new possibility.

"This could not have been done in the heat of passion. It was planned."

"Because?" he asked.

"You saw the wound," Dana prompted.

A spark of understanding flashed in Borelli's eyes. "A target point would not have created such a wound. The wound was likely inflicted by a hunting point."

"Yes, the point," Dana said. "Which is exactly the point."

Borelli smiled, perhaps at her play on words, or in appreciation for her observation.

"This means that even though the shaft might have been one used in the archery competition," Dana said, "the blade was meant to kill. This was no act of passion. It was planned. The blade had been changed to make sure it would kill."

"It's unlikely that Silvio would change out a point and use his personally marked arrow shaft. The police, after examining the point removed from Fabrizio's body, would realize this too."

"One would certainly hope so," Dana said. "Whoever shot Fabrizio left enough evidence to point to Silvio, but at the same time made it appear that he'd attempted to remove the evidence. He's definitely being framed." Dana didn't need to add more. It was evident to both of them that someone had wanted to make it appear it had been Silvio who shot Fabrizio.

Abruptly, Borelli motioned with his arm, directing Dana to take a turn. Reluctantly, she steered onto what looked more like a footpath than one intended for a vehicle. They bumped along.

"I don't involve myself directly in the business anymore," Borelli went on as if this was related to the conversation about Fabrizio's being shot. "Out of respect for Leo. But, Estella said the boy has become a great asset, involving himself in many aspects of the winery, the production. He's terribly young, but evidently doing well. He seems at times reckless." They hit a rut, then the road steepened. Dana shifted gears with a grind.

Dana thought of the condition of his cottage, which certainly looked like a boy's room. "Young men are often reckless."

Borelli smiled in agreement. "Yet, I hear he has a talent for discerning a good wine, for detecting the bouquet. Very well developed for one so young. But, perhaps that is something one is born with, a natural talent. Such skill can certainly be enhanced by proper training, but some are naturally blessed."

Passed on from father to son? Dana wondered. "The bouquet," she said, "referring to the smell." She'd heard numerous wine terms over the past few days, some obvious even to her. Aroma, nose, floral, oaky, smoky. Many of them referred to the smell as well as the taste.

"Do you know that taste is ninety percent smell?" Borelli took a whiff of his half-eaten pear as if to demonstrate, and then bit into it. "What we perceive as taste is often smell." He reached over and held the pear up to her nose. It had a pleasant, fresh aroma and he was making his point. "Take away smell," he went on, "and little is left of taste." He finished off the pear and set the core on his lap in the napkin. "Without the proper mix of sensory perceptions—smell, texture, temperature—one would be unable to enjoy the taste of a good wine, good food."

Dana got the impression he was starting in on one of his lengthy explanations to what might be a very simple observation, and she was correct as Borelli went on to describe, in an almost scientific way, how smell resulted from the volatile molecules released into the air. He explained how the cilia, which acted as chemoreceptors of these molecules, would send a message to the brain. "There are as many as ten thousand within the human nose."

"And some people have more developed receptors."

"Precisely."

"This information," Dana said, trying to steer the conversation back to Fabrizio, away from a scientific analysis of smell and taste. "About how well Fabrizio is doing as an apprentice at the vineyards, how gifted he is, this came from Leo?"

"From Estella, who does on occasion share information about what is going on in the business. Though I certainly don't intentionally go looking for specifics." He waved again, toward another turn onto another path that looked even less manageable than the one they were on.

The road had leveled off a bit, though the condition had not improved. As they bounced along, Dana thought about her conversation with Octavia, a thought that had become lost in the announcement of Silvio's arrest for the attempted murder of Fabrizio. She told Borelli about the adaptor, about Winkie wanting to speak to her, possibly about the environmental protesters they had seen.

"Is that an odd request? Why would he want to speak with you about the protesters?" Borelli scoffed. "Couldn't he purchase an adaptor?"

"I don't know, but I think he expects me to drop by today. We're driving all the way to Locri?" Dana glanced out the window. Still dark, not even a hint of daylight on the horizon as she scanned the hills to the east. "It seems we are headed in the wrong direction, and on this road, if that's what you call it, it might take much longer than a day." She laughed. "I hope Winkie isn't sitting around waiting for me. But, then, maybe he can get some writing done," she added flippantly.

"Of course we are not driving. Here, let's stop." They had arrived at a much flatter area than the hills on which the vineyards were laid out. Dana guessed they were no longer on Borelli land.

Borelli squinted at his watch. "We are early. Pull over here," he instructed her with a wave of his hand. She did and he asked, "Perhaps you'd like coffee now?" He extracted another tiny espresso cup from his pocket, removed it from the napkin and poured her a cup.

"I love a man who travels with his own coffee shop," Dana said with a grin, taking the coffee. She held it to her lips and sipped slowly. Still steaming hot and very dark, good reason for the small cups. She took a large bite of her pear, then another. "So, are you going to tell me what's up?"

But before he could answer, she heard a sound coming from a distance and then realized it was above them. She gazed up at the rotating blade of a helicopter hovering above them. Borelli opened his door, shook the bread crumbs off the napkin from his lap, wiped his lips, then wrapped the pear core in the napkin and stuffed it in the bag. When he got out and stood waving, Dana realized this was their ride. The aircraft landed with a strong whirl of wind.

Borelli introduced her to the pilot, though the roar of the blade made it difficult to hear or understand the words. They got in and fastened their seatbelts.

As they rose, Borelli explained in a loud voice that the pilot, whom he called Luigi, was retired and had once been the pope's official helicopter pilot. Then, he said they were being transported to a small private airport where they would board a private jet and go on to Locri.

If Dana was supposed to be impressed, she was.

After a short flight, they landed on a narrow landing strip and boarded a small jet, piloted by another retired Vatican employee. Borelli had evidently made friends and some valuable connections during his Vatican days.

They continued on for a couple of hours, Borelli taking a nap, Dana staring out the window of the plane, gazing down at the flickering lights of Italian villages, then daylight and billows of cottony clouds.

She thought of the first time she and Father Giovanni Borelli had spoken to one another, sitting side by side on a flight from Rome to Prague, one of life's serendipitous meetings. Though their paths had crossed previously once before when he was sent from the Vatican to Boston to take part in an investigation, that flight had been their first face-to-face encounter. He had not introduced himself at the time; in fact, he had played a little mind game with her, which she'd found rather irritating. Now, four years later it was difficult to believe they had become good friends.

Dana's stomach lurched as she felt the abrupt dip of the small plane, the sea of clouds giving way to a large expanse of water. As they descended, she was aware that they were over the Tyrrhenian Sea and the boot kicking the island of Sicily.

A car, without driver, waited for them.

"The Vatican?" Dana asked.

"No, Rent-A-Car," Borelli replied with a sly grin, obviously proud of a plan that, so far, had come together beautifully. He opened the car door and found the key hidden in a compartment above the visor.

Dana took it she was driving again as Borelli handed her the key and then went around to the passenger side.

"Very well executed," she said. "Now what? We're going to traipse around town asking everyone on the street if they know a young man named Fabrizio Rossi?"

"I'm not sure that's his real name."

Dana wondered how Borelli intended to discover anything about the young man if he wasn't using his real name.

Borelli fussed a bit with his clerical collar. Obviously, she was correct—he was going on this mission as a priest, though she doubted there was anything spiritual involved.

"You've certainly put a plan together," Dana said. "But I'm confused how this part will work."

"We will find out where Fabrizio came from and why he is working for Leo."

For a brief moment, Dana questioned what they were doing, this independent snooping without consulting or sharing with local law enforcement. Or confronting either Leo or Estella. But, if they could discover something that might explain what had happened at the Borelli Vineyards . . . Dana's reporter tendencies were taking over—her desire to be one step ahead of the others. To get the scoop.

Borelli pulled his phone out of his inner jacket pocket. As Dana kept one steady eye on the road, she glanced over. He was flipping through photographs.

"Here," he said. "I took this of Mia and Fabrizio a week ago before all of this unpleasantness took place."

He showed Dana a picture of Fabrizio, grinning into the cellphone camera, Mia next to him smiling. Two friends? Or brother and sister?

"Always start at the local church," Borelli said, matter-of-factly. And then he added, in a more serious tone, "From baptism to burial, everything starts and ends at the church."

They parked near the central piazza, then walked a short distance to the church, asked a man strolling by where the local priest lived. He pointed down the street, and they continued from there.

"Father Giovanni Borelli," he introduced himself to the woman who answered the door. He spoke rapidly and Dana could only make out a few of the Italian words, but she could get enough feel for the conversation that she knew Borelli had made an impression on the woman, and with his clerical collar they were welcomed in and shown into a reception room.

Shortly, a man entered. Borelli stood to greet him. The man was dressed casually, not like a priest. He wore a button-down, collared shirt and tan slacks. He was several years younger than Borelli, perhaps in his mid-fifties. Borelli introduced Dana, though she wasn't sure what he said about her, or if he explained why she was accompanying him. The two men carried on a brief, apparently friendly, conversation in which Dana picked up the name *Fabrizio Rossi* and the word *nonna*—grandmother—along with the name Flavia Rossi.

The younger priest shook his head several times, which Dana could see was a denial that he knew who they were or recognized the name. But when Borelli pulled out the phone and showed him the photo, even though the priest said, "No," Dana could tell by his nervous blinking that he knew the boy.

Borelli thanked the priest, and they left.

"He knew him," Dana said.

"Yes, of course he did. In a small town like this, the priest knows everyone, even though the men seldom attend Mass on Sunday. The grandmother, I'm sure, is a member of the parish. I can see her now, sitting in the front pew, rosary beads slipping through her fingers. And so could Father Antonio Tortorella."

"Where now?" Dana asked.

"Lunch," Borelli answered without hesitation.

They returned to where they had parked near the piazza. There were a number of coffee bars, restaurants, and small shops in the area. They stopped in front of several, Borelli carefully reading the menus posted outside, then glancing inside as if looking for someone he knew. Dana understood a good meal was extremely important to Borelli, but she could also see whoever was inside was just as important.

Finally, they stopped at a place that certainly wasn't as nice as several others they had seen. Though the afternoon carried a bit of a chill, several brave young people sat outside. Inside, the restaurant was crowded. An older man slid a pizza on a wooden paddle into a large open oven. The dense air smelled of garlicky sauce, sausage, and yeasty pizza. The wait staff was young, two boys about seventeen and eighteen moving quickly about, attending to the customers. Dana realized that this was exactly what Borelli was looking for. If anyone here would recognize Fabrizio, it would be his contemporaries.

They ordered a large pizza margherita to share, each an *insalata verde*, two glasses of a local wine. From the interaction between their server and the young girl bussing the tables, who could have been a little sister, Dana guessed that this was a family-owned business as were many in these small Italian towns.

Their meal was eaten leisurely, with some lively chatter between

Borelli and the server. The owner, who Dana guessed to be the father, came out to chat, and receive Borelli's compliments. It wasn't until they had finished eating their meal, then a dessert of chestnut ice cream laced with Marsala, and were sitting with coffee, did Borelli pull out his phone and show the server the photo.

"*Si, si,* Fabrizio Calaberoni," the boy offered without hesitation.

A lively, friendly conversation took place between the boy and the priest before Borelli asked for the bill. Dana knew he was a generous tipper, and this was confirmed when the boy smiled widely as they got up. *"Grazie, grazie,"* he said, waving with an appreciative bow.

As they left the restaurant, heading toward the car, Dana said, "He knows him, and his name is Fabrizio Calaberoni, not Rossi."

"Yes, raised by his grandmother, Flavia Calaberoni. The boy said he went to school with him when they were young. Then the grandmother sent him away. He was a clever boy and she felt he needed a better education than what was offered in a small community in Southern Italy. The boy said he saw him early this summer, then he left again. He wasn't sure where he'd gone."

"Does the name Calaberoni mean anything to you?"

"Yes." Borelli paused. "It does. Calaberoni is the name of a wealthy and powerful family in the area."

Just the way Borelli said *family*, the tone of his voice, emphasizing the word, along with the words *wealthy* and *powerful*, Dana thought she understood. Yet, she had to ask to be sure.

"Mafia?" she asked and Borelli nodded.

CHAPTER TWENTY

After a long morning of frustration, waiting for a visit from Dana Pierson, waiting for Giovanna, absent without explanation, Winkie Dalton refilled his coffee cup for the umpteenth time and went out for a stroll, sipping as he climbed one hill, then another. He enjoyed walking about the estate and was getting a real feel for the land, particularly after Giovanna had taken him out for several hours Sunday afternoon. Yet, he regretted not having rented a car in Rome, accepting the offer of transportation from Octavia Fleenor and the Borelli Vineyards.

Before he left America, Giovanna had offered to provide transportation from Rome. He had declined, thinking he would rent a car. But when he arrived, he was too tired to drive, and when Octavia offered the ride he'd said yes. It had been his intention to spend his time getting acquainted with the land as well as the landowner, Giovanna Veronesi, and he'd thought, in his groggy, mind-altered state upon his arrival, that he didn't need his own vehicle. But now he felt stuck without a car, inadvertently also without a phone. It seemed as if he had been sucked back in time.

Other than the woman who had prepared his coffee and meager breakfast that morning, it seemed he was the only one in the villa. Andrea had the day off and Giovanna had gone into town. This information had come from a conversation with the kitchen helper. Winkie wondered if Giovanna was meeting with her lawyer, away from the estate, to clear up any issues before the three of them met at 4:00 that afternoon.

He returned to the house and found the woman in the kitchen, preparing what appeared to be his lunch, a sandwich of thick bread, tomatoes, mozzarella and salami. She ushered him into the dining room and he sat alone at the large table to eat in silence. He carried his own dishes back to the kitchen and thanked the woman, then headed upstairs to his room where he pulled out his file to go over the notes he'd made, highlighting the points to bring up with the lawyer later that afternoon. He'd had the advice of his attorney back home, and she'd offered to accompany him to Italy. But, Winkie knew this was one journey he must make alone.

After about fifteen minutes, thirsty, he went down to the kitchen for a bottle of water.

The young woman, carrying a tray, was stepping into what Winkie had assumed was a pantry because of its proximity to the kitchen. He could see now it was an elevator. She wasn't aware of him, and even as she struggled with the tray he did not offer to help. The tray contained a covered plate, and what appeared to be a pot of coffee, as well as a coffee cup. The door slid closed.

From his observations over the past several days, Winkie had surmised that the servants left at night, that they did not live on the estate, that he was the only occupant on the second floor, that Giovanna's room was on the main level. Sunday, after they came back from a stroll on the property, Winkie had asked for a tour of the house, but Giovanna had hesitated, saying she was very tired, perhaps they could do it later, reminding him that the third level was no longer being used. He had noticed that the main staircase led no farther than the second floor.

Yet, this woman seemed to be taking something to one of the upper levels.

He lingered a moment, and then he stepped outside to see if Giovanna had returned. She hadn't. Curious he went back into the house. In the kitchen he found the girl, cleaning up.

"I go now," she said. "Signora come soon. *Si?* Signora say okay I go." Though it should have been obvious now that Winkie spoke Italian, the help seemed to insist they struggle along in English.

"Water? *Acqua?*" Winkie asked.

"Si, si." She got him a bottle.

He returned to his room. He looked out the window and saw a car stop in front of the house and pick up the girl. As soon as they were out of sight, he returned to the kitchen. He stepped over to the elevator door and attempted to open it, realizing right away that it was locked. A key was needed to enter. After searching through a number of drawers and cupboards in the kitchen, keeping an ear and eye alert, he found a box that contained several sets of keys, some loose, some clipped onto a number of key chains as if a key had not been discarded since the sixteenth century. He took out the keychain that appeared to contain a nice selection of various keys, both old and new, guessing it might be his best bet. The elevator had to be a more recent addition, at least within the past century. None of the keys were marked or labeled.

After trying a handful of the most likely looking keys, he was able to unlock the elevator door. The panel in the elevator also required a key. He searched through the collection in his hand and found the one he was looking for easily as it was much smaller than a door key. The elevator ascended slowly and laboriously with a groan that gave Winkie pause, but he was determined to go up to the third level.

The door slid open and Winkie stepped out. Quietly, he walked down the hall, peering into the first room which was empty and dark, windows shuttered and boarded. He stepped back into the hall and entered a second room and found the same—empty, not a trace of life or even furnishings. Obviously, the upper level had been out of use for some time. It was fairly cold in the hallways and Winkie guessed during the winter months it would be prohibitive to heat, good reason for keeping it closed up. But, the kitchen girl had definitely brought something up and he was positive that there was no one else on the floor where he was staying.

The corner room just above Winkie's was also empty. He walked across the hall, knowing the bathroom would be here if the floor plan was identical to the one below. When he tried the door, he found it locked. He sorted through the keys and after several attempts, he found one that fit. Slowly, he unlocked and opened the door. The room was dark, but a familiar smell permeated the air. It was a smell he remembered from his father's last days. He flicked on a light. Medicines lined the vanity. Then he noticed a door leading into another room. This was not identical to the floor plan on his level. The bathroom on his level was a separate room with entry from the hallway only, constructed for shared use of those occupying the bedrooms on that level.

Winkie stepped to the partially opened door leading from the bathroom, pushed it open and gazed inside.

A very old man, extremely thin, back to Winkie, stood over a long table, hunched, hip bones protruding. Winkie remained still, observing. He could see the tray the girl had brought up, on a table next to the bed. She had removed the silver dome over the plate, but the food remained untouched. A small bed was pressed against the wall in one corner of the room. A beam of light from the unboarded window threw a shaft across the neatly tucked covers.

The old man scratched his head, a disheveled mass of thinning gray curls. After some moments, he turned slowly. He looked at Winkie, not startled at all to see him. The man was neither surprised nor embarrassed, though he wore not a stitch of clothing. His stomach bulged like the swollen belly of a starving refugee, and his arms were thin, any muscles he might have possessed long turned into sinewy threads. He started toward Winkie, his gait unsteady, his penis swinging, without any hint of modesty, without any effort to cover himself. He approached Winkie as if he were greeting a friend.

"Vieni, vieni," he said, motioning. "Come, Vincenzo. I have a plan. Come look at the map. I have a brilliant idea for a new planting. It will make better use of the south exposure. We must expand if we are to continue to be the most profitable producer in *Provincia di Siena*." He smiled and reached for Winkie's arm, like a small child coaxing a playmate to come along.

Winkie returned a cautious smile but said nothing.

"Come, come," the man repeated. "Come, Vincenzo."

Arm in arm they crossed the room, then both gazed down at the map spread out over the table, as Lorenzo Veronesi explained his plan to his older brother, Vincenzo Veronesi.

CHAPTER TWENTY-ONE

As they drove from Locri to the private airport where they had picked up the rental car, Borelli and Dana tossed about a number of thoughts and concerns regarding the fact that a son of one of the most powerful families in Italy was now making his home on the Borelli estate, living in a modest cottage.

"Do you think Estella knows about Fabrizio's family?" Dana asked.

"Wouldn't she have to?" Borelli said, not answering Dana's question, but throwing out one of his own. She could see he was confused and uncomfortable with the possibility that the mob had infiltrated the family business, or perhaps been invited to become part of the Borelli Vineyards. Dana recalled Borelli's earlier comments about the recent large capital investments and wondered if the business had come to a point where it would accept mob money to keep operating. But, would they send an eighteen-year-old boy, a not-quite-yet man, to look after things? Another thought, which Dana was hesitant to suggest—the possibility of using a legitimate business for money laundering.

Nervously, Borelli ran his fingers over his bald head, then clasped and unclasped his large hands. Pressing against his left temple as if suppressing a headache, he said, "We've heard rumors, often when a winery changes hands. But nothing substantiated."

"You're talking about the Mafia's attempts, through legitimate purchase, to become involved in the Italian wine business?"

"The Mafia has been known to sell bogus vintages," Borelli said, veering off in another direction. "In recent years some producers have gone to digital, encoded labeling for the finer vintages, which makes this more difficult."

Dana could understand how Borelli's thoughts were circling round and round with confusion, illusion, and disbelief. But how did this relate to Fabrizio's being shot, if it did, and how did it relate to the wine destruction and Paolo's death in the Borelli cellar? And what about Borelli's suspicion that Fabrizio was Leo's son? To Dana, this seemed now to be highly unlikely.

"Possibly an extortion plot." Borelli's mouth twitched as he spoke. "Which would mean others might have been threatened? Might have paid a fee to protect their wine?"

Borelli, too, seemed to be attempting to tie what had happened in the cellar to the mob, but Dana wasn't sure that it did. If others had been threatened, wouldn't Fabrizio be the enforcer, rather than the victim? Maybe, like Paolo, Fabrizio was just in the wrong place at the wrong time. But that still left a large question as to why he had come to Montalcino.

"We're a close community," Borelli went on. "If others were being threatened, this would be known."

"Why is Fabrizio Rossi, or Calaberoni, working as an apprentice, quite a good one according to your sister, in a legitimate family business?" Dana asked. "*Your* family business. And why was he shot? Because he knows who destroyed the wine?"

"I'm not sure about any of this . . . I can't imagine if Fabrizio is Leo's son—"

"That he would allow him to be raised by a Mafia family?" Dana finished Borelli's thought. "Maybe you've been on the wrong track all along. Just from the little I know of Leo, I don't think he would allow this to happen."

"No, I don't believe he would," Borelli said, blinking nervously. "But this might make it easier to explain why Fabrizio has come to work for Leo." His voice cracked, and Dana understood the possibility that his nephew would allow the Mafia to infiltrate the family business would be much more difficult for Borelli to accept than the possibility that Leo had fathered a child outside of his marriage.

Winkie and Lorenzo Veronesi stood over the map, which looked like something produced by hand in the fifteenth century. From the lengthy walks Winkie had taken over the past few days, and the digital and Google earth maps that had been provided by the attorney Raffaelo Sabatini, as well as Giovanna's guided tour of the land, Winkie could see it was fairly accurate.

"If the weather continues to cooperate," Lorenzo said, "we should have another good harvest."

"You should eat your lunch," Winkie said to the old man like a dutiful big brother, or perhaps a child speaking to his aging father.

"Oh, yes, so nice to have it delivered," he said as if he'd sent out for a pizza.

Carefully, Winkie rolled up the map, went over to the tray, poured a cup of coffee for the old man, then brought it, along with the sandwich, to the table. He pulled up a chair for Lorenzo and motioned him to sit.

"We'll talk after you have something to eat," Winkie said kindly, and Lorenzo did not protest. "Are you cold? Could I get you a blanket?" Winkie glanced toward the bed. It didn't seem to be as chilly in the bedroom as in the hallway, perhaps because there was an unshuttered, unboarded window letting in some natural light and sun.

"No, I'm fine," Lorenzo said. "Will you join me, Vincenzo?"

"No, *grazie*. I've eaten already."

Lorenzo, who had been standing the entire time as they studied the map, sat in the chair, spread a napkin over his bare lap, and slowly began to pick the sandwich apart, separating the bread, the tomatoes, the cheese, the salami. He bit into the bread. He took a sip of coffee.

After a few moments, Winkie heard footsteps in the hallway, though Lorenzo did not appear to be aware. When a key clicked in the door and it opened, Winkie no longer felt like the big brother or even a dutiful son, but like a child caught where he had no business being.

"I see you've met my brother, Lorenzo," Giovanna said. Her words carried no anger and only the smallest amount of surprise.

"Yes," Winkie answered, "we've been going over some plans for the vineyards."

"This is very good," Lorenzo said, holding up a tomato slice, then taking a bite. He looked at Giovanna. "They serve very good food here." A dribble of tomato juice slid down his chin. "Vincenzo brought this up for me."

Giovanna did not correct him. She sat down on the bed and eased off her shoes, rubbing the heel of her foot. She gazed pensively over at her brother as he continued to pick through his lunch, then at Winkie, who stood beside Lorenzo. Though Giovanna was obviously studying the two men, Winkie didn't think she was angry with him. He couldn't read her expression. Perhaps resigned. No one said anything more until Lorenzo told them he was finished. A substantial amount of the deconstructed sandwich remained on the plate.

"It's time for your nap," Giovanna said, rising. She pulled the covers on the bed back and helped her brother settle in. "Are you warm enough?"

"You're a very nice, girl," Lorenzo said politely. "But, I'm very sorry, I can't remember your name."

"Giovanna," she said.

"Oh, yes," Lorenzo said. "The same as my sister."

"Yes, the same," she said and smiled sadly. She placed a hand gently on his forehead, gazed at him affectionately, then bent slightly and gave him a peck on the cheek. She picked her shoes up off the floor, looping the straps over her fingers. "Push the button on your alert if you need anything." She pointed to a looped cord on the nightstand, with what appeared to be some kind of call button attached. Winkie guessed the cord was intended to be worn for easy access. It was obvious that Lorenzo couldn't be talked into clothes, let alone a device around his neck. "I'll be here all afternoon," Giovanna said, "and Lucia will bring your dinner up this evening. You must try to eat."

She motioned to Winkie, pointed to the door, indicating it was time to leave. He placed the coffee pot and sandwich leftovers back on the tray and carried it out.

"I apologize," said Winkie as Giovanna locked the door. "I was curious. I wanted to see the rest of the house."

"The crazy brother in the attic." She walked quickly ahead, her bare feet light along the wood planked floor. She glanced back at Winkie, holding the tray, then stopped for him to catch up and they continued down the hall side by side.

As they approached the elevator Giovanna said, "If you are concerned, I do have power of attorney to conduct any business."

"I'm sure Raffaelo Sabatini has attended to that."

"He, Lorenzo, was living in a facility in Rome. He had become quite unmanageable. Refused to eat anything. As you can see, he is still very sweet, but he tends to wander. One morning they found him out on the highway. Very confused."

"And naked?"

Giovanna smiled. "That's the least of my concerns. But the locks, they are necessary. I'm afraid he might hurt himself or get lost. The modesty has left him completely."

They got on the elevator.

"He thought I was his brother," Winkie said. "Your brother.

Vincenzo."

Giovanna said nothing as the elevator clattered down with a jerking sensation. It came to a halt and they got off in the kitchen. "As you have observed," she said, "he's very confused."

"Do I look anything like Vincenzo?" Winkie asked.

The question seemed to startle Giovanna. Her shoulders stiffened. She did not reply. "Thank you for carrying the tray. Please set it on the counter."

Winkie did as he was told.

Giovanna said, "Raffaelo Sabatini will meet with us in the library at four. I will see you then."

"Yes, four in the library."

"I, I . . ." Giovanna started, then paused as if weighing her words. "There have been a few changes to what we originally spoke of. I'll leave that for Raffaelo to explain."

Winkie had never actually talked to Giovanna about the possible contract, as all business had been conducted through the attorney. But, Winkie was definitely curious about the changes Giovanna spoke of.

He returned to his room, knowing no matter what the terms, he would make a deal that afternoon. Soon he would be the new owner of the Veronesi estate and vineyards.

CHAPTER TWENTY-TWO

The small jet was waiting for them, and then the helicopter. It was late afternoon by the time Dana and Borelli landed near the spot where they had left his truck earlier in the day. He had napped intermittently on both flights and Dana had plenty of time to sort through what they had learned in Locri about Fabrizio's family. She wasn't sure that Borelli was ready to let go of the idea that Leo was the boy's father, but this latest revelation had thrown so many additional questions into the mix. If the mob had somehow been involved in the wine destruction, who had shot Fabrizio? His own family? A rival family?

Maybe Inspector Alberto DeLuca was right; Silvio Gallo had shot Fabrizio. Maybe the attempt on Fabrizio had nothing to do with the mob or the wine destruction. But still, wasn't it likely that these two events were related? As Borelli had said, it was generally rather quiet around here.

They thanked Luigi, the helicopter pilot, and started back to the estate, Borelli again directing Dana as she drove along the hillsides and the unmarked paths.

"I apologize," Borelli said, "that your holiday has turned into— I don't even know what to call it."

"Yes, you could have planned this all much better," Dana said, throwing Borelli a sympathetic smile, which he returned.

"Yes, if I'd planned better, I could have delayed all this unpleasantness until after your visit." His smile faded. "Thank you for your help."

Dana shifted gears as they climbed. She wasn't sure how much help she had been so far, but she sensed that Borelli couldn't go to family, and he obviously didn't want to leave this solely up to local law enforcement. Dana thought of Mia, how sad she'd been last night as her father took her up to her room. Dana had developed a real affection for her. She truly liked Mia and sensed that she liked Dana, too.

"Mia likes you," Borelli said as if pulling the thought out of her head. "Thank you for spending time with her. She misses her mother and it is nice to have a woman, a younger woman, to spend time with her. Estella is old-fashioned, and Mia has always been close to Renata, but a young girl . . . I'm pleased that you are here for her."

"What made you think of that?" Dana asked. "Of Mia?"

"I don't know. Well, truthfully,"—there was an uncomfortable hesitation in Borelli's tone— "I considered asking earlier, but I felt it an awkward situation, and I was unsure if it would be appropriate to bring it up. Even now I'm reluctant to—"

"What?" she demanded.

"When you came downstairs, as we were preparing to leave for dinner in Montalcino, your scent, your perfume. You smelled exactly like Mia's mother."

Dana took in a deep breath. It was Mia who had chosen her perfume. Dana never wore perfume. There were so many possibilities, so many interpretations that could be put to such a gesture. Was it because Mia liked here? Or wanted to sabotage her? Dana remembered riding home in the van, sitting next to Leo. It was Mia who had encouraged Dana to sit next to her father. Oddly, as she looked back on the evening, Leo seemed unaware that she smelled like his wife. The wife he had lost. If he had noticed he might have taken this as something she had done on purpose. To seduce him? To bring up memories she had no right to bring back? But Dana would not have known this was his wife's perfume. Now, she certainly didn't know what to tell Borelli.

"I had no idea," she finally said, but before she could add more, they hit a bump in the road. Then Borelli's phone rang.

He glanced at his screen and deemed it important enough to interrupt this awkward conversation. He listened attentively, saying but a few words. When he ended the call, he said, "Paolo's funeral will be Wednesday morning at the estate chapel. Renata would like me to say Mass. The autopsy revealed that the cause of death was drowning."

"In Borelli Brunello," Dana whispered, and Borelli nodded.

"A substantial amount of wine in his lungs. According to Leo, Inspector DeLuca believes, based on the time frame, the amount of time it would take the barrels to empty, whoever perpetrated the crime most likely had left the cellar before Paolo came in."

"Though whoever did this will be held accountable for Paolo's death."

"As it should be," Borelli said.

As they neared the road that led back to the villa, Dana thought of Winkie Dalton.

"I'd like to go speak with Winkie Dalton."

"Yes, I believe you should. I'll go with you." He motioned toward the main highway. Dana wondered if she should go alone, considering how secretive Octavia had been about this request, but she felt more comfortable taking Borelli with her. A million thoughts were now twisting through her head. Fabrizio. His family. Mia. Her mother's perfume. Leo. Winkie Dalton. She knew Borelli, too, had much to ponder and they spoke little as they continued down the highway, then turned off on the road that led to the

Veronesi Vineyards.

"To think I haven't been up here in almost fifty years," Borelli said. "Now twice in just a few days."

"You used to visit often?" Dana asked.

"For a time, yes."

She remembered what he had said on their earlier drive up the hill to deliver Winkie. How it had once been the liveliest estate in the region.

"Stop," Borelli said abruptly. He held a hand to his chest, breathing heavily. "Stop the truck for a moment."

"Are you okay?" Dana asked, slowing gradually, pulling over. He had suffered a heart attack four years ago, and now her own heart jumped at the thought that he might be having another here on the bumpy road to the Veronesi estate. "Do we need to go to the hospital?"

"No, no, of course not," he said indignantly. "I'm not having a seizure or heart attack. I'm fine." He sucked in air, blew out several puffs, then laughed nervously. "I'm fine," he repeated with a swallow.

"Are you sure? We can turn back."

"No, no."

"I could take you home." They remained motionless, gear shift in neutral.

"No, let's continue. It's just indigestion," he said with a surly tone. "We had a rather large meal in Locri. "I'm fine," he assured her, topping it off with a convincing burp as if proving it was indeed indigestion.

He didn't sound fine, Dana thought.

"Ancient history," he said as if talking to himself. "Many years ago."

"What are you talking about?" she asked. It was obvious that something about heading up this road was causing Borelli substantial stress, though she hadn't been aware of such a reaction when he'd come up with her to deliver Winkie Dalton.

"I know she has returned to attend to some business. When we drove up to drop Mr. Dalton off, I was unaware that she was back home." He ran his fingers through his balding scalp, over the top of his head in a nervous gesture.

"She? A woman?" Dana wanted to know more.

"Yes." Borelli took in another deep breath, but he was smiling. He motioned her to proceed, and he seemed okay now so Dana shifted into gear and pulled back onto the road.

"Giovanna Veronesi," he said, "though that is not her legal name now. She's been married several times. Once to a Romanian prince." Borelli snorted out a derisive laugh. "Though she will always be Giovanna Veronesi here in Montalcino. Gia." His tone had shifted, the final word slipping out gracefully, almost a whisper, spoken with true affection. "The lovely Gia Veronesi. Our names even the same, the feminine, the masculine, as if we were meant to be together. I was Gianni back then. Gia. Giovanna. Giovanni."

"You were sweethearts?" Dana didn't know why she was using such an old-fashioned word, but she couldn't bring herself to use the word *lovers*.

"I was studying secular law at the time. In Rome. I came home for a break from my studies and saw her at Mass." He laughed again, but now it carried more than a hint of pleasant recollection. "I had seen her as a child. She was younger than I and this was the memory I had of her. A pretty little girl. But that summer, when I saw her at Mass, she had matured into an exquisitely beautiful woman. I was hesitant to speak to her—our families were not known to be friendly, and though I was much slimmer then, my hair dark and full." He ran his hand over his temple as if smoothing his hair. "I spoke to her after Mass. We started—" Borelli shook his head, but he was smiling.

"Dating?" Dana asked.

"Getting to know one another. Becoming friends. We fell in love. At least, I thought we did." He raised his shoulders, closing his eyes for a moment as if to imply that he had been duped. "The families had always objected to such a union. The Veronesis held themselves above others. Royal bloodlines they claimed. Her family objected to any possible union between a Borelli and a Veronesi. Yet, we were determined. We became engaged. We would move to Rome, away from the families. I would continue my studies."

"But you never married."

"No, we did not." Borelli looked up toward the Veronesi villa as it came into view. "Well, here we are," he said, lightly, but cheerfully, and then, "Yes, perhaps you are right, I think I'd like to return home."

CHAPTER TWENTY-THREE

"I understand this particular aspect of the contract is something new," Giovanna said, "but it has never been your intention to live on the estate?"

"I have no background in wine production, as you both well know." Winkie glanced from Giovanna to Raffaelo Sabatini, who sat opposite him at the large desk in Giovanna's library. "I will hire a wine consultant, then someone to run the winery, oversee the day to day production. But, I definitely intend to spend time on the estate, particularly in the months when my children are on breaks from school."

Because of the poor condition of the house, major renovations would be required, and Winkie had considered this in negotiating the contract. All three understood it was the land, particularly the portion registered to Brunello production, that made up the true value of the Veronesi estate. Several areas would have to be replanted, crews hired, but Winkie had not seen the condition of the house as being a problem. It would be an expensive endeavor to renovate, but he rather liked the idea. Yet, this new aspect of the contract would require some thought.

"We do have others, you understand," Sabatini told him, in his deep, official, authoritative voice, "who are in a position to make an offer." Sabatini was an individual whose phone voice did not match his actual person. During the several times Winkie had conversed with him over the past eight months, he'd pictured Sabatini as being tall and distinguished, with graying temples, dressed impeccably. In person, Sabatini was short and plump and bald and wore a suit with visible wire hanger marks protruding from the shoulders that might lead one to believe it had been hanging in the closet for years, seldom worn.

"I'd like time to consider," Winkie said, though in his heart he had decided he would do anything to have this property. But, he was astute in business matters, and he knew not to let his heart overrule his mind. At least, outwardly.

"By the first of next week," Sabatini suggested. He raised the pen which he'd held in his hand through the entire conversation, though he had yet to use it.

"I'm leaving for home on Friday, but I can certainly call from New York to finalize anything." Winkie wondered if that was giving away too much. Perhaps he should not have used the word finalize. He glanced at Giovanna and could see something in her eyes and then in the manner in which she bit down on her lower lip that she, too, wanted him to have the property.

"Oh, which reminds me," Giovanna said, motioning to Sabatini.

The man looked puzzled at first, but then he unzipped a pocket in his briefcase which sat on the corner of the desk and pulled out an electrical adaptor. The lawyer handed it to Winkie.

"Grazie."

Sabatini clicked his pen and placed it in the inside pocket of his jacket, then rose. "We will expect to hear from you by the first of the week. Call if you have any questions. It's been a pleasure, Mr. Dalton." He reached out and shook his hand.

Winkie took the adaptor up to his room and plugged in his

phone waiting for it to charge. As he sat, he thought about the request Giovanna had made. It would be part of the contract, but he knew it was a personal request. She wished to have a life estate in the house for her brother, which likely meant Giovanna would stay too, until Lorenzo passed.

Winkie waited until his phone was sufficiently charged to make his calls. Audra was especially interested in the business aspects of his trip to Italy, what was happening in negotiations, and Winkie told her they were closing in on a deal. Sam was more interested in the romance of it, the poetic side of owning land in Tuscany, and Winkie told him about the long walks he'd taken on the property, how beautiful and peaceful it was.

After he hung up, Winkie decided to go out, leave his phone to finish charging. Giovanna's car was still parked out front. So was Sabatini's.

Winkie made his way along the steep incline of the nearest vineyard. The sun appeared low in the sky, and he guessed the American reporter would not show up. He wondered if Octavia had delivered his message. How likely was it that the conversation he'd overheard had anything to do with what had happened on the Borelli estate anyway? He'd been so out of touch for the past few days—no newspaper, no cellphone.

Yet something, maybe his sense of basic decency, was pushing him toward going to the police himself. On the other hand, he did not want his name splashed all over the news. He had come to Tuscany on a mission, and he did not want the entire world to know until he was ready.

Curious, Winkie strolled on to the area where he'd seen the two men conversing. It was a substantial walk from the main house, but he'd now decided, based on his recent study of the maps, that it was Veronesi property.

He stopped some distance from the buildings, eyes scanning the area. A light wind ruffled a nearby tree, a pair of doves cooed, but he detected no sign of any human life nearby. He approached the first building. Again, he stopped and listened before testing the door. Nothing. Not a sound or indication of others' presence. The door opened with ease. Dark inside, his eyes needed to adjust. A mouse scampered across the floor scratching the worn wooden planks. The walls were lined with dilapidated shelves. A couple of rusty bikes, both with flat tires, leaned up against one wall. There were no vehicles inside.

Again, he thought of Dana Pierson. He no longer needed the adaptor, but he wanted to talk to someone about what he had overheard. Should he speak with Giovanna? No, not yet.

He glanced back over toward the two rusty bikes, then a bicycle pump hanging behind them. He pulled it off the wall and pumped up the tires of the bike that looked most substantial, and then wheeled it out and hopped on. He was used to riding a bike in the city, but not bumping along the hills of Tuscany. As he crested one hill with great effort he nearly tumbled over, his foot slipping off the pedal, catching himself just in time. He stopped for a moment to look over the landscape. He could see the Borelli villa from here, but he knew this wasn't a good idea, riding the bike over the irregular hillside, with nothing more than a dirt path here and there. He could also see he'd have to navigate around a thick grove of trees. He should go back to the road leading to the highway. Though little of the Veronesis' road was paved, it was better than attempting to pedal over the hills.

Getting back to the road required more effort than he had imagined. Darn, he should have brought a bottle of water, but when he'd left the house, after his meeting with Giovanna and Sabatini, after speaking to both his children, he merely wanted to get out, breathe some fresh air and think.

When he finally arrived at the road that wound down the hill to the highway, he saw an old beat up truck making its way toward him, stirring up dust. As the truck approached, he could see that Dana Pierson was at the wheel. She was alone in the vehicle. She slowed, rolled her window down and held up an adaptor, no doubt the one Octavia had promised him.

"You're a little late," he said.

"Late for what?" she replied. "How about a ride? Could you use a ride?" She glanced up at the sky. "Not much daylight left. By the way, nice bike."

"Nice truck," he replied, shooting one back at her. He was straddling the bike, both he and his mode of transportation covered with dust, and he was damned thirsty. "What I could really use is a drink."

"Well, then hop in," she said. "Throw your bike in the back. I could use a drink myself."

CHAPTER TWENTY-FOUR

"Dusty road," Dana said as they turned onto the highway. "Could use some paving or at least throw on a handful of gravel." She glanced over at Winkie, sitting in the passenger side of the truck. "Where'd you find the bike? Haven't seen one like that in years."

"In an old abandoned garage," he said, combing his hand through his disheveled curls, glancing out the window. "I've always believed in conserving energy." He looked at her now.

"And you were coming after me, frantically pedaling down the road to get that adaptor for your phone."

"And you were coming up the road to find me," he replied.

"Your request certainly piqued my curiosity, the fact that you asked for me as your delivery person."

"By the way," Winkie said, "I was able to obtain an adaptor by other means. I no longer need it, but I'll return it to Octavia when I get home."

"I was surprised you were so desperate to get your phone charged since you're here for a quiet place to write. How's the writing going?"

"I'm on my way to accomplishing my goals," he replied. "As for the phone, I need it to keep in touch with my children. I'm often away on location and it's important that I'm able to speak with them frequently."

"Oh," Dana said, softening toward Winkie at the mention of his children. She realized now that he most likely had been attempting to contact his children when she picked him up in Rome. "How old are your kids?"

"Sam is eighteen, first year at NYU. Audra's a senior in high school." He went on to tell her about his children, how creative and thoughtful Sam was, what a beautiful, bright girl Audra was. Dana could tell he was proud of his children and she sensed he was a dutiful dad.

He asked if she had children and she just said no. It was easier than explaining.

They found a wine bar in Pienza, a small village a short distance from Montalcino, away from the Borelli and Veronesi estates, after Winkie suggested they find a private spot to have an uninterrupted conversation.

A trio of elderly men stood at the bar, against a backdrop of colorful bottles of liqueurs, brandy, whiskey, and wine. Otherwise, the place was empty. Dana and Winkie sat, facing one another across a scratched wooden table. Winkie asked the server for a large bottle of water, two glasses, and then, without consulting one another, they each ordered a beer.

"Is this okay?" Dana said with an ironic laugh as the drinks were delivered. "Drinking beer in the heart of Tuscany? At a wine bar?"

"It's Italian," Winkie said, raising his bottle of Peroni in a salute. He laughed too, then took an enormous gulp, followed by a swig of water. "I don't know if guzzling wine is proper, so yes, I believe so. I'm damned dry."

Dana took a good gulp of beer herself. Something about the yeasty, hoppy smell reminded her of her dad. Not that he was a drinker, but when he took her to the ballpark when she was young, they'd order hot dogs, he'd have a beer, Dana a root beer. Most of the time, at least one of her brothers would go, but those outings with her dad, when it was just the two of them, were her favorite memories of growing up.

"Octavia told me you wanted to talk to me," Dana said, finally getting to why he'd requested she contact him.

"Yes, I did. I do. I understand a substantial amount of wine was lost recently by the Borellis." His voice was low, serious. "A man died. A murder?"

"Not intentionally," she replied, curiosity mixing with anticipation now, wondering if Winkie knew something about what had happened at the Borelli Vineyards. "It's believed that he came into the cellar at the wrong time. All the spigots on over a dozen barrels had been opened. He slipped and hit his head on the metal rim of one of the barrels."

"He died from the head injury? Hit his head on a barrel?"

"He drowned." Dana wondered if she should have revealed this, but the information was all in the autopsy report according to what Leo had told Borelli during their phone conversation.

"How . . . there is . . . is there not sufficient drainage in the cellar? Enough wine accumulated to drown a man?" He chased the words with a chug on his now almost empty beer.

"Several bottles from the racks in the same cellar were smashed and the glass clogged the drains."

Winkie's eyes narrowed as if this revelation had put a new light on what he was about to share with her. "So vicious." He motioned the server to bring another beer. He shot Dana an inquiring look. She shook her head, indicating one was plenty.

Winkie said, "Remember when we were coming from Rome and getting near the Borelli Vineyards, and we saw the group of protesters? The man with the tam, the grubby beard, the one who came up to the van?"

"Yes, of course I remember," Dana answered. "I was in the

passenger seat and he put his face right up to the window, slapped the van violently, then made an angry gesture as we pulled out. That face is imprinted on my mind."

"That's why I wanted to talk to you. Because you saw him. Everyone else in the van was asleep."

"Other than the driver, Claudio."

"Yes, that's true." Winkie seemed to give this some thought. "I saw him again, the protester."

"Along the highway?"

The server arrived with Winkie's beer. *"Grazie,"* Winkie said as the man set it on the table, then left. "On the Veronesi estate. I saw him twice. The first evening I was there, he drove in, parked and came into the house. I don't know how long he stayed. I fell asleep. Later Giovanna Veronesi said a group of environmentalists was interested in buying the vineyard."

"The Veronesis are selling?" Dana asked with mock surprise.

Winkie nodded. "Then I saw him again the following day, near a group of rundown buildings some distance from the house. He was speaking with another man. They were talking about an old man, a wine cellar."

"What else did they say?" Dana asked eagerly.

Winkie hesitated, rubbed his lip, took a slow drink of beer. "I wasn't taking notes at the time. But, I believe they said something about a woman being involved. When they mentioned a cellar, I thought they were talking about a cellar there at the Veronesi Vineyards. But, yes, something about an old man, but I can't remember exactly what they said. It wasn't until the next day, when I ran into Octavia and she told me about the destruction in the Borelli cellar, about the old man being killed. When I overheard the conversation, I had no idea, but later—"

"After you spoke with Octavia."

Winkie nodded. "The man, not the protester, but the other man was cursing, swearing, quite angry." Winkie paused again as if trying to remember. "He called the protestor a *cretino*, an idiot. He said there was no need to destroy the bottled wine."

"The bottled wine?" If the bottles had not been broken, Dana realized, the drains would not have been clogged, and Paolo would not have drowned.

"I believe that's what he said."

"There were two people?"

"Yes, the young man we'd seen along the road, and another, a bit older, I believe. I'm not sure. I didn't get a good look at his face. The man's back was to me most of the time. He wore a cap."

"They didn't see you?"

"No, I'm sure of that. He was taller than average, taller than the younger man. He was wearing a jacket. Maybe blue. No, I'm not sure of the color. Could have been green. A darker shade. Nothing that would stand out."

Dana tried to contain herself, not ask too many questions, just let Winkie talk.

"He wore jeans, but he looked much better dressed than the protester, giving me the impression that he was the person with authority. He spoke that way, too. Yes, he was definitely the one in charge, because it seemed the younger man . . . well, he was getting a scolding, for lack of a better word. The older man was upset."

"With the younger man, the protester?"

Winkie nodded.

"Better dressed," Dana said. "But, wearing jeans?"

"The younger man's jeans were faded and frayed. Well, you remember how scruffy he looked?" Winkie scratched his head absently, bit his lower lip. "The other man, his jeans were the color of new denim before it goes through the wash several times." Winkie paused a moment to think. "Something else they said. The grubby fellow, he asked about another payment and—"

"A payment?" Dana swallowed her breath.

"At the time I assumed it had something to do with a payment for wine, not—"

"If you think this might be related to what happened at the

Borelli Vineyards, why are you passing this information on to me rather than going to the police?"

"I'm not sure it has any connection to what happened." Winkie glanced around the small bar, blinking nervously, and Dana followed his gaze. One of the men standing at the bar had left, the other two were chatting with the bartender, who was also the table server. He shot an attentive glance toward Winkie who indicated with a wave that they were fine. "I'm headed home in a couple of days, and I haven't publicized the fact that I'm here in Italy."

Dana wondered if there was more to this than Winkie was letting on, or if he was just concerned about his celebrity status. She'd always thought celebrities were all about publicity, but Winkie obviously didn't want to be connected with any of this.

"Since you saw the man and can describe him," Winkie said, slowly, running his finger along the rim of his bottle, then looking up at her hopefully, "I thought you could go to the police."

"Me?" she asked, voice rising, stunned by this request. "You expect *me* to tell them I overheard this conversation?"

"No, I'm not asking that you do that. But, you are well versed in protecting your source." A quick grin flashed across his face, then faded just as quickly.

"Oh?"

"Octavia told me you're a reporter, a journalist. Surely you know how to protect your source."

"You know I'm not working right now. I'm on vacation."

"What a vacation," he said with a shake of his head.

What a vacation, indeed, she thought.

They finished their beers, Winkie paid, and they walked back to the truck. They didn't talk much as they headed toward the Veronesi estate. Dana was attempting to sort through what Winkie had told her. Two men conversing. Reference to a woman who was involved in whatever they were talking about. Another payment.

When they arrived at the turnoff to the estate, Winkie said, "I'd like to ride the bike from here." He motioned toward the bed of the truck. Dana guessed he didn't want anyone seeing her deliver him to the estate. But she had some concerns about him riding in the dark. It wasn't like the bumpy road was lined with street lights.

"I'd be more than happy to drive you and your bike up to the top."

"No, no, I'm fine."

Dana got out and helped him with the bike.

"You'll pass this information on to the authorities?" Winkie asked, straddling his bike.

Dana hesitated. "Well, someone certainly should," she said, feeling an instant weight of frustration that expanded through her entire chest as she watched Winkie pedal up the hill into the darkness.

CHAPTER TWENTY-FIVE

Dana drove up to the Borelli villa, anger now overtaking the frustration she'd felt at Winkie's request. If she went to the police and refused to name her source, they might not let her leave. Her initial feelings were directed toward Winkie, but now the irritation was turning inward on herself. She should have insisted Winkie go to the authorities. She felt physically ill. She had to talk to Borelli.

Passing several vehicles, some marked police cars, others with press logos, no one stopping her—obviously recognizing Borelli's truck—Dana parked in the garage. Claudio was there, cleaning the interior of the van he'd taken to deliver the guests to the airport in Rome.

"Buona sera," she greeted Claudio as she got out of the truck. He glanced up with a scowl and muttered something she didn't understand.

When she arrived at the house, Dana glimpsed into the living room, then the library, looking for Borelli. She went to the kitchen, finding Mia coming in from the garden, arms full of fresh autumn produce. She set her bundle of zucchini, yellow squash, and tomatoes on the counter, then washed her hands. A thin woman appeared to be preparing dinner.

"We miss Renata," Mia said. "She'll be back next week, after the funeral." Mia spoke quickly to the woman in Italian, then switched with ease back to English to address Dana. "We had to get some additional help to come to our rescue while our guests were here." Mia smiled warmly at Dana. "Forgive me. Yes, you are a guest, too, but perhaps we do not have to impress you as we did the wine distributors."

Dana liked the idea that she was being treated like family.

Mia introduced the woman as Lala and explained she often assisted in the kitchen. "But without Renata we're running late, and I'm trying to help. Don't count on a gourmet meal this evening."

"No impressing required. May I help?" Dana attempted to calm the anger toward Winkie swelling inside her. For Mia's sake.

"Thank you, but no need. Lala can finish up."

Dana shot Lala an appreciative smile, then she and Mia left the kitchen. Dana wanted to ask her about the perfume, but she knew she couldn't do it. She'd already decided that. For some reason, the girl had chosen her mother's perfume, but Dana would not bring it up unless Mia did.

"Have you seen your Uncle Giovanni?" Dana asked as they walked down the hallway. She wanted desperately to talk to him about her conversation with Winkie.

"Not for several hours."

"What did you do today?" Dana asked.

"The same," Mia answered. "Nothing much."

Mia sounded like Dana's oldest nephew. Was this the standard young teen's answer around the world? Dana wondered if Mia had gone back to school. Dana had the feeling that Leo would want to keep her on her regular schedule as much as possible.

"What about you?" Mia asked. "What did you do today?"

"Your Uncle Giovanni and I went for a drive, a little outing."

"Good idea to get away. The press has been snooping around, though the police are trying to keep them at a distance."

Dana couldn't tell if Mia was excited or fearful about the increased activity.

"I know how that works," Dana said. "The press is just attempting to get the news out to the public, to keep them informed. If the authorities allow them on the property, that's where they will be. No one has bothered you?" she asked with concern.

"No. I believe my father is seeing to that."

Dana had also noted that none of the tourist vans had been on the property for the past several days. This loss of business certainly added to Leo's problems, which included not only the destruction of his prized wine, but protecting his daughter and mother.

"Where did you go?" Mia asked.

Dana wasn't sure how to answer. She didn't want to bring Mia into any of this, though she knew the girl was curious, especially to know more about what had happened to Fabrizio. But, Dana didn't want to lie either.

"Around the estate, then we headed south."

Mia seemed to be okay with this. "I met Fabrizio's grandmother," she said. "She came to visit my grandmother." Mia and Dana stood in the foyer at the base of the steps. "Grandmother is not doing well. She has hardly been out of bed." Mia glanced up.

"I'm so sorry," Dana said, putting her hand on Mia's shoulder. "I hope she feels better soon." Dana wondered again if Estella knew about Fabrizio's family. His grandmother had come to visit, and Estella had introduced her to Borelli as an old friend. She had to know. "Fabrizio's grandmother wants to take him back home?" Dana asked. *To his mafia family*, she wondered.

"I'm sure she does, but I overheard Grandmother and Fabrizio's grandmother talking. Grandmother told her how well Fabrizio is doing here, how much we would all like him to stay when he recovers."

"I'm sure that makes you happy."

Mia smiled. "Yes, we all like having Fabrizio here. I'll see you at dinner."

"Yes," Dana said, "see you then." She started up the stairs.

"Oh, I almost forgot," Mia said as if an afterthought had just fluttered through her mind, "Marco was looking for you."

"Marco Dardi?" Dana asked, turning back. She realized since dinner last night, all the activity today, she'd barely given the charming, but perplexing Marco any thought. "Did he say what he wanted?"

"He didn't, but I think he left for home about an hour ago."

"Oh," Dana said. She thought of how flirtatious Marco had been at dinner in Montalcino, how he'd suggested they get together later. Yet, he'd taken off without making any plans. Why was he looking for her? Was it personal, or did he have something to share with her about what had happened in the cellar? Neither of these made much sense. If he had something to share, shouldn't he be sharing with the police? He most likely had no idea that Dana and Borelli were conducting a little investigation on their own. Or did he?

CHAPTER TWENTY-SIX

When Winkie went down for dinner, he found Giovanna alone in the dining room, deep in thought, her eyes fixed on the painting of the Virgin and Child. The wall sconces on either side flickered, creating an illusion as if the Madonna were alive. Serene, almost expressionless one moment, and then a mere second's lapse and it seemed as if her lips had lifted into the slightest smile.

"Buona sera," he said, startling Giovanna.

"Buona sera," she replied graciously, turning, motioning him to sit.

"Raffaelo has left?" Winkie asked as he pulled out his chair.

Andrea came in carrying a tray with a bottle of wine and two glasses. He lifted the glasses from the tray and arranged them on the table. Then, with a gesture verging on theatrical, he held the bottle, label forward for Giovanna, then Winkie, to examine, like a sommelier in a fancy restaurant. It was a ten-year-old Veronesi Brunello Riserva. Giovanna nodded, Andrea extracted the cork with an old-fashioned corkscrew and poured a small portion into each glass.

"*Grazie*, Andrea," Giovanna said as he dipped in a slight bow and left the room. Giovanna turned to Winkie, picking up the conversation. "Yes, Raffaelo left some time ago."

"But not until you met with other prospective buyers," Winkie said.

"I'm sure you've never been under the impression that you were the only party showing an interest." She was not offering this as a question, and Winkie nodded because he had never thought this the case.

"There are several buyers," she said. "Some have sent representatives to examine the land, not even bothering to come themselves." Her lips quivered in a little motion of disdain that indicated she would not consider offers from these prospective buyers. "Several corporations have expressed a serious interest, but Veronesi would be sucked into a larger business. It's important that the brand, the label, stay intact. Raffaelo has some true concerns about several of the prospective buyers' suitability. And, of course, as you know, any buyer will be closely examined by the *Uficio Agricolo Imprenditori*."

Winkie was well aware of this, but he had no doubt he would pass any required tests and meet all standards to become an Italian farmer. He was sure that the financial capabilities of each party expressing a serious interest had been carefully examined by Sabatini. Yet, Giovanna seemed to imply something one step beyond this. She wanted someone with a personal affection for the land. Winkie wondered how closely he himself had been vetted. He guessed very closely and wondered if Giovanna was aware of the most significant aspect of his reason for being here.

"Am I the only one whom you've invited to stay at the estate?" Winkie asked.

"I believe you invited yourself." A smile slid across her lips.

"You accepted my invitation." He was about to ask why, but he decided to withhold the question.

"It is important to me that I pass this legacy on to someone who truly cares for the land. The money, yes this is important too. The most recent offer has come in substantially greater than your latest offer."

"I assume you'll share this information with me?"

Giovanna did not answer. She stared at the bottle of wine, then glanced at the two glasses, perhaps wondering if the time had come to drink. Slowly, and fondly, she ran her fingers along the gold DOCG seal on the neck of the bottle. "One of the final Riserva vintages produced from vine to bottle on the Veronesi estate," she said, meeting Winkie's eyes. "It is my wish that, with the sale, the full production of Veronesi wines will be reinstated."

"My wish exactly," Winkie said.

"It is my understanding that you produce, often script and star in your own films," Giovanna said thoughtfully. "You have been successful."

Winkie nodded, though he did not see Giovanna's remarks as questions. She was letting him know she had done her homework, that she saw him as a viable buyer, one capable of successfully running a business.

"I surround myself with good, capable people," he said.

"Very important for the success of any business," she agreed.

"Perhaps I need to know what your latest offer is, so I might respond." He wondered if she thought she had him right where she wanted him. She understood how much he wanted this land, this villa, this winery.

"Raffaelo has warned me about meeting with potential buyers without his legal counsel. Without his physical presence." She touched the base of one of the wineglasses, then ran her hand along the stem. "He was not happy when he learned you were staying here. He feels my judgment might be tainted."

"Are you one to have your judgment tainted, Giovanna?" Winkie asked.

She slid one of the glasses toward Winkie and motioned for him to take the first taste. Slowly, he swirled the wine, held it to his nose, then took a small sip. The rim of the wineglass was thin as paper, smooth as ice, though the deep red liquid slipped with warmth and comfort into his mouth. He nodded approval.

"Am I one to have my judgment tainted?" she repeated his question. "I've been known to lead with my heart." She swirled her wine, gazing into the deep red, bringing it to her nose, then finally sipping. "But, in truth, my greatest failures have come when I did as I was instructed by others, when I failed to listen to my inner self."

"A rather romantic notion," Winkie said. "I often find just the opposite, that I have failed in the biggest ways when I listen to my heart. I've been married twice," he said as if confessing a weakness. "Hardly a record in Hollywood terms, but I'm not one to accept failure. I truly loved them both. Maybe I fall in love too easily. I was leading with my heart and look where it got me."

"Two beautiful children," she said without hesitation.

"Yes." He nodded in agreement.

"I can outdo you with three," she said with a laugh. "Marriages that is, not children. I've been married three times. I left the first one. Married another before the annulment went through. They are all dead now. Oh, I suppose I thought I was in love each time. But, not in the truest, deepest sense. Sometimes a woman does not have the opportunity for choice. I see this is not so much a problem for the younger women now. Many have choices, satisfying careers, as well as families. But, I felt I had little choice in many aspects of my life. Sometimes a woman feels she is not in charge."

"But here at the Veronesi Vineyards, you are certainly in charge."

"Yes. Now. As I've told Raffaelo many times, though he often resists. Sometimes he speaks as if he is the owner, that we must sell to the party of his choosing. Yes, I am in charge, but only because my brother Vincenzo is dead, and has no heirs. Because my brother Lorenzo . . . well, you met my brother Lorenzo."

"Yes," Winkie said, "which brings us back to the added clause in the contract. I'm curious—have you presented this to other buyers?"

Giovanna sipped her wine and Winkie could see that she did not intend to answer this question. "You have until the first of next week to consider," she said amiably. "Of course, contingent on your meeting our highest offer."

"I agree," Winkie said cheerfully.

"You agree?" she asked.

"I'll meet the highest bid. And I agree to the life estate for your brother Lorenzo." He raised his glass, offering a toast.

"Oh," Giovanna replied. She didn't seem surprised, and yet she did, her eyes wide, her hands to her lips, as if to hide her true feelings. She did not raise her glass to his.

"There are some provisions I'd like you to consider," he said cautiously.

"I'm listening," she replied stoically, attempting to keep her emotions in check, to control the quiver in her voice.

"I'd like to begin some renovations on the first and second floors of the villa. I would like to do these as soon as possible. I'd wish to stay here in the house, along with my children, whenever we visit. When we've finished the lower floors, Lorenzo can move down and we will renovate the third floor so that he will have a suite of his own as long as he wishes."

Giovanna listened.

"You, of course, can stay whenever you wish, though help will be employed constantly to care for Lorenzo."

"You are being overly generous," Giovanna said and though she did not add the word, why, Winkie could hear it in her tone.

"I'd like your input for your own bedroom," he continued, "as well as throughout. I want you to be comfortable. It's a beautiful home and I do not wish to make any drastic changes, but merely preserve and bring it back as close to its original state as possible."

Giovanna was quiet for some time as she tried to maintain her composure, blinking nervously, lip trembling. She nodded as if agreeing. "You do understand if such renovations were to receive my personal blessing, the Italian government would also wish to become involved. Permits. Permissions. Municipal. Provincial . . . and on and on, as is the norm here in Italy."

"I understand," Winkie said. "I know this may not be a particularly quick or easy process." After a moment he continued, "I'd like to keep your household help on, those who wish to stay. Any laborers who have remained through the rough patches. I know others will have to be employed. I will hire a consultant, someone to oversee production. A business manager on site. I wish to have your suggestions on all aspects of this." He looked directly at Giovanna to gauge her reaction.

She took a slow thoughtful drink of her wine, then met his eyes. "Like one big happy family," she replied with a tremor in her voice just as Lucia stepped into the room with the *primo piatto*.

Neither Estella, nor Borelli, joined them for dinner, so it was just Dana, Leo and Mia. Lala had prepared a delicious dish of the fresh veggies Mia had brought in from the garden, served with pasta and bread. Leo joked that this evening this would be the *primo* as well as the *secondo*.

As they ate, Leo explained that his uncle had gone into town to meet with Renata and her family, to talk to them about the funeral, which would take place in the family chapel on Wednesday morning.

"The vigil will be tomorrow, Tuesday evening," he told Dana. "Uncle Giovanni would like to take you to visit Florence tomorrow. Early, to ensure he is back home in time for the vigil. About seven?"

Dana nodded, but she wished that Borelli didn't feel obligated to entertain her. Yet, she desperately needed to talk to him, to share with him what Winkie told her about the conversation he'd overheard.

"How is Fabrizio today?" she asked Leo.

"His grandmother is here," he said, which Dana knew because both Borelli and Mia had told her. "No one but family is allowed to visit."

Family, Dana thought, studying Leo closely for any reaction, then glancing toward Mia who had participated little in the dinner conversation "Surely that will help in his recovery," Dana said.

"It has been reported in the news," Leo said, "Fabrizio being shot. Silvio's arrest. Reporters are attempting to tie it to what happened in the cellar. But, it seems the police still believe that the two incidents are unrelated."

Dana didn't see how this could be true. She waited for Leo to add more, something about the boy's family, but he didn't. She sensed that Borelli hadn't told Leo anything about what they'd discovered in Locri.

"Any further word from Inspector Alberto DeLuca," she asked, "regarding the wine loss and Paolo's death?" She thought of what Winkie had told her, and for a brief moment considered sharing this with Leo, but caution advised her to wait. She didn't want to bring it up with Mia at the table, and she wanted to talk to Borelli first.

Leo said, "I believe they have interviewed everyone who has been on the estate over the past week, including any tourists who toured the vineyards, based on our lists of those who signed up in Montalcino. Many of them have left for home."

"Has Carlo Porcini been found?" Mia asked. "Everyone knows he was upset when Fabrizio moved into the cottage."

"Yes, working in a vineyard near Montepulciano," Leo answered, pushing the last of the pasta around on his plate with a piece of bread. "I know he has been questioned, but I know nothing more than that."

"He hasn't been arrested, then?" Mia asked.

"No," Leo answered, but Dana couldn't detect if Leo thought he had anything to do with the wine destruction or not.

"Inspector DeLuca is considering the possibility of another producer?" Dana asked.

"They have been interviewing the members of the Consortium. According to Alberto, tips have been coming in, and they are sorting through those, but I sense they have discovered nothing of value. In a community of this size, much is gossip."

"Have there been any threats to other producers?" Dana asked.

Leo glanced at Dana with a puzzled look, then shook his head. "The remaining bottled wine on the racks has been tested for fingerprints, along with shards from the broken bottles, though any detectable prints most likely belong to those involved in bottling the wine, arranging it in the racks. All employees. Many have been with us for years."

"I wish I could go with you," Mia said, turning to Dana. "To Florence tomorrow."

Her father waved a finger at her. "School tomorrow. You may stay home on Wednesday. It is important to Renata that you are at the services."

"Yes, of course I want to be there for Renata." There was more than a hint of irritation in Mia's voice. She was obviously insulted that her father thought he had to tell her that. "If I miss one more day," she said, directing her words to Leo, "it would make little difference. You know I can catch up."

"School," he said firmly. "You will have time this weekend to have fun at the *Sagra del Tordo* celebration."

"How can we speak of fun?" Mia said harshly, tossing her napkin on the table and rising to leave.

Dana threw a glance at Leo, who said nothing, but looked exhausted as if he had no energy for more words. Dana wondered if they could truly join in the celebration. She knew the *Sagra del Tordo*, particularly the competition, could not go on as planned. The archer everyone expected to win was sitting in a jail cell accused of attempted murder.

Back in her room after dinner, Dana tried calling Borelli, but no answer. Filled with nervous energy, she checked the local news using an online translator. As Leo had told her, Silvio's arrest had been reported, though the police had made no ties to the two events at the Borelli Vineyards. The reporter seemed to imply that the police were hiding something. There was no mention of Fabrizio's family.

She checked her emails and saw that both of her brothers and her sister-in-law had replied to the one she'd sent. Their messages were brief, telling her to have fun, a few details from her oldest brother about her nephew's soccer game. No one mentioned the events of the past few days in Montalcino, for which she was relieved. The news had evidently not made headlines in the States.

She decided to do a little research on the Calaberoni family. She found a few articles in English, enough information to determine that Borelli, as usual, was correct. The family was known in the region as having participated in questionable and sometimes ruthless business practices.

Translating several Italian articles, she pieced together a family tree for Fabrizio. His parents, deceased, his grandfather—the spouse of the grandmother, Flavia, who had raised the boy—also deceased. Father and grandfather, both killed in what Dana was sure were mob hits from rival families. She found no mention of Fabrizio himself and wondered if someone—his grandmother perhaps—had taken great effort to keep the boy out of the press, out of harm's way.

Borelli had not suggested they share what they discovered in Locri with the police, which contributed to the agitation roiling inside her. Was Borelli concerned that the reputation of the Borelli Vineyards would be tarnished should it be discovered they'd hired a son of the Italian Mafia? Even if this had no connection to what had happened in the cellar, or to Fabrizio's being shot? Or was there something else going on?

CHAPTER TWENTY-SEVEN

Unable to sleep, Dana got up before five a.m. Her mind pulsed with a confusing jumble of what she had seen, heard, and learned over the past twenty-four hours—Borelli and Dana's discovery in Locri, then the conversation she'd had with Winkie. The police should be aware of this information. But, first, she needed to talk to Borelli.

She hopped in the shower, dressed, and then sent an email to her brothers, on the chance they'd read something online or reported on the TV news or in print media.

> Don't know if the info on what has happened here in Montalcino at the Borelli Vineyards has come to America yet, but just assuring you I'm fine. Will write later when I know more, but for now, don't mention this to Mom.

Aware that this cryptic message might piss her brothers off, she hesitated for a moment, then hit *send*. At least if they read anything about the recent events, they would know she was okay.

She went down before 7:00, surprised to see Borelli already in the kitchen, filling a thermos with coffee.

Dana asked about his meeting with Renata, how she was doing. When he told her she was doing okay, Dana could see fatigue in the tightness around his eyes. She didn't mention how desperately she'd been attempting to get in touch with him, or how she had barely slept last night. She asked if he'd spoken to Estella about what they had discovered in Locri, and he shot back with a defensive, "Not yet."

Dana remembered in Prague, how Borelli had, quite honestly, slowed things down in their investigation in his attempt to protect a good friend. She wondered if this was exactly what was happening now. She didn't push this thought any further, but instead shared what she'd learned from Winkie. She described the man whom she and Winkie had both seen protesting along the highway.

"It's possible," Borelli said pensively, as if carefully processing the information, "that this might relate to what happened in the cellar. Those involved in environmental concerns have been known to use violent tactics, but generally they take full credit to bring their specific causes to the people through the media."

"When a man dies in the process, when this was not planned or anticipated, they might suppress any claim to avoid being charged for murder." Dana caught a vague nod from Borelli, who was packing a bag with fruit and rolls. "You still want to go to Florence today?" she asked.

"Yes, of course," Borelli answered, handing Dana the bag, tucking the thermos under his arm. "You cannot visit Tuscany without a trip to *Firenze*."

Reluctantly, she followed him out to the garage. There was no sign of Claudio. As they pulled out, Borelli said, "Tell me, did Winkie describe the other man in the conversation?"

"He said he was tall, wearing jeans, a blue or possibly green jacket, a cap."

"That's an ambiguous description, and it could describe half the men in the province of Siena." Borelli poured coffee from the thermos and asked if she'd like a cup. He'd brought more driver friendly cups this trip; but, even at that, Dana would wait, as maneuvering coffee and the manual shift might be more of a challenge than she was up to this morning.

Borelli withdrew a napkin from the bag, arranged it on his lap, then pulled out an orange and offered it to Dana.

"You peel. I'll drive," she replied, then, "Winkie said the older man's jeans looked new. Not faded like the environmentalist's, who was grubby and unkempt, with a scruffy beard and frayed jeans. And Winkie described the older man as having had a sense of authority about him in the way he dressed, in the tone of his voice."

"The mastermind of the plot?" Borelli dug a thumb into the fruit and began to peel off the thick skin. "If indeed this conversation relates to what happened in the cellar."

"Possibly," Dana replied. "Does this description fit Carlo Porcini?"

"Just the opposite. Short, stout. Like a mushroom." Borelli laughed. "New, unfaded jeans? Not Carlo, and hardly something to go looking for. Everything is new at some point," he added flippantly. "I believe it takes some time, a number of washings, for jeans to fade."

Dana doubted Borelli had worn denim in his entire life. She moved on to another thought. "Winkie also overheard them speaking of a woman being involved."

"Young woman? Old woman?" He handed her a slice of orange. "We would need more than that to go on. There are a number of women in Tuscany, too," he said tersely.

Dana slid the orange slice into her mouth and sucked. Even if a woman had been involved in the plot, without more information she knew this fact was not much help. But she couldn't let go of the idea that this conversation had taken place on the Veronesi estate, which was now being offered for sale by the owner, Giovanna Veronesi.

"Something else Winkie overheard," she said, "the protester asked about a payment."

"A payment?" Borelli perked up considerably "If this relates to what happened in the cellar—"

"Someone was paid to release the wine," Dana said, completing his thought.

Borelli nodded. "He's taken this information to the police?"

"He is unwilling to do that," Dana replied, then reluctantly admitted he had asked her to go to the police.

"No, no," Borelli said firmly. "Winkie must share this information. Do you have his phone number?"

"No," Dana admitted with regret. She had not thought to get Winkie's number. *Contact information*, she chastised herself, *always get the contact information*.

Borelli wiped his fingers on his napkin, then pulled out his phone, pressed a number and spoke rapidly. Though she did not understand the Italian, Dana gathered he was leaving a message, as there were no pauses to indicate a two-way conversation.

She threw him a puzzled look. *Did he have Winkie's number?*

"I left a message for Leo," Borelli explained, slipping the phone back in his pocket. "I told him to talk to Alberto DeLuca about the protesters who have been sighted around the vineyards lately, particularly the one you saw."

She shot him a look of concern.

"I didn't say *you* saw him, or mention Winkie," Borelli replied calmly, sensing her apprehension. "I merely said there had been concerns about their aggressiveness. It's likely the police have already questioned these people who might have reason to do harm to the winegrowers. I'll talk to Winkie. He must share this information. It's ridiculous for him to think you should be the one to do it." Borelli motioned for Dana to turn off the highway onto the road to the Veronesi Vineyards, and she realized they were going *now*—to talk to Winkie. Evidently, Borelli had decided this was important enough to dismiss his fears of an encounter with Giovanna Veronesi.

As they started up the hill, then continued along the bumpy road, Dana remembered something else Winkie had said.

"Winkie told me the older man was angry, calling the other man an idiot for breaking the bottled wine."

"Because the old man would not have died," Borelli said, his words slow and measured, "if the glass had not clogged the drain." He gestured for Dana to take a turn onto a side road. "Let's leave the truck here." They parked and got out.

Borelli's eyes darted about as they walked. It was a quiet morning, no other life in sight, except for a chirping bird here and there. About five minutes later they approached the back entrance to the villa, and Borelli knocked on the rough wooden door. Dana wondered if this was the door Borelli had used many years ago while courting the beautiful young Giovanna Veronesi. As she gazed up toward the two upper levels, windows boarded up on the third floor, she imagined a lovesick girl waving down to her Romeo.

They waited some time for an answer. Finally, a distinguished looking man, about Borelli's age, appeared. He was well dressed, well groomed, with a stiff posture. He stared at Father Giovanni Borelli, then greeted him with a *"Buon giorno."* The two simple words came out with a lifting of his chin and more attitude than Dana would have expected. She guessed this man knew the history of the Veronesis and the Borellis. Did he think that Borelli had come to claim his one true love? Oddly, Dana rather liked this possibility.

After an exchange between the two men, the man shut the door firmly, and Borelli motioned to Dana that they were leaving.

"Andrea," Borelli said roughly. "The man never liked me. I think he had an eye on Gia himself. Perhaps he believed her marrying a servant was one step up from marrying a Borelli." He cleared his throat, then coughed. "He said neither Signora Veronesi nor Signor Dalton was available."

"Maybe he was telling the truth." Dana glanced at her watch. It was just half past seven. Most likely they were still asleep.

Borelli didn't bother to reply. He was obviously miffed—she could practically see steam coming out of his nostrils. He motioned back to where they had parked.

In light of what had happened over the past several days, along with new revelations and obstacles, Dana thought Borelli might suggest they cancel their excursion to Florence, but he did not. They spoke little as they got in the truck, and then returned to the highway. Borelli gazed out at the landscape, as Dana increased their speed to keep up with the flow of traffic.

"I have a suggestion," Borelli finally said. "Let's set this all aside for a short time and enjoy the day."

They exchanged glances, no further words. Both of them knew this would be impossible.

CHAPTER TWENTY-EIGHT

Arriving in Florence, they went directly to the Uffizi, where in typical Borelli fashion they bypassed the long lines and went to the entrance where Borelli had prearranged their tour. They spent several hours, lingering before works of Botticelli, Caravaggio, Michelangelo, the priest providing the expected commentary. Later, they crossed the Arno River, strolling over the Ponte Vecchio, the old bridge, lined with shops sparkling with gold jewelry. Crowds of tourists moved slowly, gazing at window displays, or stopping to take pictures of the river and city. Dana thought Borelli might have had an ulterior motive for coming to Florence, but it appeared he truly was attempting to make this trip part of her holiday excursion.

After lunch at a café near Santa Croce, they walked through the piazza and visited the church. Outside again, they stopped to watch a street performer, a man with bushy white hair, wearing dark slacks and vest, a white long-sleeved shirt rolled up to his elbows. A makeshift stage had been constructed in the square, and half a dozen marionettes were posed lifeless, sitting in chairs around a table in front of a curtain. It appeared each of these motionless figures would come to life only as the result of the efforts of the single puppet master. Standing elevated behind the curtain, he began manipulating one of the puppets, a character with a long nose, easily recognized as Pinocchio. The wooden boy danced and cavorted, performing for a small crowd, mostly adult tourists.

A child, about three, dashed across the square, toward the puppets, tripping on the cobblestones, falling, hitting his knee on the hard stones. Blood oozed from the gash as the child wailed. He did not seem to be accompanied by an adult. Dana moved closer, pulling a tissue from her bag. She knelt down by the boy who continued to sob. Making eye contact, she held out the tissue, not wanting to frighten him by touching him. From behind she heard a voice, and then a young woman was beside Dana, wrapping the sobbing child in her arms. Dana handed the tissue to the mother who dabbed the boy's knee, blotting the blood even as she attempted to draw his attention away from his injury as the puppet master moved one of his marionettes closer to the boy in an effort to do just the same. Within moments the child was laughing.

The mother turned to Dana. *"Grazie, grazie,"* she said.

"Prego," Dana replied.

As she watched the boy and mother, now enjoying the marionettes, Dana felt a fierce stab to her heart.

After the performance, both she and Borelli placed some coins in the puppet master's hat as he made his way through the crowd.

They started out of the piazza. As they walked, Dana thought of the morning, just a few days ago, when they had dabbed the blood off of Mia's legs. *Poor motherless child*, she thought. Then her thoughts turned inward. *Poor childless mother*. Dana would have done anything to protect her own child, and yet she had lost him. She had not protected him. One night he simply vanished.

She thought then of Fabrizio, the morning she and Borelli had seen him in Montalcino with his friends when he'd swaggered over to speak to them. Such a handsome, confident young man. Then the night Mia had found him, soaked in blood, a broken arrow protruding from his strong, young body, as he clung tenuously to life.

"You okay?" Borelli asked.

Dana glanced at him, realizing they hadn't spoken since they'd left the Santa Croce Piazza, that they were now approaching the Duomo. She had been so deeply into her thoughts, it was as if she had disappeared. Perhaps he had also sunk inward, replaying what had taken place over the past few days. Though they had agreed to clear their minds to enjoy this time, such an effort was impossible.

"Something about seeing the little boy hurt, his crying," she said. "Sometimes something so small, something that will soon be forgotten and heal quickly, brings up—my own child." The words came out much easier than she would have imagined.

Borelli knew the story. She had told him one evening in Prague.

She had replayed the events of the day before Joel had disappeared, over and over in her head trying to find something, a detail missed. And she had repeated the story more than she could bear to the police officers in the days after. Then for years she barely spoke of it.

They were visiting her mother at the time. It was Easter. Joel was only three. It was nine years ago. He had simply disappeared during the night. He was sharing a room with one of his cousins. There were no clues. Cold case, they called it. He had never been found. No body. No closure, as trite and painful as the saying had become.

"One thought triggered another," Dana said quietly. "I thought of Mia. How sad for her to grow up without her mother."

Father Borelli said nothing as if he wished Dana to continue. This was something she liked about him. At times he talked too much, but he seemed to know when to remain silent. As a priest, he could easily offer something. Words about God's will. About a higher plan. She appreciated that he did not.

"Then I thought of poor Fabrizio," she continued. "Raised by his grandmother, who surely loves him. And I was thinking— you know a mother would do anything to protect her child." She glanced at Borelli who silently nodded in agreement. "A grandmother, too."

Dana thought of her own mother, her son's grandmother. Joel had disappeared while they were visiting Dana's mom. Dana knew her mother carried an overwhelming sense of guilt, as did Dana. They had not protected this precious child. This common, yet separate, guilt had created not a connection, but a rift between Dana and her mom. And a constant fear. Her mother's fear that Dana, too, was out in the world without protection.

"A mother. A grandmother," she said, voice low. "She would do anything to protect her child, her grandchild. And, I believe this is exactly why Fabrizio has come to the Borelli Vineyards. His grandmother's desire to protect him."

"From the only life that would be his if he remained in Locri," Borelli said. "A life, which if he were to continue would most surely result in constant threats. A legacy of crime, possibly his own death." They had stopped walking and stood now in the Piazza del Duomo, the Cathedral of Santa Maria del Fiore hovering above them. The piazza was crowded with tourists, and yet they were alone in conversation, the two of them.

"His grandfather, his father," Dana said, turning to Borelli. "Both murdered."

Again, Borelli agreed, not in words, but something in his eyes, across the set of his mouth.

"It is a mother's wish that her child finds happiness," Dana said, "a productive, rewarding life. And what better and more honorable pursuit in Italy than making wine."

"So simple an explanation," Borelli replied. "Keeping this secret makes sense. I have no doubt that Estella would agree not to reveal anything about Fabrizio's family. Even as a child, Estella was an accomplished keeper of secrets." His mouth curved as if recalling a memory. "I was usually able to get it out of her. But, I knew if I told her a secret, she could be depended upon to keep it."

"Do you think Leo knows? About Fabrizio's family. His family connection?"

"I have no idea," Borelli said, motioning. They began to walk again. "To be honest with you, sometimes Leo seems to exist in his own little world."

"Has he always been like this?" Dana agreed that sometimes Leo seemed to be far, far away, detached from what was going on around him. Oblivious to his own daughter.

"Not so much, as I recall, though you must understand I have spent most of my adult life away from home. But, noticeable with Leo, after his wife, Teresa, became ill. Four years ago. Her diagnosis came during the harvest season. Leo spent months with her in Rome for treatments, chemotherapy, and she did well for a while. Then two years later, also during the harvest, we lost her."

"This must be a painful time of year for him," Dana said in a low voice. Joel's disappearance on Easter made this holiday unbearable for her.

"Yes," Borelli said. "Before this great loss, Leo seemed to be much more involved in life, in the business. Now he spends his time in the office, his efforts put toward marketing, distribution, which in this modern age is a full-time job." Borelli bit down on his lip, scratched his balding head. "Leo's wife loved the production aspect of the business, the vineyards, the cellars. She had a natural ability to taste the wine. To smell the wine. To discern. Maybe it was too much for Leo after she passed. Yes, I think that is when he became detached. Leo himself was quite ill at one time. Fighting an infection as I understand. Not life threatening, but it set him back. I'm not sure at what point Marco took over the process of the winemaking completely. Paolo, the younger Paolo, always handled the agricultural aspects, the grapes."

"But you said the younger Paolo, Renata's husband, passed away."

"Yes."

"So, who is doing that now?"

"For a short time, Marco was doing it all. He hired a new viticulturist."

Dana remembered they'd been briefly introduced to the viticulturist by Marco during the vineyard tour. No, actually they had just run into him during the vineyard tour, but Marco had made no formal introduction. "How did Paolo die?"

"Suicide."

"How sad." Dana thought of poor Renata, losing her husband to suicide, then her father-in-law to murder, perhaps an unintended murder. "Was it?" She stopped and met Borelli's eyes.

"Was it what?"

"Do you think it was suicide?"

"I wasn't living here at the time, but I was called home."

"To bury him?"

"The local parish priest refused. Suicide has long been held in the Catholic Church as the final, great mortal sin. Taking one's own life is a serious rejection of God's love and mercy."

"You didn't believe it was suicide?"

"I had no reason to think differently, but I believe every man, and every woman, is entitled to a Christian burial. No one, save for God himself, knows what goes through a person's broken mind to motivate him to take his own life. It is not for you or I, or anyone, to judge another."

"You're a good man, Borelli," Dana said softly.

"That, too," he said lightly, "is for God to judge."

As they drove out of Florence and onto the highway, Dana considered what Borelli had said about Leo. She'd certainly noticed a detachment. Dana knew all too well how loss and grief could take one away from life, sadly away from those who needed you, those who remained. Her grief over her own loss had been so severe her marriage had not survived. Maybe it would not have survived under happier circumstances either. In Prague she had found something. She herself had almost lost her life, and she'd realized how much she had wanted to live, something at times she had doubted before. Though she'd never considered suicide, at times her life had felt meaningless.

Borelli had been there. In Prague. Maybe this was what had connected the two. Borelli had also had a life-altering event touch his life in the city of Prague.

They spoke little as they continued toward Montalcino. Dana knew Borelli thought her theory about how Fabrizio had come to the Borelli Vineyards to learn the trade was valid. But many questions remained unanswered, and she was well aware that she and Borelli were not ready to let any of this go.

"Will you take me to the police?" Dana asked. "To pass on the information that Winkie shared with me?"

Borelli gave this more thought than Dana felt he should. She didn't want to go alone.

"Winkie must share this information," Borelli said firmly.

"Maybe if we visit at a more reasonable hour," Dana suggested.

"The vigil for Paolo is this evening," Borelli replied. "Tomorrow after the funeral, I will go with you to speak with Winkie."

As they continued on, Dana picked up speed, thinking Borelli was in a hurry to get back and prepare for the evening vigil, that this was the reason they would not go to see Winkie now, yet when they got close to Montalcino, he directed her to take an alternate route. They turned at a sign for the *ospedale*. The hospital.

"We're going to visit Fabrizio?" Dana asked. "Mia and Leo both said only family members were allowed to visit."

"Perhaps they will allow a priest," Borelli said.

Dana wondered if Fabrizio was well enough to answer questions for the police, who seemed convinced that they had arrested the man who shot him.

At the hospital, she followed Borelli up to the front desk to ask for directions to Fabrizio's room. Though Dana could not understand the words passed back and forth between Borelli and the receptionist, she could see the woman was uncomfortable with his request. Her fingers moved anxiously along a register, and then a keyboard, her eyes jumping up, blinking nervously as she scanned a computer screen. The agitation seemed to transfer to Borelli. His voice was growing louder, more demanding. Finally, he turned and motioned for Dana to follow him.

"He's not here," Borelli said.

"What? He's been released?"

"She was not particularly forthcoming with information." Borelli stomped through the lobby, speaking louder than one normally would in a hospital. A woman sitting, checking her cellphone, looked up with alarm.

Lowering his volume, Borelli explained, "She was unable to find a patient under that name. As if he had never been here. Hopefully, he is still alive." Borelli hurried with heavy footsteps toward the exit.

Dana followed. "Maybe Inspector DeLuca thinks there is some danger, a continuing threat to Fabrizio, and had him secretly moved."

"Possibly."

They were about to leave the building when Dana noticed a girl, sitting in the lobby alone, hand pressed to her forehead, shoulders quivering, long dark hair streaked with red obscuring her face. When she looked up, Dana could see it was the girl she and Borelli had seen with Fabrizio, the same girl she and Mia had seen with Silvio. She sniffed and wiped her eyes, then her nose.

Dana tried to recall her name. *Elena?* Yes, Elena Moretti. "That's Elena," she told Borelli. "Silvio's girlfriend."

Borelli's eyes darted through the lobby as he started toward the girl, Dana at his side. As they approached, Dana said softly, "Elena?"

The girl looked up, eyes wide, rimmed with red. Dana could see she was puzzled that this stranger knew her name. Then, glancing from Dana to Borelli, then back to Dana, a flicker of recognition crossed her face.

In Italian, Borelli said words that even Dana could understand—"We are friends."

The priest sat next to the girl, who said little at first, but then opened up, words flowing freely, even as she rubbed her eyes, wiped her nose with the back of her hand. Borelli spoke to her in a kind reassuring voice. From his inflection, Dana guessed he was asking questions. The man could be a master of inquiry. His tone remained calm and unthreatening.

After several minutes, Borelli patted the girl's shoulder, sat silently for a moment, then rose. Dana followed him out to the parking lot.

"Please translate," she requested.

"At first she was incoherent. Blubbering. Babbling. She said he's disappeared. No one knows where he is, and she is afraid he's been murdered. Elena said it was her fault. That she and Silvio had a fight and she was trying to make him jealous."

"By flirting with Fabrizio?"

Borelli nodded. "And then she told me that she and Silvio had worked it out. They were back together."

"And she blames herself for Silvio shooting Fabrizio."

"Not for shooting Fabrizio, but for being blamed for shooting Fabrizio. She said he would never do that." They got in the truck.

"The police have obviously identified the arrow as Silvio's," Dana said as she started the motor.

"I asked her about that, and she told me that he often lost arrows while practicing. They've set up a target range against the hillside near the olive orchard on the estate where Silvio's father works. Elena said she's gone out with him on occasion. They always looked for arrows in the orchard. After a while, if they couldn't find them, they would give up."

"So, someone could have found one of the arrows and used it to shoot Fabrizio and put the blame on Silvio."

"That's what she claimed."

"I find that difficult to believe," Dana countered as they pulled onto the highway. "If Silvio is such an ace shot, he'd be, at the least, hitting the target, if not the bullseye each time. He wouldn't be losing arrows in the orchard."

"Very good, Ms. Pierson. Unless he enjoyed taking Signorina Moretti out into the olive orchard." Borelli grinned, and then continued, "I asked her just that, and she said that often when they went out to shoot, Silvio would let her try her luck."

"I see. And, she wasn't the greatest shot." Dana could visualize the girl, her thin, youthful figure erect, her slender arm, pulling back on the bowstring, arm stretched, arrow fletched, Silvio leaning in close, his arms wrapped around her, guiding, teaching. The arrow flinging forward, missing the target, dropping too soon, or zipping quickly into the depths of the orchard, into the deep dark forest, never to be found, even after repeated attempts by the young lovers to locate the lost arrows. "Silvio is being framed for shooting Fabrizio. Whoever shot him wanted the police to believe this was related to a love triangle, not to what happened in the cellar."

Borelli nodded in agreement.

On the ride back to the estate, Borelli pulled out his phone and made a call. He carried on a short conversation in which Dana caught the names, Francesco, Fabrizio, DeLuca. She gathered he was speaking to his friend, retired police officer Francesco Treponti.

Finishing the conversation, Borelli said to Dana, "Francesco told me the word going around is that Fabrizio disappeared from the hospital during the night. It appears the grandmother has disappeared, too. There's talk of both having been abducted or murdered. No wonder the woman at the reception desk was nervous."

"Do you think his sources are good?"

"I'm not sure," Borelli said with concern.

"If Inspector DeLuca has anything on the ball, he knows Silvio didn't shoot Fabrizio, and someone might still have good reason to get rid of him. The police might have moved him for his safety."

"Yes," Borelli agreed again. "There are several possibilities why Fabrizio and his grandmother might have disappeared."

CHAPTER TWENTY-NINE

Both of Dana's brothers had responded to her email messages. With the time difference between Boston and Italy, a real-time back and forth email conversation was difficult. She could see they had each responded hours after she'd sent the email early that morning.

Her younger brother Ben wrote that he would need more information to determine what it was he shouldn't mention to their mom.

Her older brother Jeff said he was troubled by her confusing, non-informational email, so he googled Borelli Vineyards, found a recent online article in Italian, and used a translation program. The article was attached to his email.

Dana scanned the translated article, realizing it was the one that had first appeared in the Italian news. Quotes from DeLuca about the cellar destruction, the old man's death, as well as Leo's quotes on the value of the wine, but nothing about Fabrizio.

"Please respond," Jeff wrote. "Pammie and I are concerned. Can you call?"

Dana knew it was now afternoon in Boston. She could probably catch Jeff at his office, but she didn't think the loaned cellphone she'd been using was set up for international calls.

She hit *reply* and typed, "Hey, just want to let you know I'm fine. I see you've read about what's happening here at the Borelli Vineyards. Otherwise, I'm having a great time!" She thought about adding a smiley face, but decided that wouldn't be appreciated. "I'm not in danger. It's late here. I'll email more tomorrow."

Within minutes, she received a reply from Jeff.

"Maybe you should head home," he suggested.

"What? And interrupt my vacation?"

"Knowing you, Dana, and knowing about your collaboration with Father Borelli in Prague," a message came back, "I seriously doubt you're spending your time sightseeing."

"We spent the day doing just that in Florence," she replied.

"Let the police figure this out."

"I'm fine," she wrote. "Really. Mom doesn't know what's going on, does she?"

"You know she still gets her news from *The Globe*, the print version, and there's nothing there." Dana could almost see and hear him take in a deep breath.

"Well, thank goodness someone still reads a newspaper."

"I'll keep an eye on what's reported here. Be careful."

"Give Pammie and the kids my love. Please call Ben, let him know I'm fine."

"Keep us informed."

"Will do."

The next day, the morning of Paolo Paluzzi's funeral, Dana found coffee and an assortment of bread set out in the kitchen for breakfast. Lala and a stout, middle-aged woman were busy preparing a lunch for those who would attend the services in the family chapel that morning.

"Prego," Lala said, motioning for Dana to help herself to coffee and bread.

"Grazie." Dana grabbed a cup of coffee, added warm milk, then placed a roll on a plate and stepped outside onto the patio adjacent to the private gardens. The chill in the air swept through her, but she wanted to stay out of the way of Lala and her helper and also have a quiet, private place to think. She placed the plate and coffee on the small wrought iron table and pulled out a cushioned chair where she would have the best view of the landscape. She cradled the warm mug in her hands and looked out toward the garden and the backdrop of Tuscan hills. Previously she'd looked out on this vista only through the kitchen window, and this shift in viewpoint presented a different perspective. In the distance, she could see a large three-story medieval building, and she realized it was the Veronesi villa. From where she sat it looked majestic and imposing, not rundown and falling apart like it had up close.

She thought of Giovanna Veronesi and Borelli's reaction to the possibility of seeing this woman. Dana wanted to know more about Giovanna. Borelli had obviously been in love with her, and Dana was curious about this ill-fated match.

She pictured Winkie pedaling vigorously on the old dilapidated bike. Darn, she should have asked for his cellphone number. Though Borelli had offered to accompany her later that afternoon to convince Winkie to go to the police, Dana felt an urgency that caused her stomach to turn.

As she sat sipping her coffee, the door from the kitchen opened and Dana turned to see Mia step out. She wore a mid-calf, long-sleeved, black dress. Her thick, dark hair was pulled back in a barrette.

"Buon giorno," she greeted Dana in a quiet voice as if they were sitting in church. "It's a beautiful morning." Mia gazed up at the sky, which was clear, save for a few wispy clouds floating high above the horizon.

Mia pulled out a chair and sat. Dana wondered if she knew about

Fabrizio's disappearance from the hospital.

"There will be a small family group this morning, a few employees," Mia explained. "Zio Giovanni believes your prayers would be appreciated, but it is up to you whether you wish to attend. We will then go to the cemetery for—" Mia bit down on her lip, and Dana didn't know if she was searching for the proper English word or attempting to hold back the tears. Dana reached out and touched the girl's hand, and Mia offered a small appreciative smile in response. "A lunch will be served in the dining room after we return from the cemetery, so it will be a late lunch," she continued formally.

Borelli had shared most of this on the ride home from the hospital last night. He'd gone directly from the villa to the family vigil in town. He explained that he probably wouldn't see Dana until later the following day, as he would spend time after the burial and lunch with Renata and her family. Dana had eaten dinner alone, feeling the vigil too intimate for anyone other than family and close friends. She'd never met Paolo. She planned on attending the funeral, only if there was room for her in the small chapel, but she didn't feel it would be proper for her to be included in the lunch. Paolo's family wouldn't even know who she was.

"Thank you," she told Mia.

After several long moments, Mia said, "My mother's services were at the church in Montalcino. She had many friends. The chapel would not have been large enough to hold them all."

"She was much loved," Dana said.

"Yes," Mia replied with the saddest smile. "Sometimes I have a difficult time remembering her—how she looked, how her voice sounded."

Again, Dana touched Mia's hand. She, too, knew how these physical details would slip, even as you tried desperately to hold them close. She didn't think she would ever forget the sound of Joel's voice, the way he giggled. His pale blond hair, his soft skin, that even at three had an innocent, baby-like smell. But sometimes she could not pull up these memories. And then, often she thought of how his voice might sound now. His laugh. Not a little boy giggle, but the hearty, or perhaps shy, laugh of a pre-teen. And his hair most likely would have turned a darker shade as he grew, like Dana's, like her brothers'.

She thought of Leo's comments about raising a strong-willed teen. Would Joel have grown to be a strong-willed boy? She hoped he would. Only in her mind could she make him grow older.

The clouds had billowed and were moving across the sky, creating a crisscross pattern of light and dark green on the hills, rows of vines running in opposite angles to the strips of shadows created by the clouds. Dana could see from the touches of gold and orange that some of the vines were beginning to turn.

"I must go now," Mia said, releasing Dana's hand, standing.

"I'll only enter the chapel if there is room. The lunch, maybe it should be just for family and close friends? I'll see you this evening." She wished she could be there for Mia. But, the girl had her family.

"Yes, I understand," Mia said, then bent to kiss Dana on each cheek before she left.

Dana took her cup and plate to the kitchen, thanked Lala and her helper, and returned to her room, slipped on her new skirt and one of her blouses that was neutral enough for a funeral. Then she went down, lingering in the hallway as half a dozen people she didn't recognize filed into the chapel. After a while, she stepped inside. The chapel was very small with only eight wooden benches, four on each side of the aisle. The back pews were full, the front two were empty, saved for family. In the third pew, she spotted Claudio and Marco Dardi, wearing the same well-tailored suit he'd worn to dinner. A woman sat by his side. *His wife?* It hadn't crossed Dana's mind that he might be married. In her semi-romantic imaginings, she hadn't imagined a wife.

Even sitting, the woman appeared to be on the plumpish side, not what she would have envisioned for Marco, if she had in fact envisioned Marco with a wife. He had not brought her to dinner at the restaurant in Montalcino. Maybe this had been considered a business obligation. But, Dana had been invited and she had nothing to do with the family business. Had it been completely in her mind that he had been flirting with her? He'd been attentive to Octavia, too. Some men were like that. Flirting with every woman they encountered. The woman leaned into him, and he put his arm around her.

Seeing Marco stirred up thoughts that Dana realized were hardly appropriate for a funeral. Was she attracted to married men because it was safe? No possibility of commitment. In Prague, she'd been half in love with the married detective that she and Borelli had worked with. Maybe her mother was right—Dana surrounded herself with unavailable men.

Then unexpected and unbidden, her mind looped back in time to her failed marriage. Andrew Monaghan. Drew. A vow, spoken in church, a promise that was supposed to last forever. After their loss, a loss they had shared, but a pain they were unable to share, Dana had sunk into herself, while Drew had reached outside of the marriage.

Forcefully, she pushed these thoughts from her head as Father Borelli appeared, a solemn spiritual leader in his black vestments, attended by two servers, a boy about eight or nine, another several years older, both still young enough to look like angelic choir boys in their black cassocks and white surplices. They were followed by six sturdy men, slowly and somberly supporting the shiny wooden casket as they moved down the aisle. Renata followed, grasping the arm of a woman who looked like she could be her sister. Another man and woman, perhaps family, maybe Renata's brother and wife, walked directly behind them. At the back of the procession, Estella, looking thin and drawn, grasped tightly to Leo's arm. Mia was on his other side, proceeding erect and brave, her face showing no emotion.

Leo stood close to his mother as if to prop her up, rising, kneeling, standing as the ceremony progressed. Dana could see he was more concerned about his mother than his daughter. Those who put on the braver face are sometimes ignored, Dana considered as Marco's description of the Sangiovese grape came to her again—*thickly skinned, but so delicate, the fruit.*

About ten minutes into the service, she sensed someone standing beside her and shifted her gaze to see Inspector DeLuca, his eyes scanning the interior of the chapel. He nodded at her, running a finger over his thick, white, broom-like mustache. She wondered if he was searching the crowd, looking for the killer, like a cop in a movie. And then she noticed, his eyes focused on Leo and Estella, and did not waver.

As Dana, too, gazed at Leo, attempting to comfort his mother, she realized that he might fit the description that Winkie had given of the second man in the conversation he'd overheard. Then she thought of what Borelli had told her about the substantial capital investments reducing the businesses profits over the past few years. She thought about Octavia asking Leo about the insurance.

She glanced again at DeLuca, wishing she could pull every thought from his mind and compare them to those that were running through hers. Should she follow him out and tell him about the conversation she'd had with Winkie? She wondered if the police had removed Fabrizio from the hospital, or if he was still there, under a protective eye. Or dead.

Father Borelli's deep, gravelly voice echoed through the small chapel. Though Dana could not understand the Italian, there was a comforting rhythm in his words. As he spoke, Borelli maintained eye contact with those closest to Paolo in the front pew, and Dana knew that he preached from his heart. There was no hint of what she had come to think of as Borelli's *pulpit voice* with its self-important, listen-to-me tone.

The police inspector had slipped out. Dana wondered if he was headed to the cemetery.

The mourners filed out of the church. Marco escorted the woman down the aisle. His eyes met Dana's briefly as he offered a quick nod of recognition, but nothing in his expression that she could read. Nothing to say, *sorry I didn't mention the wife* or *I like you, I really like you.*

The funeral procession, the hearse, and several cars filled with mourners left the estate for the burial and graveside services.

When everyone had departed, Dana went up to her room and changed into her jeans and walking shoes, grabbed her bag and went out. She knew she had several hours before she and Borelli could get together and visit Winkie with the intention of convincing him to go to the police, but she felt an urgency. She headed to the garage, passing two parked vehicles, a man she recognized as one of the officers who had been inside the house the night she and Mia had gone to Fabrizio's cottage. No one stopped her or questioned her.

She hoped she would find the garage unlocked. She didn't think Borelli would mind if she borrowed his truck. She'd been driving it for the better part of the week. The building was locked.

She wondered how far the Veronesi estate was from where she stood now. She guessed the actual distance—a straight shot from here to there—was much closer than the drive down to the main highway then up the road to the Veronesi villa. The house could be seen from certain areas of the Borelli estate, particularly the spot where she'd sat that morning in the garden. Walking would certainly be possible, though getting there would be much quicker if one had a vehicle, which she did not.

She started over the first hill, taking the path that ran alongside the nearest vineyard, circled around, then down into a dip. Soon she came across a grove of trees, a mini forest. Not olive trees, nothing that would produce a crop, but oak trees, starting to turn, adding beauty to the landscape. She stopped several times to rest. Now and then, she'd catch a glimpse of the top of the tall, three-story Veronesi villa, and then it would disappear completely. When it reappeared, it seemed as though it was getting farther away, rather than closer.

The wispy clouds of the morning had thickened and darkened, and she was soon staring up toward a threatening sky, ready to pour down on her at any moment. She hoped that the services at the cemetery had finished, that the family had returned to the house for lunch. She felt a drop fall, then another. She had slipped on a sweater when she went back to her room to put on her jeans, but it would provide little protection if the rain got any heavier.

Which it did within minutes. Some distance ahead, she saw a cluster of buildings. She hurried toward them. As she got closer, she saw they were rundown, possibly abandoned. One, from the large vehicle-sized doors, looked like a garage, the other possibly a wine cellar, though this seemed an odd location as she hadn't seen any vines for some time now.

She tested the door. It was unlocked and she hurried inside, closing it quickly behind her. As her eyes adjusted to the dim light, she saw it wasn't a cellar, but a facility that had been used to bottle wine or possibly just to store supplies. Several empty bottles, in the required dark green Bordeaux glass, sat on a shelf under a broken window, which let in enough light that she could make out a layer of dust on both bottles and shelves. She scanned the area. Flat cardboard packing boxes sat on another shelf, next to a small container of corks, many broken or falling apart from age and deterioration.

She found an old wooden crate, similar to those she'd seen in the display windows in shops in Montalcino. After testing it for sturdiness, swiping away a thick cobweb, she sat to wait out the storm. The rain slapped on the roof and Dana saw it was leaking at a far corner. Her eyes bounced around the interior, noticing more crates, faded black stenciled letters on the sides of several. She stood and examined the box she was using as a stool. She was surprised to see the stenciled words—Veronesi Vineyards—and realized she had crossed over onto Veronesi land, though she had not scaled over or ducked under any fences. She walked over to the window on the opposite side from where she'd approached the building, gazing out through the foggy glass, moisture trapped between two panes. A short distance away she saw what looked as if it could have been a productive area at one time. Vines stood, darkened by the recent rain, overgrown, unpruned.

The rain continued to fall, though it sounded as if it had let up. She'd sit a while longer just to make sure.

When finally the rain subsided to a slow, low pitter-patter, enough that she felt it would be safe to continue without getting drenched, she stepped over to the door and pulled it open. About to go out, she hesitated at the sound of a car motor. She gazed down the rutted road, damp from the rain. An older model Volvo made its way toward the abandoned buildings. It stopped in front of the garage. She could make out the silhouette of a man, sitting in the car, head tilted at an angle as if reading something. Or possibly staring down at his phone.

Shortly, the motor revved again and the Volvo pulled forward. From the window, Dana could no longer see the vehicle, but she heard the motor turn off, the car door open, then shut, and she could tell it was close. The door on the building rattled, then it opened, revealing an outline of a man in a shaft of dim, damp light. Why would someone be coming here to an old abandoned building? Suddenly, she thought of what Winkie had told her about seeing the two men and the description he'd given of the location. She sensed it would be unwise for the man to see her.

Quickly, she ducked and crawled quietly to the nearest cover, under a bench just a few feet from the wall, next to a large rack. The building was dark enough that she hoped he wouldn't see her, that the electricity had been turned off, that he wouldn't flip on a light.

The man stepped deeper into the room. Though she could not make out the details of his face, she saw that he wore a familiar tam and sported a scruffy beard. The environmental protester!

He hurried over to a desk in the far corner, slid out a drawer, yanked out what appeared to be a false bottom, pulled out an envelope. Letting out a yelp of delight, he flipped through the envelope's content, counting out loud. *Uno, due, tre.* Dana could see he was counting money. He stuffed it in the pocket of his long, hooded jacket. Dana took in a deep ragged, nervous breath, and held it, praying he would not turn and see her. Hopefully, he had found what he'd come for and would leave.

She was sure now that this was where Winkie had overheard the conversation, outside this building. Two men arguing. Dana wondered if the other man, the one calling the shots as Winkie had interpreted it, was meeting the man here again. Or, had he already been here and delivered the money now in the man's pocket? This was the payment the men had spoken of. When she heard another motor, she bit her lip and covered her mouth.

Shouts erupted from outside. The man in the hooded jacket jerked around, stood as if paralyzed, then darted toward the back door. More shouting. Suddenly the back door opened, quickly, loudly, men yelling, the protester pivoting, taking off toward the front door just feet from where Dana hid. A shot went off. She couldn't see anything now, dust flying. More shouts. She did not understand the words, but she knew they were telling the man to stop. Another shot. One more.

Shit! What should she do?

Another man entered. Dana could make out the heavy profile of Inspector DeLuca. An officer wrestled with the downed man, both rolling on the filthy floor. Within seconds the man was cuffed. Dana could see he was shot, blood seeping onto the dusty floorboards, visible now by the misty light coming through the opened door of the building. They dragged him outside. Dana's heart thumped wildly. One of the recently arrived officers glanced around the inside of the building as Dana attempted to put together words in her mind. What would she say if they found her? She doubted they would believe the truth—that she was out walking and had stepped inside to get out of the rain. She thought about the plan that she and Borelli had made to go talk to Winkie Dalton. She prayed the police would not find her here, crouched down behind a stack of benches and boxes.

The building was soon empty, but sounds, vehicles, shouting continued outside. Dana remained hidden, listening as car doors opened, slammed shut, motors revved. She didn't move, barely breathed. She would wait until she was sure there was no one outside.

Minutes ticked by slowly, and then cautiously, quietly she made her way over to the window on her knees, keeping low. A bird chirped cheerfully from outside, but she heard nothing more. Lifting her head enough to peer through the window, she gazed out. The sun had worked its way through parting clouds. The dirt road was damp and muddy in spots. No evidence of police, protesters, or vehicles. She took in a deep breath, coughing now at the intake of dusty air. Fearing she might collapse, she remained kneeling, holding her hand to her chest as if she could slow the rapid beat of her heart. Finally, she pulled herself up, legs cramped. She crept over to the desk with awkward, unsure steps. She stared at the drawer where the man had found the cash and wondered if it was already in the officer's hands. Glancing around the dim room she made out what looked like a frayed towel hanging on a rack next to a sink in a corner of the room. She stepped cautiously across the room and grabbed the towel, stiff and dusty, then back to the desk and wrapped the cloth around her right hand, not wanting to leave fingerprints. Slowly she opened the drawer from which the man had extracted the cash. Empty. She lifted the false bottom. Nothing. She was sure the money the man had taken from the drawer was a payoff for his part in the wine destruction. Obviously, the police had come here to apprehend him.

She was grateful they had not discovered her here in the abandoned building on the Veronesi estate, but she would definitely go to the police now. She wondered again if Giovanna Veronesi had been involved. Could she have been the woman the two men spoke of?

Just as she slid the drawer back in, the door tore open. Dana turned and gasped. Alberto DeLuca stood before her holding a gun pointed directly at her. She would not have to go to the police. They had come to her.

CHAPTER THIRTY

Winkie, Giovanna, and Raffaelo Sabatini strolled together down to the local branch of Giovanna's Rome-based bank after lunch in Montalcino. The money from Winkie's Italian account, set up several months earlier, had been successfully transferred to the Veronesi Vineyards' account.

Winslow Antonio Dalton was now the official owner of his own Tuscan vineyard and winery. He knew there was much work ahead, but he hadn't been this excited about anything in years, and he was eager to get started.

Giovanna had told him at breakfast that morning that she accepted his offer and invited him to lunch that day in Montalcino. When they met Raffaelo Sabatini in town, Winkie gathered, from the attorney's distant demeanor, that he had advised her against accepting the offer, as other prospective buyers were still looking at the property. But Winkie could see that Giovanna was as pleased as he himself. This was a decision she had made from her heart. Was it possible she knew?

Driving back with Giovanna to the villa, after having said their farewells to Raffaelo, Winkie felt the muscles around his mouth stretching into a smile so broad his face ached. He glanced at Giovanna but he could not read her expression, and then he noticed a tear slip down her cheek.

What a bittersweet time this must be for her. The home where she had grown up. A business that had been in the family for centuries. Yet, he, Winkie Dalton, had rescued the family business. The Veronesi Vineyards would continue to produce; the family label would not die.

She turned to him and said, *"Grazie,"* even as she brushed the back of her hand across her cheek. Then she smiled and said it again. "*Grazie* for coming."

He should speak to her now, reveal why he was here, now that they were alone, confined within the moving vehicle, papers signed, money transferred. He had been both dreading and looking forward to this day, but suddenly now that the time had come, he found himself unable to speak. Just as he was forming the words in his head, words he had rehearsed for years, an uncomfortable lump lodging deep in his throat, a dark vehicle passed them. Winkie glanced over and saw in a quick flash, the face of a woman in the back seat, caged, behind a grate. Was he imagining, hallucinating? The vehicle passed so quickly, he doubted he could see what he thought he saw. He glanced at Giovanna who stared straight ahead, eyes on the road.

As they turned off the highway, headed toward the Veronesi villa, Winkie tried to dismiss what he thought he had seen. But the image would not leave him. Had guilt conjured this image? Guilt that he'd barely considered until now. The woman was Dana. The vehicle, possibly the dark car that had come up to the house his first evening. Even then, in the waning light, he thought the two men who emerged looked like police officers.

As they pulled up in front of the villa, Winkie knew there was something else he must do before returning home.

"May I borrow your car?" he asked Giovanna.

Her expression was both stunned and confused. "What's going on?"

"I'm not sure, but there is something I need to take care of."

She sat quietly, pensive for some time and then she said, "If I can trust you with my vineyards, my winery, my home, everything I have held dear, yes, I believe I can trust you with my Mercedes. But, you must return it. This wasn't part of the deal. Please, an old woman is certainly entitled to one remaining indulgence."

Dana was patted down, her bag, which amazingly she hadn't lost in the confusion and activity, was confiscated, and she was shown into a small, dark interrogation room. Stark grey walls. A plain rectangular table with nothing on it. One stiff wooden chair on one side—where Dana was forcefully directed to sit, an officer clutching her by the upper arm—two identical chairs on the other side. One occupied by Inspector DeLuca, the other by the thin-faced woman who had acted as interpreter the night Dana was questioned after she and Mia had gone to Fabrizio's cottage. The woman stared across the table at Dana, then cleared her throat. A musty smell permeated the room, yet at the same time, the confined space reeked of cleaning chemicals and perhaps a human odor, the sweat of a guilty party. Or someone innocent, like Dana. She felt the moisture on her forehead and reached up to brush aside her hair.

"You are an American?" the woman said in English.

"Yes."

"What is the purpose of your visit?"

"Holiday. Visiting friends." Dana had answered all of these questions before, in one of the two interviews she'd already sat through. A third interview now and Dana was beginning to feel as if she were a suspect. She knew this wasn't good, and she had the feeling that this was a more serious interrogation. The chief himself was presiding, aided by the translator in a dark suit and starched white blouse, her posture and demeanor stiff. DeLuca himself looked like he'd been wearing the same wrinkled suit for the five days since the investigation had begun.

"Why were you in the building this morning?" the interpreter asked.

"To get out of the rain."

A quick verbal exchange between the interpreter and inspector, who brushed his thick mustache with his fingers as they spoke. The woman leaned in closer and stared into Dana's eyes.

"What brought you to that particular place?"

Dana explained about the funeral, which the inspector was fully aware of because he'd stood next to her in the back of the chapel.

"I had the afternoon free, the Borelli family members were attending the graveside services, and then a lunch at the villa, so I decided to go for a walk."

"In the rain?"

"It wasn't raining when I started."

"That is a considerable distance from where you are staying," the interpreter said, apparently on her own volition.

"Is that a question?" Dana asked, and then wished she hadn't.

The interpreter conferred again with the police inspector. "Did you see anyone enter or come out of any of the buildings?"

Dana didn't want to lie—it wasn't as though she were under oath, but she'd heard some frightening things about the Italian judicial system. They seemed to be treating her as a witness, not a suspect. Yet, she wasn't sure. Maybe they thought she was meeting the man there, the environmental protester whose name she didn't even know. She wondered if the police had had this man on their radar all along. Did they think she had something to do with the money waiting in the desk? She was sure they had searched the man and found the cash. Then DeLuca had seen her closing the drawer of the desk. He'd ushered her out of the building without words, gun in her ribs, and walked her down the road about a quarter of a mile to where an unmarked car sat waiting for them.

Dana sat quietly, thinking she should probably shut up, say no more. But, this might make her look guilty. Guilty of what? Did the police think she'd placed the money in the drawer?

Now, she wished she'd contacted the police immediately after Winkie told her about the overheard conversation. She shouldn't have gone to Florence with Borelli, shouldn't have agreed to wait for him to talk to Winkie again. She could tell the police now, but that might make her look even more suspicious because she had not come to them sooner.

"Did you see anyone come in or out of any of the buildings?" the translator repeated impatiently, with every implication she thought the witness was being uncooperative. Dana's heart beat quicker with every breath, her mind raced with possible answers, but no words could pass up through the lump in her throat.

"Do I need a lawyer?" she finally asked. She could hear the nervousness in her voice, even as she attempted to stay calm. She took in a deep, deep breath and could almost smell, then taste the remains of the dust from the deserted building. "May I have a drink of water?" she asked.

A few words passed in whispers between the inspector and the interpreter.

"Do you wish to make a call?" the woman asked.

Who would she call? She didn't know any lawyers in Montalcino, in all of Italy for that matter. Did she need one? Borelli had studied secular law before he became a priest, but that was years ago, and he surely didn't have a license to practice now. But he could advise her, tell her if she should share everything she knew—what she and Borelli had discovered together, what Winkie had told her. She was fully aware that she was much deeper into this than she'd ever intended.

"Yes," she said, "I'd like to call someone."

CHAPTER THIRTY-ONE

After he returned home from spending time with Renata and her family at Renata's apartment in Montalcino, Giovanni went directly to Estella's room. She was in bed, but awake, staring out the window, an open book by her side. When she turned, he could see, from her pale cheeks and the dark circles beneath her eyes, that the exertions of the day had worn on her. She had attended the Mass in the chapel, though not the graveside services or the lunch.

Estella said, "Renata, such a sad day for her."

"Yes, very sad."

"I'm glad that her sister is here for her, as well as her brother and his wife."

"They've been very helpful."

Giovanni sat down on the edge of the bed, unsure of how to start this conversation.

"I have some questions about Fabrizio," he finally said. He didn't think that Estella knew the boy had disappeared from the hospital. Giovanni had the feeling, from the conversation he'd had with the woman at the hospital, that the authorities would make every effort to keep this quiet as long as possible.

"What do you want to know?" Estella said with a mixture of exhaustion and resignation.

"What relationship does Leo have with the boy?" Though he'd been ready to let go of his suspicions several times over the past days, he needed to know for sure.

"They get along very well. Fabrizio has become a true asset. He is interested in every aspect of the business from vine to bottle to marketing. He has been studying the history of the vineyards, looking closely at yields from each vineyard over the years. The quality of each harvest. An amazing boy. He has the nose," she said proudly. Speaking of the boy seemed to have given her a jolt of energy. "Put the boy to a blind test and he can pinpoint the exact area where the grapes were harvested."

"Impressive," Giovanni said.

"A true asset to the business," Estella repeated. "I do hope he is able to return to work soon."

"As do we all." Giovanni gazed down, running his fingers along the stitched rose pattern of the comforter on Estella's bed. He looked up. "It seems as if Leo has taken a liking to him, grooming him to take over the business. Almost as if he were family." He emphasized the word *family* to make sure Estella understood his concern. "Again, is there something I should know about this relationship? Is there more between the young man and Leo than we have been told?" He stared directly into Estella's eyes.

His sister laughed lightly. "You are asking if he is Leo's son? Why, of course not. You met his grandmother, Flavia. You're asking me if I'm his grandmother, too?"

Giovanni certainly thought that Estella spoke of the boy as if she was just that. Bragging about Fabrizio as if she were a doting grandmother.

"If I were his grandmother," she said, "don't you think I would be aware of this? If this were so, I would acknowledge the boy."

"Even if it hurt Mia? Knowing her father had betrayed her mother."

"I don't know where such an idea, such nonsense came from. No, the boy has no such ties to the family," she said indignantly, "but we would all be proud to claim him as our own."

Giovanni studied her for several moments. He always thought, from the time they were children, that he could tell when his sister was lying, which she was seldom known to do. He knew she was telling the truth. As Dana had pointed out, it was ridiculous to think that Leo would allow his son to be raised by the Calaberoni in Locri.

"It was through you that Fabrizio came to work here?" Giovanni asked. "Through your friendship with Flavia?"

Estella nodded, picked up a glass of water on her nightstand and took a slow drink.

"Tell me about it," Giovanni said.

Estella swallowed, bit down on her lip, then spoke. "I told Leo that Fabrizio was the grandson of a dear friend of many years. I explained the boy had been in a situation where he could possibly end up in a bad place. His parents deceased, living with the grandmother. I told Leo that I assumed he'd been in some kind of legal trouble, but there were never specifics and I didn't ask. Obviously, nothing serious enough to involve incarceration. But, he was headed down the wrong road. He needed to get away from some bad influences, his grandmother told me."

"This is what you told Leo?" Giovanni snorted, put off by Estella's use of such euphemisms to describe the boy's mob connection.

"Yes, exactly."

"And he looked into the boy's background no further? Just let the young man come into the business. Snooping around in the vineyards, the cellars, taking a look at the company records?"

"Leo agreed to give him a month, then depending on how he was doing we would continue from there. But from the day he arrived, it was clear it would work out. Leo never questioned keeping him on. Fabrizio, he's a good boy," Estella said, sounding exactly like Fabrizio's grandmother, Flavia.

"You've known all along that the boy is a Calaberoni?"

Estella took in a deep breath, straightened her posture, even as she sat in bed, and then pinched her lower lip as if she might refuse to answer his question. She picked up the glass on the nightstand, put it to her mouth, but then set it down without taking a drink. "I knew Leo would not approve if he knew, so I told him just what I have told you. It is the truth. Flavia and I are still friends. Leo is a compassionate person, willing to give the boy a chance, and much more accepting of what his mother tells him than—"

"Than your brother?"

Estella appeared as if she were about to laugh, but she didn't. "I'm not sure what took you so long to figure this out."

"Well, the boy's being shot certainly hastened my inquiries. As you know, I've tried to stay out of Leo's way, which hasn't always been easy."

"Yes, yes, I'm aware," Estella admitted with resignation.

"Do you have any reason to believe that Fabrizio's family connections have anything to do with what happened in the cellar? With the boy being shot?"

"No, I don't. Flavia has assured me that no one knew about his whereabouts. She wished for the boy to start a new life, to have an honorable profession. He was doing so well. Until all this."

"Do you know that he has disappeared?"

"From the hospital?" Estella asked, but there was no alarm, no surprise or fear in her voice. Giovanni detected only a slight smugness, a pursing of lips, lifting of chin, and he realized it was Fabrizio's grandmother who had removed him from the hospital. And Estella knew of this plan. Flavia had taken him someplace safe. Her motivation, the same as why she had brought him to the Borellis in the first place. The grandmother's intentions in both—to protect the boy.

As Giovanni left Estella, he knew he had to share this conversation with Dana. She had realized why his grandmother had sent him here, and Giovanni had not. Did it have something to do with her being a woman? But where had Dana taken off to now? He liked her adventurous spirit, but he feared it might get her into trouble.

He hadn't seen her since the funeral services in the chapel that morning. He knocked on her door, then went down and through the main hall, glancing into the living room, the library. He tried Dana's cellphone, but no answer. He headed out to the garage, his uneasiness growing. She was resourceful and maybe she'd decided to go out on her own. Maybe she'd gone to the Veronesi villa to talk to Winkie. Then a thought crossed his mind that made his stomach turn—if whoever had released the wine, had also shot Fabrizio, might they also go after anyone attempting to delve deeper into what was behind these horrendous acts?

His phone rang. He didn't recognize the number on his screen, but he sensed he should answer. There were few who knew his cellphone number.

"Pronto."

"Father Borelli," a frightened, barely recognizable voice replied. "I'm in trouble. I need your help."

CHAPTER THIRTY-TWO

Just as he pulled up to police headquarters in Siena, a dark blue Mercedes with ROMA plates pulled in next to Giovanni Borelli.

A man jumped out, hair disheveled, eyes wide. It took several beats for Giovanni to recognize Winkie Dalton.

"Father Borelli," Winkie said, panting as if he had run all the way from the Veronesi estate rather than driven in what Giovanni suspected was Gia Veronesi's car. "Is she okay? Dana?"

"How did you know she was here?"

"I was driving home—no, I mean back to the Veronesi estate from a meeting in town and . . . She's been arrested? I hope I didn't have anything to do with this."

"You are now willing to speak with the police about what you overheard?" Giovanni asked.

"You know?" Winkie's brows rose, eyes blinked.

Giovanni felt the heat rising along his cheeks. He was about to explode, and Winkie clearly sensed this.

"Yes, yes, of course I'll speak with the police," Winkie said.

"Then wait here," Giovanni commanded, pointing back to

Winkie's—Giovanna Veronesi's—Mercedes. "Until I get inside and have time to sort out what is going on. Why they have brought Ms. Pierson here to police headquarters. I don't want to walk in with you," he snorted.

"Yes, of course," Winkie replied, aware that Giovanni had no time for discussion. "How long should I wait to go in?"

"Your cellphone number," Giovanni demanded.

Winkie rattled off his number.

"I've got it," Giovanni said with irritation, tapping his temple to tell Winkie he had memorized it. He knew it would be more efficient to enter it into his phone, but he didn't know how. Mia had set up his contact list for him. "Take a drive down the street if you have to." Giovanni glanced around the parking lot, relieved that they were the only two in the general area. "Don't mention her name," he added firmly.

"Dana?" Winkie asked.

"Yes, dammit, Dana," Giovanni snapped, glaring at Winkie. "On second thought, I don't believe calling you would be wise. Leave, then come back in two hours."

Within minutes Giovanni was inside speaking with Dana in a private conference room.

"You had no problem getting in to see me?" Dana asked, rubbing her temple. Giovanni thought she looked awful. Forehead damp with sweat, blotches of dirt on her face. She brushed nervously along the thighs of her pant legs as if trying to remove something. "As my legal counsel or my spiritual counsel?" A nervous smile slid quickly across her face.

"No, no problem getting in," he said. "Tell me what happened. Tell me exactly what you witnessed." He emphasized the word you, hoping she realized what he was implying.

Dana nodded, and then she explained she'd gone out for a walk, it had started to rain and she'd found an abandoned building for shelter. She saw a man retrieving money from a desk in a building and recognized him as a man she'd seen protesting along the highway.

"Then the police showed up." Her voice cracked. "They shot him." She rubbed her eyes.

"Shot him?" Giovanni attempted to calm his voice. "Killed him?"

"I don't know," Dana replied in a shaky voice. "I don't know if he's dead. They dragged him off. He was screaming."

"Was he armed? Did the man have a weapon?"

"No, I don't think so."

Giovanni reached out, placed his hand on hers.

"I didn't see a gun." Dana's eyes darted about the room. "It's on the Veronesi property," she whispered, "the same place where—"

Giovanni held up a hand to stop her. He did not want her to mention the conversation Winkie had overheard and shared with Dana. She seemed to understand.

"How do you know it was on the Veronesi property?" he asked. He was sure the police were aware of this, too.

"Wooden crates and boxes, printed with the Veronesi name and logo."

Giovanni gave this considerable thought, but he said nothing.

"Thank you for coming," Dana said, her voice much calmer now. Then, again she whispered, "I find the Italian legal system rather frightening. Do you think they are . . .?" She glanced around again, and Giovanni knew she was concerned about it being bugged, too.

"The police have additional questions. They will allow me in the room with you. Tell them the truth. You've done nothing wrong. Tell them exactly what *you* saw today. Nothing more." He lowered his voice, hoping she understood they wouldn't ask about Winkie. They had no knowledge of that yet, no knowledge of her being privy to this information. "Tell them the truth, the truth of what *you* saw today."

For the next hour, he guided her along through the questioning, the interpreter jumping in now and then, though Giovanni carefully explained to Dana each question as DeLuca spoke.

She described what she had observed on the Veronesi estate that afternoon. There were no questions about what Winkie had passed on to her, just as Giovanni had hoped. When they asked why she did not reveal herself to the police as being in the building, Dana flinched and Giovanni realized this might make the situation look bad for her, especially if they followed up with a question about Dana looking in the desk.

"Obviously," he said in his most threatening voice, "she was in shock, frightened. You had just shot an unarmed man, right in front of her."

"I was frightened," she said, following his lead. "I came into the building to get out of the rain, then the police came through, guns blasting, a man shot, noise, blood. The police dragging this man, who had been shot, across the floor." Dana's voice quivered. "I was frightened," she said again and Giovanni could tell this was no act.

"In shock," he said firmly, and everyone in the room could see this was all turning back on the police officers. "She had just seen an unarmed man gunned down in cold blood. She was merely an innocent and frightened witness."

After the interpreter translated both Dana's and Giovanni's final words, Inspector DeLuca nodded, and the questioning was over.

"If you have no further questions," Giovanni said, "I'd like you to release Ms. Pierson."

Within fifteen minutes, they were on their way back to the Borelli estate. They had not seen Winkie inside the police headquarters or outside, but Giovanni assured Dana that he would soon be there and share with the police what he had seen and overheard, that he would not implicate her.

"Do you trust him?" Dana asked, voice still shaky.

"I do," Giovanni replied. Dana shot him a doubtful look. Giovanni had Winkie's number, but he had decided not to call him. He did not want Winkie's number showing up on his cellphone or his on Winkie's. "I believe I have a reliable sense of judgment when it comes to people," he said. "Take you, for instance. I knew you were a good person from the beginning."

Dana's brow rose, but she smiled. The beginning of their relationship had taken place before they met. She had been part of a team with *The Boston Globe* that had written a series on the sexual abuse cover-up in the Archdiocese. He had been sent by the Vatican, not to expose these terrible acts, but to set up a system to prevent this from happening again. Often, he felt he had not done enough, but he had taken his mission very seriously, an emotional challenge. He and Dana had not come face to face in Boston. They had met years later in Prague.

"It's been quite a day," he said.

"Yes," Dana agreed, rubbing her head. "Did the graveside services, the lunch go well?"

"Yes, the family was very appreciative," he answered, and then, "Let's stop and get dinner before we return home. The offerings this evening, I'm sure, will be leftover lunch."

After calling home to let them know they would not be there for dinner, Giovanni and Dana stopped for something to eat. Over dinner, Giovanni told Dana about the conversation he'd had earlier with Estella.

"You no longer believe that Fabrizio is Leo's son?"

"It was perhaps an unreasonable thought all along. But it made no sense that the boy had come to us with no background, no real reason for being here. But, you were right," he admitted. "He was sent here to keep him away from the family business. And, in a sense, he has become part of the Borelli family business, a valuable asset according to just about everyone."

"But no one seems to know where he is."

"Again, it appears the boy has been moved for his protection."

"Thank God he's okay. He was moved by his grandmother? Estella told you this?"

"She didn't need to. She obviously knew Flavia had taken him from the hospital."

"Then, she still believes he is in danger," Dana said and Giovanni nodded.

At the police station, Winkie was asked if he wished the professional translator be present, but he opted against this. The conversation he'd overheard was in Italian and he wanted them to know he was fluent. In the presence of Inspector DeLuca and another officer, he proceeded to explain what he had overheard. He described the two men the best he could.

Inspector DeLuca asked, "Why did you not come to the police earlier if you had information that might be related to a crime that happened several days ago?"

Winkie explained that he had been cut off from the world as he had no TV, no cellphone, no internet access for several days.

DeLuca nodded, then asked, "Did the Borelli Vineyards provide transportation for you from the airport in Rome?"

Winkie caught his breath, hesitated, took several moments to form an answer. Then he explained exactly what happened, how he had run into a friend from New York who had offered him a ride. He gave them the name of Octavia Fleenor and explained she was with a wine wholesaler and here on a visit and purchasing trip to the Borelli Vineyards. She could be contacted if they wished to corroborate his story.

DeLuca scratched a note on a pad on which he had recorded very little of the conversation. Winkie was starting to wonder if he needed a lawyer. He thought for a moment about calling Giovanna Veronesi, particularly if the officers continued this line of questioning. He had come here voluntarily; couldn't he leave at any time?

DeLuca asked, "What is the nature of your visit to Tuscany?"

He considered offering the same answer he'd given Dana. "I've just purchased a vineyard."

"Veronesi?" DeLuca asked, the line of his mouth tightening.

"Si," Winkie replied. "Yes, the Veronesi Vineyards."

"When are you scheduled to leave?"

"Friday," Winkie answered.

He could see the police officer did not like this reply, but he made no request that Winkie change his schedule.

The second officer in the room stood, left, then came back with a laptop, sat down and turned it on. He clicked on a video and the three men watched. It was blurry, not a professional job by any means, but Winkie could see it was a video of the protesters from the group he and Dana had seen along the highway. After watching for a moment, he recognized the man he had seen along the highway, the man involved in the conversation he had overheard and just described to the police.

"Do you recognize any of these people?" Inspector DeLuca asked.

Winkie pointed at the man.

"Anyone else?" DeLuca motioned for the other officer to replay the video.

"No," Winkie answered after carefully watching a second time. "The other man is not in this video."

After a few more questions, DeLuca prodding for a more thorough description of the other man—Winkie telling him he did not get a good look at his face and had already described him as best he could—the interview ended with a request for Winkie's contact information, both in Italy and at home in the States.

As he went back out and got into Giovanna's Mercedes, he realized that the back of his shirt was drenched with sweat. He had so carefully planned this trip to Italy, but he hadn't planned on getting involved in anything like this.

CHAPTER THIRTY-THREE

Earlier in the day, Winkie had thought about suggesting that he and Giovanna go out for a celebratory dinner, but his visit to police headquarters had interrupted his plan. Maybe, he considered now, Giovanna wouldn't care to celebrate. Her emotions after the paperwork was signed seemed to be a mixture of sadness, elation, and relief. The family business would be saved, her brother would have a home, and Winkie had invited Giovanna to keep her living quarters intact, with any upgrades she wished. Though her home was in Rome, Winkie knew she wouldn't leave permanently until her brother Lorenzo was gone. Winkie and his children could visit anytime they wanted. It was theirs now. He would begin right away with his search for the wine consultant, managers for both the vineyards and villa renovations.

On returning to the estate, Winkie found Giovanna in the kitchen. He told her about the angry protesters along the highway, about the conversation he'd heard just outside an abandoned building on her property, and explained that he had gone to police headquarters to share this information. He didn't share with her that he'd felt no obligation to do this until he saw Dana in the back of a police car. He didn't mention Dana at all.

"Those abandoned buildings would certainly be a fine place for a secret meeting," Giovanna said. "They haven't been used in years. You think the motivation for the wine destruction was environmental?" she asked.

"It's possible," he replied.

"The police were here the day it happened," Giovanna told him. "I'm sure they thought I was involved. Such a plot would involve more energy than I have." She sighed with exhaustion. "I'm ready for a rest."

"Yes, me, too," he agreed.

"I will see you at dinner, then."

When he went down for dinner, the table was set for three. Winkie wondered if Raffaelo Sabatini was still in Montalcino, if he would join them. This prospect disappointed Winkie as he'd decided this evening he would tell Giovanna the real reason he was here. Yes, this evening.

Within minutes, she stepped into the room, her brother Lorenzo by her side, arms locked. She looking elegant as always, in a long skirt and silk blouse, he fully dressed in a nice suit that hung loosely on his slight frame. Slowly, taking small, careful steps with Giovanna's assistance, he made his way to the table. Winkie helped Lorenzo and Giovanna with their chairs, then sat.

"We are celebrating tonight," Giovanna said, her hands clasped before her.

"Yes, a family celebration," Lorenzo said, grinning at his sister, then at Winkie.

The conversation was light as they began enjoying their meal, drinking wine, a decade old Veronesi vintage. But soon talk shifted to vineyard updates, hiring a consultant, advice from a surprisingly lucid Lorenzo on several who might fill this role, though Winkie wondered if he was reaching into the past to pull up these names.

They lingered after the last plate was taken away, again discussing Winkie's plans for bringing the vineyards back to full production. Lorenzo seemed to understand that Winkie had just bought the family business. Yet, at times he referred to him as Vincenzo, thinking he was his brother. Winkie guessed if Vincenzo had lived, the family might have been able to keep the business running.

When Lorenzo announced he was ready for bed, Winkie asked Giovanna if he might escort her brother upstairs. She smiled and said, "I believe Lorenzo would appreciate that. And so would I."

They were accompanied up the elevator by Lucia, who administered Lorenzo's nighttime medications, then left the two men alone.

"Thank you, thank you," the old man said, sitting on the edge of his bed. He had taken off his suit, which Winkie hung in the closet, as well as his undergarments, which he had folded neatly on a chair near the window.

"You'll be warm enough?" Winkie asked, knowing he would not question the man's desire to sleep au naturel.

"Yes, thank you. You're staying here now. Are you?"

Winkie wasn't sure who the old man thought Winkie was now or which *here* he was talking about.

"I'll be leaving for home, back to the States Friday." Winkie was grateful that the police hadn't insisted he stay longer, but at the same time, he felt a deep sadness to be leaving.

"Back home?" Lorenzo asked after taking several moments to carefully consider this.

"Yes. I have two children. They are almost grown now, one in her last year of high school, one in college. And, truthfully, I miss them."

"You'll have to bring them here."

"Yes, definitely. They'll love it here."

Lorenzo plumped his pillow and pulled the covers back, and then crawled under the blanket, head propped on the pillow like a child waiting for a bedtime story. Winkie was tempted to kiss him goodnight on the forehead.

"Children?" Lorenzo asked puzzled. "No, no, we have no children. No heirs." Then the man's eyes flashed as if with recognition, and he seemed to be studying Winkie very carefully. Lorenzo's rheumy eyes moved slowly over Winkie's face, settling at first on his mouth as if he wished him to speak, as if Lorenzo knew there was more to be shared. But when neither man spoke, Lorenzo's gaze shifted to Winkie's eyes and held tight.

"It is so good to have you home," the old man finally said in a quiet voice, a tear sliding down his weathered cheek.

"Yes," Winkie said. "It is very good to be home."

It was late by the time Dana and Borelli arrived back at the estate. Dana had taken over the driving duties after they left police headquarters. She certainly didn't want to be stopped for having an unlicensed driver at the wheel. Borelli had dozed off as soon as they left the restaurant where they'd stopped for dinner.

"Father Borelli." Dana nudged the priest as they pulled up in front of the villa. "I'm dropping you off here." He opened his eyes and gazed about in a stupor.

"Yes, very good. Thank you," he said, blinking, not fully awake. She guessed if he had been, he'd object and insist on going to the garage with her. Without further discussion, he got out, trudged up to the door. Dana wondered briefly if he could make it safely inside and up the stairs to bed. When he turned just before he stepped inside and motioned her on, she felt reassured.

She hoped that the garage was still unlocked, which it was. She pulled in and parked the truck in its regular spot. Just as she was about to leave, Claudio stepped out from a dark corner, startling her. He nodded, but he offered no words.

"Buona sera," Dana said. Was it just her imagination or was Claudio popping out or up every time she was around, merely to offer her a glare of disapproval? She started back to the house.

A near-full moon hung in the dark sky, casting a glow along the hillside in the distance. She stopped, scanning the landscape, evening lights twinkling at nearby estates and villas. Then she noticed the headlights of a vehicle, then another, coming up the road. Lights on both flicked off as they got closer, then stopped in front of the villa, rolling in slowly. Watching from the shadows, Dana could see a man exit from the lead vehicle. She was too far away and it was too dark to make out the details of the man's face, but in the faint moonlight she could see the man's broad shoulders and thick form, and she knew it was Alberto DeLuca. The second man, the driver, exited the car. Much thinner than the lead detective and moving with an uneven gait as he made his way around the car to where DeLuca stood, Dana recognized him as the younger detective who'd come to the house the morning that Mia had discovered Paolo in the cellar. The two men stood conversing, even as another three jumped out of the second vehicle. They approached the building on the newer section of the villa, where the visitors' center was located. Someone opened the door from inside and the group entered, all except one who remained outside as if standing guard.

Soon, a light flicked on inside and she was quite sure this was the window in Leo's office. The blinds were drawn and she could see only faint slats of light. She gazed up to the second level of the villa where the bedrooms were located. Nothing but darkness.

She waited silently, not moving from where she stood, safely away from the building. She heard an owl hoot in the distance, then her own shallow breathing. She waited.

About half an hour later, a man exited the building, carrying something. As he approached one of the parked vehicles, opened the trunk and slid it inside, she could see it was a computer. Another man came out, also carrying what was clearly another computer. What was going on? The police were obviously interested in something on one of the Borelli's computers. Why had it taken this long to come for the computers? Possibly some type of warrant was required. Or had the man shot and arrested on the Veronesi property that day pointed to someone inside? A member of the Borelli family?

CHAPTER THIRTY-FOUR

Giovanna was sipping a glass of wine, staring up at the portrait of the Virgin and Child, light flickering on the two figures, when Winkie returned after telling Lorenzo goodnight. He sat and poured himself more wine.

"Do you believe in the Virgin Birth?" Giovanna asked, her eyes not leaving the painting. "You're Catholic?" Her gaze shifted toward him.

"I was raised Catholic."

"In New York? You were born in New York?"

Winkie's heart beat violently against his ribs, then moved up, throbbing in his throat, then splitting and rushing into his ears. His entire body pulsed with a rhythm so forceful he felt he might explode.

"I don't know," he said. "I don't know if I was born in New York." It was now or never, he thought. "My birth certificate shows New York as my birthplace, but I don't know if it is authentic." He paused, hoping she might say something now, unravel the mystery.

When she said nothing, he felt as if the silence might swallow them both. "Does the date January third, 19—"

"Yes," she said before he could finish his question. In the dim light, she looked like a frightened young girl. "Yes, January third is a special day for both of us." Her voice was so low he could barely hear her words.

An even heavier silence descended on the room.

"January third," Giovanna finally said, "your birthday."

"Yes," Winkie replied.

"You've had a good life?" Giovanna asked, her gaze low as if she were closing her eyes.

He didn't want her to feel guilty about what she'd done. He just wanted to know why.

"Yes," he said. "A kind mother, a good father who always provided for us. Grandparents who doted on me." She looked at him now, eyes moist. "Cousins I loved as brothers and sisters. I always suspected there was something my parents were not telling me. I didn't look like anyone in my family. I didn't *think* like anyone in my family." He laughed lightly. "My mother used to tell me I was the smartest one of all the cousins, the most curious. I believed her, too." He shook his head, grinning. Giovanna bit her lip. "Not that my family wasn't intelligent, but … just something different about me. I knew it from an early age."

"Did you know when you were a child? Why you were different?"

"I discovered after my parents' deaths. I knew my grandmother and grandfather, my mother's parents, were from Italy. But I came across something very strange as I was going through my father's papers after he died. A schedule for flights to and from Italy. They were in Italy for almost three months, according to the papers. I found it particularly odd because I was born during that time, and I'd always been told I was born in New York, which couldn't have been the case. My birth certificate said New York. I couldn't figure it out, but then I realized if they would lie to me about where I was born, they might have been lying about everything."

"But, you loved your parents? They treated you well?"

"Yes, very much. Very much. But I needed to know."

"How did you find out?" she asked, and he felt how desperately she was fighting to speak, to control her emotions.

"Eventually, I hired a private investigator. It's amazing what money can buy. And time." He paused, not wanting to go into detail of how he discovered what he now knew. "Did you know when I arrived? When I arrived here at the Veronesi estate?"

"Did I know you were my son?"

There. She'd said it. *My son.*

"Did you?" He too was trying to keep the intense emotion out of his voice, to keep his tone low. He wasn't angry with her. He just needed to know.

"Raffaelo brought me your biography when you first made the offer on the winery. He knew how particular I was about selling the business and home, how it was important to me that I know everything about prospective buyers. Not just financially, but . . ." Her voice trailed off and again she was unable to look at Winkie. "Yes, I noticed your birthdate. At first, I thought it merely a coincidence. I rented your movies. I watched every one."

"You hadn't seen them before?" he asked with mock offense.

She smiled. "I knew you were an American actor, but no, I had never seen your films."

"Well, what did you think?"

"It was very odd, watching you. I knew you were acting, but there was something familiar. They were dubbed, so I couldn't hear your voice. Your real voice. I knew I had to meet you."

"This is when you invited me to come stay here to look over the estate and vineyards. Did Raffaelo know?"

"No one knows why I invited you to come. At first, I thought you might be claiming your birthright, but then . . . I don't know, it seemed we got along so well, and I enjoyed your company. I wanted it to be true. Not that you were here to take the estate, but I wanted it to be true that you were . . ." Again, she bit down on her lip, and Winkie could see she was having a difficult time continuing.

"Tell me," he said in an unthreatening voice, coaxing her along, "the circumstances of my birth." He couldn't ask, why did you give me away? But, that was exactly what he was asking and Giovanna knew it.

She ran her quivering hand absently along the edge of the table, then placed the other over it to keep it still. "I don't want to hurt you," she said, taking in a deep, ragged breath, and then exhaling slowly. For several long moments, Winkie thought she was going to deny him this knowledge, about his birth, his father, his heritage.

"I was engaged to be married," she said. "To a boy—no a man—my parents did not approve of."

"My father?"

Giovanna held up a hand. "Please," she said quietly, "I have never told this to anyone. Please let me tell it in my own way."

Winkie nodded. He would merely listen.

"For many years the families—mine, my fiancé's—were rivals. The Veronesi owned so much of this land at one time." Her arm swept across the room, indicating the draped window that looked out onto the vastness of Tuscan hills and vineyards. "The family I speak of, they were nothing more than *contadini*, according to my father."

Serfs, Winkie thought. *My father was a serf.*

"They, my parents, saw them as much less than the Veronesi. But times change, powers shift. The power is always with the land. Much blood has been shed over land. The original family property, almost half of what is now the municipality of Montalcino, was once owned by the Veronesi. Over the years, those who had been tending the land were able to become landowners too. Those who use the land wisely will prosper. Those who use it with love will find great happiness." He could hear in her voice how much she loved this land. Her home.

"Just months before the wedding," she continued, the tone of her voice shifting once more, "my mother and I went to Rome for a final fitting of the wedding dress. She could see that I was determined to marry and had come to the point she was helping me with the planning. My mother noticed that the dress did not fit properly. The seamstress was quiet as my mother admonished me for gaining so much weight, as the woman carefully clipped away at one seam then another, repinning. Then it dawned on her—my mother—as surely the seamstress knew. A woman in the business of fitting brides would know."

"That you were—"

"Yes. Pregnant. I had been denying it myself. Praying that it was not true, though the signs were all there. Unable to face the . . . I'm so sorry, I'm so sorry." She began to weep. Winkie reached out for her hand, but she pulled it away. "I don't want to hurt you," she said. "Please, understand that. I didn't want to hurt him either."

Winkie nodded, forced himself to remain still.

"My mother flew into a rage, said that I had been defiled, that the boy I loved was nothing more than a lowly rapist. That he had dishonored the family. That we would be unable to marry in the Church. That the child would be—" Giovanna wiped a tear from her cheek. She sniffled, brushing the back of her hand against her nose.

A bastard, Winkie thought. "But, you married him? Against your parents' wishes?" he asked hopefully, because he wanted this to be true. Inwardly he was shouting, *then why did you give me away?*

"No."

"But you loved him?"

"Yes, very much. But I knew . . ." She stopped again to gather herself, taking in a deep breath, straightening her shoulders. "I wrote him a letter. I knew he would come after me if he knew, if he knew the truth, but I would disgrace my family. I would disgrace him. I knew to keep him away I had to hurt him deeply. I wrote that I had found someone else. Then I wrote that I had found someone much more interesting than him. That my life would be one of boredom if I married him.

"My mother was pleased that I had called off the marriage, my father particularly so, though he did not know about the child." She wiped a tear. "I am so sorry," she apologized again. "He did not know about *you*. My mother took me to a distant family member who tended me, then when you came you were taken away. A good family. They said a good family would take you as their own. I was not told you would go to America." She reached up and ran the back of her hand along her cheek.

"But you did not try to find me?"

"I was told that you were with a good family." She was sobbing openly, loudly now. He reached for her hand again and this time she let him grasp it as if she needed someone to hold onto, to tell her it would be okay.

"But why, if you loved him, why did you not marry him? You just gave me away. Why did you not marry my father? Could you not defy your parents?" He wanted to be kind. But he didn't understand. He wanted to understand. His voice had grown louder, even as his throat tightened.

"Please, please," she said as if begging, and then again, "I'm sorry, I'm sorry." Her face had gone pale, her eyes hollow. "I could not marry your father."

"But why?"

"I could not marry your father, because . . . because your father was my brother Vincenzo."

CHAPTER THIRTY-FIVE

They sat in silence, both emotionally drained from what Giovanna had revealed.

I am the bastard child of incest, Winkie thought, though the inner words were wrapped in numbness. He could not believe this was consensual. Surely, Giovanna's brother had forced himself on her.

"My family detested my fiancé," Giovanna said, voice low, little more than a whisper. "My mother should have known it was not his child. We were allowed no time alone. Always an escort. Always someone overseeing our meetings. Oh, we were able to sneak a minute alone here and there." Her mouth turned up slightly, almost a smile, though her lips quivered as she spoke.

"So, he could be my—?"

"No. Our love was not fulfilled in that sense. We had decided to wait. He had placed me upon a pedestal." Winkie could see she was about to cry again. He didn't want that. He could see how deeply she had been hurt.

"One night, Vincenzo came into my room," she said. "Uninvited."

"You don't have to—"

"Please," she begged, and he could see that she needed to speak of that night. She needed to finish. "I knew he had been drinking. His breath. His words, slurred. He said that I had disgraced the family, that I would never marry a Borelli . . . he said I would never marry him. Because he would not accept a woman who had been tainted." She was crying again.

A Borelli? Winkie thought. This was the first mention of the family name of her fiancé. It seemed now as if it had slipped out, as if Giovanna didn't realize she had uttered the name, as if she were protecting him. *Borelli.* Now Winkie understood why she had asked about the Borelli van bringing him up to the estate that first day. It was not about a rivalry. It was about a lost love.

"You don't have to go on," he told her again. He wasn't sure he wanted to hear. Could she understand that? Winkie knew he would need more time to take this information in, to accept it as who he was. What he was. He ached for her, Giovanna, his birth mother, for the pain she had had to endure. He understood now why she had done what she had done.

Neither spoke. They sat silently, but he knew the conversation was not yet done.

"He raped you," he finally said, voice low. He wanted to give her the words so that she would not have to say them.

"I'm so sorry, so sorry."

"It wasn't your fault," he said, and again she sobbed, and he knew this is what she needed to hear. She had never told anyone, and she had never heard these words. He rose from where he sat at the table and stepped closer to her, kneeling beside her, taking her hands, holding them firmly, staring into her eyes. "It was not your fault," he said again.

CHAPTER THIRTY-SIX

Dana waited until the police returned to their cars and were a good distance down the road before entering the house. Borelli had left the front door unlocked for her and she crept quietly up the stairs and into her room. She considered waking Borelli to tell him what she had seen, but she realized she needed to give this more thought. The police were obviously looking for something on a Borelli Vineyards' computer.

Was there something recorded in company records that might provide a motive for the crime, something that had nothing to do with the environmental protesters?

In her mind, she replayed the conversation Winkie had overheard. His description of the man meeting with the protester had been vague, but it could have been Leo. The man, according to Winkie, was angry about the bottled wine being destroyed. She'd assumed he was angry because this is what had killed the old man—the broken glass clogging the drain. But, was he angry because he'd given specific instructions to destroy only the wine in barrel, an especially valuable vintage? As Dana lay in bed, she recalled that this very wine was listed for tasting in the information that had been prepared for the Simonelli group during their visit. Borelli had given her the folder to study before she met the guests in Rome.

She jumped up, out of bed, and found the folder on top of her dresser. She opened it and leafed through quickly until she found the list of wines to be tasted. There had been no time to change the schedule. The destroyed wine was described as rich and complex, deep, ruby red, with the aromas of forest fruit, coffee, and cacao, with gentle tannins, and a velvety and harmonious taste. It had been in barrel for four years. Dana felt as if she were reading an obituary listing the attributes of the deceased. She scanned the other information in the folder; menus, history of the vineyards, articles from wine magazines, additional wines, both bottled and in oak, trying to find something that might help her.

She stopped for a moment when she came across the black and white photo of Marco, standing beside Leo. Both looked very young and eager, ready to take on the world. Marco was not particularly handsome in his youth. Maybe it was just an unflattering photo. Or maybe, like a fine Brunello wine, Marco had improved with age.

Dana closed the folder and slipped uneasily back into bed, finally drifting off.

Early the following morning, she went down for breakfast, surprised to see Estella sitting with Leo, though she looked very frail. Father Borelli arrived shortly, as did Mia. They filled their plates at the buffet set up on the sideboard.

"Inspector Alberto DeLuca was here late last night," Leo announced as they all settled in their places at the table.

Dana felt a weight being physically lifted from her. Leo was going to tell the family about the computers being confiscated.

"A man has been arrested," Leo continued, "for the destruction in the cellar and Paolo's death." He glanced at Dana, then Borelli, and she wondered if the priest or DeLuca had also told him that she had witnessed this arrest. She was having trouble reading Leo's body language, but he looked more pleased and relieved than anything. "His name is Jago DeCampo. He is with a group called *Salva la Terra*."

"The group protesting some of the practices here in the vineyards?" Mia asked, eyes wide. "This was the motive for destroying the wine?"

"Alberto believes the death of Paolo was truly an unintended result, but the man has been charged with murder. He was shot trying to escape. He is in serious condition. Alberto is unsure that he will recover." Leo's eyes slid quickly over to his mother, who Dana knew spoke little English. She guessed that Leo had already shared this information with Estella.

Borelli asked Leo, "Do you know this man? The name is not familiar."

Leo shook his head. "He comes from the south. Alberto said that he has been involved in other aspects of environmental protest."

"Does Alberto believe others were involved?" Dana asked.

"This is all I know," Leo said, and Dana sensed that this was all that Alberto DeLuca had shared. Borelli, it seemed, had shared nothing about Dana's being taken in for questioning. She waited for more, attempting to make eye contact with Leo who gazed down at his plate, tore open a breakfast roll, smothered it with jam, then lifted it to his mouth and chewed slowly. It appeared that Leo would not share anything about the computers.

No one spoke of Fabrizio until the meal was almost finished.

"Will others be allowed to visit Fabrizio soon?" Mia asked.

Dana could see Estella stiffen at the mention of the boy's name. Again, Dana glanced at Leo and guessed that he too knew the boy had been moved. Mia obviously did not.

"Soon," Leo told his daughter. "Very soon."

Mia's eyes tightened but she did not verbally protest. Did she think the boy was improving, that her father, as well as the authorities, would indeed let her visit soon?

Dana mentioned what a lovely day it was and asked Borelli if he'd like to go for a walk. He agreed and she ran up to grab her sweater.

As they strolled along the path leading to the nearest vineyard, she asked, "Did you tell Leo about my being taken in for questioning?"

"I haven't," Borelli said. "I don't believe he knows."

"Or about the conversation Winkie overheard?"

"Not yet."

"Were you aware that Inspector DeLuca dropped by last night?" she asked.

"I first learned of it this morning, as did the rest of the family. I was extremely tired when we returned from dinner. I went directly to bed, and thankfully I was able to sleep."

"After I parked your truck in the garage, I was walking back to the house. I stopped a moment to take in the view, the moon casting a glow on the landscape, lights blinking in the valley." She paused. "I hadn't yet reached the house when I saw two vehicles arrive."

"DeLuca?"

"Yes, and several other officers."

"I'm sure they wanted Leo to know right away that the person who released the wine, who killed Paolo, had been apprehended."

"They could have come earlier. In daylight."

"The man's arrest, particularly since he was injured, took some time to process. Tracking him back to the environmentalists' group, too." There was an almost defensive tone in Borelli's voice.

They continued along a narrow path, Dana attempting to sort through all of this. Borelli was withholding information from his nephew, but she wasn't sure why. He motioned and they dipped down through a grove of large, wide oaks, the recent rain having brought out their earthy smell. The tall, damp grass brushed against Dana's legs.

"I saw something else," she finally said.

Borelli stopped, turned to Dana. "Tell me," he said calmly, almost as if he were indulging her now, waiting for the next chapter of a story, the ending which he already knew.

"They took a couple of computers. I believe from Leo's office, maybe the visitors' center."

"Perhaps they were looking for employee records. We still don't know if Carlo Porcini was involved."

Dana knew if Winkie had gone to the police, which Borelli was sure he had, the police knew that another person was involved and, according to Borelli, the description of the man did not fit Carlo Porcini. "Yes, I'm sure that's all it is," she said, unsuccessfully attempting to catch Borelli's eye. She did not believe this at all, and she didn't think he did either.

As they headed back toward the villa, Borelli motioned, and they took a turn toward the cellar. As they approached, they could see two of the Borelli work vehicles parked out front. Only one of the police cars remained.

Inside, Marco Dardi was supervising a crew, cleaning out the barrels and scrubbing the floor. He approached them, wiping his hands on a stained towel. The other men scurrying about the cellar were sweating and dirty. Marco folded the towel and placed it on a bench. He smiled awkwardly at Dana, then spoke in Italian to Borelli, both glancing at Dana, and she definitely got the feeling they were talking about her. She felt terribly uncomfortable.

Marco ran the back of his hand along his forehead as if to remove beads of sweat, though there were none. "We are all relieved that this is over," he said in English. "That we are able to begin cleaning the cellar. Prepare the barrels for use again."

Did he really think this was over? Dana wondered.

The conversation soon switched back to Italian. For ease, or to exclude her, Dana wasn't sure. But she could see that whatever Marco was telling Borelli, it was upsetting him. The priest gazed about the cellar, as if looking for something, then motioned to Dana that he was ready to leave.

"What did he say?" Dana asked as soon as they were back outside.

"He said Inspector DeLuca has finished his crime scene investigation and has allowed a cleanup of the cellar."

"So, if any missed evidence was there, it isn't anymore?"

Borelli didn't bother to answer the question, but said, "He died this morning in the hospital."

"Who?" For a terrifying moment she thought he was talking about Fabrizio.

"Jago DeCampo, the man from *Salva la Terra*."

"And with him anything else," Dana said, "that might lead to the second person."

"Unless he revealed something before he died," Borelli replied. "If Winkie told the police about the conversation he overheard, if they believe it is related to what happened in the cellar, they are still looking for another person."

Borelli waved an arm and they started back toward the villa.

"For some reason," Dana said, "I had the feeling you were speaking Italian to leave me out, or maybe you were even speaking about me."

Borelli stopped, rubbed his head. "Yes, we were. I'd almost forgotten."

"Forgotten what?" she asked impatiently.

"Several days ago, Marco asked about you."

"Why?" Dana remembered one evening, several days ago, Mia had told her that Marco had been looking for her.

"He asked how long you would be here, and if he might ask you to have dinner with him one evening."

"Why didn't he ask *me*? Did he feel you had to give him your permission to ask me out, as if I were a teenage girl and you were my father? Kids don't even do it that way anymore."

Borelli laughed. "To some, our friendship might be difficult to understand. I believe Marco wanted to make sure he did not . . . let's see if I can word this correctly . . . infringe on my territory."

"Oh, yikes," Dana replied, laughing too. "What did you say?"

"I said that it would be up to you." They had reached the villa. "I apologize that I did not mention this sooner, but I have had much on my mind. I realize you have but a few days remaining, and Leo hopes to enjoy a family day at the *festa* on Saturday. Since you are scheduled to leave on Sunday, perhaps tomorrow, Friday?"

Dana surely was not going to have Borelli arrange a date for her, though she might like to spend more time with Marco. "I have a question about Marco."

"Yes."

"Is he married?"

"Why would you think that?"

"The woman at the funeral with him."

"Oh." He smiled. "That was his sister, Sophia."

"His sister?" Dana attempted to keep the confusion out of her voice.

"You thought she was his wife?"

"Well, yes, I did. His sister, she was also a friend of Paolo's?"

"She has worked here on the estate for the past several years," he said. "Sophia is our viticulturist."

Dana tried to hide her dismay as she visualized the person Marco had spoken to out in the vineyard the afternoon of the tour. He had not introduced her as his sister, or even by name. He had referred to her as the estate viticulturist. Her hair was evidently pulled up into her cap, and she wore jeans and a jacket. Dana had thought she was a man. This assumption seemed rather sexist now, but at the funeral, wearing a dress, she looked like a completely different person.

"The Borelli Vineyards, quite progressive," she said. "A woman viticulturist."

"Yes," Borelli replied proudly as if he'd chosen the woman himself. "What should I tell Marco?"

"Tell him if he wishes to ask me to dinner, he should call me."

CHAPTER THIRTY-SEVEN

Back at the house, Dana went upstairs to put away her sweater before lunch. As she hung it in the closet, her phone rang.

"Estella has been taken to the hospital," Borelli said.

"Oh, no," Dana gasped. "What—"

"She was not feeling well. Leo took her to the doctor. He tried calling me, but I hadn't taken my phone this morning, as often happens. The doctor has suggested it was the stress of the past week. She shows signs of having suffered a minor stroke."

"She's going to be okay?"

"They want to run some tests. I'm headed to the hospital now."

"May I drive you?" Dana asked.

"Claudio will take me, but thank you." She could hear a hint of apology in his voice. "I don't know that Mia is aware. I'm sure Leo wouldn't send word to her at school. It would be helpful if you would stay here. I'll keep you informed."

"Yes, please."

"If the tests go well, Leo or I will fetch Mia from school. If you'll please be available until we know more. Mia shouldn't be home until much later this afternoon and by then we should . . . if you want to go somewhere, I'll leave the keys here for you on the kitchen counter. Please help yourself to lunch. I'll take something to eat on the way."

"Wish Estella well." Dana wondered what else could possibly go wrong for the Borellis.

After a quick lunch of cheese and bread, set out on the kitchen counter, Dana grabbed her phone, having decided to go for a walk. She didn't want to leave the estate. She wished that Leo would pick Mia up, tell her about her grandmother, take her to the hospital. She knew he was attempting to protect her, but Dana didn't think this was the way to do it. Yet, who was she to judge the ways in which a parent chooses to protect a child. Dana would be available, just as Borelli had requested.

As she walked, again Dana questioned if she should arrange to leave sooner than originally planned. So much had happened since her arrival, and many times she felt as if she was in the way, an intrusion, a burden for Borelli who felt obligated to entertain her. Yet, at times she felt they were working together, moving toward a common goal. Now, she sensed something had shifted. Had she become an added burden with her questions and doubts?

It appeared that DeLuca had told Leo both crimes had been solved. The police knew more than they were sharing, or even sharing false information, implying the crimes had been solved, perfectly aware that questions remained unanswered. There was something on Leo's computer that was incriminating, possibly evidence that Leo himself had a part in the destruction. Dana shook this thought from her head as she continued on toward the vineyards, stopping at one of the locations where Marco had taken them on their outdoor tour. Her eyes scanned the landscape, and then she knelt down and swept up a handful of soil. She held it to her nose, then let it sift through her fingers.

Her phone rang. She brushed off her hands and answered.

It was Marco.

"If you are available," he said, "would you consider having dinner with me tomorrow, Friday evening?"

"Oh, Marco, I'm sorry, but I just learned that Estella has been taken to the hospital. I'm not sure if I should stay to help out, or if I should leave earlier than planned."

"I did not know about Estella. This has been a most unfortunate time for the family. Do you know why she has been taken to the hospital?"

"Father Borelli said she showed signs of having had a stroke, that they are running tests."

"Such sad news. I pray for her speedy recovery."

"Yes," she said. "It's been a difficult time for the family."

"Perhaps we can speak later," Marco told her as they finished their call.

Slowly, she headed back to the house. Approaching the villa, she saw Leo driving up.

As he stepped out of the car, Dana asked, "How is your mother?"

"She seems to be doing well." Leo looked like a man who had been completely beaten down, as if every fiber of his being had been stretched to the breaking point. How could Dana have entertained the idea that Leo had been involved in Paolo's death, the wine destruction, and possibly the attempt on Fabrizio's life?

"They will keep her overnight to monitor her condition," he explained. "Uncle Giovanni will stay with her. I want to be here to tell Mia. The poor girl has had enough to deal with over the past days." For a moment, Dana thought Leo might burst into tears. She reached out and touched his arm, not knowing what to say.

He offered her a sad, but appreciative smile. "I am not sure how much more we can endure."

"She's going to be okay." Dana was relieved that Leo would be home to tell Mia about her grandmother, and grateful that Estella appeared to be in no imminent danger.

"Yes, we will get through it," Leo said. "She will be fine."

* * *

Dinner that evening was subdued. Borelli was at the hospital with Estella. Mia had been told about her grandmother. She seemed almost in a trance as she pushed the food around on her plate. She pulled her phone out of her back pocket and, eyes cast downward, she appeared to be texting or playing a game. Dana was surprised at the girl's rudeness, but realized she'd been through so much over the past few days and was just trying to cope.

"How is the new phone?" Leo asked.

"It's a phone," she said tersely, not bothering to look up.

Leo spoke to Mia in Italian. His voice sounded concerned, rather than angry. Dana could understand several of the words. *Grandmother. Hospital. Zio Giovanni. Fabrizio.*

Mia got up and left without bothering to say anything more.

"She is having a difficult time," Leo said.

"Understandable."

"Yes," Leo said. "At least those who caused the damage in the cellar have been apprehended." Dana wondered why he was using a plural term. Had someone else from the group *Salva la Terra* been apprehended?

"Was someone else arrested?" she asked.

"Not to my knowledge. I would share this if I was aware." There was a sharp edge to his voice. "Mia asked if she could visit her grandmother, but Mother will be coming home tomorrow, so I do not believe this is necessary."

"Then she asked about Fabrizio?" Dana said. "Have you told her about Fabrizio?" *About where he came from?* Dana thought, *and have you told her that he has been taken away by his grandmother to keep him safe?* This was assuming that Leo knew all of this.

Leo pushed his plate aside and rose. "Yes, she asked about Fabrizio." He took in a deep ragged breath. "I have not shared everything about Fabrizio with my daughter, but it will likely be in the news tomorrow. A link has been made between Fabrizio and a crime family from the south."

Dana gasped, not because she didn't already know, but because Leo was sharing this with her.

"How long have you known this?" she asked.

Leo stared at Dana. His nostrils widened with a deep intake of air. "Apparently, not as long as other members of the family, as well as certain guests." He stood and Dana could see he no longer wanted to continue this conversation either.

Back in her bedroom, Dana checked online to see if Fabrizio's family connection had been reported on any online news sources. She found what appeared to be a blog, done in the sensational style of many American blogs, which Dana seldom trusted as reliable news sources. The headlines, in translation:

> Borelli Vineyards linked to mob. Organized crime infiltrates Tuscan wine industry.

No sources for the information were named. But, they had the Fabrizio-Mob connection right, whether this was truly an infiltration of the Tuscan wine industry was yet to be seen.

Dana kicked off her shoes, shoved them under the bed. She barely had enough energy to take off her clothes, pull on her nightshirt and climb under the covers. She felt exhausted, numb, and drained, but at the same time filled with so much nervous energy, she knew she would be unable to sleep.

Had Borelli told Leo about Fabrizio, or was it Estella? Maybe even DeLuca. If Leo truly hadn't known about this connection earlier, he probably had a right to be angry.

Attempting to nudge her body toward sleep, she tried counting backward from 1,000 by fives, then she attempted counting sheep, but images from the past few days, not fluffy little lambs, jumped unbidden through her mind.

She envisioned Mia sitting with her father and grandmother on the bench outside the villa, the girl's legs stained with blood and wine. Mia helping Fabrizio into the kitchen, supporting his weight, both covered with blood, an arrow protruding from the boy's body. The protester, his taunting, grubby, unshaven face pressed to the Borelli van window, and then he was creeping into the abandoned building, pulling out the drawer. Money. The police. Guns going off. Dust spraying. Blood.

Then she imagined what she herself had *not* seen. The spigots on the barrels were opened, wine gushing forth, swirling down the drains. Gone forever. But, then draining slowly because of the broken glass clogging the drains. Poor Paolo face down in the wine.

Again, she considered—what if the target was solely the wine in barrel, the Brunello, the Riserva, the most valuable wine?

She rose, went to the window and gazed out into the dark, thinking of the night she and Mia had gone out to Fabrizio's cottage. What a mess the place had been. And the smell. How thoughtful and clever of Mia to gather up clothes, the items in his bathroom.

Dana returned to her bed, but the images of Fabrizio's cottage would not leave her, pressing into her mind as she drifted off into an unsteady sleep. She smelled the rancid scent of the trash. The tang of a boy's messy room. Textbooks. Computer printouts. In her dream, she stepped into the tiny bathroom. She opened the cabinet above the sink and peered inside. A bottle of cough syrup sat beside a small plastic bottle of eye drops and a bottle of aftershave. She lifted out the dark red syrup, opened it and sniffed. Something wasn't right, but she could not hold onto the image or the smell.

She jolted upright, suddenly awake. She had to go back to the cottage, and she couldn't wait until morning.

Quickly, she threw her sweater on over her nightshirt, retrieved her shoes from under the bed, slid them on, grabbed her phone, and went downstairs and out through the kitchen door. She remembered how easily Mia had entered the cottage. A little jiggling of the door handle. She was thankful that Borelli was at the hospital with Estella because she was growing more and more suspicious that the directive for the destruction of the wine had come from within the family. But, she didn't want to suggest this to Borelli until she knew for sure. Were her thoughts merely misdirected suspicions? She understood now why Borelli did not wish to approach Leo or Estella about Fabrizio's parentage until he had thoroughly investigated such a possibility. Accusations once made could not be taken back.

Quietly, she made her way toward the cottage. The moon provided sufficient light to follow the narrow path. Cautiously she continued on, finding the cottage without difficulty. She tried the door, doing exactly as Mia had done, but it would not open. She couldn't see the lock well in the dark, so she reached for her phone to use the light, but before she could pull it from her pocket, a light appeared, like a spotlight on the doorknob.

She turned, though her heart seemed to jerk in the opposite direction. A large body moved toward her.

CHAPTER THIRTY-EIGHT

"May I help?" Borelli asked, and Dana easily recognized his voice, though she should have known him from the bulk of his figure, his lumbering movement. He wore a bathrobe over what appeared to be pajamas, slippers flopping on his large feet.

"You scared the living daylights out of me," she said. "I thought you were staying at the hospital with Estella."

"Estella was resting, so I decided to come home, get some sleep myself. Leo will go in early tomorrow." He coughed, cleared his throat. "I had barely slipped into my—" He brushed his broad hand over his robe, the belt hastily tied around his belly. "—when I glanced out the window and saw something or someone, a suspicious looking figure."

"That would be me?" Dana tugged at her sweater, realizing her nightshirt barely hit her knees, and her legs were bare.

"I had no idea it was you," he huffed. "But any activity warrants an investigation."

Agreeing with a nod, Dana asked, "Did Leo talk to you about Fabrizio?"

"He wasn't pleased that neither Estella nor I had shared what we knew about the boy."

"How did Leo learn?"

"My guess is DeLuca."

"And now the media, evidently."

"They are sure to make something of this," Borelli said, "tying the crimes to the mafia."

"While DeLuca insists that what happened to Fabrizio has nothing to do with the destroyed wine and Paolo's death?"

"I have no idea if that is what DeLuca truly believes." Borelli's shoulders rose, then lowered as if deflated. "You think there is something in the cottage that the police investigators missed?"

"The fact that they took the computer out of Leo's office seems to imply they are still looking for something."

"Perhaps." Borelli carried a large flashlight and he steadied the light on the door again.

Dana attempted to jiggle it open. "We need a key."

"Leo would have a key."

"No, we shouldn't wake Leo." Dana glanced back to gauge Borelli's response, but in the dim light she couldn't get a clear take on any reaction.

"In the office in the garage," he said, turning. "Duplicates have always been kept out there. I do have a garage key." He reached into the pocket of his robe.

Together they headed to the garage. "We must be as quiet as possible," he told her, voice low, as they approached the building. "Claudio has an apartment in the back, and I don't want to awaken him."

"He has an apartment here?" It seemed every time they had come out, Claudio was fussing around, up to something. If he wasn't out driving, he was in the garage, so it made sense that he slept here, too. "What will we say if he wakes up?"

"We'll tell him we are going for a drive."

"He won't find that odd? At this hour?"

"Oh, I've done it before at this hour," he said.

Dana laughed nervously, knowing this was probably true.

Borelli carefully unlocked the door, opened it slowly and stepped inside. Dana followed as he continued quietly toward a door at the far corner of the building. He unlocked it. Using the flashlight in the windowless office, he didn't have any trouble finding several keys on a pegboard next to a desk in one corner. A number were old-fashioned skeleton keys like one might expect to unlock a centuries-old cottage. The hooks on which they hung were marked with numbers. Borelli picked one out with confidence and, as quietly as they had entered, they retraced their steps and were soon back outside.

As they continued on to the cottage, Dana sensed a flash of light in her peripheral vision. Quickly, she turned, seeing no light, but catching a flicker of movement, something disappearing into the shadows.

"Did you see that?" she whispered, heart thumping.

"What?"

"A light, then something moving."

He glanced back, shrugged. "There are a number of motion sensor lights around the villa. Also, the wildlife is more active at night."

Dana remembered a light had flicked on when she and Leo approached the house in the dark, and she recalled Mia's description of Renata chasing the deer out of the garden with a broom. Maybe it was a deer, or maybe this was merely her hyperactive imagination.

They continued on to the cottage, which Borelli unlocked with ease. Once inside he clicked on the flashlight but kept the beam low. Dana studied the room, her gaze bouncing about as Borelli directed the light.

Stepping toward the table, but touching nothing, she could see that items had been rearranged and some removed. The letter from

Fabrizio's grandmother and the textbooks she'd seen on her earlier visit were no longer there.

"Fabrizio was taking classes at the University?" she asked. "Botany? Chemistry?"

"If he wished to make this a career, a position here, those would be the most likely choices."

"There were some textbooks on the table," she said. "One had several computer printouts stuffed inside. But I didn't see a computer or laptop."

"The internet, the reception is not good," he explained.

"No Wi-Fi?"

"The Wi-Fi only works close to the house," Borelli said and then, "His grandmother might have come to get the books. If the boy is coming back to continue his studies."

Dana wondered if this could possibly be true. Surely, if he was still in danger, the grandmother would not bring him back.

"Fabrizio used the computer in the house?" she asked.

"Yes, I suppose if he needed to do research, use the internet."

Dana knew that Borelli too was thinking of the computer the police had removed from Leo's office. There was something on that computer the police wished to examine.

Dana made her way into the tiny bathroom, Borelli following. She opened the cabinet. Borelli flashed the beam. Nothing inside but two bottles—the eye drops, the aftershave.

"What are you looking for?" Borelli asked. His eyes darted around the small space, swinging the flashlight as if he too was looking for something. A towel hung lopsided on the rack. Borelli straightened it, and Dana couldn't help but think of how anal he could be at times, but she also wondered if Borelli was searching for something she hadn't considered.

"Just checking," Dana said, "to see if we can find anything that the police might have missed, anything that—"

"Well?" Borelli snorted. He seemed impatient now, but Dana sensed it was more than that. He knew she wasn't completely sharing her thoughts. As he was not sharing his.

Finally, she said, "There was a bottle of cough syrup. It's gone."

"Cough syrup?" Borelli asked. "How strange it is now missing."

"The letter, textbooks, computer printouts, cough syrup, all missing." She glanced at Borelli and could tell he was attempting to string all of these items together.

Dana stepped out of the bathroom, along with Borelli. After another quick look through the main room of the cottage, careful not to touch anything, they started back to the villa.

They were halfway back when Dana asked, "Did you ever taste it? The wine in the barrels, the Brunello?"

"The destroyed wine?" Borelli hesitated, thinking. "There were several tastings during those many years in barrel. Yes, I tasted it. A time or two."

"And?"

"Quite good," he said. Again, the silence and dark of the night enveloped them.

"As one ages," he said after an uncomfortable pause, "the taste buds, the sense of smell, these sensual perceptions often diminish." Dana realized that was a lot for Borelli to admit, but it gave her another thought. A conversation they had several days ago when she asked if one could tell the difference if a wine was produced from less than the 100% Sangiovese. At first Borelli had seemed insulted, but he'd then admitted that very few people could tell the difference if the bulk of the grapes used were Montalcino Sangiovese. She wondered if Fabrizio was one of those few.

CHAPTER THIRTY-NINE

Giovanna drove Winkie to the airport in Rome early Friday morning. It might have been an uncomfortable hour and a half, particularly after what Giovanna had revealed, but he felt oddly at ease with her, as if he had known her much longer than the week it had been. He wondered if there was a genetic link that created this feeling of familiarity.

They talked about Winkie's plans for the business, Giovanna eager to contribute to the conversation. Winkie realized that he would like to stay longer, but he was anxious to get back and share all of this with Sam and Audra. He also had a production company to run, having put his business on hold for the past week. This morning he'd spent several hours on his phone, mostly sending text messages and emails because of the time difference between Italy and New York. He'd also made several local calls, setting up a nursing service to attend to Lorenzo, speaking to local wine consultants, getting leads on possible staff. He'd told Giovanna he'd be back in two weeks.

"I'd like to bring my children here on their next school break," he said.

"I'm reluctant to let you go." Winkie was touched by her sincerity. "When is the next break for your children?'

"Thanksgiving, toward the end of next month."

"Ah, yes, the American holiday. Do either Sam or Audra speak Italian?"

"Each a little, Audra more than Sam. I'm looking forward to you meeting them."

"Me, too," Giovanna replied, but Winkie could hear the tension wrapping around her words. "How much are you going to tell them?"

"They know I was adopted. I've shared that much with them. I will tell them that I have found you."

"But, the rest—"

"Not yet." He wasn't sure what he would tell them about his birth father. He was still attempting to understand this part himself. To sort out the strange, disturbing story of his conception. Over and over again, Giovanna had told him that she didn't want to hurt him, and he didn't want to hurt her either. He didn't want to hurt his children. He would eventually tell them, but he wasn't sure when or how.

"Do you still love him?" he asked Giovanna.

She shot him a puzzled look.

"Giovanni Borelli."

"How did you know?" she asked. He could see the muscles in her face tighten.

"You let it slip, the name Borelli. The rest I deduced for myself."

She turned at the sign for *aeroporto* but didn't say anything. He studied her face, her profile as she slowed down, reading and following the signs for passenger drop-off. They had agreed on this—she would drop him off, they would not have a formal farewell at the airport. No hugs, no kisses. No public display.

As he studied her face, he attempted to find a trace of himself, of Audra, of Sam. Maybe a little of Audra, but his daughter was blonde like her mother. Giovanna bit down on her lip, just as he'd seen Audra do when she was about to cry.

The image of the gruff-looking Vincenzo Veronesi that Winkie had seen in the American wine magazine flashed through his mind. Did Winkie himself contain some of this man's evil?

"I liked him, Giovanni Borelli," Winkie said after a while. "We had a chance to talk on the drive from the Borelli estate to your villa." She hadn't answered his question, but he really hadn't expected her to.

"Yes, I liked him, too," she finally said as she pulled into the passenger drop off area. She did not use the word *love.*

"It's not too late," Winkie said, surprising himself.

"He's a priest," she said.

"I've never believed in that celibacy thing," Winkie came back, again astonishing himself that he would say such a thing aloud.

"Well, that's encouraging that you think I'm still interested in sex." She laughed lightly.

Winkie tried to keep from smiling himself. He could hardly believe he was talking about sex with his mother. What strange mixed emotions had come into play. Yet, he knew the woman who raised him was his "mother," a woman he could not imagine having such a conversation with. He also knew that he and Giovanna were still attempting to define their relationship. Perhaps it wasn't necessary to put a label on whatever they now shared. He realized these feelings, these emotions between them, were still growing. Together and separately they were attempting to find their way.

"Two weeks," she said as he turned to bid her farewell. She had flipped the trunk lever open so he could retrieve his luggage. He sat silently for a moment, then kissed her quickly on the cheek before opening the door and going around to get his bags. He was about to cry and when he gazed into the vehicle he could see the glisten in her eyes, a reflection of his own. He turned to leave, then glanced back and smiled. She smiled too, and he walked into the airport.

On the plane, before the flight attendant came around to tell him to turn off his phone, he texted his children to let them know he was on his way home. Just as he was about to put the phone into airplane mode, he noticed a message from an unfamiliar number. *Please take a look and listen.*

He usually didn't open anything from a source not in his contacts, but he thought it might be something from the police investigator. Quickly, he flipped it on and saw it was from Father Giovanni Borelli. He'd included a link to a video file, the source Borellivine.com. Winkie attempted to open it, but it was loading too slowly.

He could see the flight attendant, shaking her finger at him, and he turned off the phone. He'd look at it when he got home. He was too exhausted to deal with the Borellis' problems right now.

Estella arrived back at the estate shortly before lunch Friday. Dana thought the woman looked remarkably well. The short time in the hospital had done wonders for her appearance. She looked as healthy as she had the first evening at dinner, a full week ago when Dana arrived.

Leo had let Mia take the day off from school, and he and his daughter accompanied Estella up to her room, where the three of them would have lunch.

Borelli and Dana sat in the dining room alone.

"Well," Borelli said after the *primo piatto* had been served, "I suppose we should finish the conversation we started last night."

Dana nodded vaguely, wanting Borelli to take the lead.

"The missing cough syrup," he prompted. "You don't believe it was cough syrup."

"It was in a bottle clearly medicinal, the label in Italian, but I didn't examine it, smell it, or taste it." She paused, waiting for a question, but when there was none, she said, "The mind becomes conditioned to seeing something as it is represented." Her words sounded so formal.

"Yes," Borelli said in a weary voice. "We tend to accept things as they are represented. A bottle is labeled cough syrup, and you assume that's what it is." Dana sensed that Borelli was thinking about more than cough syrup.

She took a drink of water, before continuing. "Later, when I replayed the scene over in my head, Mia and I going into the bathroom, picking out items to take to Fabrizio, I realized the color, the depth, all wrong for cough syrup, it was deeper, richer, redder, almost the color of—"

"Wine," Borelli supplied the word. He had yet to touch the plate of pasta shells with marinara placed in front of him. Neither had Dana. "You think it was wine? Why would Fabrizio have a small sample of wine in the medicine cabinet in a cough syrup bottle, and why would it now be missing?"

"That's what I've been trying to determine," she said.

"You believe Fabrizio took a sample of the Brunello," Borelli said, "from the barrel before the wine was destroyed."

Dana raised her shoulders, but she said nothing.

"You think there was something wrong with the wine?" There was a harsh edge to his voice. "You think the wine was tainted and that is why it was destroyed?"

"Not tainted," she answered cautiously, "but perhaps not up to Brunello requirements."

"He took this sample for what purpose?" he said, the words flat as if attempting to remain calm, as if attempting to extract information from a witness.

"What if the wine was determined to be less than the required one-hundred percent Sangiovese produced within the prescribed area of Montalcino?"

"There would be nothing *wrong* with the wine," Borelli said with more than a hint of defensiveness. "It could be relabeled."

"But it would be sold for substantially less?"

"Yes, substantially less than a Brunello," he admitted.

"If unauthorized grapes were used . . ." Dana wondered if a small amount was added early in the process, would it be difficult to taste the difference in the finished wine? Numbers ran through her head. The destroyed wine was worth anywhere from eight to fifteen million, depending on whose figures were used. What if 10%, maybe 15%, possibly 20% of the grapes were unauthorized? If such grapes could be obtained for a very reasonable price, how much extra profit might be realized? A million? A million and a half? It could be substantial, but would it be worth the risk of being caught?

"Unauthorized grapes," Borelli huffed, "in a Borelli Brunello?" He took a slow drink of wine, placed the glass back on the table and gazed into the dark red liquid. "If the wine was discovered to be misrepresented as a Brunello, if it had been sold as such, the consequences would be disastrous. The legal consequences. The reputation of the entire wine industry here in Montalcino would be tarnished if one of the major vineyards was misrepresenting a wine."

"Legal consequences?" Dana asked.

"Prison time. Substantial fines." His voice was fading, and she could see that Borelli was not pleased with what she was implying. But now that they had started this conversation, she knew they had to continue. She wanted to ask about something Marco and the Simonelli distributors had talked about—clonal studies. She guessed that through science it could be determined specifically what grapes had been used in the wine. Exactly where they had been harvested.

"Is it possible," she said, "to test, to determine by scientific analysis, the type of grape, the origin—"

"The origin of a wine can be detected, the process much like doing human DNA testing." He scrubbed his eyes with his wide palm as if something was irritating them. "DNA profiling. But I doubt that a boy taking a basic botany or chemistry class would be capable of doing such an analysis."

Dana knew that human DNA testing to determine heritage had

become popular and fairly easy to do. Now Borelli was confirming that this could be done with wine also. She agreed that Fabrizio would most likely not be capable of this. But, maybe a professor from the university where Fabrizio studied might take an interest in such a project.

"Such testing is very expensive and rarely done," Borelli added.

"So, it's all on the honor system? The designations awarded the wine based on honor?"

"There are tastings before the DOCG designations are awarded. Taste. Smell. Color. Texture. All of the sensual perceptions used in judging a wine are likely to reveal if it is not as the producer has represented it."

"Marco was talking about yields per acre. If it was learned that the yield had not been sufficient to produce the number of liters contained in the barrels, the number of bottles anticipated?" She thought about the computer taken from Leo's office.

"Such information, available in company records."

Dana didn't reply. Borelli was working through this himself.

"You think that Fabrizio became aware of such a discrepancy?" Borelli asked.

"What do you think?" Dana asked.

"The wine has been in barrel for over four years. Much before Fabrizio's arrival."

She could tell he didn't like the theory she was proposing, because it would definitely imply someone on the inside had taken part in the destruction.

"If this were the case," Borelli said, the words coming slowly and thoughtfully, "it would certainly implicate someone close." Dana could feel the pulse of Borelli's heart in his words. "Such accusations, if proven true, would be devastating . . . to the reputation," he continued, considering each phrase, "to the future of the Borelli Vineyards."

CHAPTER FORTY

Dana spent the early afternoon in her room, propped on her bed, reading online translations of the latest stories about the Borelli Vineyards in the local news. She found several articles she considered more reliable than the blog, which was taking credit for breaking the story about the mob connection.

There was no evidence presented that the Calaberonis had anything to do with the boy being shot, the destruction in the cellar, or Paolo's death, yet, the mere fact of Fabrizio's family background seemed to imply guilt.

Maybe the real story—whatever it was—might be equally scandalous. One reporter accused the police of a cover-up, which Dana thought might be true. At the least, they were not releasing all of the information. There was no mention of the money left in the rundown building on the Veronesi property, or Dana's being taken in for questioning. She exhaled a sigh of relief at that. There was nothing about the computer taken from Leo's office, no mention of books, papers, or a wine sample taken from Fabrizio's cottage.

Two arrests had been confirmed—the environmentalist's, for the wine destruction and Paolo's death, and Silvio Gallo's for the attempt on Fabrizio's life.

One article revealed that Fabrizio's whereabouts were unknown, which Dana guessed was true. DeLuca denied any mob connection in what had happened in the community, and he was quoted as having said another arrest was imminent, though so far nothing indicated the two crimes were related, and there was nothing to lead officials to believe others were in danger.

Dana rose from the bed and went to the window, gazing out. Though she could not see Fabrizio's cottage from where she stood, her imagination led her in that direction. She and Borelli were making their way to the cottage, and then her thoughts circled back in time, and she and Mia were inside. Dana wondered how much Mia knew about the latest developments. Her father was protective, but with the internet, her new phone, the girl would have easy access to what Dana had just read. Mia was clearly upset last evening at dinner. She had so many reasons to be upset, and Dana's heart ached for Mia. She didn't want to do anything to hurt her. But what if Mia's father was involved in the destruction of his own wine, Paolo's death, the attempted murder of Fabrizio?

Dana turned from the window, crossed the room, and stepped out into the hall. She knocked on the door to Borelli's room, but she received no reply. After searching for him downstairs, she stepped outside and walked quickly to the garage where she found Claudio, though Borelli's truck was gone. When she asked, "Father Borelli?" he barely looked up from the open hood of the vehicle he was working on. He grunted a few words which she interpreted to mean he hadn't seen him.

She meandered around the nearest vineyard, not really expecting to find Borelli, but feeling a need to move. A light breeze ruffled her hair, sending a chill through her. She circled back to the house. When she returned to her room and stepped in, she noticed an envelope slipped under her door. She reached down, snatched it up, and turned it over to see her name written in Borelli's hand. Quickly she tore it open.

> Please accept Marco's invitation for dinner this evening. With her prescribed medication, Estella is doing much better. We will have time with the family at the festa tomorrow before your departure on Sunday. I've spoken with Marco and he'll be by for you about seven. You may take a vehicle if you wish to go into town to shop or look around before dinner. I've informed Claudio.
> Giovanni

Well, looks like Borelli had gone ahead and arranged her date. Yet, there was something more in this message. Borelli was angry with her for her suspicions that something was amiss with the wine, that it had been destroyed merely to get rid of it and any evidence that the Borellis were falsely representing their Brunello. Was he now ready to accept what the police were telling the press—that the crimes had been solved? Whether this was true or not? Again, she thought about leaving the estate, letting the police, Borelli, and Leo—guilty or not—sort through all of this. But she knew she couldn't leave this unresolved. Yet, if her suspicions were valid it would hurt the family terribly. She couldn't bear to think what it might do to Mia.

Thoughts of Marco flitted through her mind. It made her angry that Borelli had become involved—setting up her date with Marco. What if she didn't want to go? She felt an unyielding flutter moving inside her, and she knew it was much more complicated than an arranged date. If the wine was not as represented, there were several people other than Leo who would know.

Knowing did not imply that Marco was involved in the destruction. Or that he had anything to do with what had happened to Fabrizio. But it would be impossible for the enologist to be unaware if his wine was not an authentic Borelli Brunello.

After leaving a note for Dana, Giovanni went to the garage, climbed into his truck, and started down the hill and over the hillside toward the Veronesi estate. He had not heard from Winkie Dalton since he'd sent the video but, as he recalled, Winkie was scheduled to leave Friday. It was now Friday afternoon.

The truck bumped along the road. He pulled off, knowing after about five minutes that he had crossed over the property line. He was no longer on Borelli land.

Within a short time, scraping the undercarriage of his truck several times on the rutted path, he saw what he was looking for. He pulled up to the deserted buildings. For a moment he sat, wondering what exactly he was looking for. He was fairly sure this was where Winkie had overheard the conversation, where the *Salva la Terra* protester Jago DeCampo had been shot, where Inspector DeLuca had found Dana and hauled her into headquarters. In one of these buildings someone, possibly someone from the Borelli Vineyards, had dropped off a payment for Jago.

There was nothing to indicate any of the structures were being secured. Nothing marking a crime scene where an unarmed man was shot. Giovanni got out and approached the front door of the nearest building. Twisting the knob, he found it unlocked. Slowly he opened it and peered inside.

Light slanted through a broken window, illuminating a figure. A woman stood, sorting through boxes of what appeared to be wine labels. Dozens of dusty green Bordeaux glass bottles were arranged along a shelf.

She turned. After a moment of adjusting, her eyes blinking, she focused on Giovanni. It did not appear that she was startled at his being there.

"Gia," he said. She wore a bandana over her hair. In the dim light, he could barely make out her features. Yet, he could tell, by the outline of her form, that she was still small and trim. Giovanni had never been one to rely on his looks, but now he wished he hadn't put on so much weight. He'd changed so much, she probably would not recognize him.

"Gianni?" she said, eyes squinting.

He stood paralyzed for a moment, unable to speak, and then he took a step closer. "How did you know it was me?" he asked.

"Your voice."

He had said but a single word. Her name.

They stood, neither speaking for a long moment. His throat tightened.

Finally, she said, "We've sold the vineyards, the winery, the house."

"Yes, I heard," he said as if this was the most natural conversation to have after fifty years. "An American. A movie actor. I met him."

"As I understand," she said, picking up a towel and wiping the grime off of her hands. "I'm just trying to go through some of this—I don't even know what to call it. Like going through a box of ghosts." She laughed sadly. "It was a good move, selling the business," she said as if it was necessary to explain or defend herself for selling out to an American.

"His roots are Italian," Giovanni said, contributing his approval to the deal she had struck. "I dropped by the other day. I see Andrea is still with the family. He wasn't particularly welcoming."

"Well, you know Andrea. He's likely not pleased with these latest developments. I haven't fully shared yet, but the new owner is being extremely generous about keeping the household staff on, listening to my suggestions on how we might revive the business. Would you like to come up to the house for some lunch?" she offered.

"I ate lunch several hours ago."

She glanced at her wrist, then seemed to realize she wasn't wearing her watch.

"It's well past midafternoon," he said.

"Oh, time," she scoffed with a wave of her hand. "It does seem to get away from us now, doesn't it?"

"Yes," he agreed. "It does."

"Too early for dinner," she said. "Perhaps a glass of wine."

"Yes, a glass of wine."

"Very good. I could offer you a glass of wine." For the first time since he'd stepped into the building, he detected an awkwardness, an unsteady pulse in her voice. "Please come up to the house. But you will allow me a short time to clean up."

"Yes, of course," he said, even as he thought, *you are beautiful. Just the way you are.*

They went outside. Giovanni glanced around and realized she had walked from the villa. He motioned toward his truck and then opened the door for her, wishing he had something better to offer. They laughed as they bumped up the overgrown road to the house.

"We're going to do some renovations," she told him. "Bring the house back as closely as possible to its original condition."

It sounded to Giovanni like the new owner was including Gia in any changes he was making in order to revive the Veronesi label and villa. She seemed enthusiastic, alive with the thought of such a project.

"I understand," she said, "you've had some shocking troubles over the past week. I'm so sorry. The loss of wine, Paolo Paluzzi's death. The family must be devastated."

"Yes." Giovanni knew the news had become part of the conversation throughout the entire municipality of Montalcino, that all of the producers would be relieved that an arrest had been made.

"A young man was shot?" she asked. "He was a new employee?"

"Yes, though a suspect has been apprehended. I think it's all been resolved," Giovanni said, wishing it were true. It didn't sound as if Gia had read the latest—the accusations of a mob connection.

"That's good news," she said.

"Yes, good news indeed." He realized he was smiling as they arrived at the villa, a structure as old and dilapidated as Giovanni

Borelli felt himself. But surely receptive to coming back to life, he thought as they pulled into the driveway.

CHAPTER FORTY-ONE

When Dana arrived back at the villa late that afternoon, after spending the day driving, thinking, picking up a few trinkets in Montalcino for her family back home, even a new scarf to wear that evening, she noticed the visitors' center had reopened. A tourist van was parked out front. She walked in. A group had gathered around a guide who was pouring samples of wine.

Dana glanced toward Leo's office. She started down the hall. His door was open. He looked up from his desk, then called out, "Dana."

Rising, he walked out to meet her in the hall. "I spoke with Inspector DeLuca." Leo's voice sounded both fatigued and tense. "A second arrest has been made in connection with Paolo's death and the wine destruction. Carlo Porcini has been arrested."

"A former employee. He was affiliated with the environmental protesters?"

"No affiliation with the group *Salva la Terra.* But, perhaps both with unfounded reasons to be angry with the Borelli family."

"These men weren't acquaintances?" Dana tried to keep the skepticism out of her voice.

Two men brought together, by a third person? she wondered. Borelli's description of Carlo—like a mushroom, he'd said—didn't fit Winkie's description of the person he'd overheard conversing with Jago DeCampo on Giovanna Veronesi's property.

"Joined in a common goal," Leo said, "though Alberto believes there was no intention to harm Paolo."

"This seems to have been the theory all along," Dana said. *But, what about the money left in the building on the Veronesi property? What about the conversation that Winkie overheard?* Leo had no knowledge of either or maybe he was keeping it from her.

"Have you shared this with Mia?" she asked.

"Yes."

"And the recent reports in the news regarding Fabrizio?"

"Merely the press trying to stir up more sensationalism." He shook his head dismissively. "Alberto believes that the crimes have been solved."

"I noticed the visitors' center is open again."

Leo nodded and smiled. "Yes, it seems we can get back to doing what we do best, sell fine Italian wine."

"Where is Mia? I'd like to talk to her." Dana was concerned about how the girl was handling all of this.

"Mia is with my mother now, but she will spend the evening in town with her friends"

"They're both doing okay?"

"Mother is much better, and perhaps it is good for Mia to look forward to time with her friends."

"Yes," Dana agreed. For a girl Mia's age, Dana knew friends could be helpful, often providing comfort that family could not. "I'll let you get back to work," she said.

"Yes, there is much to do, much neglected over the past days." He didn't move, made no effort to return to his desk. "I understand you have a date this evening."

For a family keeping so many secrets from one another, it was more than odd that Leo was aware of Dana's *date*. "Marco's taking me out to dinner, maybe out to see some of the sights."

"Enjoy the evening." There was a hint of something in Leo's tone that Dana couldn't quite read. He seemed a little miffed, though he smiled affably before he returned to his desk.

Dana went upstairs to shower and change. She'd decided to wear her jeans—not that she had much else to choose from. Her newly purchased skirt was too formal. Her slacks ruined. The new jacket she'd bought shopping with Mia, and the scarf she'd picked up in Montalcino that afternoon would give her jeans a less casual look.

As she arranged her scarf, tying and re-knotting to get it right, she could not get her mind off of Leo and the nagging possibility that he had destroyed his own wine. Fabrizio had been taken away by his grandmother, but could the boy still show up as a witness to point the finger at Leo? Dana realized she did not wish her suspicions to be true, especially for Mia's sake. Perhaps for Leo's, too. And Borelli. But, what if they were? There was something puzzling about Leo. As Borelli said, it seemed he was hiding something.

As she was finishing her makeup, Dana thought of what Borelli had shared about Leo. How he seldom went out to the vines, the cellars. She wondered if this detachment had something to do with the loss of his wife. Borelli had told her that Leo's wife's first bout with cancer had been about four years ago. During the busy harvest season. Then remission, then the cancer was back. Leo had lost her two years ago. Borelli had said something about Leo too being ill. About Leo turning most of the duties over to Marco.

Then Dana had another thought—grapes for the destroyed Borelli Brunello were harvested the same year Leo's wife was diagnosed with cancer. Borelli had told Dana that Leo had spent months in Rome with his wife for chemo treatments. Leo was not present for the harvest that year.

Dana glanced over at the dresser, the bottle of perfume Mia had picked out for her. She hadn't worn any since the dinner in town with the Simonelli group. She'd never questioned Mia about her choice of this particular scent. Dana remembered how Borelli had reacted, obviously aware this was Teresa Antonelli's perfume. Even Marco had taken a sniff, then shot her a puzzled look. But, no reaction from Leo. He was attentive on the drive back to the estate, but no obvious reaction to the perfume. This was more than strange.

She spritzed a dab on each wrist.

Downstairs, before going to the living room to wait for Marco, she walked down the hall and tested the door that connected the villa to the visitors' center. It was unlocked. She took a few steps until she stood before Leo's office door. She knocked.

When Leo called out, "Yes," Dana opened the door.

He looked up, surprised.

"Have you seen your uncle?" she asked, stepping closer.

"I have not seen him since earlier today when we brought Mother home from the hospital."

Dana stood near enough he could have touched her. He seemed, for a moment, startled by the proximity.

Finally, Leo said, "Tomorrow, the formal activities of the *festa* begin. I would like you to join us in celebrating with dinner in town. I believe I have convinced Mia this would be a good opportunity for family time. I have allowed her this evening with her friends." Dana wasn't sure if Leo was inviting her because she was a family guest, or if he personally wished her to come.

But one thing she was sure of now—Leo Antonelli had no sense of smell.

CHAPTER FORTY-TWO

Marco arrived, wearing jeans with a jacket, open-collared shirt, no tie. Dana had always liked this look for a man, and Marco carried it off extremely well. Her own casual attire, jeans with jacket and scarf, matched his perfectly. Someone might take note, she thought as they stepped outside, that they made a very nice couple.

"I am pleased you accepted my invitation," Marco said.

This might have put Dana at ease under different circumstances, yet, she felt apprehensive as Marco escorted her to his vehicle, hand placed gently on her back. The idea of a romantic evening was oddly appealing, yet her rational nature continued to intrude, prodding her with unanswered questions about what had taken place at the Borelli Vineyards over the past week.

Marco drove a sporty looking coupe, a European brand, an Alfa Romeo.

"I have a dinner reservation in town at eight-thirty," Marco told her, "but perhaps you might enjoy a drive."

As they took off, they spoke of Estella, what a relief to everyone that she was doing so well. Driving around the estate, covering much of the same terrain that Dana had her first day with Father Borelli, Marco explained at what point each piece of the property had come to the family.

"My father began working for the Borellis just after the war. He was instrumental in producing the first Borelli Brunello vintages, though the Brunello di Montalcino was not available to the general public until the sixties."

"You've got quite a family history here in the Montalcino wine country."

"Yes, much history," Marco said, slowing the vehicle as they started over one of the unpaved paths that ran along the rows of vines. "It is nice to enjoy the evening." He stopped, motioned out toward the distant hillside. The sun had slipped beyond the horizon, leaving a hint of pink and gold folding into the landscape.

"Time to relax," Marco said, voice low, his arm settled along the back of her seat. "Time to enjoy now that those who released the wine have been apprehended."

"It's beautiful," Dana said, realizing how much she wanted this to be true, even as her mind circled back to her suspicions.

"One of the men involved," Marco said, "a former employee. So sad that one who had worked for the Borellis would turn against them."

"What about Fabrizio?" she asked, curious why Marco would bring this up when he'd brought her to such a romantic setting and suggested they relax. "Do you believe the attempt on his life is not related to what happened in the cellar?"

"The police do not believe it is related."

"Did you know," she asked cautiously, "about Fabrizio's family? Did you know he is a Calaberoni?"

"No one knew," Marco replied, no hint of offense in his voice. "It seems this was all arranged through Estella Antonelli. Yet the press is determined to make something of this, implying his family was involved." Marco paused, shook his head. "Forgive me for this conversation. It was my intention that we enjoy the evening."

He touched her cheek, and then he leaned closer and kissed her, and she responded. She felt a stirring deep inside her, a mixture of longed-for intimacy and fear. She didn't want this to go any further. Not here. Not now. Not yet.

He kissed her again, deeper, his arm moving from the back of the seat, onto her shoulder, his hand resting near her breast.

And then her tummy rumbled with hunger. It growled.

Marco laughed, and then Dana did too.

"Perhaps I should feed you first," he said.

"Maybe so." She felt herself blush with embarrassment. *Now that was a mood breaker, or maybe a saving grace.*

"You are hungry?"

She nodded and looked at her watch. "Our dinner reservation?"

He hesitated a moment then said, "Yes, we must leave for town." He started the car, then glanced over at Dana with a grin. "Perhaps later."

She didn't reply but felt a nervous flutter that was in no way related to her empty stomach.

As they headed back toward Montalcino, Marco continued to point out landmarks, then repeated much of what Borelli had told her earlier about the history of the *Sagra del Tordo*, the festivities that would take place over the weekend, the upcoming archery contest. Neither spoke of the young man who had been accused of shooting Fabrizio, though Dana sensed that they were both thinking of Silvio Gallo, in jail now, unable to participate in the competition.

They arrived at the restaurant in Montalcino, and a young man escorted them to an outdoor table. Portable heaters glowed around the patio, diminishing the chill of the evening. As tables filled up, lively crowds moved down the street, many in costume, people chatting, laughing, caught up in the celebratory mood of the *festa*.

"The *Sagra del Tordo*, the Feast of the Thrush." Marco grinned. "Now an endangered species, so we are unable to partake of the namesake of this festival." He glanced over the menu. "Perhaps a local dish? Lampredotta?"

"Which is?"

"Cow stomach."

"Maybe something else?" She grimaced, then laughed.

"Pappardelle, an Italian noodle, with a nice wild hare sauce?"

"That sounds much better."

Marco picked out a wine, surprisingly not a Borelli, and ordered a bottle, as well as the pappardelle for both of them.

The waiter soon delivered bread, then the wine, quickly pouring a glass for each of them, before moving with speed on to the next table.

The meal came surprisingly fast, maybe due to the line of guests waiting for tables, and the server remained attentive, refilling their wine, offering more bread.

Dana had wondered if the recent events at the Borelli Vineyards would discourage travelers from coming to celebrate the *Sagra del Tordo*, but judging from the crowds it didn't seem they had. Perhaps visitors were drawn by the shocking real-life drama and, if one were to believe Inspector DeLuca, there was no further danger. Even greater reason for the locals to celebrate. As Dana enjoyed the warmth of the wine, the satisfaction of the dinner, the celebratory atmosphere, as well as Marco's company, she too wanted to believe that all had been resolved.

As they finished their meal, Marco suggested they go up to the *fortezza*.

"In the day, the view of the surrounding area is beautiful. In the evening, *romantico*." He smiled and glanced up. "The moon is almost full."

A romantic evening indeed, Dana thought, but in the back of her mind she cautioned herself.

"You seem happy, relaxed," Giovanni told Gia, realizing that being in her presence again after so many years made him feel more relaxed than he'd felt in decades. Why had he not fought harder for her? It would have changed his entire life. Hers, too. He had tried, but perhaps not enough. He'd sent a letter, and he'd often wondered if she'd received it. He hadn't known where to find her and her mother refused to speak to him. Gia had disappeared, then he heard she'd married the following year. To the man she'd dumped him for? He wasn't sure. She had said cruel things about Giovanni. She had found someone else. Yet, he knew she had not found true happiness. The marriage did not last.

They had spent the afternoon, and now evening, talking, sipping wine, nibbling on cheese, bread, salami, and olives, though it was now well past dinner time. They had spoken of the area where they had grown up, memories of the carefree life they had led as children, the fact that they had both lived in Rome for many years, yet had not once crossed paths, and now how strangely their lives had circled back to where they had begun. They did not speak of the reason for Gia's breaking off the engagement.

"You like this buyer?" he asked her. "This Winkie Dalton? You trust him?"

"Yes, I do. I think he will revive the label. I've put a lot of thought and research into this decision." She lowered her eyes as if studying the glass of wine that sat on the table before her. "Perhaps we can compete with the Borelli label again," she added with a smile, looking at him now, a bit of a tease in her eyes. Giovanni realized that she had not changed at all. Gia's smile. It was in her eyes as much as on her lips. She took a sip of wine.

They sat in the kitchen of the villa, not in the formal living or dining room. A young girl had prepared a plate of antipasti, and Andrea had brought in a bottle of wine from the cellar. Stiff and formal, he shot Giovanni an unapproving look, but as a good employee, the man said nothing.

"Due to the generosity of the new buyer," Gia said, "I'll be able to visit whenever I wish. And . . ." Her lip quivered and she took another small sip of wine as if this might settle her nerves. "Lorenzo is here. His health is not good. I'm sure even back when we were children, there were always those horrible stories. The crazies in the

Veronesi family. We now understand much better about . . . Lorenzo suffers from dementia. As did my grandfather. Lorenzo was in a facility in Rome, but he didn't do well. I brought him here. He is doing better. We've made arrangements to have him cared for here at the villa."

"The new owner has agreed to this?" Giovanni couldn't hide his dismay. "An unusual arrangement."

"Yes, perhaps unusual." Again, she lowered her gaze.

They were both silent for many moments, Giovanni contemplating how to continue this conversation. He didn't want to leave. There were so many things he wanted to ask her.

"Will this terrible rivalry now die?" he said in a playful voice.

"The Borellis and the Veronesis? You believe with a new owner things will change?" Her voice, too, bore a hint of good-natured banter.

"So, what was it all about, Gia?" he asked, his tone taking a serious turn. "We both grew up with this, a stupid rivalry that began years ago."

"So long ago." She sighed. "The past generations, my father, grandfather, your grandfather. You know the Veronesis used to own as far as the eye could see. I think it was more a rivalry of land." She gazed out the window. "Isn't it strange how something like this could go on for so long, the younger generations not even knowing what it was about?" She turned, held up her glass. "To the end of the family feud."

Just as he was about to raise his glass in a toast, Giovanni's phone sounded, the chant that indicated a message.

"Gregorian chant?" she asked, amused, eyebrows raised.

He reached into his pocket, with the intention of turning off his phone, but he could see it was a message from Winkie Dalton. The new owner of the Veronesi Vineyards. How odd that they had just been speaking of him. CALL ME IMMEDIATELY, the message said. All in caps, which Mia had told Giovanni meant the sender was shouting! Finally, Winkie must have viewed the video Giovanni had sent him.

Giovanni rose, his heart beating so fast he feared Gia could hear it. She gave him a puzzled look, somewhat fearful. "I must make a call," he told her.

He stepped outside, taking a deep breath, realizing when he sent Winkie the message he'd most likely been on the plane on his way home. Had he had time to view the video? A video taken from the Borelli family vineyard website. A tour of the vineyards conducted by Leo Antonelli. Giovanni had sent it with the realization that, though Winkie could not identify the man, he could possibly identify the voice. Giovanni pressed the call button.

"Father Borelli, thank you for calling right back." Winkie's voice was anxious. Giovanni could not speak. "I played the video you sent me," Winkie explained. "The man I overheard, I recognized the voice."

Giovanni felt a lump in his throat, a turn of his stomach, realizing he would have to act on this now. It was Leo's voice.

"It's the enologist introduced in the video," Winkie said. "Marco Dardi. I'm sure he is the man I overheard speaking to the environmentalist. I easily recognized the voice, and, as I watched the video, the tour your nephew and Marco did through the vineyards, the way he carried himself, his mannerisms. The man I saw and heard was Marco Dardi. I have no doubt. I'm calling Inspector DeLuca, but I wanted you to know first, as I'm aware the effect this could have on the Borelli Vineyards."

"Yes," Giovanni said sadly. He knew this might be devastating to his family business. And he knew, just because the man Winkie had overheard was Marco Dardi, this did not mean that Leo was innocent.

"Why," Winkie asked. "Why would the man wish to destroy his own wine?"

"I do not know," Giovanni said. But, he did. Dana was right. The prized Borelli Brunello did not meet the standards set out by the Consortium, the requirements set to win the prized DOCG designation. If they had relabeled the wine, the loss would have been in the millions. If the wine had gone to market as a Brunello di Montalcino and the deception uncovered, their reputation would have been destroyed. The legal consequences would have been devastating. Fabrizio discovered that the wine had been degraded and almost lost his life because of this. How had it gotten so out of control? Giovanni could not believe Leo was involved, but how could he not have known?

CHAPTER FORTY-THREE

When Dana and Marco arrived at the *fortezza* he suggested they get a bottle of wine. The two glasses she'd had with dinner were more than enough for Dana, but she did not object. As Marco explained they could access the upper level of the *fortezza* through the enoteca where they could buy their wine, Dana noticed a trio of girls, arms linked, enter the courtyard. They all wore skinny jeans, boots, and short leather jackets, looking very much alike, though the girl in the middle, the smallest, was the prettiest of the three. Mia, her jeans fashionably tattered with a hole in one knee, looked darling, and she looked happy. One of the girls giggled, then all three were laughing.

When Mia noticed Dana and Marco, her mouth turned downward. Unlocking her arms from the other girls, she walked over to where they stood.

"Buona sera," she said, glancing from Dana to Marco. Her smile was uncomfortably forced. "You are enjoying the evening?" Was Dana imagining that as Mia kissed her on each cheek, she took a

little sniff? Dana still didn't know what Mia's intention was with the gift of perfume.

"It is a lovely evening," Marco said.

"Yes," Mia said, then, "I hear that Carlo Porcini has been arrested. The police believe . . ." She paused as if thinking, considering her words carefully. "The police believe he, along with the environmental protester, released the wine."

"Yes," Marco said, "tonight we have reason to celebrate."

Mia stood quietly, then she glanced up at the sky, clear with a sprinkle of vibrant stars. "Tomorrow," she finally said, "we'll celebrate the *festa* as a family. We hope that Grandmother will be well enough to join us for dinner. It has been difficult for her these past days. Now, with the police catching those awful men who did this . . ." Mia studied Dana, then her eyes slid to Marco and tightened, then back to Dana. "Dana, I hope you will join us, too."

"It will be wonderful if your grandmother is able to go," Dana said, "and I'd love to join the family."

"So good to see you," Marco said to Mia.

"Have a lovely evening," Mia said, her smile taut and uncertain. She turned abruptly and joined her friends, who had been giggling and talking to a trio of boys while they waited for her.

"It is good to see Mia enjoy herself," Marco said, and Dana wondered if he was truly unaware of the shift in her mood when she spotted them.

When they reached the enoteca, Marco went to choose the wine, while Dana perused the pictures and posters on the wall from past years of the *Sagra del Tordo*, even as she reflected on Mia's demeanor. She was smiling and seemed happy. Until she spotted Dana with Marco. Something was bothering the girl.

The older pictures were in black and white, but the more recent showed the brightly colored flags and banners, the costumes of archers and medieval maidens of the modern-day celebration. An image of a young man in one of the photos caught Dana's eye. He wore the colors of the Pianello quarter, faded to a pale blue and white. His face seemed oddly familiar, which puzzled Dana—how could she recognize a young man from many years ago, in a place she'd never visited before? Then suddenly it struck her. The same man appeared in a photo in the folder Borelli had given her to study the history of the Borelli Vineyards.

In the photo on the wall, as in the one she'd reexamined two days earlier, the man's thick dark hair had yet to be touched with silver. He smiled into the camera, quiver over his shoulder, bow in hand. Dana yanked her phone out of her pocket to snap a photo.

"Yes, that's me."

She turned. Marco grasped a bottle of wine in one hand, two empty wineglasses, upside down, slipped over his fingers in the other. His smile was identical to the one in the photo on the wall.

"It was not as competitive then," he said, "I was not as skilled as the young men now."

Like Silvio Gallo, Dana thought. Silvio Gallo, who has been accused of shooting Fabrizio. A knot tightened in her chest.

"You enjoyed it?" she asked, voice steady even as her mind raced with possibilities.

"It was fun." Marco handed her the bottle. "Buying a bottle of my own wine!" he said with a grin. With his now-free hand, he reached over and snatched the phone out of hers. "No phones," he said lightly. He dropped it into his pocket. "Let us ascend!" He held up the wineglasses. Dana's heart pulsed rapidly, then even quicker as he took her hand and they climbed the steps. "Let us imagine we are living in a simpler time," he said, "when lovers were not interrupted by such electronic devices."

Dana laughed nervously, attempting to remain composed, confused if it was her growing suspicions, the romantic overtures—his warm hand grasping hers—or both that were causing the intense heat that now surged through her.

They arrived at the upper level. The moon hung bright in the sky, illuminating the valley that stretched before them. Marco released her hand, pointing out the stars, the twinkling lights blinking in the surrounding hills, marking villas, vineyards, and farmland.

They stepped up to the rampart, a narrow walkway surrounded by low stone walls and a more recently added metal barrier.

"Val d'Orcia," Marco said.

Perched on the hillside, in ancient times the fortress would have provided a view of approaching enemies from the valley side where they now stood, access to the city on the other. Only a handful of visitors strolled the rampart on the Val d'Orcia side of the fortress. Dana peered down at the steep drop, then stepped back, turning on the narrow stone path to study the inner courtyard below where people sat drinking wine, sitting at wooden plank tables. Others milled about, many making their way to the enoteca, some leaving the confines for busy cafes, shops, and outdoor vendors in the city. She could see Mia and her friends, chatting with the boys who had joined them. Dana scanned the rampart on the opposite side, where figures, little more than silhouettes, were visible in the moonlight and lights strung along the rail. Many pressed against the outer rails, gazing down at the city, the Piazzale della Fortezza below. Singing and shouting drifted up. *Borghetto. Ruga. Travaglio. Pianello.* Revelers chanting the names of the teams to compete in the upcoming archery competition.

Marco pulled the cork from the bottle, which had been opened and recorked at the enoteca, and poured them each a glass. Realizing there was no place to sit, Dana was about to suggest they go back down when he set the bottle on the stone wall and held his glass up in a toast. "To Montalcino. To Brunello. To Miss Dana Pierson. To the continuing success of the Borelli Vineyards."

He clicked his glass to hers, gazing into her eyes.

A breeze sent a chill through Dana. The heat had left her completely. She was freezing, shivering, and Marco noticed. Gallantly, he took off his jacket and draped it over her shoulders, a gesture so gracious she tried to dismiss the thoughts turning through her head.

"Better?" he asked.

"Yes, thank you."

She took a small sip of wine, pulling Marco's jacket closer around her body.

A family of four, a father, mother and two small boys, poking each other with toy bows, excused themselves as they made their way around Dana and Marco.

"Claudio has been watching you," Marco said after they'd passed.

"Why would he do that?" she asked, confused.

"He has been unhappy since your arrival." Marco's voice was so light and carefree it sounded as if he were about to tell a humorous story.

"I've noticed, but why?" Claudio had seemed fine on the drive to gather the guests at the airport, but his demeanor changed with the request that they deliver Winkie Dalton to the Veronesi estate, and Dana had thought maybe that was the source of his hostilities. She sensed that Marco was about to offer a different theory.

"He has seen you and Father Borelli together. Late at night." Marco paused as if to gauge her reaction. "Half dressed," he added.

"Half dressed?" What is he talking about? And then she realized—Borelli had been wearing his pajamas, robe, and slippers, and she'd pulled her sweater over her nightshirt, but hadn't bothered to put on her jeans when they went out to Fabrizio's cottage. Is that what Claudio considered half-dressed? Dana and Borelli were sure they hadn't awakened him, but maybe they had. She'd sensed someone following them. Had it been Claudio?

"He has always had great respect for the priest," Marco said, "but when you arrived at the—"

"We are friends," Dana broke in. "There is nothing for Claudio to—"

"He's been checking odometers on the vehicles." Marco laughed as if making light of Claudio's concerns. "One day he said you put few miles on the truck and yet you were gone the entire day." Dana realized this must have been the day they flew to Locri.

"Sneaking out to the empty cottage together at night," Marco said. "You might imagine what Claudio thought. The man has quite an imagination."

Hadn't Borelli made it clear they were not romantically involved? Why was Marco telling her this? Had he found it humorous, or was he himself still concerned about Dana's relationship with Father Borelli?

Marco took another drink of wine and his glass was empty. He filled it again, holding the bottle up to offer her more. She shook her head. He set the bottle on the wall and continued, "Perhaps you and the old priest are attempting to find an answer to what has happened at the Borelli Vineyards. Searching for something in the cottage?" His voice was neither demanding nor coy.

"Haven't Alberto DeLuca and his team settled all this?" she replied, twisting her mind back to the possibility that Marco too was sincerely attempting to determine if DeLuca's conclusions were correct.

A young adventurous-looking couple with backpacks stood next to them on the narrow rampart. After gazing down, a quick, animated conversation, exchanging a kiss, they turned and left.

Marco took a drink of wine, his eyes fixed on her. "You and Father Borelli do not believe that Inspector DeLuca has solved these crimes?"

"You don't find it odd that two devastating events—the release of wine, the attack on Fabrizio—occur at the same time, and the police see no connection?"

He was quiet for many moments, rubbing a hand over his chin, then through his thick hair, as if running the thought through his mind. He glanced down at her wineglass. "You do not enjoy the wine?"

"It's very good," she said, "but, I'm certainly no expert in judging the quality of a wine. Is that something one learns from experience? Or is one born with this gift?"

"Perhaps both." He placed his wineglass on the wall and stepped closer, touching her lower lip. His finger was smooth and warm. "I could teach you." His other hand ran down along her hip. His touch, his words were edged with a dangerous pulse, confusing Dana as her feelings shifted from attraction to fear and back again.

She cautioned herself, then said, "Could one distinguish a wine produced from the Sangiovese of Montalcino?" *Don't*, Dana told herself, *don't go there*, but it was too late, she already had. "From one that was merely being represented as a Brunello?"

There was an uncomfortably long moment of quiet. Marco said nothing as if he too was weighing the direction in which he wanted the conversation to proceed. "You believe this relates to what has recently happened?"

Dana swallowed the lump in her throat, pushing it down. Her stomach roiled.

Marco said, "The man protesting what he considered the vineyard's harmful practices, an extremist surely—along with a past employee upset with his dismissal—destroyed the wine. The motive was revenge. What else would it be?" His tone had shifted slightly as if he were defending himself against an accusation that she hadn't made. Did she dare continue?

A chill wind whipped through Dana's hair. She pushed it behind her ear as she pulled Marco's jacket tighter and felt her phone in the pocket. "Maybe we should go down," she suggested. "before we are blown off the rampart." She laughed nervously, glancing around. Most of the brave souls on their side had retreated to the warmth below. One elderly couple huddled together, gazing out toward the lights of the valley.

"But such a romantic setting," Marco said, arm waving toward the moon, eyes taking in the numerous blinking lights from the villas and wineries below. He grabbed his wineglass and took another swallow. "Ah, to destroy a perfect wine," he said sadly, raising his glass, gazing at the dark liquid as if studying the color.

"What if it was not a perfect wine?" the question slipped out, even as Dana told herself, *Stop!*

He laughed. A puzzled look spread over his face, brow furrowed.

"The art of winemaking," she turned the words over slowly. "You spoke of math and science," she said, knowing how dangerous her words might become.

"Ah, yes, you listen well." Marco nodded. "Winemaking is an art, but the math and science, equally important."

"What if someone discovered the grape harvest that year was insufficient to produce the quantity of Brunello in the barrels?"

"Unauthorized grapes were brought in?" Marco asked with interest as if such an event could have happened without his being aware. "You believe the yield was increased by adding unlawful grapes? Leo would not consider such deception. A true Brunello is made only from the Sangiovese of Montalcino," he said calmly. "The science?"

As if this thought had just entered her head, she asked, "Could the origin of the grapes, the wine, be determined through scientific analysis?"

Marco shook his head dismissively as if this was ridiculous. What sounded like a firecracker went off. Dana jumped, and Marco put a light hand on her arm as if to reassure her, before taking a step back, eyes darting from side to side.

"The tourists," he said, "not as brave as you and I."

Then she noticed that the last remaining couple on the valley side of the *fortezza* had gone down. Crowds were chanting below from the opposite side. *Borghetto. Ruga. Travaglio. Pianello.* Loud music blasted up. A pop pierced the air. A dog barked. Then another.

Marco surveyed the rampart on both sides, then he gazed down below them. Dana slipped her hand into the pocket of the jacket, grasping her phone, lifting it enough to glance down furtively, thumb moving quickly. *On. Camera. Video.* She coughed to mask the sound as it clicked. Marco looked back, seemingly unaware as Dana dropped the phone back into the depths of the pocket, hand shaking. If she'd fingered correctly, the video camera was on, recording nothing but darkness inside the pocket. But the audio would record their words.

"We are alone," Marco whispered, stepping close again, pushing his body into hers, backing Dana against the rail. He kissed her, deeply, almost violently. She could barely breathe.

Then he stepped back and lifted the bottle from the stone wall and poured more wine into her glass, and when it rose to the rim, he continued to pour until the bottle was empty.

"So sorry, please," he said, as if suddenly aware of what he had done, not noticing until the wine slid down the side of the glass, on to her hand, on to her jeans.

He pressed his fingers to her damp leg. His touch shot through her. Her heart jumped.

"So sorry," he apologized again, hand lingering. Surely, he wouldn't harm her, Dana thought. If this was his intention, he could have done it much earlier when they were alone in his car on the hillside. It would make no sense for him to bring her to a public place with the intention of harming her. Yet, *she* was the one prodding him. How foolish she was to start such a conversation. But, there were tourists, local celebrants everywhere. Yet, oddly now, as Marco pointed out, they were alone on this side of the fortress.

Dana felt a catch in her throat and swallowed hard. Slowly, she took a step back, knowing the stairs down to the courtyard were just a short distance behind her. But he reached for her and caught hold of her arm with such force that her wineglass dropped and shattered.

"Father Borelli knows," she said quickly. "And Fabrizio." She struggled to release herself from his grasp, but he was much stronger than she.

With his free hand, Marco grabbed her wrist. He pressed closer, again almost taking the breath out of her. "Fabrizio has nothing but theory. The wine has been destroyed."

"He took a sample," she snapped.

Marco smiled. "The sample, Fabrizio's sample, perhaps it has been destroyed, too."

"The police have Leo's computer."

"There is nothing incriminating on the computer." His voice was rough, and sweat formed on his forehead, even as Dana shivered. "Leo's precious records reflect only the amount in the barrels. Only the amount of wine that could have been produced from the Sangiovese harvested that year." His voice was low and tense as he tightened his hold on Dana's wrist and arm. "Even if such a plot existed, Father Borelli will protect the family name. He will say nothing to harm Leo."

"Leo didn't know." Her voice quivered. "He had no part in the harvest that year. Teresa Antonelli was ill and Leo took her to Rome for treatment." Dana had to continue now that she had started, and she had to put her thoughts into words. She prayed she'd fingered the right buttons on the phone to record their conversation. She felt the rough shards of glass beneath her feet. Over Marco's shoulder, she saw a movement, little more than a dark silhouette, creeping along the rampart.

Marco glanced back, but any sign of life had disappeared. There was no one there. No one at all.

"Unauthorized grapes were brought in without Leo's knowledge," Dana's voice rose, "and someone removed the excess wine with the intention of making a profit on the side from the additional wine." Images, words, explanations of the process of making this precious wine shot through Dana's head, especially what Marco himself had shared, and she knew he had added additional grapes to increase the yield, then at some point he'd removed the excess wine for his own benefit.

"Who might that be?" Marco snorted.

"The enologist with the help of the viticulturist." The realization intertwined with her words—Sophia Dardi was the woman! "Your sister."

"How very clever you are." Marco laughed. "But, the police will never believe that Leo was unaware. Tasting the wine, Leo would know it was not a true Brunello."

"Leo can't taste the wine," she said and Marco's eyes tightened with anger. "Because he has no sense of smell."

Marco's breathing was shallow as was hers. "You are correct. Leo would not know a Borelli Brunello from a cheap American table wine," he hissed as he pushed her up against the rail again. She could see, even in the dim light, the veins in his neck bulging. The rail pressed into her back. "A few truckloads of unauthorized grapes, already fermented, to increase the volume, so easily done with Leo gone from the estate. But, the brilliance of the plan—the fermented Sangiovese grapes were removed early, before any tainting. The stolen wine is a perfect Brunello, aging now in the required oak barrels."

"On your very small farm." Dana could see he took this as an attack on his manhood. His nostrils flared.

"Yes, aging in *my* barrels. Do you know what it means to see others take credit for what you have produced?" He'd taken her bait and the words came rapidly, with such anger she thought he might choke on them. "The Borelli family increasing their wealth year by year, while my father, then me, laboring our entire lives. Little better than the life of a serf."

Another series of firecrackers exploded. The crowds chanted from the piazza. If she called for help, no one would hear.

"Much celebration. Many drinking," Marco whispered into Dana's ear, his voice almost calm now. "Sometimes, too much celebrating becomes dangerous." Even with her pulsing rise of adrenaline, Dana realized how easily he could force her over the wall. She reeked of wine. Her clothes were saturated. He would claim she was drunk, that she fell.

He slapped a hand over her mouth, stifling her scream. His grip on her wrist cut into her. She bit hard and he pulled back with a snarl.

With all her strength, she clawed at him, attempting to pry his hand from her wrist, even as she saw a figure move rapidly toward them in the darkness.

Dana made out the faint silhouette, the small, slender girl.

"Mia, no," Dana cried even as Mia kicked at Marco, catching him in the groin. Dana yanked herself free as Marco reached down in pain with one hand, taking a swing toward Mia with the other. Dana caught his arm, protectively forcing herself between the two. Marco took another swing at Dana, striking her on the side of the head as she clawed at him, and Mia tumbled to the rough stone. A sharp snap pierced the air, the girl screamed, and an even louder blast exploded as Marco grabbed once more for Dana, catching only air as he fell, as she dropped to her knees wrapping Mia protectively in her arms.

CHAPTER FORTY-FOUR

Within seconds, they were everywhere. Police. Broken glass crunching beneath their feet. Cuffing an injured Marco, his blood spilling onto the stone. Dana still holding Mia, still attempting to protect her. The girl's arm hung loosely as she went in and out of consciousness, and Dana realized the sharp snap she'd heard was Mia's bone cracking.

"You are going to be okay," Dana whispered to her. "Everything is going to be okay."

Mia's eyes popped open, staring blankly up at Dana. "I know." Then she mumbled something in Italian that Dana was sure was, *we are all going to be okay.*

A team arrived, two of them the same young men who'd tended Mia's wounds less than a week earlier at the villa. Reluctantly, Dana released her, and they loaded her onto a gurney and carried her carefully down the steps, through the empty enoteca, out into the courtyard devoid of the earlier crowds. Dana walked by her side. She could see Marco being loaded into a response van. Within minutes, a second vehicle pulled in, and Dana realized as she glanced to her side that Alberto DeLuca stood beside her. Had he been there all along? He touched her arm and motioned her inside the van. As Dana sat by Mia's side, she became aware that she too had been injured. Blood oozed from a cut on the back of her wrist. She had felt no pain. Until now.

At the hospital they were separated, Dana escorted to a room where her wrist was patched quickly to stop the flow of blood, and then she was left alone. She waited. A woman entered and gave her a hospital gown. In broken English Dana was told to undress, though she tried to explain that she had no other injuries. Her head was starting to throb.

She complied, removing her clothes, placing them in a bag given to her by the woman, who carried it out of the room. Shivering in the hospital gown, Dana sat on the examination table and waited. Aware that Mia's injury was much more serious than hers, Dana realized how lucky she was that Marco had not thrown her off the wall. Then she realized that the loud blast she'd heard had been a gunshot. Marco had been shot.

She wondered if he was still alive. They had cuffed him. He'd been arrested. She was confused—why had the police come to the *festa*, the *fortezza* to find him when so many people were gathered in the city that evening? The rampart, the enoteca, the courtyard had been cleared. Dana felt the heat of nerves trip down her spine when she realized that the police might think she was the woman mentioned in the conversation Winkie overheard. But it was Marco's sister, Sophia. Dana knew that now. Had the police come to the *fortezza* looking for Dana, as well as Marco? Yet, she had not been cuffed. They had not arrested her. She sat now, alone. Waiting. Attempting to comprehend what had just happened.

She didn't understand why Mia had come up on the rampart and wondered if the girl had overheard their conversation, the words that Dana had hopefully recorded. This conversation would clear Dana, as well as Leo if the police suspected that either of them had been involved. But, then it came to her that in the confusion, the struggle on the rampart, the jacket that Marco had given her had disappeared. Maybe it had slipped off her shoulders. She was having difficulty remembering the details, the struggle, Mia's coming out of nowhere. It had all happened so quickly. But, she knew if the jacket was missing, so was the phone. She did not have her phone. Did the police?

Eventually, a different nurse came into the room. She took and recorded Dana's vitals, shaking her head as she put the stethoscope to her chest. Dana imagined the thump of her heart could be heard without the assistance of a medical instrument. The woman examined her wrist, then her head. In English, she asked if she had any additional injuries. Dana said no, and again she was left alone. Eventually, another woman, a doctor Dana thought, came in. Once more, her wrist was examined and repatched with tape, the modern equivalent of stitches. The doctor examined her head and asked if she needed painkillers. Dana said no. She didn't want anything to dull her senses.

It seemed at least two more hours before her clothes were returned and she was allowed to dress again. She checked the pockets of her jeans, her own jacket, searching for her phone, knowing it was not there. The phone was in the pocket of Marco's jacket, the evidence that might save her as well as Leo. Then she was escorted to another room, where she sat alone for at least an hour. Just as she was about to rise and walk through the door, official dismissal or not, DeLuca, along with the translator, entered the room. The man looked exhausted. His bushy mustache drooped as if it had not been trimmed in days, and he sported an irregular patch of grey stubble on his chin. He shot her a sympathetic look as he sat. She could see he was gazing at what was surely a developing bruise on the side of her head. From the way he studied her, she knew he was not about to arrest her.

Through the translator, he asked about her relationship with Marco Dardi. She wondered if she should ask for a lawyer, request that they summon Borelli, but she thought about what Borelli had told her earlier, *tell the truth, tell them exactly what you saw. You have done nothing wrong.*

She told them she had met Dardi for the first time during this visit, that they had no prior relationship. They asked if she knew anything about what had happened in the cellar, what had happened to Fabrizio. She told them she had no direct knowledge of either.

Looking directly at DeLuca, she said, "I recorded a conversation that will implicate Marco, that will clear Leo if he is being considered a suspect."

After a brief translation, DeLuca nodded knowingly, and Dana was sure that he was already aware of this. He had listened to the recording on her cellphone.

DeLuca and the translator left her alone and within minutes a young man arrived and escorted her to a waiting room. Borelli sat slumped on a sofa. She thought he was asleep, but then he looked up at her, eyes wide.

"Mia, she's going to be okay?" Dana asked as she lowered herself and sat beside him.

"A bad break," Borelli said. "Compound fracture. She's going into surgery shortly. Are you okay?"

Dana held up her hand. She considered saying *merely a flesh wound* but felt the situation too serious for that. "Yes, I'm fine."

"You are going to have a substantial bruise on the side of your face," Borelli said pointing. Then gently he put his arm around her, and she leaned into him feeling as if she might burst into tears. And then she did. She could feel the beat of Borelli's heart. The comfort of his presence, his strength, his largeness, reassured her. She felt safe. For many moments, they sat silently, neither speaking.

"Is Leo with her?" Dana sat erect and looked directly into Borelli's eyes.

He nodded. "Marco has been arrested. He was shot, but he's not dead."

"I know."

"Thank God you are okay," Borelli said.

"What prompted the police to come for Marco tonight? In Montalcino, with all the activity?" she asked.

Borelli took a deep breath. "Winkie Dalton recognized Marco as the man on the Veronesi property with Jago DeCampo, the man who, along with Carlo Porcini, destroyed the wine."

"How did Winkie know it was Marco?"

"I sent a video from the winery website. To his phone. God only knows how I managed to do that successfully." A smile flickered across his face, revealing a satisfaction somewhere between thankful and amazed. "Winkie called Inspector DeLuca. As soon as I found out, I too called DeLuca. I told him you were with Marco, that I feared you might be in danger."

She smiled with relief, with gratitude. "Now, why did you think I might be in danger?"

"Because you had a theory. And your theory was correct. The wine was destroyed because it was not as represented."

"Yes, I did have a theory. And I began to realize that if it was true, then Leo would be held accountable. So, I knew I had to get Marco to admit that Leo was not involved."

"And did he?" Borelli asked hopefully. "Leo had to have known." Dana realized that Borelli believed that Leo *was* involved. Borelli had alerted DeLuca to Marco's plot, to the danger this had placed Dana in, even as he suspected that Leo had played a part in the deception and destruction.

"Yes," she replied. "Leo was not aware. He didn't know that the wine was not an authentic Brunello, that the destroyed wine was tainted." She took in a deep breath. "Marco took the excess wine."

Borelli's eyes widened, his mouth dropped. "Not all of the wine was destroyed?"

"Marco admitted he took some of the wine, but he also said that his stolen wine was a true Brunello. Is this possible, when the wine in the cellar was mixed with unauthorized grapes?"

"The process is long, very involved," Borelli said thoughtfully, "with many stages . . . if a portion was removed early, the bad grapes added after that, yes this is possible. You shared all of this with DeLuca?"

Dana was so tired, she wasn't sure exactly what had been recorded on her phone. She couldn't even remember at what point she had turned it on. "I recorded our conversation on my phone. I believe the police have it, that they listened to it, that they know Leo was not involved. That somewhere Marco is storing the stolen wine."

Borelli sat quietly as if taking this all in. Then he said, "We both need to get some rest. We won't be able to see Mia until after her surgery." He rose with some effort, bracing himself on the arm of the sofa. As he stood, he said, "How could Leo not have known? How could he possibly have been oblivious to something like this? Something happening right under his nose."

Dana laughed, and then she was crying again, her emotions a jagged mixture of hysteria and exhaustion. She was so tired, but what Borelli had said—*right under his nose*. She would explain to Borelli how she'd discovered that Leo had lost his sense of smell, his sense of taste. Yet, there was so much more going on with Leo. Dana knew that the great loss he had suffered had destroyed his sense of the world in which he lived. Dana had gone through the same experience, and in many ways, she was still on this journey of survival and recovery. She understood.

CHAPTER FORTY-FIVE

On the drive back to the villa, Dana, feeling much calmer, told Borelli more of what she'd learned during her conversation with Marco.

"He's bitter that his own family was not recognized for developing the Borelli Brunello," Dana said. "I believe that this added to his motivation for what he and Sophia did."

"The Borelli's have always paid their employees very well. Especially the enologist, the viticulturist. This is very difficult to understand."

Dana could see how much this betrayal hurt Borelli, how much it would hurt Leo. A generous salary might have been useful in paying those enlisted to destroy the wine, might have been enough to purchase a small farm. But not to buy a large winery in an area perfect for raising the Sangiovese of Montalcino.

"I believe Marco had plans to buy the Veronesi Vineyards," Dana said.

"But it has been sold to someone else."

"Winkie Dalton?" she asked, and Borelli nodded.

The sun was making its way up over the hillside. Morning, Dana thought. It's already morning. Her night had been lost. She was so tired. They continued on without words until they reached the turnoff to the villa. Dana glanced at Borelli. "Do you know where Marco's farm is located?"

She could see he was giving this more thought than she'd hoped. His gaze was moving across her face, from her eyes, which she could barely hold open, to the bruise on her cheek. "I do not," he said. "Perhaps we have reached the point where we should trust that the authorities might appropriately conclude this investigation."

Later that day, Dana, napping in her room, was awakened by a knock. Slowly she sat up, rubbing her eyes, her mind and body warped with confusion as to what time, even what day it was.

"I spoke with Leo," Borelli said.

Dana rose and opened the door.

"Mia is doing fine," he said.

"Wonderful news. The surgery went well?"

"Yes. She's spending the night, perhaps not necessary, but Leo wants to take every precaution."

"Yes," Dana said. "Thank you for letting me know."

"He also spoke with DeLuca. The police raided Marco's farm this afternoon."

"What did they find?" she asked eagerly.

"That's all I know. But, this is what is being reported today." He handed her a printout from an online newspaper. She looked at the date and time and realized it was already Saturday afternoon.

Though she could not read the Italian, there was enough there, *Fabrizio Calaberoni, Marco Dardi, Fortezza di Montalcino*, that she knew the article was about what had happened the previous night. As she quickly scanned the print, she saw no mention of Dana Pierson.

"The article states," Borelli began, settling himself in the chair by the small table next to the window, "that Marco Dardi was arrested Friday evening for the wine destruction and attempted murder of Fabrizio Calaberoni. The police had cleared the upper rampart of the *fortezza*, as well as the enoteca and courtyard, so no one would be injured, although an unnamed woman tripped and fell and was taken to the hospital for treatment of a minor injury. The Inspector said additional information would be released as the investigation continued, but there was no further danger to the community."

Well, that was a familiar refrain, Dana thought, though this time she guessed it might be true. She wondered about the unnamed woman. Was that Dana or Mia? There was no mention of a child. No mention of raiding Marco's property, nothing about stolen wine.

Then another thought—what if her brothers, possibly her mother, read this article in an American newspaper or online.

"I should call my family," she said.

"Yes," Borelli replied. "I think that is an excellent idea." He laughed. "Hopefully by the time you return home, there will be no evidence of your injuries."

"I don't think I'll mention that," Dana said, remembering what had happened in Prague, the last time she'd been with Borelli.

The next morning, Dana and Borelli stopped in Montalcino and got flowers for Mia before visiting her at the hospital. Leo had spent the night.

Mia was awake, sitting up in bed, arm in a cast, looking well when they arrived. Dana arranged the flowers on the bedside table as Borelli visited and talked to Leo, who obviously had gotten no sleep at all. They said nothing about Marco, Fabrizio, the wine, but spoke mostly of the *festa*, the fact that they had missed their family day.

"I'm taking Leo for some lunch," Borelli said after a while. "Dana?"

"No thank you. I'm not really hungry." Dana guessed Borelli needed some time alone with his nephew. It was barely mid-morning, too early for lunch.

"Are you doing okay?" Dana asked after they had left.

Mia nodded. "Thank you for the flowers." She glanced over at the bouquet, a mixture of fall colors in oranges and yellows. "They're beautiful."

"From your Uncle Giovanni, too. Your grandmother sends her love. Since you'll be going home soon, she will not come to the hospital."

"Yes, I think that's best. She knows I'm okay? I don't want her to have another heart attack."

"She's doing fine. She's just relieved and grateful that you are going to be okay. Anything I can get you?"

Before Mia could answer, a woman entered the room. She examined Mia's cast, checked her vitals, nodding at Dana now and then as if she thought she was Mia's mother.

When she left, Mia said, "I can go home after lunch. I asked if they could bring an extra tray for you, too."

"Thank you. That's very thoughtful of you."

They were both silent for many moments, then Mia said, "You wonder why I followed you and Marco?"

Dana nodded. "Why did you?"

"I'm not sure. But, I didn't like seeing the two of you together. I don't even know why. Well, I don't really like Marco. I've overheard him talking roughly to employees on the estate. Then, he turns on the charm around my father and my uncle. I've never felt he could be trusted."

Mia had seen this, but why hadn't Leo? Dana wondered. Perhaps Marco felt he didn't have to put on a fake front for a child.

"Then at the *festa*," Mia said, "when I saw you with Marco, I was confused. There were so many things running through my head."

"I could tell you were upset. Did you know Marco was involved in the destruction of the wine, the attempt to kill Fabrizio?"

"I didn't." Mia bit down on her lip. "I didn't know then. But, I knew I didn't like seeing you with him. Then suddenly, your scent—

I realized why I had chosen that perfume." Her jaw tightened as she pressed her lips together. A tear slid down her cheek. Dana stroked Mia's hand, then lowered herself to the edge of the bed. "It was my mother's. I didn't realize when I chose it, but I knew it made me happy. We were having fun the day we went shopping, you and I, and I . . . It just reminded me of . . . something good." Her eyes met Dana's. "I don't want you to think that I wish you to take her place."

"No one can do that."

"I hope you will always be my friend."

"I will," Dana said. She held Mia's hand. "I've lost someone very dear to me, too." Dana felt the deep emotional throb that always came when she thought of her son. Dear, dear Joel. No one could or would take his place. But she had a tender, unexpected, yet growing feeling for this sweet young girl. Dana took a deep breath. "I had a son."

"I know," Mia whispered. "Zio Giovanni told me before you arrived. He said you . . ." Mia swallowed hard. "He said I needed to know, even though he told me you seldom talk about your son. Zio said I was not to ask about him, to talk about him, unless you were the one to—"

"It's difficult." Dana felt a tear slipping from her eye now, too.

Mia tightened her grip on Dana's hand.

Dana hesitated and then she said, "His name was Joel. Joseph Leon, but we called him Joel. He was beautiful." Dana smiled at the image of her little blond, blue-eyed boy. Mia listened, offering a supportive smile in return. "He was a little younger than you. He would be twelve now."

"I'm so sorry."

"Thank you."

Dana could tell Mia was studying her patched wrist, as well as the bruise on her left cheek.

"Just a few stitches," Dana said. "And a tiny bruise."

Mia's smile tightened. "Looks like a large bruise. I'm sorry you became involved in all of this."

"No need for you to be sorry about that," Dana said. Her eyes dropped to the cast on Mia's arm. "Looks like you got the worst of it."

"That was stupid of me to follow you."

"Maybe stupid of me to go up on the rampart with Marco." Dana smiled. "You got in a good kick to the groin. That really threw him off balance."

"If you hadn't pushed yourself between us, I think he might have knocked my head off."

"We're both okay."

"We are. We make quite a team, don't we?"

"We do," Dana replied, and again they sat in silence for several moments.

"But," Mia said thoughtfully, "if you hadn't become involved, my father would have been blamed. Thank you." She sniffled back a tear.

"You overheard the conversation?"

"I know it was Marco, that my father wasn't involved."

"The police know that your father had nothing to do with any of it," Dana reassured her.

"Did they find the wine that Marco stole?" Mia had lowered her voice.

"I don't know."

"But, they will?"

"Yes, I believe they will," she said, realizing that she believed that they already had.

That evening, Leo arrived for dinner carrying a newspaper. He sat and began reading aloud, then translating for Dana. Line by line. Borelli and Mia sat patiently, and Dana attempted to do the same.

According to the article, the motive for the wine destruction was the desire to destroy a wine that might compete with the Veronesi, as Marco Dardi intended to acquire the Veronesi Vineyards. He had paid Carlo Porcini and Jago DeCampo to release the wine. Marco

Dardi had attempted to kill Fabrizio Rossi because the young man had become aware of this plot. Sophia Dardi, Marco's sister, had also been arrested as an accessory. It was officially announced that the Veronesi family business had been sold to an American movie star and director, Winkie Dalton.

Along with Carlo Porcini, Marco Dardi would be charged with the murder of Paolo Paluzzi and also the attempted murder of Fabrizio Calaberoni, who, according to Inspector Alberto DeLuca, had provided invaluable information to the police. Silvio Gallo had been released. There was nothing said about the injured woman. Nothing said about an injured child.

"There's no mention of the wine that Marco removed from the Borelli cellars?" Dana asked.

Leo smiled and held up a hand. "Several large barrels of wine have been found on Marco Dardi's farm. He has confessed that he had taken the wine from the Borelli cellars."

Leo folded the paper and handed it to Dana as if gifting a little souvenir of her visit.

"It's over?" Dana asked, glancing from Leo to Borelli, not knowing what else to say.

"Yes, it's over," Borelli replied, and Dana understood that the full story would likely never be known.

She wondered if the entire municipality of Montalcino would be content with this half-truth. The Borelli Vineyards' reputation would not be tarnished, the misrepresentation of the Brunello wine would not be revealed. The evidence of this had been destroyed. It had never gone to market.

Rather than leave for Rome on Sunday as planned, Dana decided to stay until the middle of the week. She arranged to meet her friends in Sorrento. She wanted to spend more time with Mia. They talked—about Mia's mother, the girl's concerns about her father. They talked about Dana returning for another visit, Mia coming to see Dana in Boston, how they'd be close to New York and could go there too. They went shopping, Mia aware that Dana's wardrobe had suffered considerably during her stay. Even the jeans she'd worn on her date with Marco were irreparably stained with blood and wine.

Leo was more attentive to his daughter, and Dana saw the two walking together through the garden, then into the nearest vineyard early Monday morning, before Mia went back to school.

Monday afternoon, Borelli disappeared, returning late for dinner. On Tuesday he didn't show up at all for dinner, though Leo said he had called. Dana sensed something was going on with Borelli. When she saw him, he seemed especially happy. Maybe the relief of having the problems of the estate resolved was explanation enough for his contentment, yet Dana wondered . . .

Wednesday morning as she packed, he came to her room. His light, happy mood seemed to have morphed into something else. Unusually nervous, almost fidgety, he glanced around quickly as if checking to make sure she was packing everything she'd come with and anything she'd collected during her stay.

Leo and Mia would drive Dana to Siena to pick up her rental car. Borelli had told her that he would stay home with Estella. She knew he'd come for a private farewell.

"Thank you for what you have done to help the family. For spending time with Mia."

"We've both had fun," she told him. "I'm glad I was able to extend my stay."

"You've spoken with Leo?" he asked. Over the past few days, she sensed that Leo wished a private conversation, but until that morning he'd said nothing.

"Yes, we went for a walk after breakfast this morning."

"Thank you," Borelli said.

Dana had understood that Leo needed to talk to her alone, to express his gratitude and perhaps offer some explanation for how he could not have known what had taken place at his own winery.

As they walked, she shared with Leo how she had almost lost

her job after Joel disappeared. "Truthfully, I barely remember," she'd told him, "anything that happened during the months after, even the year following . . . I couldn't do my work. I should have been fired. But, I was surrounded by people who loved me, who knew I needed time." She realized that Leo had the added burden of the betrayal of a trusted friend.

"Time?" Leo asked. "It's been over two years since I lost Teresa. Does time heal?"

"No, I can't say that it does," she'd replied, honestly. "But, eventually, you come to realize your life will be different. Nothing will be the same. Then you continue. Accept the love all around you," was the only real advice she could offer.

Now, as Dana finished her packing, Borelli seemed pensive, uncharacteristically quiet. She folded the last of her clothes and zipped her bag. "Thank you so much for inviting me for the visit."

"It is I who should thank you," he said. "Yes, and what a visit."

"One I certainly won't forget."

"Not easily forgotten by any of us." He laughed lightly and so did Dana. "Mia says you've agreed to come again. I hope you do."

"Yes, and I've invited Mia to visit me in Boston. The invitation is extended to you, too."

"Very good." Borelli picked up Dana's bag as she slipped her sweater over her shoulders. "There is something," he said, words slow and measured, "something I want to share with you."

"What is it?" she asked, even as Borelli placed her bag back on the floor.

"I'm planning a trip to Rome for a couple of days."

"Rome?"

"Yes."

Dana knew something was going on with Borelli. A simple yes, without elaborate explanation, was not his style. Unless he was hiding something. Or attempting to protect someone.

"Is there a reason you are going to Rome?"

He glanced out the window, then turned, blinking nervously. She waited for an answer, but when there was no reply, she asked, "Alone?"

"I'm not sure I'm ready to talk to anyone about this yet. Surely not my family." He didn't look at her.

"Oh?" She didn't want to push, but she was more than curious, and he obviously wanted to share something or he wouldn't have started this conversation. "You know if you tell me something in confidence," she assured him, "you can trust me."

"Yes, I believe this to be true," he said formally, then took in a deep breath. He looked at her now. "I'm going to Rome, not actually Rome, but we've rented a small, private villa outside the city."

"We?"

"Yes." Again, he blinked nervously and ran his hand over his head.

She waited for more.

He smiled guardedly. "Gia Veronesi."

Dana hardly knew what to say.

"We're . . . well, she's just sold the vineyard."

"Yes, to Winkie Dalton. You're celebrating? She's happy about this?"

"She is. There are . . . aspects of this sale. I can't speak of this just yet. That is Gia's story to tell."

"You and Gia, just the two of you?"

Borelli smiled again.

"Might that stir up a bit of scandal?"

"Yes, I'm sure it might. For now, no one knows."

Oddly, Dana didn't feel scandalized, but admittedly somewhat stunned. And honored that he had chosen to share this with her.

"I'm afraid," he said, "*you* have already helped to stir up a bit of scandal."

"Even though we are just friends," she offered, and then, "Your feelings for Gia, more than friendship."

There was something in his smile now that she hadn't seen

before. A youthful openness, perhaps. A vulnerability. Borelli was in love with Giovanna Veronesi. The thought that this love would have another chance made Dana smile, too.

"Well," he said, clearing his throat, glancing at his watch. "Leo and Mia are waiting." He leaned over to kiss her on the cheek. "You have a good trip."

"You, too, my dear friend, Giovanni," she whispered. "You, too."

EPILOGUE

1 year, 6 months later
To: danapwrites@gmail.com
From: Leo@borellivines.com
Subject: A gift for you

Dear Dana, It has been a challenging year. Circumstances have compelled me to take a more active role in the business, and this has been good. Often when walking along the vines, I feel Teresa's spirit beside me. After a lengthy search, we have hired a new enologist, who I believe will work well with the viticulturist hired late last summer. Fabrizio has been very helpful as we have gone through this transition.

Mia is well and especially happy when she receives a letter from you. Uncle Giovanni is also well. As he has informed you, he has begun the process of laicization. This is difficult for my mother to accept, but we all realize that one day he and Gia Veronesi will marry. The happy couple splits their time between Rome and Montalcino, where the Veronesi Vineyards have come back to life under the new ownership. I anticipate at some time the Veronesi wines will again compete with Borelli Vineyards.

I am sending you a bottle of Borelli Brunello Riserva from a special vintage, which might have been lost if it were not for you. We are now entering the sixth year after harvest, and the wine may officially be awarded the DOCG designation and the Brunello Riserva label.

The wine has gone through extensive analysis, as well as a number of tastings by representatives of prestigious wine publications and respected industry critics. The ratings awarded are all extremely good.

Because of the limited number of bottles produced in this particular year, it will no doubt become a coveted vintage, stored away in the dusty cellars of the most discerning collectors, taken out from year to year, merely for the owner to proclaim he owns a bottle.

I hope that you will drink your wine, share it with those you love, as this is the proper way to enjoy a good bottle of wine, and I hope that you might think of your friends in Italy who are forever grateful.

With regards,
Leo Antonelli

READERS GUIDE FOR

BLOODLINE AND WINE

Discussion Questions

1.How does the title take on new significance as the story develops? Do you see the bloodline in the title as referring to characters in the story? Were there surprises in how these possible blood relationships turned out? How does the bloodline of the destroyed wine figure into the plot?

2. At the beginning of the story Dana reflects on her friendship with Father Borelli and refers to it as *odd*. How would you characterize their relationship? What draws them together? Do they have anything in common? Do you see growth in the relationship by the end of the story?

3.The Borelli/Antonelli family takes pride in the *Borelli Brunello di Montalcino* label. How do consumers and society in general place value on labels? Do we tend to put labels on people? How might the characters in the story label one another, and do any of these perceptions change?

4. Did you question Winkie's intense desire to buy the winery? How do you see his relationship with Giovanna Veronesi developing in the future?

5. Marco describes the Brunello as a wine made for aging and worth the wait. How do *waiting* and *aging* apply to various characters in the story? How do you see Dana dealing with her own aging? Do people improve with age?

6. The author uses the sense of smell in many ways in the story. How does smell play into the plot? Are there certain smells that bring back memories for you? How do you think it would affect your life if you had no sense of smell?

7. As the story progresses, the reader learns of the past relationship between Giovanni Borelli and Giovanna Veronesi. Do you think that Giovanna reveals the true reason she called off the marriage many years ago? Can relationships survive if important facts are hidden?

8. There are numerous relationships developed throughout the story. How do you see the relationship evolving between Dana and Mia? Dana and Leo?

9. The loss of the valuable Brunello wine is an important part of the story's plot. How do the various characters' personal losses become part of the story? How does the undercurrent of Dana's loss of her son affect her relationships with others?

Kelly Jones grew up in Twin Falls, Idaho. She graduated from Gonzaga University in Spokane, Washington, with a degree in English and an art minor. She lives in Boise. Visit her website at kellyjonesbooks.com.